Every Exit Brings You Home

ALSO BY NAEEM MURR

The Perfect Man

The Genius of the Sea

The Boy

Every Exit Brings You Home

A Novel

NAEEM MURR

Copyright © 2026 by Naeem Murr

All rights reserved
Printed in the United States of America
First Edition

For information about permission to reproduce selections from this book, write to Permissions, W. W. Norton & Company, Inc., 500 Fifth Avenue, New York, NY 10110

For information about special discounts for bulk purchases, please contact W. W. Norton Special Sales at specialsales@wwnorton.com or 800-233-4830

Manufacturing by Lake Book Manufacturing
Book design by Daniel Lagin
Production manager: Louise Mattarelliano

ISBN: 978-1-324-11790-2

W. W. Norton & Company, Inc., 500 Fifth Avenue, New York, NY 10110
www.wwnorton.com

W. W. Norton & Company Ltd., 15 Carlisle Street, London W1D 3BS

Authorized EU representative: EAS, Mustamäe tee 50, 10621 Tallinn, Estonia

10 9 8 7 6 5 4 3 2 1

For Averill

[He had] the revelation, nearly religious, that the colossal scale of evil could only be matched or countered by some solitary flicker of intense and private humanity.

Whether this amounted to a loss of faith, or to the acquisition of it, was uncertain.

—Shirley Hazzard, *The Transit of Venus*

Every Exit Brings You Home

1

Jack's phone buzzed in his pocket like a trapped hornet. May's texts somehow achieved a particular ferocity of vibration.

> They are here. IN MY SPACE!!!

He hurried to his back deck, entering the heat of August in Chicago. From the top floor of the two conjoined three-flats that constituted the Jensen Grand Condominiums, he watched a white couple, early thirties, perhaps, with a mixed-race girl of four or five, emerging from an ancient white Econoline in the parking lot. RYKER FRANKE KNIFE SHARPENING was inexpertly stenciled on the van's flanks. Natasha, the building's developer, had called Jack to tell him she'd sold the final unit: a miracle, given swelling concerns in the news about toxic subprime mortgages. The couple had pulled into May's space. May, who'd never owned a car, was quick to call the tow truck if anyone violated her parking space's sacrosanct emptiness.

The man looked as if he was in a biker gang: bandanaed hair, sunglasses, scruffy goatee, the leather vest on his bare torso revealing a once-muscular body wreathed in tattoos and going to seed. Jack felt apprehensive; even more so when he saw, emblazoned on the back of the man's vest as he turned to open the van, "Fuck Al-Qaeda" above a skull and two crossed machine guns.

As he went downstairs to greet them, he cast a "Bonjour, ça va" to Bernard, a gaunt, dark-skinned Haitian, nearly toothless, sitting on the ground-floor deck outside Pauline's apartment, his gaze at once clairvoyant and confused. A large notice on the railing said, "Tanpri, pa kite galri dèyè a, Papa." *Dad, please don't leave the back deck.*

"Hello, welcome," Jack called, propping the gate open with a brick. "I'm Jack, El Presidente of this condo." Jack couldn't hide the fact that he looked Mediterranean, with thick, black curls and olive skin, but the biker's vest made him glad he'd ceased calling himself Jamal.

"Marcia," the woman said, adding in a tone more derisive than amused, "do I need to salute you?"

Tall and slender, she wore skinny jeans and a black tank top, her dirty blond hair in a spiky bob. She had what Jack thought of as Slavic features: a strong jaw (like Birdy's) and high, broad cheekbones. Her eyes prickled with a defensive fierceness softened slightly by the hazy sea-glass greenish blue of her irises. A colorful tattoo of a seductive La Calavera Catrina stared from her left shoulder while a thorny rose vine bound a dagger to her right bicep.

"No salutes necessary," he said with a laugh.

The biker removed his shades to reveal periwinkle-blue eyes as unlikely and fragile as alpine flowers. He wore a large button with DAYS SOBER emblazoned beneath numbers you could rotate to change like those on a multiple-dial padlock. He was at 0032.

"Are you Ryker?" Jack shook the man's strong but trembling hand.

"That's right. You have any blades you need sharpening?"

"I'll check."

"Could do a group discount for the whole building. And if you need any odd jobs done around here, I charge ten an hour."

Ryker noticed Jack glancing at a cluster of blacked-out tattoos across his chest. "Had a few tats I wasn't proud of before I gave myself to the Higher Power."

Marcia, picking up her little girl, interrupted sharply, "We need to get on."

"Of course," Jack said, though he slipped in, "And this is your daughter?"

"Aisha," she said impatiently, the child performing a toothy smile, as if posing for a photograph.

Ryker said, "You can probably tell she's not mine, but I couldn't love her more if she was."

"Ryker," Marcia barked, setting Aisha back down.

Jack noticed some heavy pieces of furniture. "If you need any help," he offered.

"We're *fine*." She was becoming irritated.

"Come on, honey," Ryker countered, "you're pregnant and the devil's playing fucking Jenga with my spine." Glancing at Jack, he pointed at his own back: "I think I blew out a disk getting this shit into the van."

"Pregnant?" Jack said.

"Three months," Ryker confirmed.

"Congratulations. My wife"—Jack hesitated, caught between saying it and not wishing to tempt fate—"she's pregnant too. Ten weeks."

Marcia shot him an odd look, perhaps because the way he'd said it made it seem as if he was lying. He felt he was, glancing up at the windows of his own apartment's back bedroom, where he could just make out Dimra's head. He'd left her glued to the television, watching the tail end of the civil war raging in Gaza, hundreds killed as Hamas retook control. Hard to believe the election was just a year ago.

"This is going to be a building of babies." *Inshallah, God willing*, he prayed. "Anyway, please let me help you move some of the heavier stuff at least."

"We don't *need* help." Marcia looked ready to punch both him and Ryker, her nostrils flaring, her face aflame. "We just want to *get on*."

That hornet buzzed in his pocket and he checked.

THEY ARE IN MY SPACE!! TOW TRUCK IS NEXT!

Retreating, Jack gestured up to where he lived and told them to knock if they needed anything. He joined Dimra in the back bedroom. She'd slipped on her pink silk hijab in case he invited these new neighbors for coffee, her large, gleaming black eyes freshly lined with kohl. Her hand rested tentatively upon her baby bump. It was astonishing to him that all the pain she'd suffered had left no trace in her face, with its trusting glance and the ready smile of her broad mouth. She'd retained all the youthful beauty and innocence that had caused a seismic slippage of hope in his chest at their first meeting with her unhappy parents. Only her long, slender nose, with its distinct dorsal bump, contradicted this childlike aspect with a quality that was almost aristocratic. He loved her now more as if she were his daughter instead of his wife. He might have desired to keep her locked up and safe from the world, but he didn't have to. Her anxiety and agoraphobia were worsening. She had to take beta blockers just to make it to the fertility clinic without a panic attack.

She spoke to Jack in Arabic, her rudimentary English maintained only by her connection to neighbors like Pauline and Lulu; she could hardly read in either language. She avoided Arab or Palestinian social groups, partly from shame at having no children, but mostly, like him, for fear she'd meet someone from home who might know or discover the truth about them.

She grew herbs and vegetables on their sunny deck, made labneh, hanging the homemade yogurt above the sink in cheesecloth, and shopped, when he could accompany her, at the Middle Eastern stores in Albany Park. They never ate out, lived on lentils and beans so they could save every penny from his modest salary, either to send to her parents in Gaza or for fertility treatments. His wife had suffered three miscarriages, and when she failed to become pregnant again, they tried intrauterine insemination without success before scraping together enough for IVF. Ten weeks and four days ago, Jack returned from a three-day shift to the smell of mansaf, the lamb cooking in homemade jameed. Dimra was looking beautiful also, in her least-old dress. When he stepped into their apartment, she sang their wedding song:

> *Say to his mother rejoice and be glad,*
> *place myrtle on the pillows and henna on our hands.*
> *The wedding is here, the men are all dancing,*
> *this home is my home and the rooms are all mine,*
> *We are as one, let the enemy die!*

He guessed, of course, that she must be pregnant. She turned on some lively Arabic music, and they danced a dabka until his phone vibrated.

> ARE YOU HERDING ELEPHANTS? WHAT IS HORRIBLE NOISE? TORTURE FOR ME!

After switching off the radio, they held each other, kissing in silence.

Now, turning upon him the full force of her innocence, she spoke with naked longing: "If they need someone to look after the little girl while they're moving things in . . ."

"I'd ask, but that woman's . . . prickly. Man seems okay. He sharpens knives."

She tipped her head curiously. "The Nawar bedu used to do that when they came to my parents' village."

"The girl's name is Aisha."

"They're Muslim?"

He shrugged. "I doubt it. Perhaps her father. She's not the knife sharpener's child."

Just as Jack was wondering if he should tell her the woman was pregnant, they heard a crash. Ryker had dropped one end of a ratty-looking brown couch. Hurrying down, Jack was ambushed on the second floor by May, who whispered his name sharply and beckoned from behind her screen door. A short, blockish Vietnamese woman a year or two from sixty, she was a besieged little fortress of fear and anger, expressed now in her obdurate, scowling face.

"I texted you!"

"Yes, I'm sorry, I—"

"Tell them they're in my space," she demanded.

"They're just moving in."

"Why's he lying on the floor?"

"Looks like he hurt himself."

"Is he a gangster? Where's his shirt?"

Backing toward the stairs, Jack said, "I'm heading down. I'll talk to you later."

"Parking spaces deeded. Tell them!"

Ryker lay supine on the concrete, white with pain. Marcia stood over him, sympathy vying with frustration in her face, while Aisha squatted close, singing a curative spell in a magical language, her small hand upon Ryker's forehead.

Ryker insisted he just needed to lie still for a while.

"My wife's upstairs. She'll look after Aisha," Jack said, explaining, "Cars speed up and down this back alley, and we don't want to run her over with the furniture."

Though her mother said nothing, the girl took Jack's hand, as if she'd realized early on that she couldn't add any more to the burden of her mother's life. After taking her up and handing her into Dimra's delighted embrace, he brought down some flat cushions from their deck furniture for Ryker to lie on. Jack suggested driving him to the hospital, but Ryker didn't have health insurance.

Jack spent the rest of the day helping Marcia move in. They drove back and forth from a storage facility in Edgewater. She had no interest in talking and revealed only that she worked for an agency that hired her out as a server for the pleasure cruises leaving from Navy Pier. When he expressed concern about her moving heavy furniture in such heat while she was pregnant, she ignored him. All day she avoided his eyes, her pale face flushed as much with proud anger as with heat and exertion, as if his kindness were a brutish and enslaving power.

She did ask, however, what it meant that he was condo president. He explained the condominium association and the board members, Lulu the secretary, May the treasurer. Marcia was shocked when she realized she had to pay monthly assessments.

"To pay you and those women?" she said, with her quick anger.

"Not us, no. It's for water, trash, all that stuff, and to build a reserve for maintenance."

"I don't need a reserve," she said. "I don't want to be a part of that."

"I'm afraid we all have to—"

"But I have a smaller place."

"The basement—"

"*Garden*," she corrected.

"Of course, I'm sorry. You pay a little less. Have you owned before?"

"What difference does that make?" She was sharply defensive.

"Oh, nothing. I didn't mean to pry. We're all first-time owners here, so we're trying to figure this stuff out together. We have a few issues to deal with in the building, so we're having a condo meeting on Monday at six thirty. Can you make it?"

"I suppose I'll have to."

He dreaded the painful conversation he'd need to have with her about the serious and expensive issues becoming apparent in the building.

At last they wrestled the final piece of furniture, an elephantine faux-leather armchair, into the apartment Natasha had greedily carved out of the front half of the basement. Ryker had managed to drag himself onto the platform queen that nearly filled one of the two bedrooms and was softly snoring. Light seeped in from slender windows lining the low ceilings. The bedroom windows, level with the concrete walkway along the south side of the condo, looked out at the cedar fence between the condo and the adjacent apartment building, while the windows of the combined sitting room and kitchen provided a narrow view onto the small front garden and street. Marcia's back door led into the common-area basement, which often flooded and was full of water heaters, storage units, and bicycles. Her front door opened into the landing for a stairway leading up to the condo's street entrance. This area, fermenting all the stale cooking smells from the units above, also contained the building's water pump inside a framed-out-but-never-completed closet.

After setting the armchair into place, both of them sweaty and breathing hard, Marcia surveyed her new home in a way that made Jack ashamed of the disparaging eye he'd cast over an apartment that should never have been built. It was her first moment of vulnerability, her mouth falling softly open, her eyes filling with a dreaminess befitting the blue-green sea glass of her irises. He recognized the feeling in this look but hadn't experienced it for a long time—that sense of a fresh start, of anticipation for a new self and fate. This place was hers; she was proud of it. And yet he couldn't help something rousing in him as he observed the dark bib of sweat between Marcia's breasts, the elemental tattoos guarding her broad and naked shoulders, her flushed face yielding in this moment to hope.

She glanced at him then, and he sensed she was trying to muster the courage to thank him. Instead, she asked what the little gold book was, pointing to the pendant that had slipped out of his shirt during the move.

"It's the Quran."

It hung on a long chain, so he proffered it, and she took it into hands he now noticed were beautiful. "What does it say on the front?"

"It just says 'Allah,' God. You can open it."

She delicately slipped off the clasp to reveal the verse. "And what does that say?"

"My mercy embraces all things."

She nodded. They were standing close enough now that their heads were almost touching. Closing it up, she set it carefully back upon his chest.

"I'm not religious," he admitted, "but someone gave this to me in a moment when I needed kindness, and that's"—he felt embarrassed now, oversharing—"why I wear it."

"You don't believe in *anything*?"

He thought for a moment. "Faith."

"Faith in what?"

"I don't know." He shrugged, wondering how they'd slipped into this place. "Just faith."

"That doesn't make sense," she said. "You have to have faith *in* something."

Suddenly, footsteps overhead made a sound like that of an ax biting into a tree trunk, the explosive crackle, creak, and whine of the old floors recalling that tree in its deafening collapse.

"Fee-fi-fo-fum," Jack joked, the shock of the noise causing him to react with inappropriate levity.

"What the fuck!" Marcia cried out.

"That's Ken," Jack said. "We have a condo rule that you have to take your shoes off inside. I'll remind him, now you're here. The floors are a bit creaky, I'm afraid."

"Creaky?" She stared at him, appalled. "It sounds like the whole fucking building's going to collapse."

Jack, sighing, explained, "Natasha, the developer, had her workers hide the creakiness of the floors using spray foam and wedges of cardboard, but it didn't last long."

They now heard a trickling sound they realized was Ken peeing, followed by the flush and rumbling evacuation of his toilet through the soil stack in the wall; everyone's flushes would echo through that pipe.

"Oh," Jack remembered, "and I should tell you that it's essential only toilet paper goes down the toilet. You have an ejector pump for your sewage. One of our developer's men flushed a rag down your toilet once and it blocked the line so sewage was pumped up into Ken's apartment and flooded back down here."

Marcia stared at him with pained perplexity, and he realized this probably wasn't the best time to line up future nightmares behind the one she was currently experiencing. Just as Jack was thinking things couldn't get any worse, the entire apartment filled with the sound of a dozen pigs being brutally slaughtered.

"And *that* noise," he had to shout, "is the water pump. I'm afraid we have issues with water pressure." What he meant by "issues" was that if more than a couple of people were using water in the building, it dwindled to a trickle, usually at the instant you'd soaped your face in the shower.

Marcia sat heavily on her sofa, the fight briefly knocked out of her, her hands sandwiching her face as if in a subdued but somehow more hopeless iteration of *The Scream*. The mortal agonies of the pump finally ceased, replaced by Ryker muttering anxiously to himself in his sleep and the ethereal clang of Ken's Tibetan singing bowl from his dojo above.

"We'll sort this out—I mean the water stuff and the pump—hopefully in the next few months," Jack said.

Her hands dropped from her cheeks, anger returning to harden her face. "You'd better." She looked at him almost with hatred as she stood.

By "we" he'd meant all the condo owners, including her, but this wasn't the time to quibble.

"Where's Aisha?" she demanded.

He said he'd bring her daughter down, but she followed him up the back stairs. He sensed that Marcia was desperate for the redoubt of her love for Aisha. They entered into the warm, buttery smell of ghraybeh, the sound of his wife singing and Aisha laughing. Jack kicked off his shoes, but Marcia didn't take the hint and clomped with urgency up the long hallway, past their three bedrooms toward the great room at the front. Hurrying after her, he felt the angry vibration of his cellphone. May maintained a no-tolerance policy to noise.

Marcia stopped at the end of the hallway, as if she feared entering the great room itself, her face reddening again. Dimra sat on the couch under the front windows, bouncing Aisha on her lap. Jack felt obscurely ashamed. The great room, with its grand fireplace and fourteen-foot ceilings, larger than Marcia's entire apartment, was currently awash in magical evening sunlight through a green surf of maple leaves. For the first time he was glad for the poverty of their furniture, IKEA's very cheapest, most of it fifteen years old, as well as for the mismatched carpet remnants on the hardwood floors to soften the creaking. On the walls hung a framed poster of the Al-Aqsa Mosque and the Dome of the Rock, a colorful epoxy Hamsa hand to protect from the evil eye, and a cheap framed canvas print of the al-Fatiha in calligraphy—meaningless cultural signifiers to fill space.

Dimra stood, her face almost supernaturally radiant, lifting Aisha onto her hip as if she'd carried children all her life; and Aisha, that mixed-race child, with her brown eyes and dark-olive skin, looked more hers than Marcia's.

"We made cookies!" Aisha shouted.

"Come on, we have to go," Marcia scolded, not taking one step into the great room.

Dimra, acutely sensitive to anyone's discomfort, carried Aisha over and handed her into Marcia's arms before gesturing back into the room. "Please, sit, welcome. Cookies, they are ready in five minutes. I make Arabic coffee. Invite your husband."

"He's not my husband," Marcia said, the sharpness she'd intended blunted by Dimra herself, who stood with her body almost touching Marcia's. It's hard to be angry with someone who seems to see in you nothing but the light of God.

"We really have to go."

"But Mommy, we made cookies."

"Please stay," Dimra begged. "Minutes only. You take the cookies. Take, take, please." But the instant Dimra lay her hand gently on Marcia's rose-bound dagger, Marcia flinched as if she'd woken from a trance.

"We have to go," Marcia insisted, and clomped back down the hallway. As Aisha began to howl, Jack noticed the copper scorpion clutched in the little girl's hand. Hurrying after them he said, as delicately as possible, "Can I have my scorpion back, habibti?"

He felt awful, Aisha entering full-blown toddler grief.

"What?" Marcia snapped.

"My scorpion." He pointed.

Marcia pried it from her daughter's reluctant hand, causing the little girl, impossibly, as if a drill boring through marble had hit granite, to shift to a more elevated pitch of grief. As Marcia thrust it back toward Jack, the little girl reached for the scorpion and him as if she were being dragged to hell.

Shutting the back door behind them, he felt the buzz of more angry texts from May.

WHO IS WALKING WITH SHOES? LIKE EXPLOSIONS IN MY HEAD! $50 FINE IS NEXT!

Jack returned to his wife, standing at the end of the hallway, stunned.

"Did I do something wrong?" she said.

"I'll take a Tupperware of the ghraybeh down to them a little later."

She removed the cookies from the oven. "I must cook them proper food."

"No, no, we don't want to be too intrusive."

She turned to him, her eyes glittering. "What a lovely little girl."

"We'll have our own lovely child soon enough."

"Inshallah." She looked afraid, and without closing the oven or switching it off, she hurried past him to their bedroom, shutting the door gently behind her. He followed, stepping exactly where she'd stepped on those areas of the hallway floor that didn't creak, so as not to disturb the web of May's acute senses, the thick carpet remnants worn in those places to faded stepping-stones. But he stopped at the door. She'd be in bed, crying, still feeling the body of that child against her, remembering the three she lost. Feeling helpless, he returned to the great room, taking one of the cookies and slumping into the PELLO armchair, its cushion sagging through the back despite his wife's stalwart efforts to Velcro it to the frame. The sun was setting behind the apartment building opposite, its last light a golden libation through the canopy of leaves. He needed to text an abject apology to May sooner rather than later but was wired and exhausted, still too full of the day, of Marcia. He was working a late flight to Charlotte–Douglas in a few hours, the first leg of a four-day trip.

Glancing around, he no longer viewed their apartment with Marcia's eyes. She'd seen its size; he saw its poverty. He could hardly imagine how they would afford a child. Dimra's food was delicious, but he ate so many beans he could fart on command. They never turned on the air conditioning or heat and in the winter sat huddled on the couch under dozens of blankets, him reading while she watched Al Jazeera or one of her Arabic soaps. Only at the Eid Al-Fitr celebration marking the end of Ramadan might she rub spices into the skin of a halal chicken he bought at a place on California Avenue. He'd drive to this butcher through a neighborhood of Orthodox Jews until men with sidelocks dangling from hoiche hats and bewigged women strolling beneath billboards merging the American and Israeli flags transformed into mosques, men in thobes and kurta pajama, women in abaya or shalwar kameez. You could choose your chicken, touring those hapless prisoners in cages at the back of the store, have your victim brought to you naked, headless, still warm, with her neck and tasty organs in a plastic bag, and return home to the smell of ma'amoul cookies.

Though he didn't observe Ramadan himself, he would always have to be home on the night of the twenty-seventh day of the fast, Laylat al-Qadr, the Night of Power, the most holy night when the Quran was revealed to Mohammed (*Peace be upon him* still echoed in Jack's head). Dimra would have filled two dozen Tupperware containers with food to distribute to the homeless. It would be one of the few occasions she'd leave the apartment, terrified as they drove around handing the food and cans of Coke to the people huddled under the bridges in the parks along Chicago's lakeshore. She would be shaking by the time they arrived home. And then, unless she was on her period, they'd have to make love at midnight, when the doorway into the world of God would briefly open. She would pray then, like a person possessed, into the small hours, murmuring, "*To Allah belongs the dominion of the heavens and the earth; He creates what he wills. He gives to whom He wills female children, and He gives to whom He wills males. Or He makes them both males and females, and He renders whom He wills barren.*"

The sun slipped behind the apartment building opposite, the moon like a fingernail paring in the gunmetal-gray sky. Lifting out the brass Quran pendant, he recalled Marcia's beautiful hands, the hazy aquamarine of her irises, the smell of her darkly spiced perfume mingled with her sweat, the two of them standing so close in that hallway.

= 2 =

The late flight to Charlotte didn't start well. A woman clutched Jack's arm as he was checking everyone for takeoff and told him that her son was deathly allergic to nuts, particularly peanuts, and that the dust alone could set off a critical allergic response. She'd forgotten her EpiPen, and the only epinephrine in the onboard first-aid kit was in a large dose designed to treat heart attacks, potentially dangerous for allergic reactions. The boy, perhaps four, sitting in the seat beside her, though cherubic in appearance, with curly golden hair, had a face aged by his mother's anxiety.

Jack's announcement that nuts of any kind could not be consumed on the plane, and that they'd not be passing out the snack mix during the drinks service, provoked a general groan.

A middle-aged man, shaggily tonsured, with a scalded red face and handlebar mustache, wearing a T-shirt declaring, YOU CANNOT IMAGINE THE IMMENSITY OF THE FU*K I DO NOT GIVE, shouted, "You gotta be shitting me. Suddenly every kid's allergic!" His breath reeked of alcohol.

He occupied an aisle seat on the opposite side of the plane just two rows up from the woman and her child. Producing a bag of mixed nuts from the backpack under his seat, he shook them threateningly at her, declaring, "I will not be subject to your tyranny."

Screaming, the woman reflexively thrust her hands in front of her child as if protecting him from a head-on collision.

"Sir," Jack said, "I'm afraid you can't open those."

"I had to take out a fucking mortgage to buy these at the airport. I'm starving, and you're telling me that not only have I been stripped of my God-given fucking right to a snack mix, I can't eat what I bought."

The woman shouted, "My child could die. Die!"

"It's called natural fucking selection, lady!" the man hollered back.

"Please put your nuts away, sir," Jack said, causing a general titter in the cabin, "or I will have to confiscate them."

"I'd like to see you fucking try."

Nancy, a veteran flight attendant, now only working enough shifts to keep her flight privileges, barreled down the aisle from the back. Long-since purged by such customers of any shred of empathy, courtesy, or patience, she pushed her pinched-together thumb and forefinger into the man's face and told him she was *this* close to having him hauled off the plane in cuffs.

The passengers applauded as the man huffily returned the mixed nuts to his backpack, and they took off.

This disturbance had distracted Jack from a fantasy about Marcia. Jack was susceptible to romantic and erotic fantasies, but this desire felt unusually intense. Was it her physical strength? His sense that she could give birth to her child with the same ease as his grandmother had delivered his father, alone among the orange trees of his family's orchard in Al-Nabi Rubin? He could still smell Marcia, see the flush of her exertion, remember how those elegant hands seemed to open him when she opened his Quran, returning him to that condemned building in Gaza, the dolorous crack, the square of achingly blue sky, the smell and salt of the sea on Sofya's body, a kiss so fierce his own teeth had cut his lip and he and she had tasted blood. And, of course, Marcia had evoked Krysta—Birdy—the blond hair, the stature, the strength, though (he couldn't help smiling) Birdy had been far from elegant in those early years, and had no fierceness, every door and window to the sunny home of her being flung wide. His Birdy, whom he'd not seen in years, whose home in Lincoln Park, on a good traffic day, was less than a twenty-minute drive from his own.

Jack wished he could free himself from desire. In his youth, it had been a wolf yanking at his innards; these years later, he felt hollow, but the desire persisted, now the agitated swirl of a dust devil in the desert. Dimra suffered from chronic endometriosis: nerve pain pulsed from her lower back, her periods were hell, and severe jolts of pelvic pain sometimes collapsed her to the floor, mostly because she tried to hide it as she tirelessly performed her wifely duties. He begged Dimra not to behave like his servant, but the moment he stepped in the door, she'd be bent in front of him untying and removing his shoes, becoming frustrated if he tried to stop her. She wouldn't allow him so much as to take his plate to the sink. She rubbed his feet and his back. She ironed his socks and underwear in winter just before he put them on, to warm him. When he had an early flight, she'd be up before him, making his coffee, breakfast, and packed lunch; and no matter how late he returned, she'd be waiting to ask if he needed anything. Their home was always spotless. Her Sisyphean cleaning routine wore all the sealant from the granite surfaces and marble tiles, choked their washing machine's vent with lint, and haunted every inhale with the ghost of lemon bleach.

Endometriosis made sex painful for her, though she insisted on it both because she believed it her duty and because she never lost faith that she'd become pregnant. At least twice a week, she'd bathe in jasmine-scented water, emerging from the bathroom shyly even after all these years, her body scrupulously hairless in adherence to Sunan Al-Fitrah, though he'd have preferred it otherwise, and lay herself like a sacrificial virgin upon the altar of their bed. Her body had always been a source of pain, so it was hard for her to be genuinely sensual, but she was physically affectionate and loving. What was most difficult for him was how alone she was. Even now, he could feel her waiting for him, a burden that never allowed his heart to surface and breathe.

Worse still, the slow suffocation and suffering of the place Dimra still thought of as her home, lived as much within her as the pain of that endometrial tissue breaking its own borders to choke up her body. When that chronic war flared in Gaza, he'd return home to find her frantic, unable to contact her elderly parents, who lived in the Jabalia Camp. Often she wouldn't hear Jack come in from work, and the sight of her on the couch, hitched to their television by wired headphones, flinching at images on Al Jazeera—plumes of smoke, pancaked buildings, women howling in grief—would strike him in different ways: at times as if the television were a parasite feeding on her feelings; or as if she were a terminal patient hooked up to a machine sustaining her life with shocks of horror; or as if she were a baby connected by a poisoned umbilical to a dying mother. When he was home, she'd lie against him on the couch, flinching and exclaiming as he tried to read and not glance at images of a world they both remembered too well: the shattering roar of the Israeli jets, the plumes of their bombs; the pops and dry rattle of gunfire; the acrid black smoke of the burning tires; tear gas prickling in your pores; the barking of *sheket*, shut up, and *lekh*, move, at the Israeli checkpoints; the protesting crowds chanting, *Oh rifle branch flowering with fedayeen, I have inscribed your name, Mother, on the edge of my rifle* (while each of them muttered in the privacy of their homes, *How can the empty palm fight the iron fist?*); the curfews patrolled by Israeli sons and daughters put into uniform so they could be taught to hate Palestinians with the same murderous vehemence with which Palestinian sons and daughters were being taught to hate them; and, of course, the endless coffins washed down those narrow streets upon a whitewater of chanting people, the women wailing, beating their chests, leaving the reality of wrenching, intimate, and lonely pain in the wake of all that public performance. He begged her to turn the news off, to sever the poisoned umbilical, to find a life in Chicago where she would soon have lived longer than she'd ever lived in Gaza, but the conflict saturated her being. As she slept she whimpered and often woke sheened in sweat.

In the periods of remission, of relative peace, she watched Middle Eastern soap operas and films. A week ago, he came in to find her absorbed in *Struggle in the Valley*.

"You're watching this *again*?" he exclaimed.

Pausing the movie, she jumped off the couch, her face flickering with disappointment because he'd removed his shoes himself. Then she embraced him, as she always did, as if he'd been away for years.

She said, "You know Omar Sharif fainted when he and Faten Hamama first kissed on camera, and he fell instantly in love."

Jack kissed her cautiously, as if trying a strange new dish, then crossed his eyes, staggering, and declared he was feeling a little dizzy himself. She laughed, that beautiful, ever-surprised, and open laugh. She laughed at even his crappiest jokes, hungry for joy. When he went to kiss her properly, she set a hand gently upon his cheek, examining his face for a long while before that little chevron of frustration appeared between her eyebrows at her failure, again, to find a breach.

"You know, Omar Sharif converted to Islam for her," she said wistfully, her shining black eyes offering him, freely, access to and dominion over the entirety of her being. She could not have been more open if he were a surgeon looking at the flinching beat of her raw heart. A generosity he'd never reciprocated. Dimra offered herself in this way to everyone she met, often unsettling people with a look that seemed to see only whatever was most beautiful and sacred in them. It saddened him: she was made to love, was loved by anyone who knew her, but was caged in fear, kept by him as a djinn keeps his kidnapped princess in a cave under the sea.

"At least come back to your God," she said. "Come pray with me."

"One day."

"One day," she said, "there will be no more days."

But he did pray, as he prayed now, drifting like Morpheus through the darkened cabin of slumbering people, prayed to the raw crescent moon above the clouds, that her body would hold on to their child. A little earlier, an exhausted parent had accepted his offer to walk a crying infant up and down the aisle, and he could still feel the weight and smell of a new being, the softness of the cheeks he'd rubbed with the back of his fingers as he'd murmured a lullaby his mom used to sing him to keep evil away, *Come you to kiss him, I will not let you kiss him, Come you to harm him, I will not let you harm him*. Only a child would appease Dimra's mother.

He no longer joined his wife on Skype calls with her parents. Sometimes, though, he'd listen outside the door to these purgatorial tri-weekly sessions in the back bedroom, wincing at her mother's voice. It was as if she were painfully scraping at her own vocal cords like a child learning the violin, producing the tremulous, high-pitched minor key of the interminable ballad of her misery. He could picture her parents, both heavy now, beached upon the faded brown and orange flowers of their '70s couch, her mustachioed father, hugging his own plump belly, seditiously conveying in his glance an apology to his daughter. Her mother sat also inert, except for her hands scribing a calligraphy of despair punctuated by the wringing of the handkerchief used during her frequent bouts of melodramatic sobbing.

"Child, we have no one, nothing, as God is my witness, we live like beggars." ("We don't live like beggars," her father interjects, "and we're grateful for all you and Jamal send.") "Like beggars! Your yaba, he has ulcers big as sea urchins, and I can hardly walk, arthritis. The doctor said my bones are powder." ("He said they *would* be if you didn't take your pills.") "Powder," she insists, louder. "He said, 'If you fall, even once—*once*—you will be skin and dust only, the end of you, Khalas!' " She makes a quick, twisting slap of her palms. "In the village, may God strike me dead if I lie, the old, they didn't need to lift one olive to their mouths. And look at us here." Another bout of weeping, from which she takes a few moments to recover. "Alone, with hardly enough to eat." ("You can see we're both starving," her father says, laughing, patting his belly.) "I gave your father a beautiful son; and now we have no son." (Her father's good humor vanishes, and his heavy body seems suddenly like a boulder slowly crushing the life out of him.) "And our daughter, where is she? And when people ask me how many grandchildren I have, I say none. They say, 'By God, *none*, this is unnatural.' " (Dimra would now close her eyes, preparing for imminent impact.) "Have you prayed to God for a child, Dimra? Are you going to let me and your father die without seeing our grandson?"

Dimra was named after her parents' home village, its ruins visible from the road to Tel Aviv, its lands absorbed by Eretz, a nearby kibbutz. They fled it to escape the fighting in '48 and were never allowed back. Her mother's brother and his wife eventually made it to Chicago, where they lived undocumented, working in kitchens, their son, Wafiq, becoming a wealthy CPA. The rest of Dimra's extended family ended up in the Tel al-Zaatar refugee camp in Lebanon, all of them slaughtered in yet another of Arafat's "Palestinian Stalingrads" when the camp was besieged and shelled to rubble by Christian militias during the early years of the civil war. Dimra and her progeny were all the hope and future her parents had.

One time, Jack heard her mother say, "Is it Jamal? Is he not interested? Tell him he's your husband; he *must* make you pregnant. Tell him to make you pregnant and then he can go drink seawater." That's when he realized they'd always known; worse still, that Dimra knew.

How had he ever imagined she would not?

In his darkest and most bitter moments, Jack wondered if her parents, when they arranged her marriage to him, had known about Dimra's endometriosis, how hard it might be for their daughter to conceive.

He returned to the galley for coffee and a chat with Nancy. She couldn't wait to retire to a house she and her husband (for whom she affected a rueful, eye-rolling tolerance) owned in Cancún.

"I want to be found dead on the beach," she told him, "fat as a Thanksgiving turkey, basted and baked to perfection."

He laughed.

"By the way," she asked, "how's Krysta?"

He shrugged.

She frowned, confused. "I thought you guys were close?"

"We lost touch."

"I heard she really landed on her feet, caught herself some rich Arab guy."

"Good for her," he murmured, succumbing to a wash of prickly heat at his scalp.

Birdy haunted him. Whenever he was out in Chicago, he thought he might see her from the car, bump into her on the street, constantly believed he'd spotted her, as you do with the beloved dead. They met working a flight to Denver twelve years ago when she'd just qualified and was on reserve. Jack still had her contact in his phone, and her last text to him.

You broke my heart.

She'd never known who he was.

A scream from the cabin. "He's eating those nuts!" It was the woman with the allergic child. He and Nancy hurried down to find the man shoving nuts frantically into his mouth and leaning out into the aisle to huff deadly, nutty breaths at the howling woman clutching her ancient child's head to her breast.

3

Jack arrived home from his four-day trip a half hour before the dreaded condo meeting. Inside the back gate lay a fat Chicago rat, still twitching. After shoveling it into the garbage, he found Panther lying in the bed Jack had made for him under the deck. A feral cat who'd adopted the building, Panther was pure black and enormous, with startling emerald eyes.

"Thanks for the rat, buddy." He scratched Panther beneath his chin, provoking a thunderous purr, and wished he could just curl up beside him.

Upstairs, he found Dimra in the kitchen and wrapped his arms around her small body, pressing his cheek to her hot cheek as he told her again that she didn't need to make food for everyone whenever they held a meeting.

Laying his hand on her stomach, he softly chided, "You're stressing yourself. You need to rest." She'd never sustained a pregnancy past ten weeks.

"I'm almost done." She pulled the pita she'd baked out of the oven and slipped in a tray of cookies.

Leaving her, he slumped down on the couch in the circle they'd made from all the chairs in their apartment and strategized about how to deliver all the bad news.

He'd begin by pointing out that they were better off than many during this economic collapse. He didn't really understand all this talk of bad CDOs and MBSs. In the end, it all came down to his uncle Kassam's favorite saying: *God made this beautiful world while he was sober; then he had a few too many drinks and thought it might be funny to put the monkeys in charge.*

In recent years, banks had been throwing money at mortgagees and developers like drunken lottery winners. The developers were rehabbing buildings at a breakneck pace, cutting corners, everyone dreaming of leaping up the magical property ladder into wealth. Their own developer, Natasha, was an ever-agitated and whippet-thin woman with a fog of frizzy blond curls. A Russian immigrant, she was like a wolf who'd washed up on an island of flightless birds.

Everyone in the building paid close to $300,000 for these apartments in an insalubrious area of Rogers Park. Dazzled by the size and cosmetically impressive rehab of the three-bedroom, two-bathroom 1,500-square-foot apartments with fourteen-foot ceilings, they all made the first-time homeowner's mistake of ignoring the properties around them, the overgrown yards dotted with ancient appliances, the subsiding porches, tarp-covered roofs, and boarded-up windows.

With everyone else too terrified to deal with Natasha, Jack was voted the building's president and spokesman. She'd turn up at his door beneath that frizzy mane, effusive about the paradise she alone had made available to the owners. "This place a *shithole* before I come, dropped ceilings, can you believe it. I make you these ceilings" (raising her arms as if in supplication to them). "Isn't it beautiful? Isn't it beautiful?" she'd insist with increasing aggression. "*Beautiful.* You can breathe!" Closing her eyes, she took deep, sensuous breaths, as if she'd been released from a stinking pit into an alpine meadow. "Only thing higher, the sky, yes!" At this, she made a noise like the scream of someone slipping off a precipice into an abyss, a sound she clearly believed bore some resemblance to human laughter.

When he brought up the illegal back deck, the severe water issues, and inquired about how the basement apartment could be viable given the problems with flooding and plumbing in the building, she assured him she was putting in "special systems," as if she were a kind of Prospero, Jack thought, these "special systems" magic enacted by her Ariel, a sinister Serb called Zoran, and her browbeaten and hapless team of wordless Calibans who seemed to spend most of their time sitting in defecatory postures in the backyard waiting for instructions.

"Jack, Jack, have I ever let you down?" she'd say, and before he could respond, she'd bark: "No! I live for you. I live for this building!"

A few months before Marcia's arrival, Leo Fackler, Natasha's pit bull of a lawyer, began sending sphincter-loosening letters demanding they complete the turnover of responsibility for the building to the current condo owners or Natasha would have every right over them, from repossessing their apartments to warming her feet in the freshly disemboweled bellies of their children.

At the turnover, when Jack tried to insist Natasha sign a contract binding her to personal responsibility for the building's outstanding issues before the condo owners would sign anything themselves, her operatic performance made Lady Macbeth, Brünnhilde, and Medea seem like Victorian ladies squealing at the sight of an uncovered table leg. Natasha sang of her generous nature, her self-sacrificing goodness, sang tearfully of the splendors of her creation, "the ceilings, the ceilings!" and then hissingly plunged into ominous suggestions of her occult powers over their homes and very souls as Fackler's basso-profundo threats intensified, echoing up as if from Hades, while Natasha's husband, a rumpled little goateed man who provided in his entire crushed being evidence that nothing could withstand his wife, sang,

"Sign, sign the papers! Sign, sign and you shall be free! Just sign here in your blood! For God's sake, sign!"

After what seemed like hours of this torture, they signed. The curtain fell, the storm vanished, and they all huddled together ashamed and bewildered. Natasha, of course, immediately dissolved her company and holed herself up behind the fortress of her lawyer. Jack and the other owners made halfhearted forays into hiring lawyers to force Natasha to live up to her contractual obligations, only to be told by the ones with a conscience that it would cost them more to go to court than they could possibly gain.

Now the condo board, with Jack as its president, held complete legal and financial responsibility for a building with a leaking roof, a back deck held together with rusty nails and duct tape, showers with tiles falling off the sheetrock walls, a chronically constipated and displaced sewer line that frequently flooded the basement, and plumbing that provided so little water pressure to the top units his wife filled buckets late at night to wash with in the morning.

Through all of this stress, Dimra kept him sane, cupping his cheeks in her hands and reminding him they'd grown up in Gaza. "At least they're not bombing us, habibi," she'd say, gifting him her lovely, open laugh.

She was right. He thought of that early life in the breezeblock-and-concrete sprawl of Beach Camp, with its heart of darkness, the majlis. What had once been the legislative council building had become the seat of the Israeli military governor, surrounded by its barbed-wire fence. Beside it rose the empty pedestal of a monument to the unknown soldier erected by the Egyptians, blown up by the Israelis after their victory in '67, as if they were determined to obliterate even the dead. He recalled one night in the summer of '85 being woken by the cries of their neighbor, Nadine, and looking out of his bedroom window to see her husband, Azat, a skinny, bookish man, being dragged into the street by the IDF. It shocked and surprised Jack to see Azat naked but for his underwear. Everyone knew to sleep in their pajamas despite the awful heat, so the soldiers couldn't humiliate them in this way. As they manhandled Azat into the jeep, Jack glanced at the graffiti lit up by the jeep's headlights on the steel shutter over a storefront: "Life is like a cucumber, one day in your hand, the next day up your ass."

Azat, it turned out, had thrown a grenade at the majlis some nights before. It had bounced off the thick concrete walls and failed to explode. Betrayed by a collaborator, he received a twenty-seven-year sentence, of which he would serve nine. Jack didn't know a single family without someone in jail. His own father spent more than half Jack's childhood imprisoned. The majlis seemed to Jack like a malevolent hive, out of which swarmed the IDF in their oversized jeeps, the night patrols deliberately revving their engines and blaring traditional Hebrew songs from loudspeakers. Jack remembered all the protests following someone being shot by the IDF, or a child blinded by a rubber bullet, that eerie oceanic roar of the crowds, ending in the sight of people spilling back through the streets escaping the tear gas, covering their mouths and noses with their shirts or kufiyahs. The protests were followed by curfews, hundreds of thousands imprisoned in their hot, cramped homes from dusk till dawn. He remembered his dad often climbing onto the roof to repair the bullet holes in their water tank, since the Israeli patrols shot at them for fun. Checkpoints and searches could happen at any time, baby-faced IDF soldiers barking senseless orders in incomprehensible Arabic or rapid Hebrew. Following Palestinian unrest or an attack of any kind, patrols would kick over vegetable stands, pound on the fragile tin doors in the camps, terrifying the children, tear down the washing lines between the houses, trampling the clothes in the dirt. Many of the camp men worked as day laborers, leaving the crumbling houses and infrastructure of Gaza every morning to construct beautiful new homes for Israelis in Ashdod, Ashkelon, and Tel Aviv. Gaza was a mini East Germany, no one knowing if their neighbor was working for Shabak, living in constant fear of the night raid. And he thought of how fractured the Palestinians themselves were, their own corrupt and ineffectual leaders, no one able to control the rocket attacks that led to Israel's brutal reprisals, the gangsterish infighting of the political and religious organizations. The Israelis encouraged the Muslim Brotherhood and other Islamic groups early on, hoping their influence would weaken Fatah. These groups distributed leaflets condemning female education and encouraged attacks on infidel communists.

Then came the intifada, all that hatred and misery and thwarted love finally blowing the streets apart. Young militants threw stones at the patrols, making sure the soldiers followed them into people's houses so they'd beat up the family and smash the furniture. This ensured there'd be someone wounded and vengeful in every home.

But it often seemed to him that the greatest weapon the Israelis possessed was their power over time, all the ways in which they could steal hours from Palestinian lives. Those who weren't thrown in jail for years or decades were kept in endless lines at Israeli administrative sites to be issued permits or identification; or at the tax office, where the officers would take three-hour-long breaks, leaving people cooking in the blazing sun. They waited at checkpoints, waited to be picked up as day laborers to earn a few shekels, waited for the curfew to end so they could leave their homes, the little hourglasses of their lives emptying grain by grain.

Some went mad. Mr. Halabi's eleven-year-old son, Raja, was in a gang of boys throwing stones at fast-moving IDF vehicles, and one of the young IDF soldiers, encouraged by the others to give the boys a scare, fired his M16 over their heads. He did so just as the vehicle hit a pothole, the machine gun jumping and one of the bullets shattering Raja's skull. Just after the soldier's court-martial gave him a one-month suspended sentence, Mr. Halabi picked up a kitchen knife and headed to Tel Aviv. There he stabbed to death a young American tourist, Adam Greenberg, studying public policy at Notre Dame, and then rushed at the police, who shot him dead.

And yet, Jack also loved much of his childhood in Beach Camp, that sprawling labyrinth rife with children playing marbles or gathering teams for a raucous game of Jews and Arabs through its sandy alleyways, shadowed by sheets of corrugated iron, heavy with the scent of the sea. He remembered when he and Dimra first stood on Gillson Park Beach in Wilmette, how she said that this great lake was so like the sea, but didn't smell like the sea, as if they were in a dream. These pristine northern suburb beaches were not at all like the ones in Gaza, with trash everywhere, donkeys in the water, brightly colored kites dancing through the air, the sand packed with sunshades cobbled from planks of wood and palm fronds, the smell of grilling fish and hubble-bubbles, and of cardamom-infused coffee, sweet corn and potatoes roasting on burning embers, sizzling steam rising from the carts selling pistachios and roasted seeds, all those food stands with their fragile carnival beauty, adorned with tinsel and little lights.

At night, when there wasn't a curfew, he and his cousin Salim often slipped out to the beach. That was a time when Salim's reserve of youthful hope was so close to his surface it had leaked up, pooling slick and bright in his eyes. They would share the hubble-bubble Salim had filched from his father, Jack's uncle Kassam, who would have been passed-out drunk. They watched the fishing boats, whose lamps created a magical, illuminated path stretching far out into the sea. Jack could picture the two of them there, himself stealing glances at Salim like a girl at an older lover, while Salim remained impenetrable, implacable, his self not buried deep in uncomfortable flesh, as it was for Jack, but infusing him to the borders of his skin, his being and body as coextensive as that of an Attic statue.

Even that late, families gathered around fires. Gaza was a place without privacy, the markets jammed, the streets a river of people, especially in the crowded camp, the thin-walled houses on top of one another, all the windows and often the doors open; you heard every argument, the crying of newborns, the shrieks of mourning, the sound of Abu Ashur beating his wife in the small courtyard behind the houses. Um Ashur would pant like an anxious animal as Abu Ashur slid off his belt. Then the sound of its thwack, again and again, while Um Ashur kept as quiet as she could throughout so as to not further provoke him in this strangely mutual labor. All the listening ears around the courtyard created an unnatural well of silence, at the very bottom of which Um Ashur lay fetally curled and flinching.

Jack often heard his parents making love, his mother mostly silent, his father softly grunting, and remembered the stifled moans of pleasure of the newly married couple living in such a crowded house that they set up a tiny tent on their roof, becoming shadowy figures entwined in muted torchlight. When he and Dimra first arrived in Chicago, lying in that fancy bedroom in her cousin's house in Wilmette, they couldn't sleep for the silence.

As a child, Jack often hid in his wardrobe, reading by flashlight. It was the only place he could find deep privacy before he and Salim climbed that sandy cliff above the sea to discover Eden in a condemned and visibly listing two-story house.

Herzl, the father of Zionism, imagined his Zion as paradise, his old-new land a multicultural and pacifist utopia, free of religious zealotry. There were times in Gaza, as when Jack stepped out onto the balcony of his home at sunset to stand before that weary orange orb over the sea, cooled by the rush of salt air brought by the coastal wind at the end of a scorching day, his nostrils filling with the scent of honeysuckle winding through rusting cast iron, when he could sense the paradise hidden in every moment. On that balcony, at the restless and absolving turn of the day, the sun and moon sharing the same sky, paradise seemed so close to the surface it was easy to imagine Palestinian children letting the stones fall from their fists, Israeli children casting aside their machine guns. He could feel that ticklish thread of paradise come loose from the weave of this fallen life, a thread that could be teased out by someone with more faith than he and a steadier hand, drawn through the sun as through the eye of a needle, and through the moon, and through each star as it appeared, and then through every human heart, so that people all over the world might stop and wonder how it was that they were feeling a soft breeze, smelling honeysuckle and the salt sea. Then distant gunfire would return Jack's gaze to the scorch of burned tires in the street, and his uncle's cynicism would re-echo: *God made this beautiful world while he was sober; then he had a few too many drinks and thought it might be funny to put the monkeys in charge.*

Now Jack was in America, the great Satan, enemy of his people, whose taxpayers supported their invaders, oppressors, and occupiers, whose jets and bombs murdered and terrorized them. Whose taxpayers also (and for this, perhaps, they were hated more) supported the camps, clothed and fed them.

In Gaza, people excoriated America with one breath and dreamed of climbing its glittering Jacob's ladder with the next. They all watched *Dallas* and dreamed of big hats and big hair, of wives with childlike faces and miraculous breasts. Jack had made it here. Now he lived in a city that felt almost as profoundly segregated as the place he'd come from, and where more people were killed by guns in most years than died in Gaza and the West Bank.

Jack checked his watch. Lulu, who owned the apartment next door, would arrive first, to support him. He wondered if Marcia would bring Aisha and Ryker. May, of course, always turned up last. To keep people waiting was yet another petty assertion of her power.

Just a day after he and Dimra had moved into their apartment last year, May left a note on their front mat.

Why are you both walking like <u>big buffalo</u>?

These notes became part of his life, shifting to texts once she secured his number.

Your TV is loud AND NOT IN ENGLISH!

I'm going crazy down here! I hear you clip your fingernails. I hear you BREATHE. I HEAR YOU FART!!

Why did you THROW UP so long and so loud all night. I got NO SLEEP!

She owned a half share in a Vietnamese restaurant in Evanston, but her partner had sidelined her, so she had nothing to do, and insisted on being treasurer for the condo. She also insisted on strict condominium rules and stiff fines for any breach. He and Lulu tried to explain to her that people were struggling financially and that it was harsh to fine them $50 if they mistakenly walked into a common area holding a cigarette or were a couple of days late with their assessments, but for May, swift, severe punishment of rule-breakers was the only thing that kept chaos at bay. Of course, she never fined herself for late payments during the restaurant's frequent cash-flow issues, or when her son, Danh, who turned up periodically when he needed a place to stay, smoked in the common areas and flicked his butts into the yard.

Jack heard Lulu's gentle knock, and she entered, unfortunately followed by the sour face of Valeria, a recent live-in girlfriend to whom Lulu was entirely in thrall. Lulu, a massage therapist, the daughter of Mexican immigrants, was a pixyish dynamo with waist-length hair and the glimmer of innocent wickedness in her eyes. Before Valeria, except for dramatic earrings, Lulu used to dress casually, but now conformed to what Jack could only assume was Valeria's schoolgirl fetish. Tonight: pigtails, a tight crop top, plaid miniskirt, and high-heeled Doc Martens. Valeria, who'd recently published a novel, taught comparative literature at UChicago. She dressed with a punk/rockabilly aesthetic, a '50s-style polka-dot corset dress showing off the chaotic array of tattoos on her arms—the monochrome head of an agonized Christ bumping up against a Looney Tunes Tasmanian Devil. With her bouffant mohawk, cat-eye glasses, and studded dog collar, she resembled a dominatrix librarian.

"You guys look nice," he said.

Valeria quickly responded, "We're heading out in an hour." And then impatiently to Lulu, "No me quedaré en este lugar ni un minuto más."

Apologetically, Lulu said, "It's a double celebration. Valeria's novel has been longlisted for the National Book Award, and the University of Chicago has offered her a tenure-track position."

"Congratulations," he exclaimed too effusively, as one does when good things happen to people you loathe.

Jack's front door opened again just after Lulu and Valeria sat down.

"Hello all!" It was Gunther, who lived in the apartment beneath Lulu's, kicking off his green Crocs. He was a heavy, bearded, middle-aged white man in a plaid shirt and jeans, jolly as the Ghost of Christmas Present.

Drumming his belly in anticipation of the meze filling the coffee table, he whispered, winking, "Jack, I have something to show you. Come down after the meeting."

"Something else you've stolen?"

He laughed heartily, as he always did. "Borrowed, my friend. *Borrowed.*"

Jack had never met anyone so entirely without guile or subtext. Gunther found everything and everyone "not normal," like Lulu and Valeria, exotic and fascinating, and would stare at them as if from a great distance through binoculars. Gunther worked in cataloguing and displays at the Field Museum, and "borrowed" items from the museum archives, cycling them through his apartment: the beak of a mummified ibis, the eighteen-inch incisor of a sabertoothed cat, a petrified dinosaur egg. It was this little dragon hoard he liked to show off to Jack.

"Neat tattoos," he said to Valeria as if praising a four-year-old's crayon drawing. He'd already piled a small plate with meze, his beard littered with the crumbs of a spinach pastry. Valeria loathed him. When he first met her, he'd asked in perfect innocence if she was going to a costume party.

Ken arrived next. He was a slight, good-looking African American in his midthirties, with tiny ears high up on his shining bald head, dimples when he (rarely) smiled, and a lower lip made prominent by a slight underbite that gave him a thoughtful pout. The first in his family to go to college, he now taught science and math at Jordan Elementary. He lived alone, fastidious as a cat, his immaculate apartment furnished like a corporate waiting room. A Buddhist, he'd turned his second largest bedroom into a dojo containing nothing but a reed mat and singing bowl. Ken took his seat, stiff and punctilious, straightening his pant seams and tugging his shirt cuffs.

Pauline entered moments later, a heavy, ebony-skinned Haitian with a soft, round face and close-cropped hair. Her eyes were wide-set and slightly bulbous, their direct gaze full of sympathetic inquiry, the perfect face for a neonatal nurse who dealt all day with the parents of sick or premature children. Like his wife, she was concerned for Jack's immortal soul, adjuring him to accept Jesus as his personal savior. It had become a joke between them, with her singing "Someone's knockin' at the door" almost every time she saw him.

Another knock, and in stepped Marcia, with her greyhound slenderness and muscularity, wearing a camo tank top with black capri jeans. Though visibly nervous, she also shot Jack a look that seemed actively, as opposed to defensively, angry, and he wondered if she'd discovered more issues with her place. He introduced her to everyone, careful to refer to her apartment as the garden, not the basement, and asked her if she wouldn't mind removing her sneakers. She protested that she wasn't wearing socks but saw that both he and Dimra were barefoot, and after a hesitation slipped her shoes off to reveal every toenail of her long-toed feet painted in a different neon shade.

"Aisha painted them," she explained, glancing regretfully down.

"They look very pretty," Dimra said.

Marcia took a seat on the couch beside Gunther, pushing herself into the far corner, her face flushed.

Checking his watch, Jack considered texting May, but she finally appeared, clutching the folder in which she kept the condo accounts.

"Welcome," Jack said.

As if his greeting were a dig at her lateness, she responded indignantly, "My son's here"—an event that clearly took precedence over this insignificant meeting.

Jack instantly wondered if the basement door was locked. Last time Danh came to stay, Lulu's new road bike vanished.

"Just for a visit?" he asked.

"This is his home," she barked. "He can stay however long he wants."

As he and May took their seats, he noticed Marcia's glance, newly inflamed, fixing upon May, and before he could begin, she blurted angrily, "I'm not paying fifty fucking dollars."

"We gave you the rules and regs," May snapped. "Your stuff is everywhere in the basement. Only bikes in the common area or a fifty-dollar fine."

"I *just* fucking moved in."

"May," Lulu interjected as gently as she could, "we're a community. These rules are guidelines."

"Guidelines, what's guidelines? People pay or people don't pay, whatever they feel like!"

"Please," Jack said, "let's talk about this later. We have a lot to get through."

"I'm not fucking paying and this bitch isn't going to make me."

"You call me a bitch, I'll call the police."

"*Please*," Jack pleaded, "let's keep this civil. Look, we have a lot of . . . unfortunate things to talk about."

"*What* things?" Marcia said. "Are you talking about the water situation?"

"Yes, but Marcia, there are lots of issues with the building, and Lulu and I have spent the last few weeks gathering estimates."

Jack surveyed his list. "In order of priority, we need ten thousand for a new two-inch water line, thirty thousand for a new back deck, five thousand for a new water pump, three thousand for a stent to repair the sewer line, and twenty thousand to resurface the roof."

Ken interjected, "But at the last meeting we talked about dealing with these over time, right?"

"Unfortunately"—Jack hesitated, sighing—"one of the many things Natasha neglected to mention to us was that the back deck and water system failed city inspection. As the new registered agent, I just received notice that if both are not replaced within nine months, they'll declare the building unlivable and we'll have to move out."

"Move out!" Pauline looked frantic.

"So," Jack continued quickly, "to fix everything is sixty-eight thousand, which is about ten thousand for all the aboveground units, eight for the garden. If we were just to deal with the water and deck for now, it's forty thousand: about six thousand each, four for the garden."

"And we're all underwater with our mortgages," Ken murmured with a deep, sad breath, "so we can't get anything from the bank."

Gunther was so stunned, the forgotten wedge of pita he was holding up to his mouth wilted, spilling baba ghanoush all over his shirt.

"What the fuck!" Marcia shouted.

"But I have a plan." Jack lifted his hands to calm the room. He explained that all the contracting companies were in serious trouble, since there was now no work for them, and he was sure that in a couple of months he could find someone to replace the deck for much less than $30,000. He'd repair the leaky roof himself until they could afford to replace it. They would deal with the water and sewer situation first using their reserves, which would need to be replenished by a special assessment of just over $3,000. He hoped that some could pay this early but understood (he avoided looking at Marcia here) that money was tight, so the absolute deadline for payment was the first of April next year.

The meeting went on for another hour. By the end, exhausted, Jack hoped Gunther had forgotten his invitation. He hadn't, but as Jack was about to follow him down, Marcia said fiercely, "I need to talk to you."

He told Gunther he'd be with him in a minute. When Marcia glanced meaningfully at Dimra, who was cleaning up, Jack suggested the back deck. Forgetting her shoes, she marched down the hall and he quickly followed. They stood barefoot on the deck in the darkness, a sliver of the moon behind Marcia. He could smell cigarette smoke and guessed Danh was sitting beneath them.

"They're glow-in-the-dark," Jack said.

"What?" she snapped impatiently before following his glance down to her toenails. "Oh. Yes. Look, I didn't know about any of this fucking shit with the building. Why should I have to pay for the roof or the deck? I don't use the deck. Where the fuck am I going to get three thousand dollars?" She was shouting at him now, her face so close, their noses were almost touching.

"Look, I—"

"I'm pregnant. I've got a fucking kid. Who knows what's going to happen to my job with all this shit going on. I'm guessing there aren't going to be too many people splashing out on luxury lake cruises. And that royal fucking bitch down there—"

"We'll sort out the fine."

"What about this three thousand?"

"I'm afraid—"

"You tell me what I'm going to do. You want me to sell a fucking kidney?"

"Marcia, you have seven months. We're *all* responsible for the building. We're a community." He tried to speak as quietly and calmly as he could.

"You want me to be in a fucking community with that Chinese asshole?"

"May's Vietnamese."

"Whatever the fuck she is. And you still haven't told me where the fuck I'm going to find this money."

It was shocking and upsetting to have this woman he'd only just met screaming at him.

From a window of the big apartment building on their north side someone shouted, "Take that shit inside!"

When Marcia turned to the voice, he could see the rapid rise and fall of her chest. He met the malevolently seductive gaze of her Calavera Catrina, and glanced down again at her luminous toes. She smelled faintly of cedarwood; her deodorant, he guessed. When she turned back, he noticed how dry her lips were. She kept pulling them into her mouth to wet them, only making them drier, then gnawing at the fraying skin. He wanted to tell her to stop.

The voice seemed to have broken the spell of her swelling fury, and she suddenly reentered his flat, marched along the hall, snatched up her shoes, and vanished out of his front door. Remembering Gunther, he reluctantly headed down to his neighbor's back door on the landing below.

Danh sat on the rattan bench on May's deck, a cigarette unspooling from his trembling hand. His huge mop of matte-black hair looked as if it weighed more than his skinny body, his face tubercular and acne-ravaged. An addict, he'd spent his life in and out of halfway houses.

"Hi, Danh, how are you?" Jack didn't expect a response. Danh had never said a word to him, meeting any attempt to engage with a dull stare of contempt.

"Danh, can I ask you if you wouldn't mind smoking out front. We put a chair out there for you. It's just that if—"

"I know. That Black woman came up, asked me earlier. Not my problem her dad's gone nuts."

Pauline hated cigarettes, the one grace granted by her father's Alzheimer's being that he'd forgotten he smoked. But whenever Bernard smelled smoke or saw anyone smoking, if no one was supervising him, he'd vanish into the neighborhood to find cigarettes. If Jack was home, he'd receive a frantic call from Pauline. Everyone in the building would help, heading out to see if they could locate him.

"He's got Alzheimer's."

"We all got something, bro."

The door finally opened. "Sorry, I thought you were coming in the front." Gunther led Jack up his hallway. Gunther never cleaned his place, which smelled mostly of stale grease and whatever microwave meal he'd recently zapped, though you were sometimes ambushed by the dark umami of body odor. On the floor lay things Gunther had dropped and not bothered to pick up, the inner ring of a toilet roll, a sock, loose change, a teaspoon, all immured in a foggy web of dust. As they walked, lilliputian herds of dust buffalo scattered before them. His bedroom contained only his bed and a dresser, the distinct grease mark of his head upon the pillow. Finally, they entered his great room, filled with mismatched furniture he'd picked up at charity shops and garage sales, all bringing their own deep odor of a former life.

Gunther asked Jack to take a stool at the granite-topped island all the kitchens had.

"I have a few objects for your delectation." Gunther hurried back down the hall and returned carrying a large crate covered in a towel. Taking his place on the opposite side of the island, he settled the crate gently on the floor beside him before slipping on a pair of white cotton gloves. "I'm going to leave the best for last."

The first thing he produced was a mason jar containing a quarter inch or so of what appeared to be colored sand. "These are scales I gathered from the bottom of a recent display of now-extinct butterflies and moths."

Jack examined them appreciatively, a few of them glittering with remembered glory under the bright ceiling lights.

He admired Gunther, educating himself with an encyclopedic knowledge of everything that ever passed through the museum. But the fact that he'd never attained a higher degree meant he was still earning an hourly wage. He hauled the exhibits around and did whatever handiwork and maintenance the displays or archives required.

"Now, this next one *should* be the one I leave for last, but the other two are more fun."

He pulled out a small box, his hands trembling a little as he removed a fossil and set it down in front of Jack before hurrying around the island so they could examine it together.

"This I have to return first thing tomorrow morning. It's going to be on display next week. I think it's the most precious thing I've ever borrowed."

"A bird?"

He nodded. "They found it in Germany. Can you tell what kind of bird it is?"

It was tiny. "A finch?"

"My friend, let me introduce you to *Eurotrochilus inexpectatus*, a fancy way to say unexpected European hummingbird. Naturalists thought these little fellows were unique to the New World, which is the only place they can be found now. The oldest fossils discovered in South America are about thirty thousand years old. Guess how old this is."

"A hundred thousand."

Gunther leaned in so close, Jack might have dined on the remains of his wife's meze in his neighbor's beard. "Thirty. *Million*. Years. Old."

Jack, amazed, more closely examined these tiny bones vomited from the snaky innards of the earth.

"This discovery finally explains why there are a handful of European flowers that seem specifically adapted for hummingbirds. Can you believe they've been waiting thirty million years?"

"I'm going to bring that up when my passengers complain about flight delays." Though Jack made a joke of it, he thought of Gaza again: waiting at checkpoints, at the border, or for a curfew to lift, waiting to return to homes that were no longer there. He thought of Dimra waiting for him every day, waiting for a child. And then he thought of Birdy, and how he felt almost from their first meeting as if he'd been waiting for her for longer than his life.

Gunther carefully replaced the hummingbird in its box, that scintillant, flickering existence forever seized.

The next thing Gunther produced was the skin of a snake floating within a wax-sealed apothecary jar.

"This was in a recent exhibit of frauds and hoaxes. We had a jackalope, Piltdown Man, all sorts of goodies. The story behind this is that it was purchased by the Chicago city fathers a hundred years ago from a huckster who convinced them it had been shed by the serpent who'd corrupted Eve. Satan's skin!"

It was delicate, lacy, miraculous; you could even see where the snake's eyes had been. Jack often wished he could shed himself and be new, though he had a vague intuition that this desire, the root of the American dream, was the devil's primary temptation. The Zionists had dreamed of renewal, purity, safety; and yet fragments of the past had turned morbid, poisoning the new country, the new citizens. With a buried jolt of fear, he thought of the baby and his wife's endometriosis.

"Well, I guess you never know," Jack said.

Gunther laughed, lifting the jar to examine the skin once more before returning it. Gunther lacked the imagination (he would have said *superstition*) required for faith of any kind, except in science. He found religion laughable, but didn't recognize that there was something fetishistic about these preserved or petrified items, proof of a secular afterlife for a man sealed in the present moment of a purely material world.

"And now for the *pièce de resistance*," Gunther declared, flinging a pair of cotton gloves at Jack and making a drumroll on the granite-topped island.

As Jack slipped the gloves on, his neighbor produced a little wooden box packed with cotton batting. From this batting, he carefully unwrapped a mottled buff-colored object, which he lay gently into Jack's cupped hands. It was about the size of Jack's two palms together and not as heavy as he thought it would be. It was as if someone had fashioned a baby from clay but had then half compressed the finished infant into a ball, all the distinct limbs compacted together, one arm curled over the top of its slightly misshapen head, the other bundled beneath it, fist to chin, resembling a mini and mocking version of *The Thinker*. It was nearly crossing its legs like a little Buddha, and he could make out the toes of one foot. All the facial features were slightly flattened, so the child looked pugilistic.

"What do you think it is?" Gunther asked.

"A mummified fetus?"

"Close, but no cigar. This is a genuine lithopedion. A stone baby."

"I don't understand. Someone made this?"

"No, it's a real baby. Or was. It happens when the fetus grows outside the womb, in the abdomen, and dies; so, to stop the rotting flesh from infecting the mother, the body's defense system calcifies it. And voilà, you have a stone baby." He explained that this one was found in an American woman called Emily McFadden who became pregnant in the late 1860s. After six months she was in pain. Doctors wanted to cut into her, but she'd been a nurse during the Civil War and the butchery she'd witnessed had turned her off surgeons. She suffered abdominal pain with periodically acute spasms and became bedridden. "She carried this little fellow inside her until her death fifty years later, lactating for *thirty* of those years. She always claimed she could feel the baby moving," Gunther concluded, "and at the postmortem they found him floating in a white, odorless pus inside her abdomen."

"Him?"

"Or her."

Jack didn't know why, but the baby had immediately imprinted itself on him as a girl. He felt a strange kind of awe, weirdly mixed with tenderness, at holding Emily McFadden's child. And suddenly his heart began to beat with fear as he again thought about the child inside his wife, of the pain Emily McFadden endured, the wasted milk soaking her chemise, the phantom movements of a beloved thing turned to stone within her, as if her whole life were in unceasing labor to give birth to death. And yet this child didn't seem dead, her pugnacious little face asserting her small being.

"Pretty neat, huh?"

Jack wished Gunther wasn't with him. He could hear his neighbor's labored breathing, smell the baba ghanoush on his beard.

"I have a feeling this might end up in my permanent collection," Gunther said, gently removing it from Jack's hands and returning it to the box.

"What do you mean?"

"It was part of an exhibit of medical curiosities in the '30s, after which it was marked as missing, presumed stolen. I found it at the bottom of a box marked 'Miscellaneous Petrified Objects' in a storeroom containing uncatalogued items."

"You're going to keep it?"

"For a while," he said, rewrapping it in the batting as carefully as if it were a living infant.

When Jack returned to his apartment, he could see the light on under the bedroom door. He stood in the dark hall for a while, feeling strangely bereft, and then raised his hands and looked at his palms. Empty. It seemed as if he had never really taken hold of anything.

His thoughts were broken up by the sound of Preacher Morris screaming from the street. Preacher Morris lived in one of the Section 8 blocks near Jordan Elementary and spent his days wandering the neighborhood at all hours, fiercely proselytizing about the wages of sin and coming judgment, terrifying anyone who didn't know him.

Jack finally entered the bedroom to his wife reading the Quran. After brushing his teeth, he slipped into bed beside her, and she put the book down, looking at him with bashful curiosity.

It struck him that they never talked about the baby. They hadn't even discussed a name. It felt cowardly and neglectful suddenly, and, lifting the covers, he kissed the small bump of her stomach.

"What did Gunther want?"

"He's *borrowed* a few more artifacts."

"This is *wrong*."

"He needs them. Being trapped in a cell that has doors in it, even if they're all locked, is better than being trapped in one without any doors."

She shook her head, confused.

"Those artifacts are his doors," he said. "One of them was the skin of Satan in a jar."

Under her breath, she apotropaically murmured, "Nothing will ever befall us except what Allah has destined."

"Don't worry. It's just a shed snakeskin. It's beautiful. Wouldn't you like to shed your skin sometimes, habibti?"

To this she gave no answer, just stared at him with her lambently dark eyes, a look so familiar to him, tense with a question she was afraid to ask. She kissed his shoulder. She loved him, her love like an irradiating force. What he hoped was that her genius for devotion would shift to the child. She would meet the parents of other children and find friends here she could love, finally cutting that poisoned umbilical to Gaza.

"Just the snakeskin?" she said.

"And an ancient hummingbird." After telling her about those European flowers waiting thirty million years for what had once shaped them, the vacuum of silence created by him *not* mentioning the stone baby tonally distorted his abrupt "Marcia's toenail polish was glow-in-the-dark."

After a moment, quietly, his wife said, "She's very beautiful."

"Yes," he said, "I suppose so."

"Will you tell her I'm happy to look after Aisha whenever she needs?"

He could see Marcia's toes again, glowing out there on the deck. Shifting aside the covers once more, he lifted Dimra's right leg to kiss the silky skin of her thigh. He slipped further down in the bed to kiss her knee, then her calf.

"Would you ever wear toenail polish?" he asked, kissing her immaculate little foot.

"If you want me to," she said.

= 4 =

That night, unable to sleep, Jack went out to the couch to read but ended up just staring at the rippling shadows of leaves on the ceiling, listening to their soft surf, *The Inheritance of Loss* splayed open on his chest. He would begin a five-leg trip tomorrow: Minneapolis, San Francisco, Seattle, Dallas, back to Chicago. How many years now of diffusing himself throughout this country? Lost. He'd been lost even before he and Dimra emigrated from Egypt nearly twenty years ago.

They had stayed briefly with her cousin Wafiq in Wilmette until Jack secured a job manning a stand called Fly Fresh at O'Hare. Some months after they arrived, the first Gulf War began. One afternoon, while Dimra was out shopping, a gang of high school girls called her a towelhead bitch. One wrenched off her hijab, another emptied her shopping bags onto the sidewalk, and a big girl slapped Dimra in the face, the spell of violence broken only when a brave passerby shouted for them to stop and they scattered. This initiated Dimra's reluctance to leave their apartment.

At work, desperately lonely, Jack watched with envy the chattering flocks of flight attendants. One day, a male steward set a bottle of water on his counter. Jack had noticed him before, an attractive man with a sly, carnal smile and a raffish flop of black hair, his uniform provocatively tight. His name was Phelan, a recent Irish immigrant who'd qualified as an airline steward a few years before. He handed Jack a magical card that had just whisked him first class to Hawaii. The card also ensured a 50 percent discount on hotels. "Or a fine-looking fella like you can find yourself a friend." Phelan winked. "I'm very good at that. I fly the friendly skies, stay in friendly beds. Just think now, you can head to any gate in this airport and go."

"Go?"

"Anywhere in the world. Just go." As he retrieved the card, Phelan slid his finger across the side of Jack's palm, and with another wink, softly mouthed, *Anywhere, anytime.*

Dimra was confused. "How can you attend night school with such a schedule?" She was fixated on Jack becoming an accountant like her cousin. She dreamed of a beautiful house near the lake in a quiet, safe northern suburb.

"In time I'll have flexibility over my schedule, and we'll be able to travel. The training's free, and I'll earn a lot more than I do right now, with good benefits."

Quietly, she said, "Is this a job that men do?"

"Of course, lots of men do this job."

"I don't like to think of you serving and cleaning up after people. You could get a good job."

"This *is* a good job," he insisted, "good enough we might be able to buy a flat of our own soon," adding with emphasis, "for our child." There was nothing she wanted more than a baby, and his manipulativeness caused him to briefly suffer that hollow, off-kilter feeling he always experienced when he was behaving dishonorably.

The interview required all his courage. For nearly two years, he'd worked alone at his booth in Terminal 3, and standing still within that endless flux, he felt ever more orthogonal to the world, scoured to near invisibility. The thought of trying to sell himself to strangers made him so nervous, his underarms became swampy and he nearly walked away. One of the interviewers, an older woman, followed him out afterward. Hoping, she said, he could take a small piece of advice in the right spirit, she suggested he use a more American name.

"Jack," she proposed, laughing. "Jack's a name no one can object to. Jack is everyone and no one."

A month before his training was to begin, he received a letter from his mother. With the time difference, his work schedule, and the risk of his father finding out, telephoning was impossible. He mailed his letters to the Palestinians for Peace office where his mother volunteered, careful to write a false name on the return address.

My darling son,

All is well, thanks be to God. I wish I could send you money so you could give up this job at the airport and go to night school. I had no idea it was so expensive to qualify as an accountant. We've just celebrated the birth of Salim's second child, a boy. It pains me so much in such moments that you're not here and that Salim never mentions you. I want to ask him if he's forgotten how close you were. When I suggested he name this son Jamal, he and your father looked at me as if I were mad. Oh, my beloved boy, perhaps I am. They've named him Mazen, but he'll be Jamal in my heart, and I will love him. My son, I so long for you to have a child. I pray every day for God's mercy. Your father forbids any mention of you and because the most vital truth cannot be spoken, everything your father and I say to each other, no matter how banal, is a lie.

I promised myself this wouldn't be a sad letter, but without you I feel empty. Even my dearest friends treat me now as a woman without a son, a barren woman.

My darling, you were my miracle. I know what Dimra is going through. Please tell her it can happen. It can. You said it was hard to get hold of pigeons, but do try, and eat them as often as possible. Keep your blessed parts cool and unrestricted. Tell Dimra to eat dates and the black seed. I enclose alum for you to burn. I'm an educated woman. I know these things are silly, but what's the harm in trying? But when you have a child (God willing!), how am I to keep that from your father? How could I live with that lie?

This week I'm scheduled to have a stent put into one of my arteries, so my next letter may be a little delayed. It's a simple and safe procedure (God willing), so don't worry. My beloved, I miss you. My love to Dimra. Next time, all the chambers of my heart will be singing (not croaking!) with my blood, and I will write you a happy letter!

Your loving mother

Jack's mother had been his world. From a wealthy Copt family, she received a private-school English education with mostly expat girls in Cairo, singing "God Save the Queen" every morning and dancing around the maypole in her blazer and skirt during the hottest part of the Egyptian summer. Her father played golf at the Gezira Sporting Club with King Edward and was an adviser to King Farouk.

Jack had often sifted through the Polaroids of his parents in their youth, kept in a biscuit tin in his mother's office. In one they're protesting with other students in front of Cairo's Nahdat Misr monument. His beanpole-thin mother is almost as tall as his father, the two of them holding up a sign that says FREE PALESTINE. The raven wings of her stormy eyebrows lend a comic fierceness to a face so young. In another, she and his father lie on a lawn trapped in the weblike shadow of a tree. He's wantonly supine, his shirt halfway open, staring up through the branches with dreamy seriousness. She's on her side, her arms and legs wrapped around his body. It's an image of obliterating love, as if she wishes she could be entirely inside him or draw him entirely inside herself. Jack could imagine his father's shirt smelling of Acqua di Parma and Fatima cigarettes, the feel when she kisses him of a stubble the sharpest razor can't subdue for long. But the most poignant picture is of her in a mountainous place—Jordan, perhaps, or the West Bank. She's sitting on rocky ground cradling a Kalashnikov. Wearing a pale blouse, capris, and gladiator sandals, her hair tied back with a Chanel scarf, she couldn't look more out of place. It's a haunting picture, as if she's in a dream where someone has set the machine gun into her arms, saying, "Here is your baby." Her expression of confused tenderness has somehow shifted her from girl to woman.

For her family, it was as if, in marrying her father, she'd wedded a chimera comprised of the three most abject creatures on Earth: peasant, Muslim, and Palestinian. When they cut her off, she moved from a gated mansion in Zamalek to a four-room house in the most crowded refugee camp in Gaza, Beach Camp, adjacent to Gaza City. Though she converted to Islam for his father, the camp women viewed it as shameful to marry outside one's clan and shunned her. The camp was a hermetic world, all the Palestinians from the same town or village clustered together. It was a compressed soundscape of the lost paradise, from the singsong accents of those from Simsim to the lazy burr of Bir Salam. The refugees brought with them all their old class and tribal prejudices: those from Burayr derided those from Simsim as notorious thieves; the former merchants and businessmen of Majdal looked down their noses at the fellaheen rubes. If a visitor was searching for someone in that maze of alleyways, all you needed was the person's surname. If called Shamalla, they were from Beit Daras, and you'd tell them to head west and take a hook down the alley past Abu Rushdi's falafel stand.

The camp women shunned his mother not only as an outsider but also for her fine-boned beauty, immodest dress, and film-star Egyptian accent. She smoked in front of the men, even argued with them. Their hard-bitten wives gave her little quarter. Many called her, derisively, Princess, and there were a few who couldn't hide their delight at her struggle to conceive. One particularly bitter woman nicknamed her Um la Shay, Mother of Nothing.

It didn't help, either, that one of the few things his mother brought with her was an extensive library. When Jack finally arrived, he was everything to her. With Jack's father so often in jail, Jack slept in her bed until he was a teen. Rather than send him to the overcrowded UNRWA school, she hot-housed him. Jack was speaking English with a BBC World Service accent, Parisian French, and his mother's upper-class Arabic by the time he was seven. With each other they spoke an idiomatic patois of French, English, and Arabic. They both learned Hebrew, and later Jack taught himself German in case he ended up at a university there, as many Palestinians did.

An Anglophile, like her father, she had selected no Arab writers for her library, not even Naguib Mahfouz. She immersed Jack in the classic children's stories she thought would appeal to boys, *Treasure Island*, *Kidnapped*, *The Hobbit*, *The Chronicles of Narnia*, but he also loved *Anne of Green Gables* and *Little Women*, and quickly transitioned into adult novels by means of *Jane Eyre*, *Kim*, *Rebecca*, and *Oliver Twist*. Cuddled up in bed together, each read a chapter at a time to the other. During *War and Peace*, Jack became so absorbed in the lives and struggles of bearish Pierre, gloomy Nikolai, and vivacious Natasha, it would disorient him to leave the house, expecting britzkas in the broad boulevards of St. Petersburg, not donkey carts cluttering the camp's narrow alleys. In the house, they lived as if within that literature. Jack was a great mimic, and both he and his mother would slip into Dickens's characters, the two of them performing skits as they made dinner or cleaned the house, declaring the wind was in the east, that they were mere children, and so very, *very* 'umble.

Mocked and punched a few times by the camp boys, Jack quickly learned to switch to the coarse demotic of the streets the moment he stepped out of the door. It was an absurd bell-jar life. While the camp filled with black smoke, tear gas, and shouts of protest, he and his mother would be sobbing over the death of Beth March, Little Nell, or Lennie Small.

In Jack's early teens, his father returned after a three-year stint in prison. As ever, it was as if a drop of oil had entered to split their emulsion. Jack's father was a shocking bolt of pure masculinity. He banned their patois, furious at them for being so infected by the languages of their colonizers and betrayers. He also became furious if Jack tried to help his mother with the cooking or cleaning, shouting, *Are you a boy or a girl?* Jack and his mother behaved like secret lovers, embracing quickly as they passed each other in the hallway, whispering in their illicit language. When his father was inevitably arrested again, Jack felt a treacherous complicity with the Israelis. In some deep, confused way Jack did love his father, and yet when he was gone, something fragile and vital in Jack could return to life.

But after his father left that time, his mother insisted he was too old to share her bed and no longer returned his embraces with her usual hungry affection. She shooed him out of the kitchen if he tried to help. Gide and Genet vanished from their bookshelves, as did *Twelfth Night*, *As You Like It*, *Orlando*, and *Maurice*. His father had clearly said something about his unmasculine manner. For Jack's sake, his mother wanted to break the bubble of their life together, realizing that her son needed to face the reality of his existence as a Gazan man.

Jack began to worry that something was wrong with him. He lived as absolutely in the desires and frustrations of the women in those novels as of the men. When he practiced the secret habit, he often imagined being both male and female in the same climactic moment, like Adam dreaming of the Eve inside him.

By this time, his mother had learned that long pants and a voluminous blouse were not enough to stop the women calling her a safra. She cooked bread in a taboon, washed clothes by hand. She no longer looked men in the eye or let men into the house when she was alone. She never disagreed with her husband in front of other people, and during his Fatah meetings vanished after serving the coffee. She adapted herself to being alone during his incarcerations, joining the hundreds of camp women on the buses to the various jails that held their men. She also established literacy and numeracy workshops for women, set up a children's daycare for those who had to work because their husbands were in jail. She studied Israeli law and teamed up with Israeli peace groups to eke out a modicum of justice from a world where the police and judges were your enemies. Establishing friendships with liberal Jews and NGO workers, she grew less lonely, but in the camp she was still an outsider. She became stouter, her face fiercer and more masculine. While the strange dream of the Kalashnikov baby had shifted her from child to woman, this was the next stage of life, the long-besieged state of the women in the camp. She came to understand why they laughed so much and learned to ride the waves of that laughter with them through their stormy lives.

During the violent Land Day demonstrations in '84, Jack's mother saw from their balcony a neighbor's twelve-year-old son being chased by an Israeli patrol. By the time she got to the boy, he was being shoved and slapped by a young IDF soldier. She pushed herself between them as women flooded the street. The soldier had a bleeding contusion under his left eye, no doubt from a stone the boy had thrown. Though feeling sympathy for this frightened Israeli child in his uniform, in Hebrew, she said, "Your mother must be proud of you beating up little boys." In a blind fury, the soldier slammed his palm into her face to get her out of his way, hitting her nose, which bled profusely. Jack ran into the street calling for her but was gang-tackled by four of the women and shoved back into his house. They knew he was at much more risk for arrest and violence than the women who now crowded the street, screaming at the nervous soldiers. The injured soldier again tried to wrench Jack's mother out of the way, but she shoved him back. The next time he took hold of her, she slapped his shoulder, finally inciting him to twist the offending arm behind her back. Cuffing her, he shoved her into the jeep and they roared off. When she returned after a five-month sentence, a crowd of women gathered outside their house. Clapping in rhythm they sang the kind of call-and-response songs you heard at village weddings, one of them improvising verses in praise of her heroism.

Jack had been moved by this, but perhaps more so by the sight of his mother as she stepped out of the taxi. He was struck by how much she now resembled many of the women around her, her body heavy, a burden and a fortress; nothing left of the ardent, beanpole girl. Her movements, even her breathing, were aquatically slow, as if she'd adapted to a different medium and sense of time.

Now the camp women called her Princess without derision: it had become her nom de guerre.

Jack would sometimes look in on her sitting with her back to him in the tiny office carved from a section of his parents' bedroom. He often found her staring out of the window into the central backyard they shared with other houses, webbed with washing lines. A lonely figure. She and his father were once inspired by Algeria, Cuba, and Vietnam—righteous struggles pitting bombs hidden in women's baskets against fighter jets. But this was hardly the Che Guevara life she'd imagined. His mother's battles began with a hammering at their door, a woman's voice calling up, "Um Jamal, Um Jamal!" His mother would sit with her petitioner, who was sometimes frantic, weeping, tugging at her own clothes: a husband who'd taken work abroad wasn't being allowed back into Gaza; the vague charge of "suspected terrorist activities" was preventing a work permit from being renewed; a son or daughter had been arrested. She would sit patiently, like a mother absorbing a little child's punches and screams following some pain or fright. When the woman calmed, his mother would outline the next steps, the forms she would help the woman fill out, the minister his mother would contact, the NGO that might help. Her once burning desire for decisive action had become this tiny room full of petitions, papers to file, calls to be made. No righteous war, just a grinding inquiry into where a prisoner was being held and under what charges, or the Kafkaesque pursuit of a single elusive stamp on a permit.

When Jack caught her staring out of the window, he wondered if she was thinking of the life she'd given up. She might have ended up in Paris or London, a doctor, a lawyer, a writer, a professor, a person for whom the trouble in the Holy Land was merely the irritation of a single fly buzzing around a pristine home, a few columns in *Le Monde* or *The Times* provoking a sighing resignation. And it seemed to him that in these moments she embodied all that had been lost in this crushing struggle. Not just the tens of thousands killed, but the millions of thwarted, suffocated lives, the sheer waste of ambition, talent, and hope. "All this wheat used not for bread," as his mother once said, "but to stuff a ragged mattress."

Her other burden, of course, was his father. Each time his baba returned, he seemed darker, more compacted, more silent. All the passionate storminess of his parents' early years together was gone. She never confronted or argued with him anymore but provided the soft tinder of her loving attention to reignite the embers of his masculinity. Patiently, she would coax him out of the jail cell that still lived in his being and body. And when she finally said, "Why don't you shave, my beloved," Jack knew to leave the house so they could have privacy.

Jack and his mother usually exchanged a couple of letters a week after he settled in the United States, but a week passed without another letter from her, then two, then three. A few days before his airline training was to begin, he telephoned his home. At his father's gravelly "Alo," Jack said, "Baba."

His father hung up. Jack immediately called again, but the phone wasn't answered. He felt frantic, not knowing what to do, but the very next day he received a typed letter from the Palestinians for Peace office. Flooded with relief, he tore it open.

> Dear Mr. Shaban,
>
> My name is Lara Keefe. I worked at Palestinians for Peace with your mother, and today opened your letters addressed to her here. I'm assuming you know by now, but in case you still don't, as your letters indicate, it grieves me to tell you that she passed away during an angioplasty operation a few weeks ago. She had a beautiful soul.
>
> My sincerest sympathies,
> Lara

It was a mercy at first that his grief should be so quickly overrun by a burning hatred for his father. The letter Jack wrote him didn't include a salutation because he couldn't bear to write "Father."

> I just found out that my mother died a month ago. Her friend told me she died during an operation, but I know it was because she

was unfortunate enough to marry a man who took her from a life of happiness and privilege only to suffocate her with his failure, bitterness, and misery. Dimra and I have a happy life in a beautiful home here in Chicago, and I thank God every day that our newborn son, Fayez, will never know you. If he ever asks about you, I'll tell him you were a coward who died of shame in '48. I'll tell him you were nobody.

He intended to stamp and mail this at O'Hare's post office, but the line was too slow for him to make it to his shift at Fly Fresh. When he returned home, he threw the letter into the back of his filing cabinet, less sure about mailing it, though he still felt desperate to wound his father, to be a son worth losing.

The letter remained in the cabinet, and though at first his anger had eased his grief, it seemed now to trap it in him, increasing its pressure, as if he were a person with nausea unable to vomit.

In the few days remaining before the start of his cabin-crew training, Jack's entire being filled with a numbing silence of such pressure it made his ears buzz and pop. His body felt puppetlike, an object of pathos and grotesque fascination.

His training class consisted entirely of childishly excited young women. It was like surviving an artillery attack only to stumble into a fireworks display, all these bright, happy faces banging, whizzing, fizzing with sparks, detonating shock waves through the meat of him. He had no idea how he managed to remain upright, let alone speak, but when it was his turn during the initial introductions, relying on his gift for languages and mimicry, he replaced his BBC World Service English with a Midwestern accent and introduced himself as Jack, born and bred in Chicago.

The trainees quickly bonded, but Jack found himself choking on his words, unable to make eye contact. He declined their invitations to social gatherings and his fellow trainees formed a united glacial front against this rude, weird man.

He hoped the job itself would pull him out of this quicksand, and in those early months on reserve, even as he removed plastic bags of used diapers shoved under seats, he could feel a faint sense of possibility whenever the plane took off, freeing him to an empire of clouds. And yet he remained an inchoate being, unable to find his voice, his tongue so deeply rooted there was no unearthing it, even to reciprocate small talk. He was like a boy who'd arrived late at summer camp, after all the groups of friends had been established. No one even knew he was married. In Egypt, desperate for money, he'd sold his wedding ring. He spent his evenings in interchangeable hotel rooms behind endless doors in labyrinths of gaudy industrial carpeting. Alone in those sterile beds, he'd often cry like a child.

= 5 =

Startled by a shout, Jack removed Desai's novel from his chest and leaned over the back of the sofa to peer into the street. Preacher Morris again, hurrying through fractal shadows like a man harried by demons, shouting for humanity to repent. As Jack lay back on the couch, the trees swelled to a frantic boil before soothing to a simmer on the ceiling.

How had he survived those crushing early months on reserve? One night, in his and Dimra's first apartment—a grimy ground-floor studio in Park Ridge—he'd been shocked awake by someone screaming. It was as if lightning had struck his spine, igniting the memory of his own torture and shame. Operatic sex, as it turned out, from the apartment above. Dimra found him shivering in the bathroom. He couldn't, of course, talk to her about what was wrong, what he'd done. Jack woke each night after that in a cold sweat, poisoned with self-loathing, and struggled all day to keep himself above the surface as the undertow of the past grew increasingly strong.

A few weeks after that night, the first leg of a six-day trip took him to San Francisco and he found himself on the Golden Gate Bridge, contemplating the swirling waters of the bay. Suicide had become an obsession as he moved through a landscape of fast-moving trucks, tall buildings, and deep rivers. Dimra understood he was in crisis, but without the confidence or strength to ask what was wrong, she only became more fearful of the American world she assumed to be the cause of his affliction. Whenever he returned home, she met Jack with an anxious, pleading look he couldn't assuage. She'd wrap herself around him at night as if trying to draw out the poison with her body. She was all that kept him from killing himself because he couldn't imagine what she'd do without him.

Then, toward the end of his third month as a flight attendant, Jack was waiting to board an early plane to Dallas when a new crew member, Lawrence, walked straight up to him and said, "Well, *ha*-lo, handsome, what are you, Italian?" Lawrence didn't wait for a response, plucking woundedly at Jack's thick hair, "God, I *hate* you."

Lawrence was the first flamboyant gay person Jack had ever encountered, a large, heavy white man, his receding hair buzz-cut, a slender rope of beard demarcating his face from his smoothly shaved double chin. His lips seemed always pouted as if he were almost but not quite satisfied, and his eyes managed at once to be sleepy and to pulse with lewd suggestiveness.

With Lawrence you could either be the audience or join the performance. He always made a beeline for Jack, roasting him slowly upon the spit of his smoldering looks. No more was required of Jack than a nod or smile, but it was, at last, a connection of a sort. Though only a sexual object in Lawrence's bold glance, this trumped the shadow in the mirror. Hardly the demiurge Jack might have selected, but you can't choose your maker.

Lawrence invariably pointed out male passengers apparently thirsting for Jack. Jack would just laugh it off. On their fourth time crewing together, Lawrence said, "Girlfriend, did you see that cowboy in 22F? His eyes were playing pattycake on your ass and he had a bulge bigger than the Texas Panhandle." Jack suddenly found himself responding in his best Texan accent, "Well, then, I s'pose I'd best prepare myself to be lassoed and hog-tied. Yee-haw!" for which he was rewarded with the full force of Lawrence's lewd smolder.

Just like that, all the ice in Jack's throat broke up. It finally freed him, the burlesque sexuality, the kabuki expressions and flamey idioms, Jack developing an affect just a little more subdued than Lawrence's. He and Lawrence mocked the difficult passengers by imitating them, and developed a pantheon of stock characters, Jack becoming Helmut, the obsessive German who insisted on selecting the size of the piece of ice he wanted for his drink; Lawrence becoming Gloria, the Dallas oil wife with that alien face of late-stage plastic surgery, getting drunk and disorderly in first class. They'd improvise skits, Helmut and Gloria in bed together (Lawrence made everything sexual) and set the galley at a roar.

With variously tempered versions of this new self, Jack began finally to connect to his colleagues. That's when he grew close to Manny, whom he hadn't realized was gay. Manny was slender, almost gaunt, in his late thirties, with reddish-blond hair and an anxious, ascetic face. He'd grown up a Hasidic Jew in Skokie, the very neighborhood Jack drove through to buy his Eid al-Fitr chicken. Like Jack he was estranged from his family. "No getting around Leviticus 20:13," Manny said with a particularly Jewish shrug. "For years I was tortured that I was carrying an abomination within me. The primary task of Orthodox Jews is to replace the dead of the Holocaust. I remember my rabbi quoting the Sefer ha-Chinuch, which compares the homosexual act with marrying a barren woman." He laughed with sad irony. "At least I'm not a barren woman."

Manny couldn't bear Lawrence's parody of sexuality, his incapacity for intimacy. "He's nearly forty and still a virgin. There's something deeply wounded and terrified crouching inside all that performance," he told Jack. "Still, it might have saved his life." Many of Manny's friends had died of AIDS, and his partner, Brett, was on AZT and a new drug called saquinavir. "You know, I was actually a little disappointed when my test came back negative. It felt like a kind of Passover." He wrung out a wry smile. "But my love was with the Egyptians."

It was with Manny that the lies began, as a backstory for whomever this was he'd become. When Manny asked if he had a partner, Jack created one named Mario, based on Salim. He could feel himself plummeting into these lies. Fearing he might reach a point of no return with all the new crew members he was now connecting to, he gradually lowered the flame on his queeny affect and became a gifted listener, asking questions in part to avoid answering them. Remembering everything he was told, he incubated people's confidences. By the next encounter, they'd sprout into an illuminating connection or a fresh line of inquiry. A relationship with Jack, as with a therapist, was a relationship with oneself, and luckily most preferred this to a truly reciprocal intimacy.

Then, a dozen years ago, Krysta Vogel appeared, fresh out of flight-attendant training, a twenty-one-year-old blond Midwesterner from Eau Pleine Wisconsin, a town of 700 people, all white. She wasn't yet beautiful, her features still inchoate, with plump cheeks, a sharp little retroussé nose, and a broad cleft chin, but she was tall, buxom, glowing with vitality, her deep, husky voice a sexy surprise. Makeup caked a face often wrought with exaggerated, almost emoji-like expressions, dissolved by an orthodontically immaculate smile. It was the face of someone who seemed never to have known a moment of true suffering.

"Your surname means 'bird' in German," was the first thing Jack said to her after being introduced by Manny.

"Well, Mom says I have an appetite like a gannet and a voice like a crow, so that makes sense," she said.

That evening in Denver, they went dancing with a couple of the other crew. He loved how unselfconsciously and badly Krysta danced, as if she'd learned all her moves from a dancercise class. Emily and Lisa laughed at her, not unkindly—they thought she was goofing around—and Krysta was innocent and good-natured enough to laugh with them. Emily and Lisa didn't dance so much as wiggle sensuously upon a hook, and soon caught themselves a couple of young men, leaving Krysta and Jack together. Jack loved dancing, and was a natural, Krysta trying to mirror his moves. When she staggered off to order her sixth mojito, he became concerned, since they had an early flight. Gently taking hold of her hand, he suggested they head back and she nodded enthusiastically.

At her hotel-room door, before he could say, "Sleep well," he found her lips pressed to his, her arms around his neck. A wonderful soft kiss tasting of mojitos. It took all his resolve to pull back.

"We need to get to bed, Bird-Girl," he said. "I'll see you in the morning."

The image of her confused, bereft face haunted a sleepless night. At breakfast, Krysta slumped sheepishly down opposite him, her plate piled to overflowing from the buffet. She'd just rolled out of bed, sleep crusting her eyes, crease marks rivering her cheeks, her unwashed and slightly greasy hair wrenched back into an exploded chignon. She wore baggy sweats and a tentlike Green Bay Packers T-shirt, her face even younger without makeup and bearing the weight of a hangover. Jack never found Dimra in any kind of personal disarray, her body always smooth and scented, her hair glossy. She used matches in the bathroom, denying him the privilege even of her most intimate smells.

"I'm sorry," she said.

It was in that moment, putting a hand on her arm and telling her with a smile not to worry, that he realized with a lurch of his heart that he was falling for her. It was more than just sexual. She seemed so open and vital to him, a font of joy to quench his parched heart. He loved her unabashed appetite, her Junoesque physique, her clumsiness, her innocence and courage. She was a tomboy just coming into herself as a woman.

He soon found out she had four older brothers and one younger, and he was wrong in his assumption that she hadn't known suffering.

Her favorite brother, Kyle, was killed at thirteen years old by her eldest brother, Noah, in a hunting accident, Kyle's absence (and Noah's presence) becoming a black hole at the heart of every family occasion after that. Still, as the only girl, she was adored and spoiled by everyone. It was this he loved most in her: her expectation of love. There was no greater strength in the world.

"I just ran into Emily," she said.

"Oh, is she coming down?"

Krysta laughed. "She was actually just getting back."

"Oh."

She went quiet, digging idly at her food. He knew immediately that she'd said something to Emily, who must have told her he was gay.

She said, "Do you have a . . . partner?"

He nodded, and it took him a second to remember the name he'd given Manny. "Mario."

She seemed at a loss for a moment, and then said brightly, "Have you ever seen *Three's Company*?"

"I don't really watch TV."

When her amazement emoji had been dissolved by her lovely smile, she gathered herself and said, "There's a Jack in it, but he's only pretending . . ."

"Pretending?"

She flushed deep red. "Oh, I'm sorry, it's a stupid show," she said. "I'm so sorry."

"Krysta, you don't have anything to be sorry about."

"I mean I didn't realize."

He nodded.

"It must be hard now?" she continued.

"Hard?" Then he realized what she meant and admired the brave naïveté of this question before he remembered her kiss, warm and deep, and realized she might be worried—terrified. All at once, that endemic shame rolled through his nerves, the swallowing flex of the constrictor that had already squeezed out so much of his life. Last night an object of desire, this morning one of mortal fear, her perception of him turned upon its head, everything explained, right down to the quality of his dancing, his gentle manner and capacity to listen. And now she might read incipient and deadly sickness into the hollows of his face.

"Yes," he answered quietly, wondering with amazement at how he had arrived at this place. "I don't have it, if you're wondering."

"Oh no," she said, "I . . ." Suddenly putting down her fork, she laid her hand over his and squeezed it. "We can be friends, yes?"

"I'd like that."

Soon they were inseparable, Bird-Girl becoming Birdy. Her cousin worked in scheduling, so they had a lot of success bidding for the same trips and explored the cities they flew to together. He helped her through her determination to throw herself into the world. She was very young, and for a while this was about drinking and sex. He often held back her hair while she vomited into the toilet, and a few times, worried, stayed with her in her hotel room. One afternoon in Boston she banged on his door, charging in when he opened it, frantic, convinced she'd contracted herpes after a drunken romp with an engineering student the night before. She told him she had a blister on her hoo-ha, tugging down her sweatpants to show him before he'd even closed the door. He stopped her, and they caught a taxi to a walk-in clinic, where for four hours she lamented her now-unmarriageable state until she was reassured by an overworked and irritated doctor that it was just mild skin trauma from overvigorous activity.

She had an affair with a Delta pilot that consisted of five-minute assignations in a janitorial closet on Concourse C in O'Hare. Jack asked her if she actually enjoyed it. She shrugged. "It's exciting," she said, "and now I'm aroused by the smell of cleaning fluids, which helps me get my housework done."

Jack talked to her a few times about her drinking, but she said she was young and having fun. Constantly worried about her, envious of the men she met, he was no longer enjoying his role as mother hen. It came to a head when they joined a few colleagues at a sketchy little dance club in Houston. As the music and lights pulsed, Birdy slammed tequila shots at the bar with a couple of the other girls, but they soon left, since they all had an early flight. Birdy became so drunk, her face looked as if you could smear it with your hand. When he tried to convince her to leave, she told him to go ahead. He retreated to a table in a dark corner to keep an eye on her, feeling exhausted and dissociated from it all, the whole place throbbing and pulsing like the aura before a seizure. He noticed Birdy talking to one of the bouncers, who was buying her drinks, a huge guy with a shaved head. Jack slipped off to the bathroom, and when he returned couldn't see her or the bouncer. After searching the club, he ran out of the front entrance to check the street before realizing the bouncer couldn't leave. He asked a woman to check the restroom, then pushed through a door close to the DJ's booth to find an emergency exit propped open by a brick and went through it into an alley. The bouncer, having jammed Birdy against the wall between two industrial steel garbage containers, was tugging down her tight jeans.

"Hey!" Jack shouted, terrified the bouncer was going to beat the crap out of him, but it was as if he'd snapped the man out of a hypnotic trance. The bouncer stared with confused fear at Jack for a moment and then back at Birdy, slumped and too drunk to be aware that her pants were around her knees. Then he strode quickly back into the club and slammed the fire exit shut. Jack hurried to Birdy, catching her just as she stumbled forward and fell to her knees onto the concrete of the filthy alley, vomiting pure liquid over the front of Jack's pants and shoes.

The next morning at breakfast, while Birdy sat in front of him looking bloodless and wrecked, he told her he was done going with her to clubs, and that if she ever drank like that again, their friendship was over.

6

Jack was surprised and delighted to see Manny on the Minneapolis flight. He hadn't crewed with him since the U.S. invasion of Iraq over four years ago. Disillusioned with America, Manny had switched to long-haul international flights with vague notions of living abroad.

"So funny," Jack said, when they stole a moment in the galley. "I was thinking about you last night."

"Glad to hear it. How are things with Mario?"

"Same as ever." Jack hated to be trapped in this ridiculous lie.

Manny's expression of sympathetic inquiry provoked Jack to say, "He feels more like my brother than my partner."

"You'd never leave him?"

Jack shook his head. "I could never do that."

When his silence failed to elicit more, Manny, setting his cool, pale hand on Jack's, whispered, "I can't say I haven't imagined us together."

Jack met his friend's gaze. No one would immediately think of Manny as handsome: his scrub of rusty hair receded from a furrowed forehead that expressed his intelligence as if it were a migraine; but his nearly invisible eyebrows gave his ice-blue eyes a startling nakedness, and his slender lips were exquisitely shaped. Beautiful.

Putting his free hand over Manny's and squeezing it gently, regretfully, Jack said, "How about Brett?"

Manny withdrew his hand, took a weary breath, and said, "Well, he's being . . ." He stared at the galley floor. "I guess 'self-destructive' is the word."

"He's always been a bit like that," Jack said. "I remember you telling me what a struggle it was even to keep him on his meds."

Manny shook his head sadly. "Now he's got into the meth scene."

"He's taking meth?"

Manny nodded. "Followed by what Brett describes as 'piggy sex with strangers.' It's become a bit of a fad among gay men."

"After everything he's been through?"

Manny raised his hands palms-up, hopelessly. "When he tested positive all those years ago, we believed he was dead. We flew to Italy for a farewell tour, blew his savings and most of mine. We held his funeral, all his friends delivering eulogies. We'd all created this poignant story of his life as he was about to join the tragic legion of the dead. Then he was put on this drug trial and didn't die. Everyone tells me its survivor's guilt. I think in part he's just embarrassed." Manny laughed ruefully. "But it's exhausting to be with someone who's lost the capacity to invest in or even imagine the future."

"I'm sorry," Jack said.

Manny nodded gently. "I'm back on short-haul because I can't trust him on his own for too long. The thing is, I want to leave him, but it's so hard to leave someone after such intensity. He essentially died in my arms upon a hill in Tuscany at sunset. The whole AIDS thing made a kind of performance out of our lives; and now the audience has drained away, and it's just me and him on the stage trying to figure out the next scene."

Manny's broad, resigned smile gave Jack permission to smile also.

"By the way," Manny asked, "are you still in touch with whatsername, that jolly blond giant from Minnesota?"

"Wisconsin. Krysta. Married now; two kids."

"You're not in touch?"

A woman appeared in the cockpit. She was a little heavy, with an owlish face.

"Can I help you?" Jack asked.

"The Arab gentleman next to me is praying," she murmured nervously.

"Praying?"

She was clearly deeply embarrassed, but no less afraid.

As the woman slipped into the bathroom, Jack wandered up the mostly slumbering plane until he came to her seat. The man beside her looked Afghan, with a hennaed beard, and was davening as he murmured a sura Jack recognized, despite the man's nearly incomprehensible Arabic. "*And to your Lord direct your longing. And when my guidance comes to you, whomever follows my guidance will have no fear, nor will they grieve.*"

Their eyes caught, and Jack greeted him in Arabic. The man apologized that he didn't speak Arabic well, much to his shame, so in English Jack said, "I'm sorry, I didn't mean to disturb your prayer."

The man then glanced at the empty seat beside him, and leaning toward Jack whispered, "Please tell the lady I'm afraid of flying."

When the woman returned to her seat, Jack thought that this was just the kind of story Birdy would have loved. And he would have loved to tell her.

When Jack arrived home, he found Dimra shucking prickly pears in the kitchen. For once, she didn't come to him, kiss him, or insist on helping him off with his coat and shoes. He guessed she was distracted by Israel's blockade of Gaza, punishment for the election of Hamas. Egypt, too, had closed its border.

"Are you all right?" he asked, kissing her forehead.

"I talked to Mama on the phone." She looked like someone hopelessly searching for a recognizable landmark in dense fog. "Baba can't get his medication or insulin. No fuel, no electricity. There's hardly any drinkable water."

It struck him that Dimra must have left the apartment to buy the prickly pears, and he declared with happy surprise, "You went out."

The television was on but silent, showing eerie satellite pictures of smart-bomb explosions in Iraq, the earphones still connected, lying on the arm of the couch where he could imagine she'd spent much of her day as an exposed nerve.

"I'm trying," she said. "I found these in the Mexican grocery store across the road."

Like Jack's mother, Dimra could shuck their spiny skins in an instant, pinching them between thumb and forefinger, decapitating and splitting them, rolling the bright-red fruit free of its covering. She sliced the flayed fruit and slid a piece into his mouth: faint taste of bubblegum and watermelon, slightly mealy. He preferred them cold.

"They don't taste like the ones from home," she said, sighing.

"Not as sharp, but not bad; just different."

"These were Nafiz's favorite." She glanced up at him, the fog clearing. Even sad, her eyes remained full of her vital and loving energy.

She returned her gaze to the red stain on the cutting board. "This was the day they found him," she said. "He'd been missing for a week."

She'd never spoken about her brother.

"Mama tried to teach him to shuck them, but he was too impatient and clumsy, kept getting the spines in his fingers."

She settled a red-stained hand on her belly, and he lay his over hers.

"These have no spines." She raked her other hand through the small bowl of fruit as if she wished they could defend themselves.

Her sadness unsettled him, reminding him how lucky he was that Dimra was usually so loving and sunny, making no demands, trusting him unreservedly.

"If it's a boy, inshallah," he said, "we can call him Nafiz." Jack, too, had been named after a dead brother.

"No." She looked at him almost with fear.

To change the subject he said, "It's a beautiful day. Why don't we take a walk by the lake, get you out of this apartment for a while."

It was a ten-minute drive to the lakefront in Evanston. Dimra, who was afraid of Rogers Park, though it was one of Chicago's safest neighborhoods, loved Evanston's east side, along the lake. In Evanston, the first of the wealthy white northern suburbs, you had to pay to access the beaches, $8 per person. The fence that separated the beach from the lakeside park had become a de facto color line: Black, Hispanic, and immigrant families on the grass of Dawes Park; middle-class whites on the beaches themselves. In Gaza, the beach was one of the few saving graces for the poor.

As they approached Northwestern University, Jack noticed cop cars and television trucks parked along Sheridan. They could hear chanting and the husky bark of a megaphoned voice. As the lakefill came into view, they found themselves, as if in a dream, moving toward a sea of Palestinian flags and protest signs: *Stop Strangling Gaza; Halt the Palestinian Genocide; Cease Funding Racist Israel; From River to Sea, Palestine Will Be Free.* They slowed, their hooked-together arms tautening, but were like meteoroids caught inexorably in a planet's gravitational field.

The crowd was a mix of citizens and students. A bearded young man wearing a checked kufiyah wrapped around his neck stood at the highest part of the lakefill with a megaphone shouting demands for Northwestern to divest from Israel.

They entered a cluster of small tents set up by pro-Palestinian organizations and passed a female field reporter he recognized from ABC 7 News talking on-camera. A young woman holding a clipboard emerged from a tent marked STUDENTS FOR JUSTICE IN PALESTINE and asked them if they were members of the BDS movement. He and Dimra, surprised that someone in the bizarre apparition of this protest had spoken to them, remained silent until a man in the American Muslims for Palestine tent explained in Arabic, "It's a movement calling for a boycott on Israel, as well as disinvestment and sanctions."

They nodded, and Dimra, addressing the girl in her heavily accented English said, "No, we don't belong."

The girl, who had a purple mop of hair and a nose ring, explained their mission at a breathless pace, always referring to Israel as "Apartheid Israel." Jack could see Dimra nodding as the girl spoke and then she took the pen the girl handed to her and signed both the petition and a membership form. The girl rewarded them with a button depicting "BDS" within the Star of David, and a key ring with an image he remembered from graffiti in Gaza. It was Handala, a cartoon icon, a Palestinian Peter Pan forever stuck at ten years old, the age the cartoonist who'd created him had been during Al-Nakba. The figure was turned away, his hands clasped behind his back, an image of poverty, anonymity, and helplessness.

A woman wearing an abaya and hijab called in Arabic from the Palestinian American Council tent, "Where are you from?"

Jack felt unable to speak, but Dimra seemed to have become excited, and said, "Gaza." Jack thought of what it meant to Dimra, given all the time this deeply social and loving woman had spent alone, enduring years of stifled physical and emotional pain, wired into the news of the Middle East, to find herself suddenly surrounded by people for whom her life was not something to be ashamed of.

The woman was from Ramallah, and she and Dimra began to talk. Moments later, Jack felt a tap on his shoulder. It was the reporter from ABC 7 News, an attractive Asian woman, looking for someone to interview, her cameraman at the ready behind her. "Sir, where are you from?"

"Oh, I'm just from Rogers Park," he mumbled in as discouraging a way as he could, "out for a walk."

The woman from Ramallah called out, "This lady, she's from Gaza, and she's named after her parents' ethnically cleansed and destroyed village." The woman almost pushed Dimra in front of the reporter, saying in Arabic, "Tell her, tell her."

After the reporter had talked to Jack's wife for a short while, she nodded at the cameraman, and instantly the world's eye was upon Dimra. As she spoke about her parents' expulsion and their current suffering during the blockade, she became increasingly impassioned. "The Jews treat us like animals; our deaths mean nothing to them, really. They make Gaza a concentration camp. Jews are like the Nazis," she said. "As God is my witness, this is how they behave."

Jack wanted to pull her away, to stop her saying Jews when she meant Israelis, to stop her saying anything. He felt as if he were an American watching this on television, looking at this Middle Eastern woman in a hijab saying just what you'd expect her to say, inarticulately, and with her heavy accent, the kind of woman who would have been dancing in the streets with the rest of her tribe as the Twin Towers melted. The reporter thanked her and, turning to the camera, said, "That was Dimra Shaban from Rogers Park, a woman whose very name is a legacy of this bitter half-century-old conflict."

The moment the camera was lowered, a young man wearing a *Chicago Sun-Times* press pass buttonholed his wife for fifteen minutes, holding up a voice recorder. Jack could see how excited Dimra was, like a tipsy teenager at her first party, everything spilling out of her. After that, she signed up for the Palestinian Women's Association of Chicago, exchanging numbers with the woman from Ramallah. It then occurred to him that as frightened as he felt about her interview, this might help her out of their home and into a life of her own, one with purpose, where she could find a friend or two, and of what a huge weight that would lift from his shoulders.

As they walked back to the car, he said, "Are you going to join any of those groups?"

"I don't know." She was almost too quiet to hear, and on the car ride back, she began to look stricken and nearly nauseous.

The moment they stepped into the flat, she hurried into their room. He made them both tea. When he entered the bedroom, she was lying under the covers. Sitting on the bed, he ran his hand gently through the silky dark curls of her hair. He could see the quickened pulse of her heart in the vein of her neck. She couldn't have been more electrically awake but had closed her eyes like a child who believed that the world and its dangers could only exist if her eyes were open.

Her interview ran on the local news that evening, her "Jews like Nazis" comment picked up by numerous media outlets. The next day, her image and interview were in the *Sun-Times* with coverage about the protest. Dimra, who looked like she was suffering a hangover, refused to look at either. As she was making breakfast, their home phone rang. When she picked it up, Jack could hear the screaming voice even from where he was sitting at the kitchen island. She put the receiver down, backing away from the phone. Moments later it rang again, and continued ringing for days: *antisemitic jehadi bitch, Nazi whore, fucking terrorist, you should be raped and your children gassed.* Their phone number and address had been posted on several internet sites. Crudely doctored images of her appeared online with a Hitler mustache or dancing on a pile of bodies in a concentration camp. Jack took a week off work, changed their home number and diverted the flood of letters and packages into the garbage

After that it became almost impossible to convince her to leave the house.

7

A few weeks later, on a late September day frigid with the breath of imminent winter, Dimra lay against Jack on the couch. She was watching news footage of Israeli missiles striking an evacuated block of apartment buildings near the Jabalia Camp, from which rockets had been fired into Israel. He was trying to read *Half a Yellow Sun*, but noise leaked from her earphones as irritating as the buzz of a mosquito, punctuated by her pained exclamations and rhetorical questions in a voice she didn't realize was loud, "Why does Hamas keep firing these rockets? Don't they care that people's homes are being destroyed?" The two of them were each resting a hand on her bona fide baby bump. This was his first full day off in two weeks and seeing that bump for an extended period had set off a little frisson of hope. He'd started to allow himself even to imagine a child, always a girl, bringing joy to them both. And yet he couldn't help feeling the child was being poisoned by these images, dreaming of corpses coated in concrete dust, and might emerge like Little Father Time, joyless, morbid, and wishing only for death.

Slipping off the couch, he threw on his coat and retreated to the back deck to sneak a cigarette, swearing he'd quit once the baby was here. Ryker's van was parked at an odd angle across Marcia's and May's parking spaces and he wondered how soon May's outrage would cause his phone to spasm. He shuddered to think what it would be like once they had a child running up and down the hallway. May infected their whole life. At times he hated her, but a few months ago, Jack came up the stairs to find an older Vietnamese woman sitting on the rattan bench outside May's back door, smoking. Shooting him a shrewd glance, she said, "You Jack?"

She was May's business partner, Kim. She wanted to buy May out of the restaurant. *She's useless, how you say dead sticks.* Deadwood, he corrected, laughing. May kept turning her down, and Kim was angry, claiming she'd looked after May in Saigon, *Found her in the street like a little stray cat.* May was a village girl, escaping an arranged marriage to an ugly old man. Kim told him that in the village, they called girls "flying ducks" because the family has to feed them only for them to fly off. *So they force you work like water buffalo until you marry some village man and become a water buffalo for him.* Kim herself had escaped both an abusive husband and the VC, who were putting pressure on people in her village to fight the GIs. Turning fondly nostalgic, she told Jack she became a taxi dancer, loved it, loved the war. *No pimps or nothing. Sex only if you want. Girls help each other. Plenty GIs go round.* She wrote to her mother that she worked in a dress shop, sent her money to keep her happy. *Best time my life, fat and happy.* May had a sad-country-girl act. GIs would buy her expensive drinks, and she'd skim half the cost. Then she met a nice GI, Paul, and became pregnant with Danh, but three days before their marriage, Paul stepped on a mine. Kim made a puff sound to indicate him vanishing into thin air. When Jack asked how they got out, Kim said they didn't, not at first. Here she went quiet, her eyes glazed. Finally, she huffed and told him that after the war, things were real bad for the bar girls. She, May, and little Danh spent a year in Phú Quốc Island Prison. Then a reeducation camp outside Da Lat. *They starved us. Guards rape all time, all time*. She waved her arms about her head as if these rapes were maddening mosquitoes. *Worse than prison. Terrible for Danh, bastard American boy.* Then they almost died taking a boat to Malaysia. And the refugee camp, she said, was worse than everything. *Things we have do get food terrible, terrible.* She was half hugging herself at this point, rocking a little, staring with a wincing expression at the boards of the deck. Then she shook it off, as if irritated at herself for her weakness, telling him they finally got to Chicago, Uptown, which she said was a real slum then, drugs, gangs, and she and May opened a little noodle place on Argyle and eventually moved up to Evanston. Kim stood up suddenly, smoothing her dress, telling him to convince May to take her offer. When Jack said that he didn't have any sway over May, she looked incredulous. *She talk about you all the time. Trusts you. She listen to you. She says you a good man.*

Jack was freezing, and after a quick cigarette returned to the couch. He tried to sink back into Adichie's novel, but the sectarian slaughter in it felt a little too close to home. Dimra let out a loud *Haram*, and murmured the Surah Ash-Sharh as she watched a woman weeping and tearing at her abaya in front of a shrouded and bloody corpse.

He wished Dimra would read. He loathed television. Jack's family had owned one of the first televisions in the camp, a heavy battery strapped to its back. Neighbors would crowd into their house to watch momentous events or *Dallas*. Most vividly he recalled the old men and women responding to any setback to Palestinian hopes with a glancing slap of their hands, declaring, "Khalas, we're finished. Bye-bye, Palestine." His wife said it even now, subjecting herself to death by a thousand cuts, murmuring, "Bye-bye, Palestine. Bye-bye, Palestine."

At Jack's birth, the news would have been of Black September, the bloody eviction of Palestinian militias from Jordan, most flooding into Lebanon to further destabilize that already fractured country; and of the death of Nasser and his pan-Arab dream (*Bye-bye, Palestine*).

Jack would have been toddling around his parents' feet when Palestinians starred in the first fully televised terrorist attack at the Berlin Olympics. This culminated in half the Israeli athletes being machine-gunned, the other half turned to Pompeiian ash by a grenade flung into an Iroquois helicopter. All of this on an airfield just a few miles from Dachau, where 65,000 Jews had been slaughtered less than thirty years before.

Jack was starting to use full sentences during the Ramadan War, the Israelis caught napping as the Egyptians breached the impenetrable Bar Lev Line, the Syrians swarming through the Golan Heights, until the Israelis pushed back, advancing almost to the suburbs of Cairo and Damascus (*Bye-bye, Palestine*).

He could vaguely remember their house crowded to watch Arafat addressing the UN in '74, just before the screen flooded with the horrors of the Lebanese Civil War, including the siege of Tel al-Zaatar, where Dimra's entire maternal family were among the 15,000 slaughtered by the Christian militias of le Front Libanais.

Seven years old when Menachim Begin's cadaverous face loomed on the screen. Jack hadn't understood why everyone was so appalled that this man had been elected Israel's prime minister (*Bye-bye, Palestine*). Soon after, their precious television was almost destroyed by his father's flung shoe when it dared convey images of Egypt's President Sadat shaking hands with Begin at Camp David (*Bye-bye, Palestine*). Followed by his uncle's cynical laughter at the sight of these two men receiving the Nobel Peace Prize just before the Israelis invaded Southern Lebanon in a brutal campaign that turned many of the Lebanese Shia villagers into homeless refugees.

When he was eleven, he'd watched a confused Sadat onstage saluting the very men come to assassinate him. Though many celebrated his death in the streets of Gaza, his father and mother weren't cheering, any more than they cheered the images of ecstatic Iranians welcoming the Ayatollah Khomeini back to Tehran.

Then Lebanon filled their screens again as Begin and Sharon's invasion began, thousands slaughtered as terrified Israeli troops shot and bombed everything that moved. He'd never forget the images of the bloated fly-wreathed bodies in the Sabra and Shatila Camps, or of the Palestinian fedayeen being shipped out of Lebanon in a great parade, showered with rice and flowers, as if they were the victors (*Bye-bye, Palestine*).

He was seventeen when a truck accident in the Jabalia Camp set off the dry tinder of the strip, making Gaza world news as this flared into what would come to be called the intifada. His friend Thaer was privileged enough to be televised on CNN having his arms and legs broken by the IDF when he was caught firing ball bearings at Israeli helicopters with his slingshot.

He and Dimra were in Egypt when the Palestinian Declaration of Independence, written by the poet Mahmoud Darwish, was declared by Yasser Arafat in Algeria. Dimra had seemed excited, hopeful, which baffled him. All Jack knew was that the Palestinians would suffer for it, which they did, Israel enforcing a two-week curfew in Gaza, with all the phones cut off, nearly a million people imprisoned in their homes.

He and Dimra had arrived in America just before the coalition liberation of Kuwait. As the attack began, the awestruck news commentator described it almost tearfully as beautiful.

After Gorbachev opened the borders of the Soviet Union, he and Dimra watched a million Russian Jews pouring out of passenger jets at Ben Gurion, a new vanguard of settlers for the West Bank (*Bye-bye, Palestine*).

Then came Oslo, and Jack could hear his uncle's mirthless laughter from beyond the grave when Rabin, Peres, and Arafat received the Nobel

Peace Prize in 1994, the same year Baruch Goldstein, an Israeli immigrant from Brooklyn, blew up and gunned down scores of Palestinians praying in the Ibrahimi Mosque. Hamas retaliated with a car bomb that blew up a bus, killing eight, in Afula, and a week later, a bomb on a bus in the Hadera bus station, killing five. After Oslo, the illegal Israeli settlements grew at an accelerated rate, the camps remaining as miserable as ever even as fancy hotels were constructed on the beaches. The new Palestinian Authority was just the old political elite returning to control the Palestinians, foreign aid and donations siphoned into their private bank accounts. Jack couldn't help but think of everything his parents and those who'd fought for a better future had suffered, and of all those who'd lost their lives either literally or because they'd been jailed for so long or had never managed to climb out of the grinding poverty of the camps.

The result of Oslo was no state, no democracy, no freedom from occupation. Soldiers, tanks, checkpoints, guard towers, pillboxes, barbed wire, land confiscation orders all continued apace. Then Yitzak Rabin was assassinated by a right-wing fanatic, to be replaced half a year later by a political slimeball called Netanyahu, whose rallies had included effigies of Rabin being hanged.

Churning onward to those tired images of Ehud Barak and Arafat with Clinton at Camp David in 2000, all of it as meaningless to the Palestinians as every other agreement, presidential photo op, and Nobel Prize.

The Second Intifada began in that same year, the man who'd instigated it with his march on the Al-Aqsa Mosque elected prime minister. Ariel Sharon, the Bulldozer, resembling a dissolute panda, disgraced after his monstrous campaign of slaughter in Lebanon, was now Israel's leader, implementing a deadly crackdown on the intifada with assassinations and a suffocating siege.

Dimra's mother telephoned whenever there was rioting, a raid, shooting, or bombing. Dimra often had the phone on speaker. From it, Jack could hear her mother's weeping and adjurations to God, explosions and the crackle of gunfire leaking into their American life as Dimra watched Apache helicopters firing missiles, bulldozers destroying homes, and the bloody aftermath of Palestinian suicide bombers penetrating Israeli cities, providing justification for more walls and barbed wire. They watched the Israeli Army destroying Palestinian homes, uprooting old-growth trees to create security zones and exclusive-use roads to ensure the safety of Israeli settlers. All over the West Bank, Palestinians were increasingly severed from their farms, homes, water sources, families, cut up into smaller and smaller cantons, prisoners in their own land as the Israeli settlements swelled (*Bye-bye, Palestine*).

Three years after Sharon's election, Jack returned from a two-day travel leg to find Dimra weeping. "The old man's dead," she said. Jack's legs went suddenly so weak he had to pull the stool from the island to sit. It surprised him, since he had no love for Arafat and his corrupt cronies. But Arafat was a man who'd stepped out of buildings in Beirut seconds before Israeli bombs had pancaked them, a man who had to dodge Arab bullets as frequently as those fired by Israelis, a man whose life was forfeit equally for every concession he made as for every one he didn't. A man as empty and absurd as Mussolini, as brave and holy as Omar Mukhtar. Arafat had no power. All he could be was obdurate. All he could do was refuse not to exist. Jack and Dimra watched the chaotic funeral, Dimra sobbing quietly beside him (*Bye-bye, Palestine*).

In 2005 they watched the great charade of Sharon withdrawing the settlements in Gaza, the world watching the Israeli military in conflict with rioting and weeping settlers. Then in early 2006, Palestinians, sick of rife corruption and nothing changing, voted in Hamas, a group responsible for suicide and rocket attacks, opposed to Israel's very existence, Gaza becoming explicitly what it had been for so long implicitly for the Israelis, a hostile territory under siege. In June, Gilad Shalit, an IDF soldier, was captured using tunnels beneath the border. The Israeli response was brutal and collective, Ehud Olmert declaring he wanted to make sure no one slept in Gaza at night, blowing up the power plant and water lines, stopping fuel shipments, preventing the presence of journalists. Again, Dimra's parents suffered horribly. Financial institutions were boycotted, so he and Dimra couldn't even send them money.

It had always been the same, nothing but bad news. It had been *Bye-bye, Palestine* since 1967, since 1948, since the Holocaust, since 1917, since 1897 . . .

Jack was astonished that his wife continued to be freshly horrified, and it struck him that it must be because she still, impossibly, held out hope. As far as Gaza and Israel were concerned, his heart was stone. That didn't mean, alas, that he was without feeling. That stone heart incubated in him as an alien mass, indolent, but heavy and obstructive.

As Jack picked up his novel again, he was startled by the buzz of his phone.

> That CRIMINAL is lying in the basement stairwell! HIS CAR IS IN MY SPACE. We are not a garbage can for HOMELESS PEOPLE! Is he DEAD? POLICE NEXT!!!

Jack found Ryker passed out in the shallow concrete stairwell in front of the basement door. He must have driven home drunk. He was freezing. Jack shook him awake, but he wasn't coherent. Hurrying through the basement to Marcia's back door, Jack gently tapped on it with no success. He phoned her, but she must have switched off her cell, so he used Ryker's key to enter, softly calling Marcia's name. When she suddenly appeared from her bedroom in boxers and a tank top, he averted his eyes, since the thin material of the latter left little of her pregnancy-swollen breasts to the imagination.

"What the fuck are you doing in here?"

"It's Ryker. We need to get him inside."

She followed him through the basement, and when she saw Ryker, said, "He's not coming in my home in that fucking state."

"He's freezing."

From an area of the basement piled with Ryker's possessions (provoking numerous ignored fines from May), she pulled a foldable sun lounger.

"We can't put him on that, not in the basement."

"It's that or fucking leave him there."

Jack hooked his hands under Ryker's arms and Marcia took his legs. He was a big man, 230 pounds at least.

"Be careful you don't strain yourself," Jack said.

"I'm fine," she snapped.

The sun lounger groaned beneath Ryker. Marcia fetched a heavy old duvet and as she flung it over him Aisha appeared.

"Fuck," Marcia snarled under her breath before shouting, "Get back to bed!"

"What's wrong with Ryker?"

"I said get the fuck back to bed. I'll be in in a minute."

"Don't worry, habibti," Jack said, "he's just camping."

Aisha glanced at him with a sad sophistication beyond her years, as if she'd prefer the rudeness of her mother to his condescension. For a moment the little girl didn't move, testing the tender edges of her mother's chronically inflamed patience before slipping back into the apartment. Out of the open basement door, he and Marcia glanced at the sunrise blossoming pink in the branches of the massive oak in the garden of the house across the alley.

"You got a cigarette?" She must have smelled it on him.

Trying not to sound judgmental, he said, "You're okay to smoke?"

"You got one or not?"

Jack retrieved the two-month-old pack from his jacket pocket. He smoked rarely. In certain moods and moments, he needed one. They left the basement and sat side by side on the deck stairs. She drew in the smoke thirstily. When the chill set off an involuntary shiver in her, he slipped off his jacket and hooked it around her shoulders, causing Marcia to glance at him with a suspicion that betrayed just a touch of curiosity. In her world men were not gallant. Jack *was* gallant, instinctively, but not entirely in that action, evoking the dreamlike feeling that he'd removed not his jacket but his skin.

Desire had knocked him off-kilter. He loved her strength, the athletic veins rivering her arms, hands, and slightly bunioned bare feet. He loved how harshly weathered by her life her features were, the unexpected softness of her sea-glass eyes, naked without makeup, raw with exhaustion. He loved (as he loved it in his wife) the gravid changes in her body, her breasts' clear blue veins and darkened, enlarged nipples. Even loved, as she drew in another breath of smoke, her eyes closed in angry, almost vengeful pleasure, her resentment of this new life colonizing her body.

"I tried to bum one from that Asian kid the other day. He told me to fuck off."

"That's May's son."

"What's his deal?"

"Addict: meth, heroin. She's spent everything she has on treatment programs. Got kicked out of his halfway house, so he's back with her, at least for a while."

"Gives me the fucking creeps."

"I'm always worried when he's here." Jack knew he was being indiscreet but thought she should be warned. "Things go missing: Lulu's bike, our new lawnmower, people's packages."

"Can't you kick him out?"

"There's no proof."

She took a thoughtful drag. "Everyone's life is shit sometimes, but

I don't get people turning themselves into fucking zombies. Ryker was in the machinists' union, earning eighty thousand a year. Spent two months' wages once having a solid-gold medallion made with "One year sober" on it. He wanted a goal. Five weeks is as far as he's ever got."

The sun lost its purchase in the branches of the oak and the fatty tissue of low clouds, its bloody smear draining as it suffused itself into a sterile, ecumenical brightness.

"You have any bad habits?" she said.

He shrugged. "I do kill people, but only if the voices tell me to."

She stifled a smile, glancing at him, their eyes meeting for a dangerous instant too long before she looked away.

"Don't you ever just want to escape yourself?" She sighed, instantly answering for him, "Of course not, Mr. Fucking Perfect El Presidente." A sudden change of tone: "That reminds me, our shower, it won't get hot. It's fucking miserable."

When he told her it sounded like she needed a new shower cartridge, estimating $150 for the plumber, she dropped her head to her knees.

"It's Aisha's fifth birthday tomorrow. She wants this life-sized animated golden retriever toy that costs a fucking fortune, and I have to buy all the shit for a party with her preschool friends. At work they're pissed I'm pregnant. They've put me on food prep and cut my hours. Every month something wipes me out. No way in fucking hell I'm going to come up with that three thousand by April."

They both startled at May's voice shrilling above them: "Stairs are a common area. No smoking. Fifty-dollar fine is next!"

Jack stood up, apologizing as May's eyes fixed on him with scalding suspicion. He felt he'd been caught in an indiscretion, sitting shoulder to shoulder with this half-naked woman wearing his jacket.

"Where's knife man?"

Jack was desperate for May not to come down. If she found Ryker in the basement, he'd never hear the end of it.

"He's fine, May; he's in bed."

"We are not a homeless shelter. Next time I'll call the police."

Marcia, who'd remained on the steps smoking, said, not even half under her breath, "You're such a fucking Nazi."

"I heard you. You're smoking while pregnant. I should call social services to take your baby away."

"Come on, you guys," Jack pleaded.

Marcia stood so she could look directly up at May. "Go ahead, call them, tell them to take both my kids, and that useless fucking drunk. Make my life a whole lot fucking easier."

"You have a *dirty* mouth. You're *dirty*. I feel sorry for your children."

"And you're such a great mother. Your druggie son's a fucking thief."

May cast Jack a look of shocked betrayal. Pointing into the parking lot, she shouted at Marcia, "Your car's still in my space. I'm calling the tow truck right now." She vanished and they heard the slam of her screen door.

"Why is she such a *fucking* bitch?" Marcia sat on the stairs again, her flushed face turned up to him. Suddenly she closed her eyes, tensing, as if she were trying to swallow, not nearly for the first time, an indigestible bolus.

Sitting back beside her, Jack told her he'd move the van and come down once Aisha had left for preschool to see if he could clean out her old shower cartridge. Marcia opened her eyes, and he noticed the vaguest softening pulse in her defensive hostility, like the shadow of a spindly cloud upon a harsh and arid landscape. He was acclimatizing, becoming aware of this landscape's brave and at times delicate life amid the scourged rocks; of it as a place perhaps not entirely without hope or mercy.

Jack returned to Marcia's apartment a few hours later. As he worked on her shower, she sat with her legs pulled up into her chest on the closed toilet seat, dressed now in black capri leggings and an old T-shirt with Popeye on it. He asked if Ryker was okay, and for a while she didn't answer, contemplating the floor tiles in a way that reminded him of a beggar he'd seen in Egypt staring at a reed mat before her upon which she'd arranged a broken doll, a cracked jug, a used Bic lighter. Passersby left piastres, but none took the meagre final possessions of her life in exchange; it may have been for this very reason that the woman met every donor, especially those who called down the blessings of God upon her, with a look of hostility.

Finally, she spoke. "Ryker called his sponsor, who came and took him to a nearby meeting," adding with flaccid irony, "One day at a time."

Jack wondered if Ryker's chaotic life helped Marcia feel in control; if, without him, she might be the one found lying in a stairwell.

"I told Dimra about Aisha's birthday. She loves being with kids. She really wants to bake a cake and cookies for the party. She said she could do mini pizza bases and then all the kids can make their own pizza." He tried to relate this as nonchalantly as possible. When he glanced back at her, he glimpsed fear like a surfaced fish vanishing quickly beneath her anger, and she shrugged.

"Great," he said, "I'll tell her."

Marcia returned her gaze to the tiles. "Birthdays and Christmas are hard because Aisha always brings up her dad."

"Does she see him?"

"Not if I can help it," she said. "Bastard forgot to tell me he was married with three kids."

"Oh."

"Yes, *Oh*. They were in Nigeria at the time."

"That's where he's from?"

She nodded. "His brother was involved in a failed coup and was executed. Chike was rich out there and I guess some government official wanted his properties and money, so this guy said Chike was also involved. He got asylum here. His wife and kids were still there in his parents' hometown when he met me, waiting for their visas. He tries to give me money sometimes. He wants to see Aisha. *Fuck* him."

"And this baby?" He'd wondered if it was Ryker's.

"Chike confessed about his wife and kids the day before I found out for sure I was pregnant again."

"Does he know?"

She shook her head.

Trying to sound neutral, Jack said, "You don't think it would be better for your kids to know him?"

"That's what that bastard wants, to have his fucking cake and eat it."

Even more gently, Jack pursued, "Couldn't he help you with the three thousand?"

"I'd rather be fucking homeless," she said, though after a beat she added with less heat, "He just qualified as a long-distance truck driver and has to support three kids and that poor bitch he's also lying to."

After another moment, she said, "Could *you* lie to someone like that?"

Jack wasn't sure if this was rhetorical until she went on, "He was at Aisha's birth. We named her after his fucking grandmother."

"And Ryker?"

"I've known him since high school. We've dated on and off for years."

"You have family?" he said.

"Mother and sister. Dad left when me and my sister were little. Don't blame him. My mom's a fucking nightmare. I had to live with her for a while after I left Chike. I'd rather die than do that again. She's in a shitty Section 8 apartment near the airport. I swear you could almost touch the planes when they go over. One bedroom the size of a closet. Can't breathe in there for the fucking smoke. I don't ever remember her without a cigarette in her mouth. Got emphysema. She's on oxygen, takes sucks of oxygen between sucks on these foul-smelling bootleg cigarettes she gets from some Hispanic guy she used to fuck in high school."

"Is it just the smoking?"

Widening her eyes, Marcia shook her head as if the list of iniquities was just too long to get into. "She shouldn't have had kids. We were taken into foster care for a while because my sister called the cops on a guy she was seeing who was sexually abusing us. Mom was so fucking pissed at her."

"I'm sorry," he said. "You in touch with your sister?"

Staring again at the tiles, it took her a moment to respond. "Kelsey married a stockbroker, lives up in Highland Park, has her own real-estate franchise. Changed her name to something high-class, Colleen, Colette, something like that. She has a daughter, Felicity—must be sixteen or seventeen now—and I remember Kelsey telling me she was going to give Felicity everything we didn't have: private school, music lessons, all that shit. Felicity was like a big-deal softball pitcher; she was being scouted by colleges in middle school.

"I remember one time when Chike and me were living in this attic apartment in Albany Park, Kelsey and Felicity came to see Aisha just after she was born. I guess Felicity would have been twelve. And when I was in the kitchen, I heard her whining to her mother that our place stank, and Kelsey telling her they didn't have to stay long. When Chike got back from his shift, all they could see was that he was a Black guy, an immigrant fucking taxi driver. They don't have Black people in Highland Park. I wanted to tell them he had fucking servants in Nigeria.

"Anyway, I'd been cooking all day, but Felicity wouldn't eat a thing and looked around her like she was in a sewer. My sister had to all but force her to hold Aisha. I know she was just a kid, but I kind of hated her. And I could see my sister judging everything as well. I'd made this pavlova dessert. Took me fucking hours, but they both said they didn't want it. Then I saw Kelsey checking her watch when she thought I wasn't looking, and I just kind of lost it, told them to get the fuck out.

I changed my number so my sister couldn't call me and haven't talked to her since. I don't think she even knows where I live now. She and my mom don't talk. I saw an interview with Kelsey in the *Tribune* a few years ago because she organized a walk for MS. In this article she said that when Felicity was fifteen, she started getting this tingling in her limbs. She got real tired, started missing her pitches. Turns out she has MS. Not the worst type; the one that comes and goes, but it's progressive. You want to know what a bitch I am? When I read this, I felt"—she looked as if she were steeling herself to eat something nasty for a bet—"joy. I felt happy. Isn't that shitty?"

He glanced back at her, her bare feet together, knees hugged into her chest, as if she were trying to fold herself into nothing.

"That is pretty shitty," he said.

"All my sister ever did was marry a fucking rich man."

He managed to get the cartridge out.

"Here's your problem." He showed her the small twig he'd found in the shower valve. She didn't pretend to be interested.

As he began to reassemble the faucet, she said, "I bet you've never done anything shitty."

"Everyone has."

"So, what shitty things have you done?"

He shrugged. "Lots of things."

"I bet your wife hasn't."

"I think you're probably right."

"It freaks me out how nice she is."

He didn't know what to say to this. Just as he finished securing the shower handle, she said, "I thought all male flight attendants were gay."

"I can do plumbing. How could I be gay?"

She wasn't going to let it go. "So?"

"So?"

"Are you on the down-low?"

She was staring at him with just a hint of viciousness, like a beautiful mean girl in high school. It struck him that Marcia had said too much, been too intimate, and this was a kind of defensive revenge: the forcing of a shameful secret upon him—as if he needed any more of that.

"I'll turn the water back on and we can see if it works."

When he walked past her to exit, she was staring down at the tiles again: used Bic lighter, cracked jug, broken doll.

8

He found Dimra still hooked up to the television. She lifted an ear cup. "Did you fix it?"

"Yes, yes," he said. "It was the cartridge. There was a twig in it, probably from when they replaced the water line." He was overexplaining, feeling nervous, as if hiding something.

She nodded.

"I'm going to read in bed," he said, but she'd already replaced the ear cup, absorbed in images of masked Islamic Jihad militants firing rockets into Israel.

He tried to read a little more, but the image of Marcia perched on the toilet seat kept intruding, her lovely long legs in those tight capri leggings hugged into her chest, her sharp, angular face beneath that gush of spiky blond hair, the way she lay her chin on the plateau of her knees, staring at him, a passionate anger in her soft blue-green eyes.

Dimra never questioned him about anything. Though she clearly wanted Jack to confide in her, her glance ever-hungry, she never pushed him to speak about his past or his life outside their home. He thought of how palpably Birdy had come to exist in the silence between him and Dimra. After Birdy's near rape at the nightclub and Jack's ultimatum, they'd grown closer. Birdy stopped drinking entirely, and for a while they spent all their free time together, wandering the cities or just sitting in one of their hotel rooms chatting, playing poker for pennies, watching the TV comedies she adored for their content and he adored for the way she leaned back against him on the bed as they watched. Often, they fell asleep together. It was a halcyon time. But alcohol was then replaced by a new intoxication: love. She shifted to more serious relationships, and he was forced to endure all the intimate details as she spoke with the wonder-blinded eyes of someone recently inducted into a cult.

For seven months, she dated a New York corporate lawyer, Markus Sherwood, who slipped his number into her hand on a flight to L.A. She spoke blissfully of their trips to his sprawling Victorian mansion on the beach in Kennebunkport. He bought her jewelry, including a diamond ring, and told her constantly he loved her. One morning a free local magazine called *The Berkshires* was delivered to the house and she came upon a photo-feature showing the recent attendees of a Republican fundraiser in Manhattan. There stood Markus, flanked by his painfully slender blond spouse and their two girls. Birdy said she felt like his fun off-roader, ridden hard at the weekends before he returned to the sleek silver Mercedes of his wife.

Then came Simon Eberhart, a six-foot-two pilot with those B-movie leading-man looks that seem as much an incarnation of stupidity as crossed eyes and goofy teeth. From a small town in the wilds of Indiana, he was very Christian. Jack found him impenetrable. When the flight crew were sitting around chatting in the lounge, Simon would afflict himself with a stiff, genial smile, sometimes winking at someone for no apparent reason, his laughter at any humor always a fraction too late. And yet he was more comfortable in the anonymity of groups. As soon as you were alone with him (he and Jack had once shared a taxi) he became awkward, tense, seeming almost angry. But Birdy was determined to fall in love, and told Jack that Simon was the only man she knew with a deep faith in God and a six-pack. Simon talked of marriage and children, and though they'd been naked together, he didn't want to go all the way until God sanctioned their union. She said he was loving, gentle, and very open when they were alone.

Then came the thirtieth birthday party of one of their colleagues in an Elmhurst crash pad, where Simon, a teetotaler, guzzled strawberry daiquiris he didn't realize were alcoholic. Flushed, he joined the dancers, becoming looser and wilder as the evening wore on. Jack could see that Birdy was a little surprised at this unbridled Simon, drenched in sweat, staring at the world ravenously as he began to understand this thing humans called fun. A little later in the evening, Simon, sweaty hair plastered to his forehead, whispered to Jack that he needed to show him something, and led him through the kitchen into a small mud room at the rear of the house.

"Something out back?" Jack said, confused.

Panting rum and strawberries, Simon shushed Jack with a finger to his lips, as if involving him in a childish prank. Suddenly, he thrust his mouth at Jack, who fended him off.

Stepping back, sobered, Simon insisted, "I'm not gay. I'm really not. You won't tell Krysta, will you?"

Returning to the party, Jack said his goodbyes, pulling away from all the hands trying to keep him there, including Birdy's, as he caught sight of Simon's stricken face at the kitchen door.

Jack didn't tell Birdy what happened, only provided comfort when Simon broke up with her a few days later.

Then, during a fateful flight to Florida, she served a cocktail to Nick Monaghan from her hometown, on his way to bag himself an alligator. Nick had been her dead brother's closest friend, and she'd nursed a crazy crush on him almost since she was out of diapers, a dreamboat athlete with the perfect girlfriend, Jenny Orville, whose doting father owned three farm-supply stores. But now Nick was hers! Birdy could hardly believe it, as if she'd tamed a unicorn, and was stupidly in love. For a while Jack didn't see Birdy, since she bid her schedule to spend as much time with Nick as possible.

Six months later, Nick drove Birdy home following an abortion, assuring her that if he ever desired to be married or to have children, she would be his choice, but he realized now he wanted neither.

Just days after this, Birdy and Jack had crewed a flight to Mexico City. Jack did his best to comfort her. Dimra, like now, had been pregnant, and he'd allowed himself to feel a little excited about the ten-week ultrasound booked for his return, trying not to think of her two previous miscarriages. Dimra called him the morning of his third leg to Houston to tell him she was spotting. Convinced she was going to lose the child again, he'd never felt more trapped in his lies. When Birdy began expressing regrets about her abortion, Jack excused himself with a headache. He could hardly sleep that night, but Dimra called him in Seattle just before his last leg to tell him that the doctor had explained that it was only a subchorionic hemorrhage. The bleeding was nothing to worry about and would stop. His relief was nearly ecstatic, and he again allowed himself to ascend to the fantastic belief that within seven months he'd be holding his child. But how could he keep that from Birdy? How could he continue this strange double life?

When Jack returned from that trip, he found Dimra lying in bed. He flushed the clotted bloody mess of the miscarriage she'd left in the toilet and scrubbed the toilet bowl with bleach.

Forced to hide his grief from Birdy, he struggled to extinguish the little flares of anger he sometimes felt at her obliviousness. Sick of loving Birdy, something in him wanted to hate her rather than hate himself, to sacrifice her upon the altar of his grief and shame, but he couldn't have borne the loneliness of that. He reminded himself this was all the result of his lies. Enervated by his sadness, he was further exhausted by how devastated Birdy was about Nick.

Her anger spilled into work. A couple of times, he had to step in between Birdy and an irritating passenger because she was about to blow. But after a month of him holding her while she cried and ranted, her old self began to return.

"Did I tell you Nick only has one testicle?"

"You did. More than once. And I wasn't interested the first time."

"It's ginormous, like a submarine."

"Shut. Up."

She laughed, which was good to see. They sat side by side on her hotel-room bed watching a show she loved called *Seinfeld*. He could smell the cherry-red polish she was daubing on her fingernails. She'd just finished her toenails, her toes separated by wads of tissue paper. She wore only her faded Packers T-shirt and panties.

"That's killing your brain cells," he said.

"Less brains you have, the happier you are." She gave him a cross-eyed, ditzy look.

She'd pulled her hair up into a messy chignon. She'd lost her puppy fat, her face transitioning from child to woman. In some ways he'd been a mentor to her, convincing her to use less makeup, to dress more fashionably, and to work on her manners, particularly her wolfish way of eating, acquired from living in a pack of hungry boys. Their bodies were pressed shoulder to shoulder, knee to knee. While snorting a laugh at one of Kramer's explosive entrances, she farted.

"Oh God," he said, putting his hand over his mouth and nose.

"Oh, come on, they smell like roses."

"Freshly manured."

In these moments, he knew he filled the place of her brothers. She'd told him he reminded her of Kyle, the sensitive one in the family. He wanted to lean forward and kiss her knee, to kiss her neck; his heart fluttered like a wounded bird. Love had become a chronic sickness. He'd called his wife Birdy a few times, and though he saw the name fall like a stone into her well and ripple faintly out of her depths, she said nothing.

Birdy became unabashed in front of him, talked to him from the bathroom with the door wide open while she was peeing and thought nothing of being half-naked or naked, once throwing off her bathrobe to properly dry herself while he kept his eyes assiduously on the Weather Channel. A few times they wrestled over the remote control. He was amazed by her strength, after a childhood of such bouts, and loved her girlish squeals and reddening face, loved being able to hold her down and mock her, the two of them panting on the bed, their hot faces pressed together until she finally called uncle. Then he had to sit with his knees pulled up to hide his arousal.

After a moment, she said, "I wonder if it's a bit different for you, I mean the feeling."

"Different?"

"I mean you don't want your boyfriend's baby; you don't have dark thoughts about going off the pill without telling him."

"I suppose not."

"You *suppose* not. I mean when someone brings a baby aboard, something inside you doesn't jump up and down screaming, *Baby, baby, baby*, does it?"

It took him a second to remember to shake his head.

"Do you ever want a child?"

He gave an indeterminate shrug.

She frowned at him, becoming serious. "Jack, I tell you *everything*. I know hardly anything about your life."

"What do you want to know?"

"Have you ever been in crazy sexy love? I can't imagine it."

"You can't?"

"You're just so wise and calm. Have you?"

"Have I what?"

"Been in crazy sexy love? *Please* tell me."

After a moment, he said, "Once, yes, when I was very young."

"Details, details," she demanded excitedly, imitating George from *Seinfeld*.

"It was in Egypt." (He'd told Birdy he was Egyptian). "We were fourteen, fifteen. We used to meet in a condemned building."

"And that was crazy sexy love?"

"It was; and it was *mucho* forbidden, of course. It felt like the sex Adam and Eve might have had before they were kicked out of Paradise."

"They had sex?"

"What, you think they gardened all day?" He smiled, lost in his own memories. "Afterwards we'd go swimming in the sea."

He realized his mistake, but also that she didn't know that Cairo wasn't on the sea and was too innocent to be suspicious.

"What would have happened if you were caught?"

"Same thing that happened to Adam and Eve."

"What about Mario? Do you love him?"

He was quiet for a moment. "I love . . . him, yes, but it's . . . difficult."

"Please tell me," she begged.

"He's always waiting for me, and I can feel him waiting for me?"

"Waiting for you?"

"Just . . . he's not very independent, and he wants to do everything for me; he even wants to take off my shoes when I come into the apartment."

"Is that like a fetish thing?"

"No, no," he snapped, angrier at himself than her. "It's not like that."

"I'm sorry," she said, shocked. He was never angry.

"I just feel a little trapped."

"Even though you love him?"

"Yes."

He was upset now, sitting on a hotel-room bed as a gay man next to this half-naked woman he loved while another woman he loved, two thousand miles away, waited for him. How was it possible that he could love this silly girl beside him, who seemed to have had no education, who read the same three novels in high school every other American was forced to read alongside a Shakespeare play—the one, she told him, where the Black guy kills his girlfriend. Not only didn't she know Cairo was not on the sea, she had no idea that Egypt was in Africa, and all she seemed to know of American history was a rhyme about Columbus sailing the ocean blue in 1692 (1492, he'd corrected her). On the long flights, she read lurid romances with titles like *Sweet, Savage Love* and *The Flower and the Flame* with such childish absorption she'd twitch, whimper, and yelp, like a dog dreaming. And yet still—*still*—every time he saw her waiting with the other attendants in the lounge, all his nerves tautened and lifted, like hair to static electricity.

9

On the day of Aisha's party, Dimra spent all morning baking, including a huge chocolate cake decorated with dogs chasing M&M balls. Jack was worried about her overdoing things, but she was happy, no doubt projecting herself forward into her own child's life.

Just after the party began, Jack, heading off for a three-leg trip around the Midwest, came upon Marcia sitting on the deck steps, smoking.

"How's it going?" he asked.

She shrugged. "They're eating now. Why the fuck do little girls have to scream like that? *Jesus.* And do you know what that asshole Ryker got Aisha?"

He shook his head.

"A puppy. An *actual* fucking puppy. Some guy at AA's dog had a litter. That fuckup thought he was doing me a favor because I couldn't afford that animated Labrador she wanted. Like I haven't got enough to deal with."

"What are you going to do?"

"Break her fucking heart and get that asshole to take the puppy back."

Jack said he was sorry. As he walked away, she called in a voice that surprised him with its softness, "Jack, I'm not always like this. I can be fun sometimes."

He laughed, and then she laughed also, a miraculous laugh, as if any one of us could enact the Devil's promise, shedding our tight old skins to become the person we want to be.

When Jack opened the back gate, he nearly collided with a man clutching a creepily realistic Baby Alive doll. About Jack's age and height, very dark-skinned, he was strikingly handsome, with wideset eyes above prominent cheekbones. He wore a brightly embroidered Kufi hat. Chike, it had to be.

"What are you doing here?" Marcia called, jumping up and hurrying to the gate. Jack was caught between them.

"I tried the front," he stammered nervously.

"That doesn't answer my fucking question."

Chike had noticed her belly. "You're pregnant again?"

"No, I'm just fucking fat."

For all her anger and bravado, she glanced away from Chike's shocked, interrogatory look.

"Sorry, I'll get out of here," Jack murmured, but Marcia, taking his arm, pulled Jack into her.

"I just want to see her," Chike said.

"Get the fuck out of here!" she shouted.

From behind them came Dimra's gentle voice calling up from the basement stairwell, "Marcia, we're going to do the cake."

Glancing back, Jack could see that his wife was confused and troubled by the way Marcia was clutching him.

"Will you give her this?" Chike proffered the baby doll. "You don't have to say it's from me."

"Give it to one of your other kids." Slamming the gate in his face, she followed Dimra inside.

When Jack opened the gate again, Chike, who was almost out of the parking lot, hurried back to hand him the doll. In the exchange, Jack pressed something on the doll's foot that made her giggle and say "Mama."

"My children are too old for such things." As Chike turned to leave, he hesitated again. "She's pregnant, yes?"

Jack nodded, and at Chike's desperate look, added, "Four months."

"It's your child?"

Jack shook his head. Chike's gaze seemed to turn inward to bleakly assess a landscape clearly impossible to traverse.

"She shouldn't be smoking," Chike murmured finally, and left.

Three days later, when Jack returned, his final leg delayed six hours by tornados, he found Dimra sitting sideways on the couch in nothing but one of his T-shirts, her bare legs pulled up into her chest, a garbage bag spread beneath her. Watching the sunset through the trees, she resembled one of Edward Hopper's archetypal women, lonely and half naked at a window. He felt suddenly trapped in a banal nightmare, numbness suffusing his limbs and head, causing him to hesitate a moment too long before he joined her, sitting as close as he could, wrapping his arms around her knees. The plastic felt squalid. The sunlight in the dark leaf canopy resembled smelted iron in slag. They could hear the proselytizing screams of Preacher Morris on Birchwood, God the cudgel of repentance. Strangely, Jack suddenly wondered what awful thing Preacher Morris must have done to be so passionately focused on the world repenting its sins, as once Jack idly wondered what shameful thing Jesus might have done to have preached forgiveness and journeyed so inexorably to his own sacrifice.

He hugged her knees harder, kissing them, and finally she told him that an hour ago she started cramping and bleeding. She sat on the toilet and felt something coming out, so she put her hand between her legs and caught it.

"It's the baby," she said. "I didn't know what to do with it; if I should save it or . . ." Preacher Morris was directly under their window now, his percussive adjurations causing her to wince. "It's in the bathroom."

"I should take you to hospital."

She shook her head. "It's over now. Will you do something with it?" she asked as Preacher Morris's voice ebbed.

On his way through to their bedroom's en-suite, Jack was disturbed by the sight of the Baby Alive doll on the bed. In the bathroom, he discovered what had come out of Dimra in a soap dish. It wasn't a four-month fetus and must have been dead for a while. He tipped the mess of blood and the sac into his hand and ran it under the faucet until the fetus lay glistening in his palm. He could make out the swollen head, the tiny, blood-filled eye, its neck just forming, its small limbs folded into its body. It sickened him that she'd been alone. She'd only mustered the confidence a week ago to tell her parents she was pregnant. Even her mother, she said, had managed to look joyful—something Jack couldn't imagine.

Strange little shucked oyster of life, of their life, his and Dimra's, and the lives of all their ancestors, back to fish and ammonites and whatever came before, now a glutinous glimmering, a half human, half aquatic being lying in the palm of his hand. His phone pinged with a text and vibrated. He tipped the fetus into the toilet and flushed, then washed out the soap dish.

He sat on the toilet lid listening to the cistern refilling until the final silence. When he heard Dimra enter the bedroom, he remembered the text.

> Dimra has been crying so much. ALL DAY!

May must have seen his car in the lot.

He texted back. "She lost the baby. She's okay." He then texted Lulu and Pauline.

When he came out, he saw that Dimra had transferred the garbage bag to the bed, and was sitting on it, leaning back against the headboard.

"Why's that doll here?" he asked.

"A friend of Marcia's found her a temporary job covering for someone as a receptionist at one of the downtown hotels, but she's got all the late shifts. She doesn't trust Ryker, so I've been looking after Aisha when she goes to work."

"You shouldn't be doing that." He was suddenly furious at Marcia. "Is Aisha sleeping here?"

She nodded. "It's okay, I like having her here."

He thought of the physical stress of looking after a five-year-old and could feel himself blaming Marcia for the miscarriage. When he moved the doll to sit next to Dimra, it giggled and bleated, "Mama."

They sat silently for a while, until Dimra said, "It wets its diaper."

"What?"

"The doll. You feed it and it wets its diaper."

A knock at the front door. It was Lulu. Her hug brought tears to his eyes.

"She's in the bedroom," he said.

He heard them both crying then, and it struck him that Dimra hadn't found that release with him.

Pauline appeared after her shift a few hours later.

They couldn't stop Dimra cooking for everyone, the apartment filling with the smell of fresh bread, falafel, and baba ghanoush. Jack remained in the kitchen cleaning up while the women sat talking at the table. He had no appetite for food, still less for conversation, but listened. Pauline said she'd longed for a child. She'd dated a few men but didn't believe in sex before marriage so the relationships, even with men from her church, hadn't lasted.

"I'm not so hideous, am I?" she said, laughing. Lulu and Dimra loudly protested, each snatching up a hand. Pauline continued, "Manman believed there was the perfect person waiting out there for everyone." She sighed. "I feel like a lost letter, you know, mailed to my beloved, but never arriving." She laughed. "But God is my sender, so being returned is not so bad."

Dead letter. Sealed. It was strange for Jack to think of her virginal life: work, church, her father. He often thought of her in the infant ICU, as one of those minor deities that occupy the space between life and death, a gardener in a hothouse of fickle, fragile plants.

"What about you, Lulu?" Pauline said.

"I love children, but Val . . . not so much. Val told me her writing would always be her priority. The problem with being a lesbian," Lulu added, "is that you can't claim you got pregnant by mistake."

Jack feared for Lulu. Before Valeria, her apartment had thronged with friends from her old Pilsen neighborhood, shopgirls, nurses, elementary school teachers, and he would hear Lulu's voice vying with theirs on the deck, joyous and boisterous. After meeting Valeria, Lulu seemed at odds with herself, ever uncomfortable in the absurd clothes she wore to satisfy Valeria's schoolgirl fetish. When she was on the back deck with Valeria's university and artist friends, he could hear Lulu periodically making desperate attempts to join the conversation, asking questions so inept, she was like a bicycle crashing at a chokepoint of the Tour de France, strewing a couple of wrecks behind her, the main field moving swiftly around.

Everyone agreed to Arabic coffee, and for once his wife let him make it. While Jack was sure he'd never return to the crisis of being that had led him to the Golden Gate Bridge, he felt that same glacial breath of nonexistence at his neck as he stirred the slurry of coffee, water, sugar, and cardamom, becoming his mother preparing coffee for one of his father's late-night diwans of Fatah men.

He remembered Wahib, a neighbor boy he and Salim played with, who came from a family of eleven living in a one-room shack in the camp, all of them sleeping at night upon two mattresses they lifted against the wall in the morning. When he was ten, having done something naughty, Wahib was trying to escape his mother's slap and mistakenly jumped on his newborn baby sister as she lay swaddled in the plastic basin serving as her crib. Little Noor's fragile ribs pierced her small heart. After her burial, no one mentioned Noor again. Jack thought of all the suffering of the occupation and exile, of Al-Nakba and Al-Naksa, and before that of the incomprehensible horrors of the Holocaust becoming a juggernaut that crushed Palestine and inaugurated the manifest destiny of Israel, a destiny that had somehow landed Wahib upon his sister's chest creating a tiny grave surrounded by silence. A baby girl, her heart pierced by her own rib, made sense as the point upon which the inverted pyramid of human suffering balanced. All this had come to him in trying to reason that his and Dimra's was a comparatively small sorrow. And yet he'd foolishly invested in this child, imagining his daughter—it was always a daughter—into life. He'd fantasized about how much it would change Dimra to walk their child to school, to meet other parents, hosting sleepovers and parties, finally giving full rein to her capacity for love; and thought no less of being himself rooted by this love into his home, Chicago and America, into a life, *his* life, into which he'd somehow never, from his first breath of air, felt fully born.

Responding to a light tap on the door, he opened it to May's ever wary, accusative, and angry face. She thrust toward him an earthenware pot of beef pho.

"Thank you," he said, bringing the pot to the kitchen island. Dimra stood as May put her head around the door.

"I heard you crying; crying so much. So much!" She was laughing in that grating, fake way of hers.

This forced Dimra to laugh in response and say, "I'm sorry, I hope I didn't disturb you."

"So much *crying*. I heard you *all day*," she continued, followed by another staccato "Hahahahaha."

"Please come in, join us," Dimra said, "there's plenty of food."

"No, no; no time; I'm busy, very busy today." But she lingered, staring at his wife in painful confusion, and for a moment became tearful. Jumping up, Dimra begged her again to join them, but when she approached, May blurted sharply, "I'm giving you the soup not the pot. I need the pot. Tomorrow. I need it tomorrow," and hurried out.

When Pauline and Lulu left, Dimra wrapped her arms around Jack as he washed the dishes and asked him to come into the bedroom to pray with her. He kissed her forehead and said she should pray. He'd join her in a little while.

Just after she'd gone in, he quietly traversed the hallway and listened at their bedroom door:

Bismilla ir Rahman ir Rahim, In the name of Allah the beneficent the merciful, who granted us the opportunity to be in America.

Ya Allah, we remember that all we have, our possessions, will be left behind when we die. Our only true luxury is faith in you, and in your sure love.

Forgive me for not doing enough to help my parents in Gaza; for not being a good wife to my husband, for not providing a son. Only you know what I have suffered trying.

Ya Allah, please open my husband's heart to you. Bring him back to the faith; let your love, peace, and wisdom flood him.

When Dimra was finally asleep, Jack was too sad and agitated to join her. He needed another cigarette. Just as he reached his back door, a knock came. It was Marcia with Aisha, the little girl clutching a plush lion cub.

"You're back," Marcia blurted, continuing after an awkward silence: "They gave me another shift tonight."

"Dimra's sick."

"Is she okay?"

He almost said, *We lost our child*. Instead: "She'll be okay."

Silence again. He couldn't turn Aisha away, and stepped aside, the little girl obediently heading into the second bedroom.

"She's ready for bed. You might need to read her something. I brought a bunch of books up yesterday." Marcia wasn't looking at him. He could sense how hard this dependency was for her, and his sullen unresponsiveness wasn't making it any easier.

Finally, she glanced into his eyes, clearly wanting to ask him what was wrong, but with neither the time nor emotional resources for such an inquiry, she abruptly turned and hurried back down.

Aisha sat on the bed having selected *Lyle, Lyle Crocodile* from a pile of books in the corner. Dimra had decorated the walls with the girl's crayon drawings.

"What's your lion called?" he asked.

"That's Simba, silly."

He told her to get under the covers, and sitting beside her read *Lyle, Lyle Crocodile*, letting her turn the pages, her head falling against his shoulder, intensifying the ache of his loss.

When he finished, she looked up at him and said, "I told Dimmy she's not reading it right. She making it up."

He'd forgotten how little English Dimra could read. She was probably guessing at the story from the pictures. "She likes to make up her own stories."

He then read *Don't Let the Pigeon Drive the Bus*, and though Aisha wanted him to keep reading, he told her it was time for bed and he'd be just outside the back door for the next twenty minutes if she needed him.

Jack huddled himself on their fraying wicker bench in the freezing night, looking up at a bloodless bone moon, nearly full. He kept seeing the glistening fetus in his hand, thought of it now floating through the city's sewer system. Having invested too much in this child, he felt his whole life was abortive. He recalled that furious letter to his father, shoved somewhere down the back of the filing cabinet, claiming he and Dimra had a son. If still alive, his father would be surrounded by his cousin Salim's children. Would he be the same black hole for them as he'd been for Jack?

Jack's mother had told him his father's story, and Jack now tried to imagine little Ali, born four years before World War II in Al-Nabi Rubin, a village built around the tomb of Rubin, son of Jacob, though it was a much older pagan site, and whose bones lay in the sand was anyone's guess. Jack once overheard his father, in a rare nostalgic mood, talking about the Nadi Rubin Festival, attended by tens of thousands every August. He spoke of Sufi dervishes whirlpooling beside gipsy women undulating their sexy potbellies, and horses thundering up and down the sand as poets recited the epics. Jack's paternal family were grain and citrus farmers but made a good portion of their yearly income selling food to the festival crowd. In '48, his uncle Kassam was five, Jack's father thirteen, his uncle Ahmed fifteen, and aunt Nahla sixteen. All his father understood of the war was that foreign countries had given half of Palestine to the Zionists. In early May, an explosion shocked his father out of bed. He peeked out of his window to see one of their goats decapitated beside a blackened shell hole, its month-old kid bleating helplessly. The Hagenah was firing mortars into the village to terrify its occupants into running. His family fled to an area of sand dunes until the shelling ceased. When they returned, Abu Ahmed produced from under his bed a rusty Lee-Enfield. Jack's father felt pride that his baba was going to fight, until he was ordered to bury the rifle in the orchard.

A month later, Palmach troops rousted the family out of their home like chickens, gathering them into the yard. His father's widowed grandmother scooped up a handful of donkey dung and rubbed it all over Nahla's face, hoping this might save her from being dishonored. The soldiers laughed. While this was happening, a Yemeni Jew tried to tug off his mother's headscarf to see if she was hiding her gold under it. Another soldier, an older man who spoke French, pulled him angrily away, their scuffle halted by a shout from their tiny, austere-looking commander, who wore steel rimmed-glasses and a uniform a couple of sizes too big. This scholarly, dyspeptic man pointed south.

"Egypt," he said to Abu Ahmed in immaculate Arabic. "Go be with your Arab brothers and sisters."

The officer refused to let them take the donkey, claiming it was being commandeered for operational purposes, so they'd have to pull the cart themselves.

A couple of soldiers were left to supervise the family as they loaded the cart, one of the men stroking the ears of the baby goat their mortars orphaned. The other went to urinate against the side of their house. Ever after, Jack's father was haunted by the image of that Zionist soldier leaning on the wall near his bedroom with one hand, his urine darkening the stones. He'd never forget it because this soldier left his Sten gun propped near the door. These men had no fear of them. For all his life, Jack's mother told him, his father would regret not snatching up that Sten gun and killing the two soldiers.

The family loaded only what they could pull, together with the grandmother, into the cart. Abu Ahmed carefully locked their front door, taking his key and the Ottoman deeds with the stamp of the Sublime Porte. On the scorching journey toward Gaza, they begged food from retreating Egyptian soldiers. Streams of refugees became a river that emptied into a sea of 20,000 at what would become Beach Camp, just one of the encampments holding the 200,000 who'd fled into Gaza. It was barely more than desert. They shared a tent with two families from Lydd and Bir Seb'a before securing one of their own. Jack's father remembered the crowds of refugees kneeling at the shrine of the

Prophet's great-grandfather, Hashem, in Gaza City, praying to return home. They received a little food from the Quakers before UNRWA was established, but essentially survived on bread dipped in tea, and garlic soup with a few scavenged greens. As years passed, the tents replaced by crude breezeblock and corrugated-iron structures, Abu Ahmed remained useless, stuck, as many were, like a clock broken at the instant of a murder.

The Jordanians annexed the West Bank, and however much bad faith preceded this annexation, the king at least made the Palestinians Jordanian citizens. Egypt had no interest in annexing Gaza, rendering everyone there stateless, even the indigenous Gazans, the muwataneen. They'd never allow their children to marry a mehajera, and those living in Gaza City would rather eat cow dung than set foot in Beach Camp, just ten minutes' walk from their comfortable houses in the shade of the flame trees.

After the winter rains, Ahmed made a deal with someone who owned a truck and he and Jack's father dug gravel out of the flooded areas of the Gaza Valley to sell to concrete factories. They made enough for Ahmed to begin negotiations to buy two dunams of land. The boys, ever famished, dreamed of fresh tomatoes and ripe figs. When they told their baba, he showed no interest. But on the day Ahmed finalized the deal, they discovered the Spam can in which they kept their money empty. They went straight to their father, who told them he'd bought a hundred dunams with it. Ahmed, incredulous, demanded to know where this land was.

"Home," their father replied. He'd given all the money they'd saved, breaking their backs for over a year, to one of their old neighbors in exchange for his deed.

"You boys keep working," he said, "and when we return, we'll own half the village."

Their grandmother pushed herself between an incandescent Ahmed and their father. A little later that evening, she slipped a thick gold bracelet into Ahmed's hands.

"I was keeping this for your sister," she said, "but no one here has anything. Khalas"—she shooed away their protests—"go with God. Bring me figs and fresh tomatoes!"

During this time, Kassam, too young to be anything but a hinderance, was sent out with a tray holding sewing kits, combs, and chewing gum to sell to the Bedouin. Bullies sometimes stole his money, and he was frequently bitten by the mangy dogs guarding the Bedouin encampments. *Sensitive*, that's the word the family used for Kassam. He seemed always to be crying, seeking solace with the women, who spoiled him. In '53, when Kassam was ten, a cholera epidemic swept the camp, killing Nahla and their grandmother. Their mother began imagining snakes and scorpions in their home and sometimes flung all their food away, convinced it had glass in it. She died a year later from a stroke.

Kassam turned inward then. All day, he'd work on their plot of land, the only thing that gave him peace. In his early teens, when an aid worker gifted him a book on dryland farming, Kassam planted shelter beds of trees and shrubs to reduce wind evaporation and oriented crops perpendicular to the slope of their land. The result was more food than they could eat, sold for a good profit at the market. He also grew cyclamen, chrysanthemums, and lavender, just because he loved them. He built himself a sturdy little shepherd's hut, and often slept out there.

Jack hugged his knees tightly into himself as the last Metra rattled by, wishing he too had somewhere he could escape to. Even the moon, with its hoarfrost nimbus, looked frigid. He shook a second cigarette from his pack, though he knew it would keep him awake.

Two years after Um Ahmed's death, Abu Ahmed declared he was returning to Al-Nadi Rubin. They told him he'd be killed, but in those early years people often slipped back across the border. Then he was gone.

Though the Egyptians didn't offer citizenship, they did provide free education. Jack's father and Ahmed studied civil engineering at Cairo University during the revolution that brought Nasser to power. Joining the General Union of Palestinian Students, they became close to its chairman, Yasser Arafat. With Arafat, they spent many long nights discussing the foundation of a political party to lead the Palestinians toward a secular democracy, with an armed wing that would fight the Israelis as the Algerians had fought and defeated the French.

At one of these gatherings Jack's father met Yasmin Zohry, just sixteen. Jack could imagine that ardent, willowy girl chiding and challenging the men. She told Jack that when she first saw his father, tall and film-star handsome, as he stood to recite Ibrahim Tuqan's "My Homeland," tears flooded her eyes. She thought this was love, and no doubt it was, but they were not joyful tears, and years later she wondered if she'd received a premonition of the suffering to come.

When Jack's father and Ahmed returned to Gaza, they joined the Palestinian Liberation Army. His mother and father exchanged secret letters every week, since the marriage would have been objected to as fiercely by Ahmed as by her family. In '56, the Israelis invaded Gaza during the Suez crisis, a rout, his father and Ahmed captured. After the Americans forced the Israelis, British, and French to withdraw, the brothers, including Kassam, joined the fedayeen.

In '57 Arafat and other Gazans in Kuwait formed Fatah. Ahmed and Jack's father joined its military wing, Al-Asifah, and led an attack to bomb a water-diversion canal between the Jordan River and the Negev. The bombs didn't detonate, and they were almost killed. When the Israelis retaliated against the Egyptians for Palestinian incursions, the mukhabarat cracked down, all three brothers arrested and beaten senseless for two days. The two older brothers gave nothing away, but Kassam betrayed dozens of their comrades, carrying with him, ever after that, a heavy burden of shame.

Undeterred, Ahmed and Jack's father made an incursion from Jordan to lay mines near an Israeli military encampment. But the Jordanian secret service, determined to stamp out Palestinian nationalism, betrayed them. Jack's father survived because he had to relieve himself, squatting in nearby bushes when he heard the gunfire. From behind a cluster of sabras, he saw three of the seven fedayeen lying dead. His wounded brother was being propped up by two of his comrades. They'd been ambushed by a troop of Druze, whom the Israelis recruited as border guards. One of the Druze also lay dead. He could hear Ahmed appealing to the Druze as brothers. In response, one of them hammered the butt of his machine gun into Ahmed's face, pitching him to the ground, then flipped the machine gun around and emptied its magazine into Ahmed's body. The cry Jack's father couldn't stifle was drowned out as the rest of his comrades were gunned down.

The moment his father made it back across the river, he was arrested by Jordanian intelligence. After days of beatings and torture, he was kicked out of the country. Though he went on no more missions, he remained a prominent Fatah man.

As a boy, Jack never asked his father about all the scars mapping his face and body, but wondered which were Egyptian, which Jordanian, and which Israeli.

With the death of Ahmed, Jack's father was now free to marry his mother.

In '64, the PLO was formed, but his father refused to join, considering it a puppet of Arab governments. Instead, he invested his hope in Nasser, all those stirring speeches ringing in his ears. He joined the Egyptian Army during the military buildup at the Israeli border in '67 to stand in endless ranks of soldiers chanting *"Adwa, Adwa, Adwa, Return, Return, Return."* Nasser visited his troops like a conquering hero, a performance of victory before any battle was fought.

Days after Nasser's visit, Israel's preemptive air strike destroyed the entire Egyptian, Jordanian, and Syrian air forces on the ground, followed by an armored assault, and his father found himself scattering back through the Sinai with his unit. The Israeli Air Force hunted them down like rabbits, their armored divisions equally merciless: everywhere burned-out vehicles, trucks full of corpses, 20,000 slaughtered. His father remembered watching Bedouin collecting ill-fitting boots that had been discarded all over the desert, as if it had been a rapture rather than a rout. Yitzhak Rabin named it the Six Day War, to give it Pentateuchal and biblical significance, and all around the world Israelis were depicted as a plucky David defeating a monstrous Goliath.

The Palestinians called this June war Al-Naksa, the Setback, more a sick joke than an understatement, despite its Quranic resonance. His father believed Al-Naksa, not Al-Nakba, truly created Israel, resuscitating what had been to that point a dying dream. Jack's father, after investing all his love and hope in Nasser, was heartbroken. But he'd witnessed the Arab disease of nepotism filling the Egyptian Army's higher ranks with lazy and incompetent officers. Like so much Arab rhetoric, it was make-believe; they were children playing a game.

When it was over, the ex-military men in Gaza were ordered into Israeli headquarters and asked to serve as policemen, liaising with the Israelis for a hefty salary. His father felt this tantamount to collaboration and walked out, the weight of his reputation half emptying the ranks of men there and adding to the fat file Shabak already had on him.

With the borders now open, the first thing his father and Kassam did, of course, was visit Al-Nabi Rubin, hoping to find Abu Ahmed. But of the town only the ancient mulberry trees and the shrine with its minaret remained, holding within it the tomb with the green curtain declaring *There is no God but God, and Rubin is his prophet*. They knew for sure now that their baba was dead.

After '67, Jack's father, like most Palestinians, stopped hoping that someone else might liberate them. Using weapons stashed from the war, scattered remnants of the PLA joined members of the PFLP, the Ba'ath Party, Fatah, the communists, and the PLF to form an erratic resistance. An injection of hope came with the Battle of Karameh in '68, the Jordanians and Palestinians fighting side by side to repel an Israeli incursion. His father, though, was deeply troubled when he discovered that during the battle Palestinian fedayeen wrapped in explosives detonated themselves against Israeli tanks. He had never heard of such a thing: human bombs. They were lauded as glorious martyrs, but it appalled him that Palestinian lives were now worth so little.

And all for nothing. Two years later, Black September began a few weeks before Jack's birth. In response to Palestinian fedayeen landing hijacked jets on Jordanian soil as well as yet another of their numerous attempts to assassinate the king, the Jordanian Army attacked, slaughtering them, washing most out into Lebanon. On the day Jack was born, Nasser, who'd filled so many with his dreams of a unified Arab world, died in despair. Jack's father wept tears both of grief and joy. "My son," he declared, lifting Jack to their gathered neighbors, "will be Nasser reborn."

At last, Jack's parents could be called Um and Abu Jamal. Though his mother never managed to bring another child to term, at least she'd produced a son. She also inherited a little money from one of her more forgiving aunts. It was enough to extend their house in the camp and to buy a small place nearby for Uncle Kassam and his sweet, meek wife, Ameena, who gave birth to their son, Salim, just a week after Jack. Enough money also to establish a hardware and mechanical-repair business.

Kassam, though, had no interest in spending his life resuscitating ancient appliances. Traveling to Ashkelon, Kiryat Gat, Tel Aviv, and Rishon LeZion, he scavenged things to sell. In Gaza's souks he sold scraps discarded from Israeli textile factories as material for blankets and filling for pillows. With the profits, he bought two containers of rusty cans of tomatoes exposed to moisture at Ashdod's port. He also bought cans that had lost their labels, and food that was out of date, joining many others in Gaza's markets selling whatever the Israelis threw away.

Finally, Kassam made enough to set up a barber shop in a tiny streetfront property he bought in the camp. Installing a television and radio, he always had tea on the boil and loved talking to people. He also had the freedom to close his shop whenever he wanted to go to the family plot, its produce providing the rest of his income. His wife complained that he slept out there in the shepherd's hut half the week, reading by the light of a kerosene lamp. He developed an obsession, of all things, for landscape gardening, the walls of his shepherd's hut covered in magazine images of flower beds and gardens from all over the world. His dream was to emigrate to England.

Over the next couple of years, though, the Israelis and Gush Emunim, the Bloc of the Faithful, embarked on a mission to settle Gaza with fundamentalists. Israel confiscated a third of the prime agricultural land for a few thousand Israelis, a million impoverished Palestinians having to make do with what remained. The family plot was expropriated. It had been Kassam's little Eden. He'd filled the shepherd's hut with dried lavender, and no doubt, when he lay in it during the winter rains, imagined himself in an English garden.

The Israeli settlers received interest-free loans to set up labor-intensive operations making use of cheap and desperate Palestinian workers. With resistance operations continuing, Ariel Sharon, the Bulldozer, was put in charge of pacifying Gaza. He was as brutal as he'd ever been, a hundred resistance fighters killed, hundreds of others deported to Jordan, Lebanon, or cast into the Sinai. He wanted armored vehicles to be able to control the narrow streets of the refugee camps, so he bulldozed 2,000 homes. Beach Camp received the worst of this purge, beginning just before Black September. Luckily Jack's home wasn't destroyed, but

Uncle Kassam's was, as was his barbershop. He was offered a place in compensation in a housing project in Sheikh Radwan, providing he and his family signed a paper relinquishing their refugee status and any claims arising from it. His uncle refused, so he and his family moved in with Jack's family. Jack's father and Kassam extended the house up another story and split it down the middle, so the families could have separate spaces, sharing the roof and yard. The hardware store barely made enough to sustain Jack's family, many of their customers so poor they paid with eggs and baked goods, so Kassam became a day laborer.

A month into this work, Kassam was picked up at the area they called the slave market, where day laborers gathered to be chosen for agricultural work. With a half dozen other men, he was driven to the very settler farm that had subsumed his own plot of land. For nearly a week, he tore up what was left of his plantings, digging irrigation channels for an orchard, and converting his own shepherd's hut to a pump house for a well.

That's when Kassam started to drink. He brewed 50 proof rakija from grapes grown on the roof of their house. But then Ameena gave birth, four years after Salim, to a girl, Samira. As she grew older, Kassam all but stopped drinking, coming to love this girl in a way he was never able to love his son.

Salim could not have been less like his father: physical, kinetic, not at all academic. Jack and Salim had rioted about the camp's streets with their gang of boys ever since their scrawny bodies were barely sketched in. Puberty hit Salim early. While the voices of Jack and the other boys still screeched and boomed like little car accidents, Salim's grew so deep and percussive, you felt it like a stone thrown at your chest. Both Jack and Salim grew tall, but Jack remained smooth and skinny while Salim possessed nearly a man's body at thirteen. Jack's mother kept Jack's hair shorn, so they could quickly deal with the headlice that raced like wildfire through the thousands of children in the camp, but Salim's crazy mop fell rakishly into his handsome face. Any girl would envy Salim's large eyes, with their lush lashes, eyes that glimmered like the lit taper of a Molotov cocktail as a devilish smile curled the edge of his lips. No part of Salim ever seemed to withdraw into some deep or private place. At times he entered a kind of quiescence, but it was more as if his being had diffused itself restfully through his skin and musculature. It wasn't animal, exactly, because it revolved around a passionate will, a reckless bravery. Jack and the other neighborhood boys followed in Salim's wake as he led them into Gaza to smash the windows of Hapoalim or Discount Bank, sometimes even to throw stones at patrols, all of them scattering to hide in the orchards surrounding the city. In their rough games, Salim's body was the one with the hardest and most heartless edges. Salim was somehow a reproach to Kassam, and Jack would notice his uncle wincing at the percussive force of his son's voice as Salim commanded the boys around him in a raucous game of Jews and Arabs.

Samira, in contrast, was playing chess with her baba and speaking good English by the time she was seven. Like Jack and her father, she was sensitive, imaginative, and loved to read. Samira and her father dreamed magical gardens into being, and she came to share her father's passion for England. Her favorite book was Frances Hodgson Burnett's *The Secret Garden*. Jack often read it to her while he sat on her bed (as he'd just read to Aisha), her little head lying against him, and he could see by her dreamy, absorbed face that the Yorkshire Moors, the manor house and rain were more real to her than the camp's tumbled shanties and burning sun. One night, she said, "Do you think there's a secret garden somewhere in Beach Camp?" Jack told her he was sure of it.

One of Jack's favorite books as a child was *The Fantastic Mr. Fox*. He dreamed of enlisting all the kids in the camp to dig tunnels into the Israeli side so the Israelis would never know who was emptying their orchards and stealing their fresh-baked pastries. When he later read H. G. Wells's *The Time Machine*, his vision darkened as he imagined all the Palestinians moving underground, adapting to the dark, evolving into Morlocks as the Israelis became the Eloi, the Palestinians no more than a story to scare naughty children, but always there, like shadows. In much later years, he recalled this fantasy as Gazans riddled the border with smugglers' tunnels.

In '82 another cholera outbreak ravaged the camp, Samira and Ameena became ill, and Kassam was forced to relive the nightmare of the deaths of his sister and grandmother. He was luckier this time: his wife survived.

At Samira's funeral, his uncle was drunk and being held—constrained—by Jack's father. Throughout the ceremony he kept shouting "Mangos," laughing, "sweet as first love. Mangos. Anyone want some mangos!" When Jack asked his mother about this afterward, she told him that during those few days he was hired to clear his own plot of land, he dug irrigation channels for a mango orchard, a crop that would guzzle up Gaza's scarce water. In the camp, the water was often saline, becoming periodically so evil-tasting everyone had to switch from tea to coffee to disguise the taste. Sewage sometimes leaked into the water, causing diarrhea, and people often had to go to relatives with wells where the water table hadn't yet fallen below sea level. Cholera, she explained, usually comes from contaminated water.

Samira was far from alone as a child in a cemetery filled with small graves covered in little toys and sweets. Kassam embedded chess pieces into hers and planted it with wildflowers that blazed out every spring.

After that, his uncle was always drunk, his entire personality changing, his language laced with bitter irony: "We Palestinians are a cause célèbre, Jamal, habibi. Thousands rally in the streets of the Arab capitals, UN resolutions, international conferences, special prayers. Arab leaders hold lavish banquets in our honor. But have you noticed any change in our lives? No? Well, there's a reason for this. At these banquets, do you know what they're eating, habibi? *Us.* You see, the problem, habibi, is that Palestinians are *delicious*. Israelis, particularly, love a good roast Palestinian, but the truth is we're a delicacy all over the Arab world."

Jack began to dislike his uncle for being so weak, and for not even hiding his distaste for his son. Jack's aversion turned to hatred the afternoon Jack and Salim returned home from a Prisoners' Day protest. They were thirteen, their faces covered with wet kufiyahs, their eyes streaming from tear gas. His uncle lay on the couch. Kassam had grown very fat and was so drunk he looked as if his bones were dissolving into the sodden slurry of his body. Salim's anxious mother, chiding them, cut up onions to put under their eyes, a popular home remedy for tear gas that perplexed Jack since it only ever made things worse.

"You're going to get yourselves shot," his aunt said fearfully.

"Then our blood will water *our* land," Jack's cousin declared, parroting one of the protest banners.

At this, Kassam laughed. Hefting himself to his feet, he approached Salim in a wrestling stance. "Come on, son, I'm Israel, resist me."

As his father took hold of him, Salim laughed, thinking he was horsing around, but Kassam quickly pinned Salim on his back, sitting on his son's chest, trapping Salim's arms under his knees.

"I'm Israel!" Kassam shouted as he mimed punching his son's face repeatedly. "I've smashed your face to a pulp," he said, laughing. "Now what do you do?"

"Get off me, Baba. You're heavy. You're hurting me!" Salim shouted, his face going puce.

Jack was trying to push his uncle off, but the alcohol made Kassam a numb dead weight. Ameena fluttered around like a bird watching a fox devouring its young.

"You know what to do, brave fedayeen," Kassam shouted. "Yalla, spit at me, shout 'Samood.' I'm the hated Zionist Entity!" He imitated a pathetic kind of spitting, "Ptew, ptew. There you go, you've spat at me," Kassam declared, "ptew, ptew. And now I pound your face to a pulp again." This time he banged his fists into the floor, scarily close to Salim's face.

"Yalla, tough guy, what are you going to do?" he shouted gleefully. "Come on, spit in my face, shout 'Samood,' shout 'Revolution until victory,' shout 'Land and honor.' Now my turn," and again the vicious imitation of pounding.

Salim looked distraught, tears streaming, and finally Jack slapped his uncle in the face as hard as he could. Kassam seemed to be awakened a little, and after a moment hefted himself up and back onto the couch, words escaping him like the last wheezes of a dropped accordion, "Samood, samood, samood."

"Samood," Jack murmured, a foggy exhalation in the cold, like life leaving the body; *samood*, meaning steadfastness, that shibboleth of ultimate Palestinian victory; samood, the capacity simply to endure.

Jack now wondered if his hatred for his uncle had been rooted partly in a fear for himself. He was like Kassam: sensitive, a mother's boy, a reader, the furthest thing imaginable from his father's dream of a new Nasser. He'd cried so often as a little boy, his mother worried he might need psychiatric help. But in his tenth year of life, Jack stopped crying and woke into a strangely remote consciousness that split him from the pain of being himself. He became a watchful cipher drifting through the world. While Jack's body sprouted in height, the full expression of his being seemed impossibly far-off. It was as if he, himself, were not the *point* of his life. As if he were merely providing passage for an embryonic divinity from one end of his existence to the other.

His father, on the other hand, could not have been more a part of this world. Spending half of Jack's childhood in jail, he completed what the prisoners called the world tour, spending time at prisons in Ashkelon, Ramle, Nafha, Tel Mond, Ayalon, and the Negev. Because of his high position in Fatah, the Israelis often arrested him as a precaution before national occasions and anniversaries like Land Day or Fatah Day, since they suspected him of organizing protests. As he was being taken to the jeep in handcuffs, their neighbors would shout, "The winds cannot shake the mountain!"

His father's arrests weren't always a knock at the door. When Jack was eight, Palestinian Fatah Fedayeen landed on a beach north of Tel Aviv and rampaged through Israel, slaughtering thirty-eight Israelis, including thirteen children. The next night, an IDF patrol smashed in their door at three in the morning. His mother ran to Jack's room to put him behind her body as the soldiers flung his father to the floor, cuffed him, and dragged him out. A half dozen soldiers remained to perform the mockery of a search as an excuse to smash all their crockery and whatever furniture was in boot range. His mother would address them in immaculate Hebrew, telling them that uniforms and orders didn't make them any less the instruments of evil. Jack never understood why she did this, since it only enraged them more. On another such raid, after a collaborator claimed his father was hiding a box of grenades, they shot tear gas through the windows, smashed in the door again, and this time wrecked the entire house.

Jack could imagine vividly what would happen to his father from the stories the veterans of the jail system told. They'd take him first to the maslakh, the slaughterhouse, in Gaza Central Jail, where he'd join a crowd of half-naked men sitting with their hands cuffed behind their backs, their heads covered in hoods that stank of sweat and fear. As a child, he imagined it a weird landscape of men in grotesque and agonized poses, like the eerie shattered remains of a primordial forest, or the opening tableau of some strange modern dance. His father would eventually be thrown into a small room, tied to pipes, made to lie on a concrete floor for hours, even days. Once or twice a day, he'd be taken for interrogations where Jack didn't want to think about what would happen.

One time, when his baba returned home after one of his detentions—Jack was eight or nine—he couldn't understand why his father didn't eat with them. Later, he snuck down from his room to lie on the cold stone of the hallway and look under the gap beneath the kitchen door. He watched his mother feeding his father like a child because his hands were still too damaged and swollen by overtightened cuffs for him to hold cutlery.

Jack felt confused by his father's returns, riven with guilt because he felt miserable and resentful. His father sat most often at the table in the kitchen smoking, and Jack would forget he was in the house, this black hole of a human being who'd stay up most of the night and sleep during the day. He'd sometimes shed so much weight, Jack hardly recognized him. He almost never spoke to Jack, who wouldn't dare even to look him in the eye. He could snap at the smallest things. One time, when Jack forgot to kick off his plastic sandals and clattered across the stone flagging of the kitchen, his father dragged him to the floor by his shirt, snatched off an offending sandal, and frenziedly slapped Jack with it all over his body until his mother rushed in to stop him. With each passing year his father hardened, becoming like flint buried in the soft limestone of his family. All Jack could feel was this man's sharp edges, and he wished his father would work to the surface of their life and be lost forever. All his childhood, Jack felt himself trapped between his uncle's bitter irony and his father's astringent silence. These two men were his examples, one comedy, the other tragedy, one broken, the other indurate.

He guessed that for most, having such men in their lives would put them off fatherhood, but for Jack it was the opposite. He wanted to discover himself in his love for his child and in his child's love for him, to have a child who would never fear to look into his eyes, for whom he would be flesh and blood, rather than a piece of flint, a graven image, a stone father.

But sitting there on his deck on a frigid Chicago night looking at that moon like a hacked bone, the warm smoke of his cigarette escaping with his frigid breath, Jack's eyes spilled the first tears he'd ever shed for either of those men.

He finished his cigarette. He could see people floating through their lives in the lit windows of the adjacent apartment building, a heavy man asleep in front of the flickering light of a television. Rats skittered out of the shadows, fevered little messages flashing through the neurons of the night, and there upon the roof of the garage opposite lay the condo's feral cat, Panther, serenely declining to annihilate the rats for now. Jack quietly reentered his home, instinctively avoiding every creaking floorboard up the hall to his bedroom. Entering, he saw that Aisha had slipped into bed beside his wife, so he returned down the hall and slept that night in a child's bed.

= 10 =

Spring wouldn't come to Chicago for another few months, so Jack was glad this fragile, sunny day had wandered into March like a snow-white stallion into a herd of muddy wildebeest. He lingered in his Honda, having just returned home from a long Gulf Coast trip. Despite his seniority, he often worried about losing his job. He'd just clung on after 9/11, and now, only six and a half years later, the world teetered on the precipice of a recession worse, according to the media, than the Great Depression. He was exhausted also. On his final leg from Tallahassee, a cremation urn a passenger had slid under the seat in front of her shattered during turbulence. Jack spent most of the flight on his hands and knees, sweeping the ashes into a trash bag while the woman wept.

Though he knew he needed to muster himself, he was in no hurry to deal with condo issues. The collapse of the housing market meant everyone was strapped for cash, but he was particularly concerned about Marcia. With her newborn, Aiden, he was sure she wouldn't be able to pay the $3,000 special assessment due April 1, less than a week away.

At last, he forced himself out of the car and entered the back gate just as May emerged from the basement holding an empty plastic bag.

"Hi," he said, wondering what she was doing down there, "were you talking to Marcia?"

Seeming flustered, she balled the bag into her fist and barked with disgust, "I don't talk to that woman."

After a moment of strangely tense silence, she blurted, "The lights at the side of the building are not working. It's a liability. You need to fix it. *Today.*"

Jack knew that Marcia had sabotaged the motion-sensor lights. She'd complained that they went on and off all night, penetrating even the blackout blinds in her bedroom windows.

Jack felt heavy as he ascended the stairs, anticipating that he'd find Dimra wired to the television. The Israeli border with Gaza had been sealed entirely in the middle of January. The Rafah border crossing into Egypt had been closed since June of last year after Hamas took control following the civil war. When Hamas militants blew up part of the border wall near the Rafah crossing a few months before, half the population of Gaza flooded into Egypt, desperate for supplies. During this breach, militants smuggled Grad missiles into the strip, and just a few weeks before had fired these deadlier longer-range missiles into Israel, hitting Ashkelon. The result was Operation Hot Winter, a full-scale Israeli assault to root out these weapons, resulting in the deaths of over a hundred militants and civilians.

It was endless, endless, *endless*.

On his back doormat he found a brown envelope. It contained Valeria's novel and a note from Lulu: "Read this and you'll understand why I love her." Though he knew Valeria would soon break Lulu's heart, he couldn't help glancing at the first paragraph, finding the prose gorgeous and engaging, despite himself. He perused the cover copy and thumbed through a few more pages, as if he were wiggling the toes and pinching the cheeks of the adorable baby of a person he loathed.

Fitting then that he should find Dimra on the couch in the great room holding Marcia's five-week-old son up to her face, singing to him between kisses.

After Jack claimed his own kiss from Aiden, becoming briefly part of the phantasmagoria drifting over the mirrored river of the infant's mind, Dimra told him she was going to Skype with her parents before picking up Aisha at her pre-K. It bothered Jack that she was essentially becoming a full-time mother to Marcia's children, even if this diverted her from images of corpses being dragged from shelled buildings. Marcia had never asked what happened with Dimra's pregnancy. Immediately after delivering Aiden, she returned to her job at the hotel, using the pill to dry up her milk. Working every shift she could, often bunking at the hotel overnight, Marcia took for granted that Dimra would look after Aisha and the baby. While Aisha remained in the second bedroom, Dimra slept with the baby in the back room, so as not to disturb May in the bedroom beneath. He found it unsettling at night to be woken by the muffled sound of a baby crying and to find himself alone in bed.

His phone buzzed. He was relieved to see it was Gunther, not May.

> Saw your car in the lot. New "acquisitions," for your immediate review!

Gunther flung open his door with a look of devilish excitement. As ever, his apartment smelled stale, and was becoming dimmer, most of the bulbs in his recessed lighting burned out.

As soon as they took their usual places on either side of the kitchen island, Gunther produced from his towel-covered crate three mineral samples he'd appropriated from a "Spectacular Earth" geology exhibit: elbaite tourmaline, like rainbow-colored crystal coral; a fist-sized fire opal seizing a spectacular sunset in glass; and a bismuth specimen forming a fairy-tale Escher staircase.

Examining the elbaite tourmaline for a second time up against Gunther's dim kitchen lights, Jack said, "It's like I'm looking at the primary colors of creation. I feel as if it's not my eyes but my soul that's seeing them."

Gunther shot him a dubious look. "Those colors are just impurities, Jack: chromium, manganese, boron. As for the fire opal, it's the simplest dish that tectonic forces can rustle up, silica spiced with iron oxide. And that effect on the bismuth is oxidation. It causes light to refract in different wavelengths, and voilà, a rainbow. No soul required."

"That could be your motto, Gunther."

"'No Soul Required.'" Gunther barked out a laugh. "I love it!"

A collection of prehistoric insects in amber followed. Jack picked up a large chunk containing an ancient spider trapped at the moment it had captured a fly.

"Tantalus," Jack said. "There's a kind of immortality for you."

"The only lesson here, my good man," Gunther replied dryly, taking back the specimen to examine it himself, "is that death comes for us all. In this case, just as this poor fellow was about to tuck in."

Gunther's final sample was the fossil of a *Tumidocarcinus giganteus* crab. Jack ran his fingers over the smooth shell that seemed carved from rosewood.

"Looks as if he could scuttle right out of that stone base," Jack said.

"Can you guess how old?"

Jack shook his head.

"Twelve. *Million*. Years."

Gunther examined the perfectly preserved crab with a look that seemed almost desperate to ignite into awe; but some internal short-circuit always prevented this, and quickly sobering himself with a mock salacious smile at Jack, he said, "They suffered from parasitic barnacles that sometimes castrated the males, and when this happened the male crabs would turn into biological females. Neat trick, huh? Attack of the shemale crabs! And before you harp on about souls and immortality again, there's nothing of the original fellow here. He's all mineralized."

"What about the stone baby?" Jack asked.

"The lithopedion?"

"Do you still have her?"

"Her?"

"It, whatever. Can I have another look?" Jack often thought about the stone baby swaddled among the treasures of Gunther's dragon hoard.

Gunther rummaged inside the crate and soon Jack was again cupping the calcified child in his hands, that crumpled little pugilistic Buddha. Or Vishnu, perhaps, struggling with her universe-sustaining dream as it sours, her beautiful world becoming rife with the monkeys some drunken fool had put in charge.

Returning her regretfully to Gunther, who seemed to have lost any interest in her, Jack thanked him and exited Gunther's back door into the overwhelming stench of pot. On the adjacent deck sat Danh sharing a joint with a skinny, washed-out blond girl in cut-off jeans and a crop top. He'd seen her with Danh before, a hollow-cheeked specter with tattoos of three-dimensional butterflies settled all over her body, including one on her pale forehead above her right eye. Her body also displayed the neat striations of self-harm scars. With black eyeliner surrounding her blank eyes and cold sores encircling her pinched mouth, she resembled a human Calavera Catrina.

"Oh, you're back," Jack said, unable to hide his disappointment.

"Like a bad penny." Danh smiled, narrowing his eyes as he drew deeply from the joint before handing it to the girl. Jack spotted Pauline's father heading out the back door and hurried down.

Confused at being stopped in the parking lot, Bernard said, "Mwen bezwen sigarèt."

"Le voici." Jack handed him what remained of his own packet, as well as his lighter, and led him back to his seat on the deck, reminding him that he needed to stay and wait for his daughter.

He thought about asking Danh again not to smoke when Bernard was around, but he knew it would be useless, so he headed up, stepping onto his deck just as Lulu exited her back door. She was dressed casually, her waist-length hair in a ponytail.

"You heading to work?"

She nodded.

She was so petite, with hands that seemed too small for a massage therapist, he'd always thought, though she specialized in oncology massage, no doubt requiring a lighter touch.

"Thanks for the novel."

"Valeria's on some huge book tour. It's a bestseller now"—her tone and glance were more anxious than enthusiastic—"and a finalist for the Pulitzer."

"Oh . . . great," he said.

"Yes," she agreed, unconvincingly. Suddenly she made a face, smelling the weed, and mouthed, *Is that Danh?*

He nodded, whispering back, "High as a kite."

She rolled her eyes. "I hope everything's locked up."

She was quiet for a moment and then said with a sigh, "I wish I had some of his pot. Val just put her earnest money down for a huge duplex in Hyde Park."

Jack knew that Lulu had been ferrying Valeria around for months to view properties, since Valeria had never deigned to learn how to drive.

"It made me realize she must hate my apartment. She loves vintage. The duplex has old fireplaces and built-in bookshelves; and because of the housing collapse, she's paying less than half what I paid for this place. I mean, I know I should be happy for her, Jack—for *us*. UChicago just offered her an endowed professorship. Nearly two hundred thousand a year. Can you believe it?"

"What are you going to do with your place?"

"I told her I was going to sell it, but Val said I should rent it if I have to." She glanced anxiously at Jack. "What does she mean, 'if I have to'?"

Jack shrugged, not feeling brave enough to expose a truth that must have been welling up like a sickness in her anyway, and said, "I'm going to miss you."

She wasn't listening, still too anxiously absorbed in the answer to her question, and said, "We could have just bought old mantels and tin ceiling tiles or whatever for my place. Jack, I don't want to be in Hyde Park. I *hate* professors. I *love* this neighborhood." She was getting agitated.

He wished he could help her. "Listen, I should get back in."

Suddenly Lulu seemed to actually see Jack through the fog of her misery. Impulsively wrapping her arms around him, she said, "What am I going to do without you?"

As she released him, Lulu's face became again dyspeptic, her gaze abstracted, her hand tenderly seeking her stomach as a little dragon of anxiety gnawed at her roots.

A few hours later, during dinner, after Dimra had picked up Aisha and returned her and Aiden to Marcia, Jack's phone binged.

The text was from Ken:

> EMERGENCY! My hall is flooding with Sewage!
> It's everywhere!

As Jack jumped up, he heard someone hammering at his back door. He opened it to a frantic and furious-looking Marcia, her cami tank top covered in stains.

"I'm soaked in fucking shit!" she screamed, her eyes hot with captive tears.

He followed her down. The baby and Aisha were plopped on the couch. Sewage poured through the ceiling, mostly into the two bedrooms.

He told Marcia to take the children up to his wife. This had happened once before, when one of Natasha's Calibans flushed rags down the basement toilet, blocking the pipe. When the ejector pump continued to suck the wastewater out of the sump, the sewage surged up through the washing-machine drain in Ken's hallway, flooding down into the garden apartment.

Jack sprinted into the basement and, after switching off the pump, called an emergency plumber. He ran up to Ken, who was distraught, jamming towels into the gap under the door to his dojo.

Reassuring him that no more would be coming up, Jack helped him mop up the foul-smelling seepage, the two of them soon reeking of sewage.

When he returned to the basement apartment, Marcia was back. "Look at this!" she screamed. "This shit's all over my home. I'm going to sue you. The condo's going to replace my fucking ceiling and my floors."

May suddenly appeared at Marcia's back door, like a malignant elf.

Marcia shouted at her, "The condo's going to fucking fix this and pay for a hotel until it's done."

May said, "We're not responsible for inside your apartment. You need to use your insurance."

"Not if it's your fault."

"How is it our fault?" she said.

"That pump or whatever it is, is fucking broke and filled my home with shit. You think it's *my* fault."

"The ejector pump is only used for your apartment, so it's *your* responsibility. That's Illinois law."

Marcia turned to Jack, "What the fuck's she saying?"

Jack walked quickly over to that viciously delighted little woman choking the doorway. "May, you're making things worse," he whispered, "could you please let me handle this?"

May didn't whisper: "She has to fix this. And sewage needs professional cleanup. I looked it up. We don't pay. *She* has to pay." Finally, she left.

"What does she fucking mean, I have to pay? I have a fifteen hundred deductible on my insurance. It's the only way I could afford it."

Jack didn't feel it wise to explain Illinois condo law at the moment. "Let's just see what we have. We'll deal with it."

Marcia looked like someone unable to wake from a bad dream.

"Where's Ryker?" Jack said.

"I don't know and I don't give a fuck."

"For now, could you perhaps get some clothes and whatever else the kids need, and for you also, and come spend the night with us."

"The clothes that are not covered in shit, you mean. I'll get what I can for the kids, but I'm not leaving my home."

"Marcia—"

"I'm *not* leaving my home," she repeated firmly, her eyes again hot with brutally repressed tears.

"Okay, but if you go up now, you can have a shower and wash all the clothes that got covered in that gray water."

She huffed a laugh. "'Gray water.' You should be a fucking politician."

The plumber cleared the line and replaced the ejector pump. With the emergency fee, it came to nearly $1,000. Jack paid with his own credit card because he didn't want May to know—at least yet—what had caused the problem.

He went up to his place first. Everyone was showered, the washing machine and dryer going. Aiden lay asleep in the back room, and Dimra was putting Aisha to bed. He found Marcia on the couch in the great room looking out of the window. The sight of her wearing his wife's pale-pink abaya, with a blue towel turban upon her wet hair, sent an unsettling pulse of feeling through him. Her broad shoulders strained the cloth of the abaya, the hem just covering her knees, those long, ill-used feet so different from his wife's childlike size fours.

"Plumber's gone," he said.

"So, what happened?"

Jack sat in the PELLO armchair kitty-corner to her and prepared himself.

"Marcia, do you remember," he said as softly as he could, "when you moved in, I talked to you about nothing but toilet paper going down the toilet?"

"We *never* put anything else down there."

"What caused the blockage and wrecked the pump were two diapers."

"I didn't put a diaper down the toilet. Who would put a fucking diaper down the toilet?"

"Well, that's what was in there. It's lucky Ken returned as early as he did. As it is, his hall floors are ruined."

Fury suddenly rescued her from despair. Jumping up, she marched down the hall, the thumping of her feet no doubt rousing May from her predatory slumber.

He hurried after her into the second bedroom, where Aisha and his wife were giggling over something in a book. Dimra moved aside for Marcia, who clamped Aisha's upper arms in her hands and demanded in a low growl, "Aisha, did you put Aiden's diapers down the toilet?"

"I didn't, Mommy," Aisha said, wide-eyed.

"Yes, you did. Why?" There was a tremor in Marcia's voice.

"I *didn't*."

"Don't you fucking lie to me!" she shouted, shaking her.

Hurrying over, Jack set a gently restraining hand upon one of Marcia's arms as Dimra wrapped her own arms protectively around Aisha, Jack's phone vomiting up one ding after another from May's furious texts.

Marcia angrily shrugged Jack off, but released Aisha, who buried herself, howling, into Dimra's chest.

Breathing hard, Marcia glanced around the room as if perplexed that this nightmare seemed to be taking place amid rainbows and fairies.

"Marcia, let's sit outside," Jack softly suggested. "It's going to be okay. We'll talk it through."

When they were both on the wicker bench, he said, "I'd offer you a smoke, but I gave my cigarettes to Bernard." The stench of pot was still heavy in the air.

She removed the towel turban with an irritated motion, laying the towel in her lap and snatching away the wet strands of hair that fell across her face. "Jack, I can't pay for this. I'm doing everything I can to get that three thousand together. Why do you think I'm working so fucking hard? I couldn't even take enough time off to breastfeed my baby. Don't you think I wish every day I could be here with my kids?" Her tears finally made their escape, though he could see her working to recover her anger.

"Of course I do," he said, feeling a little ashamed now that he'd assumed she was just taking advantage of Dimra.

She hesitated again and spoke more quietly. "You know, Aisha shoved me out of that bedroom because she and your wife have a routine. My own fucking kid didn't want me there. Aisha is always telling me all the fun things they've done. When Aisha had a tantrum last week, she got hold of my phone and called Dimra. I had to fucking sit there while Dimra calmed her down. I'm losing my child. Now I'm losing my home. Jack, I can't lose my fucking home."

She scraped her tears away as if they were cobwebs she'd walked into. It appalled him how alone she was. He wanted to put his arm around her, comfort her.

"Look," he whispered, not wanting Danh to hear, "I'll tell May the pipe broke in the wall or something. The condo will pay for the ejector pump and the plumber. I have tomorrow off. If Ryker's around and . . . upright, he can help me replace the drywall. The kids can stay with Dimra. We'll cut the soaked carpet out. You'll need to clean the floor with bleach, and maybe get a small rug or carpet remnant for now. And you'll have to paint the drywall at some stage. I can help you with that too. We'll clean it up. Once you paint it, it'll be like new."

Flushed, she stared at him through stringy wet hair. The abaya had turned her into a different person somehow. He realized he'd been silent too long, as if expecting her to thank him, which he knew she didn't have the resources to do. He'd simply lost himself in those sea-glass eyes.

"So, you're staying here tonight, yes?" he said, as if it were settled.

She shook her head. "I'm just waiting for some things to dry," she said. "I can sleep on my couch."

After she left, Jack prepared himself for May and texted her that he was coming down. May's apartment was beautiful, full of exotic plants and antique furniture she'd refinished, including chairs upholstered in vibrantly colored textiles. Only the enormous television above the fireplace spoiled it, always at a low auditory boil, replacing the hearth as the flickering, mesmerizing heart of her home, Judge Judy chiding some hapless defendant. As he went to sit on her Kente-print couch, she cried out, "Stop."

She retrieved a new garbage bag out of the cupboard under her sink and spread it on the seat cushion.

"You been with dirty water."

"I showered and changed," he assured her.

"That smell. It doesn't come off."

As expected, she berated him for using his own credit card, suggested she shouldn't reimburse him, torturing him for over thirty minutes as he kept humbly quiet and apologized, until she finally yielded the check.

"Now, she has to pay for the plumber. I'll add it to this." She showed him a notebook of all Marcia's fines and late fees, totaling over $2,000.

"May," he said, as reasonably as he could, "you can't keep assessing fines she can't pay. She's working hard, trying to get the money for the special assessment. You need to be flexible."

"I don't need to be anything. Rules are rules." Producing a pen, she added the cost of the plumber to the total, nearly out of breath with eagerness.

"Rules are rules," she repeated her mantra. "She's a *dirty* person. We shouldn't have fixed it. Let her live in sewage."

"She has two kids."

"I'll call social services. They'd be better off."

She looked hard at him, that small cinched-up face in her little helmet of graying hair, and for a moment he thought about what she and Danh went through in Phú Quốc Prison, the reeducation camp, and then as refugees in Malaysia. Her voice softened and she said with something almost imploring in her tone, "Jack, we *want* her to go, yes?"

"This is her home."

She hardened again. "She broke the pump, so she has to pay."

"She didn't break it." He wasn't good at lying but tried to keep his eyes on hers and voice steady, hoping she didn't understand how the plumbing worked. "There was a crack in the pipe and it broke in the wall."

She was incredulous. "The pipe's broken? No, it was blocked, like when Natasha was here."

"No, it's this screwed-up plumbing."

She snatched up the invoice he'd given her, but Jack had removed the page the plumber added with his explanation about the diapers.

"Nothing here about a break," she said.

"The plumber just explained it to me."

"Call him," she demanded. "Call. I'll talk to him."

"May, I'm just telling you what he told me. The pipe in the wall broke. He fixed it."

For a moment she looked as if she were about to punch him. "What broke it? Did a diaper break it?"

"Diaper?" Had she somehow talked to the plumber? But Jack was with him the whole time. "It was a broken pipe. I saw it myself."

"*Something* broke it!" she shouted, but was luckily distracted by her son entering the back door. Jack could hear him and his girlfriend laughing as they stumbled up the hall and into the kitchen.

"We're hungry, Ma," he said.

"I'll make something, bring it to you. Go!" She waved them irritatedly away.

They were sluggish, moving like walruses, but finally wound themselves back down the hall.

Jack took his opportunity and stood.

As he was leaving, she said, still looking furiously thwarted, "The motion-sensor lights. I told you. They're not working. They're a liability. They need to be fixed today, *now*."

He nodded and, not wanting any more trouble from her, went straight down to the concrete walkway at the south side of the building. He quickly realized that Marcia must have used a broom handle, angling the movement sensors upward to stop the glaring lights going on and off. Again, he was trapped between Marcia and May. As he was thinking about what he might do, the light came on in Aisha's bedroom, and through the low window he saw Marcia at the threshold, standing on the black garbage bags he'd covered the soaked floor with, sadly surveying the mess. He wondered if she was comparing that tiny room with the large, beautifully decorated bedroom where she'd left her daughter with another woman. Strange to see Marcia's face unguarded by its anger, to see her rest her head against the jamb as if it were the supportive shoulder of her beloved. She was barefoot and still wearing his wife's abaya, stretched tight across her chest and hips. Stepping into the room, she sat on her daughter's bed, with its My Little Pony comforter. Pulling her knees into her chest, she rubbed her tired feet as she leaned her head back against the wall to look up at the ceiling, now mapped with continents of yellow-brown stains. Desire for her raked through his nerves like fingers tugging hair with sensual force, and hard upon this rushed a tidal surge of feeling, sudden and strong enough to lift the rock of his heart, making it feel for once, if briefly, weightless.

11

That night, Jack lay alone in bed, Dimra in the back room with Aiden, who wouldn't settle. Unable to sleep, aroused and agitated, he felt like a teenager again, full of sweaty, stifled desire. Sex had been a huge problem for the boys in Beach Camp. The girls too. Six houses down from Jack's, seventeen-year-old Haya Thabet was found by her father and brother with a young neighbor, Rashid, in the house. After they beat Rashid to death, Haya's brother held her down while his father strangled her with a length of fishing line.

Yet sex seeped through all the seams of conservative camp life, and there was little privacy for most boys to practice the secret habit. When he was younger Jack contracted a lung infection and had to be transported to the Sheba Medical Center in Ramat Gan, where he'd been shocked to see Israeli doctors and nurses flirting and being so free with one another. Gazan men who went to study abroad returned with tales of sexual adventure, glutted as foxes who'd found their way into the henhouse. What came through the camp's network of Chinese whispers to the younger boys was akin to Herodotus: stories of giant Swedish women with no nipples; Frenchwomen who could produce an erotic electricity with their tongues; and drunken, sexually rapacious Englishwomen forming marauding gangs to ravage men.

Just after Jack and his cousin turned fourteen, Salim told Jack he'd discovered something and led him to a two-story house on a sandy bluff at the far northern edge of Beach Camp. Notices on the surrounding fences warned it was private property and unstable. A few years before, a wayward shell from an Israeli gunboat firing at militants on the beach struck its foundation, killing its owner, who was pruning a carob tree in the yard. The house was cleft by a lightning-like crack slicing through the plaster from roof to base. The property was now tied up in an endless court battle between two claimants from the same family, and between this family and the Israelis for compensation.

Salim led a reluctant Jack up the side of the bluff and through a gap beneath the fence. Jack balked as Salim entered the house, mewling after him that it was going to collapse. Finally, he entered, discovering his cousin upstairs in a whitewashed master bedroom, sitting on the mattress of a queen-sized bed, with a white, tufted faux silk headboard and footboard. The great crack snaked through the plaster, bisecting a square window framed in pale blue with a view of the sea.

He and Salim said nothing to the boys in their little gang. It became their secret hideout. This cavernous, whitewashed space, with its white bed and one azure opening, made it feel to Jack as if he and Salim were two new beings in an as-yet-uncreated world. The carob tree filled the space, late in the year, with its rank, seminal scent. The room provided a sense of privacy they'd rarely experienced. He and Salim would lounge on the bed reading their comics and books, Jack sitting up against the headboard while Salim lay curled at the far end like a cat, his head propped on his hand. They began to talk to each other in a way they never had, about not becoming their fathers, or who they dreamed of marrying. Salim urged him to leave Gaza. "I have shit for brains, habibi, but you, you're smart enough to make it to a foreign university. You can get out." As their talk became more personal, Salim seemed to forget himself, lying there at the foot of the bed, his taut muscularity slackening, his posture becoming unconsciously sensual. It was like the effect of sunset on the harsh and arid hills of this Holy Land, turning them supple, velvety, and inviting. That incendiary hunger in his eyes dimmed, his glance becoming, at times, almost coy. This emergent odalisque unsettled Jack. It was as if he'd been painting a portrait of his cousin, and his own perception and inspiration had now to yield to a subject coming into being that was not at all what he'd expected, almost frightening.

On one visit to the house, Salim suddenly produced a pair of female underwear and flung it at Jack.

"It's Munera's," he explained. "I stole it from her room."

"What do you want *me* to do with it?"

"Sniff it." He was astonished Jack had to ask. "That's what a woman's little fish smells like."

Jack laughed, thinking he was joking, but Salim frowned. "Sniff it," he demanded.

It was a complex, mushroomy, faintly vinegary odor.

"Do you even know what to do with a girl?" Salim sat up. A faded image of Chief Wahoo leered from his maroon Indians T-shirt.

Jack, embarrassed, shrugged. Tugging his T-shirt off, Salim made a headscarf of it and sat himself shoulder to shoulder with Jack, their backs against the headboard.

"Okay, compliment me."

"Compliment you?"

"My name is Salima," he murmured with a bashful glance, sweeping loose strands of long hair beneath his makeshift hijab.

"Well, Salima, habibti, your face is radiant as the moon, your eyes more beautiful than a doe's, your lips soft as ripe figs, your limbs turned as if upon a lathe."

Though Jack's voice was mocking, he became aware of the soft wash of the sea and the throbbing trill of the locusts, as if they were a part of his own tidal circulation. Arousal wasn't unusual—the shitty backside of a donkey could arouse him—but this arousal generated a kind of static field between their bare arms.

"Well, that's warmed me up nicely." Salim was staring into Jack's eyes, that devilish flame flaring. "Do you know what to do now?"

Jack shook his head.

"Have you ever seen tarantulas mating?"

Again, Jack shook his head.

"Well, habibi," Salim's tone became at once deeply sensuous and ominous, "while the male tries to mate, the female tries to . . . *eat*." Salim suddenly wrenched Jack down onto the bed and they grappled, laughing, hot cheek to hot cheek. Jack rolled himself on top, Salim's arms and legs wrapped around him, their crotches grinding until that shocking burst, as if a piece of agonizing shrapnel long buried in Jack's groin had been torn out, causing a blue effusion in his head as his body melted with exquisite relief. Salim kept tight hold for a moment, both of them taut and trembling before going slack, their hot flesh stuck together. Jack slipped off, and they lay side by side, breathing hard. Salim was the first to sit up, tugging off his makeshift hijab. Jack, trying to understand what he felt, what to think, glanced at his cousin, who looked as if he'd just woken from a lovely dream.

"Come on," Salim said, and Jack followed his cousin out. They washed themselves in the sea and by the time each arrived home, the sun had dried them.

How quickly all the boundaries of what they did tumbled. Though Jack never asked Salim to be the woman, his cousin grew his hair longer, borrowed his mother's headscarves, stole women's clothes from washing lines, had Jack distract one of the foreign relief workers so he could filch makeup from her handbag. With the boys, Salim was as reckless, hard-edged, and verbally percussive as ever; but in the white room with the blue window, his body and being softened, yearned, yielded. They enacted countless scenarios. Jack preferred the desperate women whose husbands were impotent, forcing Salim to play a more active part in the seduction. Salim favored the darker scenarios involving the corruption of innocent girls by salacious doctors or godless imams. Neutral territory was women married to men they didn't love, young Muna sold off to a seventy-year-old clan leader at fifteen, sweet Nisrin who knew nothing but the callused hands of her brutish husband. He and Salim learned how to kiss, how to touch with a more discursive tenderness, how to extend their pleasure.

Afterward, the sea baptized them back into Gaza, and Salim seemed to retain no residue of life in the white room. Outside the room, not once, even when they were alone, did Salim soften into that other being, mention the room, or exchange so much as a covert glance with Jack. Jack took his cue from his cousin but discovered that he couldn't be intimate in that way without emotion; and once or twice in that room, looking into his cousin's suppliant face, often a little smeared with lipstick, he felt a dizzying surge of love, a desire to declare sincerely, *You are beautiful.*

Jack was susceptible to his feelings, his mother's sensitive boy, and even in the most elaborate of his and Salim's scenarios, some part of him remained aware of the reality of the being within the hot, salty skin of Muna, Nisrin, Karima, or Rana. Jack had always been afflicted by sympathy for the world. This world was tragic to him; doubly tragic, then, that he should love it, love its struggling inhabitants, these poor monkeys, most of them not even in control of their own lives. And all this feeling was finding new expression through these imaginary lovers to their source. Every dip and arch and swell and bend and pose of Salim's body inaugurated the runes of Jack's love: the way Salim's hair fell across his eyes; the supernova complexity of his honey-colored irises; his heavier upper lip; and the knowing curl of his smile.

Once, after sex, he and Salim had stood naked at the window, shoulder to shoulder, watching an exhausted orange sun expiring into the sea, offering them a glittering path into a melancholy hell. Turning to observe Salim, that sun igniting his amber irises, Jack reached to comb back the hair that had fallen into his cousin's eyes, but Salim flinched, angry, almost disgusted, and flicked his own hair free.

It pained Jack how blank and impenetrable Salim remained outside the room. A few times Jack wandered along the shore to the house alone to stare up at the window as if his beloved might appear. When he thought of the room, it filled him with an eviscerating ache. He dreamed of it constantly and conjured it whenever he needed to escape Gaza, during suffocating curfews and power cuts, or when he was stuck at an Israeli checkpoint, or after collisions with his father's flinty edges. The only time he entered the house without Salim, he discovered that it was not the place of his dreams. Sitting upon that white bed in the pure white room, he felt erased: the room stripped him to nothing; made him no one, nowhere.

Noticing the change in his mood, his mother asked him a few times if anything was wrong. And one evening she came to his room while he was reading and sat on the bed beside him. She'd gained weight through the years, but it suited her, matching the raven-browed gravity of her noble face.

He often found it hard to meet his mother's eyes, her look frequently clairvoyant, as if she were seeing his future and fearing it, or as if she were looking through him to some distant pain of her own. Tonight, though, it was merely a troubled and sympathetic inquiry, and after a little while, she said, "Is it a girl?"

"What?"

"Is it a girl you like?"

"I don't know what you're talking about," he said, frightened by how attuned his mother was to him.

"It's all right if you like someone."

"Just leave me alone," he snapped. "I want to read."

She lingered a moment, examining him sadly, and then said, "When I fell in love with your father—"

"I don't want to know," he pleaded. "Please, Mama, I don't want to know."

She kissed his knee and left.

His and Salim's secret life in that room continued for nearly three years. It was risky, and they met at most twice a month. Over time a stabilization took place. Salim became Sofya, a married woman of duty and faith, deeply conflicted about her long-term affair with Jack. Jack and Sofya spoke (with the naïveté of teenagers) of their passionless marriages, their sexual fantasies about each other, their dreams of escaping Gaza. They fought and passionately made up. Over the footboard of the bed lay an entire stolen wardrobe of women's clothes and underwear, the lingering scent of the women to whom they belonged enhancing their encounters for Jack. These meetings were initiated by a note from Sofya, and she would be waiting when Jack arrived at the house. While this fantasy relationship deepened, a distance grew between them in their everyday lives, in part because they were so different, with Salim dropping out of school to work in Jack's father's appliance-and-repair store full-time.

When they were seventeen, a traffic accident involving an Israeli truck that killed four Palestinians in the Jabalia Camp ignited the tinder of Gaza and the intifada began. As the violence ramped up and Israeli military control grew more severe and suffocating, the curfews longer, the streets rife with IDF patrols, it became even more difficult for Jack and his cousin to meet, their parents demanding them home and safe. This only intensified their desire; they took absurd risks. With their bodies snakishly entwined in the white room, Jack and Sofya could hear gunshots, jets, helicopters, explosions, the roar of the riots. Their noses burned with the acrid stench of propellant, gunpowder, burning tires, and tear gas. Once, a funeral procession roared past the house. As the room echoed with vengeful chanting and the dry crackle of Kalashnikovs, he and Salim only entangled themselves more fiercely, becoming the forgotten dream of a burning city, lovers in a broken house.

Late one afternoon in the room, Jack, on the bed and already naked, had just removed Sofya's dress to reveal a lacy silk bra and panties. Jack would have asked where she found them but didn't want to break the spell. Suddenly they both jumped at the pop of gunfire directly under the carob tree, followed by frantic shouting and what sounded like an RPG detonating a little distance away. A massive explosion rocked the house, a shell, perhaps from an Israeli gunboat. F-15s thundered overhead, rattling the windows and the Arab voices quickly receded.

"God help us, this place is going to collapse," Jack cried out, terrified.

As he went to jump off the bed, Sofya held him back. She'd lined her eyes with kohl, her lips blood-red. Sofya, unlike Salim, was a melancholy soul, a being full of doubts and hesitations, of sudden and reckless afflictions of passion or self-loathing.

Looking sadly into Jack's eyes as if into a mirror, she said with a wistful smile, "What will everyone think when they dig the two of us out of the rubble?"

Jack flinched and ducked as another explosion seemed almost to land on top of them. "Shit, God help us."

Sofya laid her hand on his cheek and kissed him. "It's all right, habibi. If we die, at least we die together."

Rolling over, Sofya slipped off the bed and went to the window.

"I can see the Israeli gunboats," she said. Hurrying back, she snatched up her lighter, returned to the window and ignited it a couple of times, as if signaling someone on those boats.

"W'allaw, what are you doing?" Jack shouted.

"Remember when that Fatah recruiter told us about the little Black girl murdered by the American Army in the Detroit riots all those years ago?"

"What are you talking about?"

"The army fired on the building because someone lit a cigarette and the flash of the lighter was mistaken for sniper fire."

Jack leapt off the bed, dragging his cousin to the floor, and tried to retrieve the lighter from his fisted hand.

"Come on, Jamal"—his cousin was laughing now—"one Israeli shell and it's all over."

Salim was stronger than Jack, but Sofya was not, and yielded the lighter. Jack lay on top of Sofya, the two of them jammed against the wall, breathing hard, the crack rising from their wrapped-together bodies like a sapling from that naked root. Suddenly, they could hear the squeak and roar of a tank close by, voices barking in Hebrew, and the throaty cough of a 50-caliber. Jack felt the banging open of the house's front door as if a steel-toe-capped boot had kicked his tailbone. A thundering ascent. He and Salim fell into two and sat up side by side against the wall under the window, the crack now between them, Jack jamming his legs together to cover his nakedness.

"Turn your head away," Jack hissed, but Sofya defiantly faced the M16 nosing into the room and twitching between them. The soldier holding it was auburn-haired, blue-eyed, and blockishly muscular; behind him appeared an Arab-looking boy, hawklike and nearly as skinny as his rifle.

The four boys stared at one another silently for a moment, Sofya primly adjusting her bra, and then, as something was barked in Hebrew from below, the auburn-haired one glanced at the other soldier, who shrugged.

"Clear," the auburn-haired one shouted, returning down the stairs; the other soldier, with one more confused glance at them, following.

The voices diminished, and finally all they could hear was the soft wash of the sea. When they stood, Sofya kicked her heel angrily at the crack in the wall, "Goddamn this place. Why won't it fall?"

Early in February of 1988, the intifada still raged as the sun burned away winter's rain clouds, wildflowers and yellow mustard invading the vineyards, the orchards filling with almond blossoms like blood-stained snow. Jack and his father were fitting a water tank onto a roof when Karim, a little boy from their neighborhood, shouted up at them both that they needed to go home. They arrived to a crowd of men chanting patriotic slogans, some in balaclavas, firing Kalashnikovs into the air. The house was crowded with women, weeping and ululating. Jack's mother had wrapped her arms around Um Salim, who looked only half-conscious.

"What happened?" his father demanded of his mother.

"Habibi, your brother," she replied, "he was martyred at an Israeli checkpoint in front of Salim."

Salim had been arrested. The Israelis claimed that Kassam tried to stab one of the checkpoint guards and that Jack's cousin was involved. It was more than two weeks before Salim was released.

Salim looked wrecked, broken. He told them that he and his father were heading to their patch of land to plant watermelons, his father more than usually drunk. They were stopped at one of the many checkpoints, the atmosphere particularly tense because two IDF soldiers had been gunned down the day before in an ambush near Beach Camp. At the checkpoint, one of the guards, a big man with a deeply pockmarked face, told his father in Russian-accented English to tie his shoelaces, though they were already tied. Hunkering down, his father managed to untie them but was too drunk to tie them up again. A restless line of people gathered behind them, and Salim realized that this was about delaying those people as much as it was about humiliating his father. Salim finally squatted down and tied the laces for him. A few soldiers, some amused, others troubled, gathered about them, including a nervous, wide-eyed American boy, a fresh recruit, clutching to his M16 as if to a piece of flotsam after a wreck. Next, Salim's father was ordered to undo and do up all the buttons of his shirt. When this was finally achieved, the big Russian, after slipping a cigarette into his own mouth, tried out some of his fledgling Arabic. He said something to Salim's father, but the Arabic was so mangled it was impossible to understand. Kassam just stared at the guard, who furiously barked whatever it was he was saying again, repeating it with increasing anger, brandishing his weapon, alarming the new recruit, who clearly had no idea what was going on. Salim realized the guard was demanding a light for his cigarette just as this same realization sank into his father's rakija-sodden brain.

The instant his father thrust his hand into his pocket to retrieve his lighter a cluster of shots sent him flying to the dirt. The terrified American recruit stared with shock at his M16 as if he couldn't understand how it had fired, and then at Salim's father, who was staring back at him with horrified confusion as the blood from the bullet wounds in his stomach bloomed through his shirt. Salim fell to his knees beside his father. He understood enough Hebrew to know the boy was saying that it had just gone off. Salim shouted at them to call an ambulance. The big Russian ordered the others to take Salim into custody and to call for support to deal with the other Palestinians in line, who were screaming at the guards that they were murderers. Salim was shoved down over the body of his father, handcuffed and pulled away to an armored vehicle. Salim kept shouting at them that his father needed help; he was still alive. They locked him in the back. From the vehicle, he could see the big Russian searching through his father's pockets, his father staring at this man, helpless as a baby. Later, the soldiers claimed his father had pulled out the large folding knife he used to harvest cauliflower. Several armored vehicles arrived, but no ambulance for over an hour, by which time, he'd bled to death.

Salim spent the next two weeks being interrogated. He was asked how long his father had been planning this and if he was involved. He missed his father's funeral, attended by hundreds, since he'd become a glorious martyr.

Now Salim's family was trapped. His father was a hero of Palestinian resistance, his picture pasted up with those of the other martyrs in the camp. Salim's mother received a stipend from the martyrs' fund. But just a few days after his release, the IDF burst into their house, smashing the door, trashing the furniture, and arresting Salim again. The Israelis couldn't let the family of a terrorist go unpunished.

He was released less than a week later. According to the Gaza rumor mill, one of the checkpoint guards from that night threatened to go to the newspapers with the truth if they didn't leave the dead man's family alone. It was the only explanation that made sense.

The day after Salim's return from detention, Jack found his cousin alone on the roof, sitting under the arbors of his father's grapevines, a shadowed green enclave within the concrete boxes surrounding them. It seemed impossible that this young man, looking monumental and lonely as the statue of a forgotten pharaoh, had any connection to the white room, his eyes empty as the sockets of a skull, his face expressive of the chronic spiritual dyspepsia resulting from indigestible injustice.

Jack felt as awkward as a supplicant to a stranger.

"I can help you prune these vines," Jack said.

"I'm getting rid of them."

"Why?"

His cousin didn't answer, perhaps didn't feel he needed to. They heard the crackle of gunfire, as much a part of the background now as the rattle of insects.

"I'm the head of my family now," Salim said. "With the money for Baba's death, I have enough to marry. My mother is looking for someone."

Jack felt as if a drop of icy liquid were sliding with agonizing slowness down his spine.

He thought of the clusters of grapes, miracle of sun and water, weighing down this arbor at the end of the summer. Rakija for his uncle, while his father devoured them unripe, sour, with salt.

"I won't be going to the house anymore," Salim said, with a softness of tone that indicated not tenderness but a fear of being overheard.

12

Jack slipped out of bed and crept down the hall to the third bedroom. He wanted his wife in bed with him, her body next to his. Dimra lay fetally curled in the trundle bed beside the cot, where Aiden lay performing a backward swan dive into sleep. He felt so restless, agitated, ashamed, but still stalked by a ravenous desire. As he returned to the master bedroom, Birdy appeared palpably before him. He could taste the mojito kiss of their first meeting. He thought of the wedding, that trundle bed, just like the one his wife now lay on, in the basement of Birdy's childhood home.

When was that? Just a few months after 9/11, it had to be, the flights nearly empty. All the flight attendants—those who hadn't quit—had endured self-defense training and simulations in smoke-filled cabins. He could picture Birdy's fierce face as she hunkered in front of him and said, "That bastard's getting married."

It was a late flight out of Atlanta back to Chicago. He was sitting on his carry-on in the galley absorbed in *The English Patient*.

"Which bastard?"

"*Nick*," she said, irritated by his obtuseness. "Guess who he's marrying?"

"The only person I know is that perfect girl, I forgot her name."

"Jenny Orville, six months pregnant; it's in my hometown church."

"I'm so sorry, habibti." He laid his hand gently against her cheek.

"Jack, I need you to come to the wedding with me."

"Why would you go to that?"

"I *need* to go"—her eyes became steely—"and I need you to come as my boyfriend."

"What?"

Wrapping her arms tightly around his legs as if she wasn't going to let him go until he agreed, she said, "You know that bastard told me he'd always loved me, even when we were kids. He told me Jenny was cold and materialistic and about as exciting as roadkill in bed. He talked about a house he was building as if it was going to be *our* house." She squeezed Jack's legs forgetting how strong she was.

"I'll pay for *everything*," she said. "A fancy suit and shoes, and you'll get to meet my family."

"As a fake."

"You won't be a fake. I mean, you do love me, don't you?"

He closed his novel, avoiding her begging eyes by glancing at the monochrome image on the book's cover showing the hunched silhouette of a man moving across a blasted desert landscape just beneath a slender opening into paradise. "Yes, of course I do."

"And I love you. So it wouldn't be a lie. Not exactly."

She sighed, propping her chin on his knees. "Please, please, *please*."

"I don't understand why you want me to come."

"Because you're tall and handsome and exotic and elegant, and I want him and Jenny to know I've upgraded."

"To a male flight attendant? They're going to know."

Now she shot him a sheepish glance. "Well, you don't have to be."

"I don't have to be?"

"You know when you and that heavy gay guy used to goof about, pretending to be different characters, and you'd become that English lord?"

"Are you talking about Fitzpatrick, Fourth Earl of Ridgelick, erstwhile groom of the king's prepuce?"

"Well, we don't have to call you that, *obviously*. We can just give you a nice English name like Charles."

"You want me to be a British aristocrat?"

"Just for one weekend. Everyone in Eau Plaine will be so impressed."

"You're *serious*?"

"If you do this for me, I will do anything for you. Anything, anything, *anything*."

"Do I even look English?"

"Jack, it's a tiny town in Wisconsin. They won't know."

He refused again and again, but she wouldn't let it go. She did most of the cleanup on their next three flights. She kept following him into his hotel rooms, falling to her knees and lassoing his legs with her arms so he couldn't move, begging him.

He resisted until the final leg of a six-leg marathon, a nearly empty late flight from St. Louis. They were sitting in their jump seats looking out at a crescent moon in a navy sky above a pale, salmon-colored horizon.

She said quietly, "You know, Nick broke up with me while he was driving me back from my abortion. When he started his breakup speech, I was so out of it I didn't really understand what he was saying, and then I felt something and reached between my legs because I thought I might be bleeding. When he saw me checking my fingers, he slammed on the brakes, literally *dived* over me to pull open the glove box, hitting my knees *really* hard, grabbed an atlas, screamed at me to get up, and shoved it between my legs. Only when he was sure I wasn't going to stain the leather seat of his beloved '67 Mustang did he finish his breakup speech. I wish I'd torched that stupid car. I just need Nick to know he's nothing to me."

Though Jack, of course, didn't tell Dimra the complete truth about his life at work, this trip to Eau Pleine was the first time he'd directly lied to her. While Dimra believed he was at the Holiday Inn in Portland, he was on a trundle bed in the partially finished basement of Birdy's parents' three-bedroom ranch house, which hadn't been updated since the '50s. Three of her brothers still lived in the house, two of them employed by the same small furnace and air-conditioning company their father worked for, the other a custodian at the local school. They were big, shy boys with chaw swelling out their lower lips. It was heartwarming to see her brothers and father with Birdy, how they pulled her into awkward hugs, teased her, snatched at her clothes and hair. He wouldn't have been surprised if they'd all howled in unison and run out for a romp in the woods. Her mother, however, a large Dutch woman in leather clogs whose staunch jaw Birdy had inherited, was polite but cold. She was hard-edged, compacted with unhappiness. Her homemaking energy, though tireless, felt empty of purpose in this life she couldn't forgive for the death of her son.

For this weekend, Jack was Charles de Rochefort. On the day of the wedding, he was waiting in the hallway when Birdy teetered down the stairs in stilettos. Her red off-the-shoulder mini dress, with its plunging neckline and lace trim, left less to the imagination than most lingerie. Tipping up her head and flaring her nostrils as if cuirassed in steel in preparation for single combat with her nemesis, she said, "What do you think?"

Jack thought better of saying, "I think you look like a magician's assistant," and managed to blurt, "Gorgeous!"

Suddenly appearing from the kitchen, her outraged mother demanded Birdy return to her room to make herself decent, but Birdy snatched up Jack's hand and dragged him out to the truck they were borrowing from one of her brothers. At the church, Birdy hurried to take an aisle seat toward the front, so she could level a much-rehearsed you-mean-less-than-nothing-to-me smile at Nick as he walked to the altar with his best man. Jack noticed Nick's smile freeze a little when he saw Birdy. But whatever smile Birdy reserved for the bride had no effect as Jenny Orville appeared in a modest white dress that made no attempt to hide her baby bump. Petite, with a sharp, imperious glance and masses of copper-colored hair, she was a fox in human form. Nick's voice broke with emotion as he made his vows, while Jenny's manner was that of a queen accepting abject fealty from a once-errant noble.

They followed everyone to the reception in a marquee set up in the garden of Jenny's wealthy father's mansion, and Birdy, ignoring her mother's final, desperate attempt to convince her to return home and change into something decent, defiantly teetered into the tent. After the food and speeches, a good number of people, smelling blood in the water, introduced themselves. Birdy told them she'd met "Charlie" while she was working first-class on a flight from London. Jack comported himself with the slightly louche and ironic elegance he associated with spoiled scions of the aristocracy. When someone asked if he'd ever met the royal family, he talked about sharing a room with Prince Edward at Gordonstoun (*What an absolute dunce!*) and swore that while he was with Eddy at Balmoral during one of the school holidays, the queen had goosed him in a hallway.

Finally, Jenny, whose manner was more truly aristocratic than anyone's, appeared before them both, smiled indomitably up at a towering, teetering Birdy, more flesh than dress, and with a warm hug told her she looked beautiful. Then she graciously thanked Jack for coming and vanished, leaving them routed.

Birdy, in a final rally, drained every Champagne glass she could lay her hands on and dragged Jack onto the dance floor next to Nick and Jenny. Her parents, thank God, had left by that time. Birdy tried to dance sexily, but her sense of rhythm had never improved, every thrust of her half-exposed breasts resembling a vigorous workout of her core. During the slow dances, she writhed against Jack, and after a half dozen more glasses of Champagne began to kiss him wetly and passionately.

He couldn't help but return her kisses, and Birdy quickly forgot Nick and Jenny, kicking her heels off, the two of them dancing until the small hours. When Jack drove them back, Birdy followed him into the basement. He sat on the trundle bed as Birdy shed her dress and then stood between his legs undoing his shirt as he unhooked her bra. But into Jack's mind, as if on photographic paper in a dark room's developer bath, resolved Dimra's face, her eyes bravely kindling hope and love within the stifled pain. All the lies he'd told Birdy flooded in.

Gently constraining her hands, he said, standing and reaching around to rehook her bra, that he loved her, but this could never work.

She stepped back, staring at him with frustrated anger, then pushed her hand between his legs and said, "It certainly *feels* like it could work," before snatching up her dress and stalking upstairs.

For a couple of weeks, she didn't bid the same flights as he, which he tried to make easier for her by bidding unpopular routes and schedules. Soon enough, though, he saw her sitting with the others at the gate, waiting for him. She was a little cool and snappish for a while, and he would often glance up to see her staring at him sadly. Once in the galley, she took hold of both his hands, and said tearfully, "I want this to *go* somewhere." He squeezed her hands, then released them and cupped her cheeks, telling her he believed friendship was the strongest and truest connection a person could have. Soon, they were closer than ever, their relationship growing quieter, more tender and intimate, less performative, which made it feel, strangely, as if a consummation had taken place.

Returning to the condo's master bedroom, Jack's last thoughts, as he finally drifted off, were of Marcia in the strained cloth of his wife's hijab, marooned on her daughter's little bed. His sleep, though, was fitful, disturbed by a whirl of disparate thoughts gradually unifying into a murmuration so dense it became a single realization that shocked him awake in the small hours.

May had flushed the diapers.

How had he not realized it immediately, with May turning up at Marcia's door talking about professional abatement and Illinois condo law, even suggesting diapers as the cause? May knew about the previous disaster when Natasha's Caliban had flushed rags. She, like Jack, kept a lockbox containing keys to all the apartments in case of emergencies. She knew Marcia and Ken were at work, the children with Dimra, and Ryker no longer in the picture. Exiting the basement when Jack arrived home, she'd seemed flustered, trying to hide the plastic bag that had no doubt contained the diapers. After flushing them, she must have run all the water in Marcia's apartment for a while, perhaps filling the bath and letting the water drain, triggering the ejector pump to suck the diapers out of the sump pit. Though he could hardly believe that even May could be so vindictive, the truth settled like heavy overnight snowfall.

= 13 =

After using his entire day off to replace Marcia's ruined drywall, Jack spent the next three nights blissfully alone in hotel rooms. He brought Valeria's novel with him, losing himself in its gorgeous prose. It was the story of a Colombian woman trying to make her way to America to escape her abusive husband, a member of the Gulf Clan. Lulu was right. Jack found himself spellbound. Or as spellbound as he could be while fielding May's barrage of furious texts about the back gate not latching properly. She seemed to believe that everyone in the building would be murdered in their beds before he could return to fix it.

Halfway through the novel, he realized that its substructure was that of Bunyan's *The Pilgrim's Progress*. His mother had read a children's version to him as a boy, the story of a man called Christian dwelling in the City of Destruction, burdened by humanity's sins. She told him that when she was a girl in the British prep school in Cairo, she asked a nun what was meant by the City of Destruction. The nun led her up the church's spire to an outlook over Cairo, a sprawl of minarets and pale buildings with windows glittering through the bruise-colored smog in the burning heat, and said, "Yasmin, if you look with the eyes of your soul, you will see below us a burning city. Every person in this city is on fire. They just don't know it."

It was troubling to Jack to realize that a work of art so restrained and sensitively imagined had been gestated and brought to term by the arrogant and rabidly ambitious woman he thought he knew. How could such mature wisdom lie behind so jaggedly defended a persona? He guessed this other Valeria was part of what made Lulu love her, the secret core of this puzzling partnership.

The afternoon of his return, Jack's fingers almost froze off affixing an anti-sag kit to the back gate. The mild weather had vanished, Gulag Chicago reasserting itself with a vengeance, the sun frozen within a sky like soiled ice.

While leveling the latch bolt with the strike plate, he heard the click of Valeria's heels in the parking lot. Just as he opened the gate for her—Valeria shooting him her usual haughty glance—he blurted, "I read your book."

She halted, stiffened, and he saw instantly her vulnerability.

"I thought it was wonderful," he quickly assured her.

She stared at him, flushing, eyes dilated, nostrils flaring, as if he'd just declared himself to her, not the book.

"My mother read me *The Pilgrim's Progress* when I was a kid," he said. "I could never have guessed I'd see it reimagined so brilliantly."

Looking somewhere between appalled and amazed, she said, "*No one* saw that I'd used Bunyan."

"I'm guessing there aren't many who read it anymore."

She walked a few steps away but then turned back with an expression that was apologetic, curious, and irritated at him for not being what she expected—*wanted*—him to be.

"Thank you," she said. She seemed about to go on, but at the sound of the basement door being unlocked, fled upstairs.

Marcia appeared. "I thought I heard your voice. I'm desperate for a smoke."

As he took his pack out, she said, "Let's share one. I really am trying to quit."

They sat on the deck steps, both shivering a little. She wore sheepskin moccasins, heavy gray sweats, and an enormous motheaten white cable-knit sweater he guessed was Ryker's.

"Are you looking forward to the condo meeting?" he asked, affecting conspiratorial irony, though his purpose was to remind her.

"Highlight of my fucking week," she said, "but I have to run off to work right after."

The $3,000 was due today, but Marcia didn't seem concerned.

"Who were you talking to?" she said.

"Valeria. I just read her book."

"The dyke with all those crazy tattoos? She wrote a book?" After taking a drag, she returned the cigarette. "What's up with that other one, why does she dress like she's twelve? It's creepy."

He didn't want to talk about Lulu. "You don't like Valeria's tattoos?"

"Looks like she let someone doodle all over her body. Why would you treat your skin like a fucking sketch pad?"

"Are those tattoos on your arms the only ones you have?"

Retrieving the cigarette, she cast him a sly, penetrating glance. "You want to see all my tattoos?"

He could feel himself blushing. "No, I mean, I just wondered."

She laughed, not entirely unpleasantly, and after retrieving the cigarette said, "She made a pass at me a couple days ago."

"Valeria?"

"Yeah. Do I look fucking gay?"

He laughed, trying to hide the outrage he felt on Lulu's behalf. "I don't know what that would look like."

"I thought they had some kind of gaydar thing, secret wink or handshake or whatever."

He shrugged, still incredulous and angry.

"That little schoolgirl, what's her name?"

"Lulu. She's not a schoolgirl."

"Someone needs to tell her that. She's so cute. What does she see in that troll?"

"You don't think Valeria's attractive?"

She looked at him as if he were insane. "You think she's attractive?"

"Yeah, sexy in a kind of unusual way."

She opened her mouth wide to add an exclamation point to her disbelief.

"When she made a pass, what did you say?"

"Told her I was a grown woman. Not her fucking type. Are you going to tell the little schoolgirl up there?"

Jack thought about this. "Lulu's crazy about her. I don't know how she'd react."

Marcia took another drag, narrowing her eyes forensically at him. "So, you're really not gay." She was clearly convinced enough that the question mark had all but evaporated from that sentence. "Or is it only lesbians you find attractive?"

He just sighed, giving her a forbearing look as he reclaimed the cigarette. He didn't want to smoke so much as preserve it, to keep them both here, their trembling bodies cleft for warmth.

"Oh"—she seemed to have suddenly remembered something and jumped up—"stay here." On her return, she dumped a pile of mortgage documents into his lap and snatched his cigarette away again.

"I don't really understand it," she said.

He was shocked to see that her apartment had cost $270,000, almost as much as his own. The broker had sold her a two-year 9 percent balloon loan, telling her that once she'd made the payments, she'd be able to refinance at a low rate, providing her with extremely creative "ballpark" figures.

After reading through, Jack explained, "You'll have to refinance by the end of the year. Essentially just get another mortgage."

"For how much?"

"The same amount. This is interest only."

"So I haven't paid anything off the apartment?"

"No, not yet."

"So who do I get the new mortgage from? The same people?"

"Maybe, or you'll just have to see who's interested."

"Huh," she sighed, shrugging, retrieving the documents and laying them in her lap. As she took another drag, she glanced up at the ghostly disk of the sun. Jack didn't want to tell her there was no way in the world she could refinance, given how underwater she was. The news was more dire every day, the financial structure of the entire world riddled with the termites of bad American mortgages. All over the city, developers were abandoning half-finished apartment blocks, home prices plummeting as foreclosures flooded the market. Nearly 4 million people had lost their homes.

Panther appeared, pushing his large head against Marcia's shin and then jumping up onto the documents in her lap.

"Oh shit," Marcia said, "get him off me."

"You don't like cats?" Jack reached across to scratch him under the chin.

"That thing is covered in fucking rat guts," she said, disgusted and not a little fearful as Panther rolled onto his back, purring blissfully.

"Get him *off* me," she repeated.

Delighted to see her frightened by this friendly, furry bundle, Jack lifted Panther into his own lap. "Give me some of your rat guts, my beautiful big boy," he cooed, touching his nose to Panther's.

"That's disgusting," she cried. "*Je-*sus."

She was staring at his hands, stark pale against Panther's black fur, and said, "God, I never noticed how big your hands are."

Panther, who had little interest in those who actually wanted his company, jumped off and sauntered away.

Jack examined his own hands. "I did a lot of hard, manual work when I was younger."

"Does that make a difference?"

He shrugged. "I don't know, but think of farmers' hands, quarterbacks' hands, don't they tend to be larger than average?"

"I guess." She'd almost finished the cigarette. "So where are you from?"

"A place called Gaza."

"Where's that?"

He huffed out a sad laugh. "It's between Egypt and Israel. It's sort of controlled by the Israelis. Mostly."

"You Jewish, then?"

He shook his head.

She bent down and crushed the stub out onto the concrete, which he wished she wouldn't do. Sitting back upright, she raised the palm of her hand toward him and confessed, "I have to buy men's gloves." She lifted her foot. "I can wear Ryker's shoes."

"You have beautiful hands and feet," he said, not looking at her. "You remind me of someone I used to work with; she was even taller than you."

When he finally mustered the courage to glance at her, she was examining him curiously, almost speculatively.

"How much bigger are your hands than mine?" she asked, lifting her palm toward him again.

When he raised his hand, she pressed hers to his. She then began to push, and a silly contest of strength ensued. As she pushed harder and harder, he playfully mocked her for her weakness, telling her to let him know when she actually intended to start pushing. He felt like a teenager, with butterflies and the growing ache of desire. Her fingers slipped through the gaps between his, their hands interlocking, her other hand coming up to join her effort, her body pushing against his. As she put all of her weight into trying to move his hand, he made a theatrical yawn.

A door—May's—opened above them, and she snatched her hand away. The two of them stood up, Jack's heart pounding. Moments later, they were enveloped in the thick smell of pot.

"I should go," Marcia said, and hurried into the basement. He collected his tools and, after a final check of the gate's locking mechanism, walked back up.

Danh was sitting with his girlfriend, who was still hardly wearing a thing in this frigid weather. He glanced at her web of self-harm scars and those trompe l'oeil butterflies, including the one on her pale forehead that looked as if it were about to take flight.

He ignored Danh's cynical salute.

When he arrived at his back door, he slumped down onto the bench outside and murmured softly to himself, "Jamal, what the *fuck* are you doing?" He remained there, punishing himself with the cold, thinking about what had just happened with Marcia, breathing in the gusts of skunky smoke rising from Danh and his girlfriend.

He wished his heart could be that frozen, bloodless sun, but it was still pounding, his whole body aroused. He repeated, "Jamal, what the *fuck* are you doing?" but the words had no traction, the self within himself trembling not with the cold but a lust for reckless action, for a way to tear this skin off, to live without qualm or conscience. He lit another cigarette. How had Salim been able to eradicate Sofya so quickly, to quench his own longing? Just months after his father's death, Salim married, his wife immediately pregnant. Salim worked diligently at Jack's father's business, extending the hardware store and expanding into home renovation. He sold his own father's vegetable patch and became a mirror of Jack's father, wearing a mask of sour disappointment aimed particularly at Jack.

They hired day labor to help with the heavy work, moving appliances and installing water tanks and generators. That's when Hasan became a regular. In his early twenties, his long mousy hair fell into a pale, handsome, though slightly bovine face, his sleepy-seeming gray eyes shyly elusive. He walked pigeon-toed and his body was soft and pear-shaped, though he was surprisingly strong. A few times, Hasan bumped into Jack with a gentle apology, his hand lingering on Jack's arm, those elusive eyes flashing out at Jack with unnerving boldness. On one job, Jack gashed his leg against the corner of a steel water tank he and Hasan were installing. Hasan insisted on attending to it, clasping Jack's hand to lead him to a chair, kneeling at his feet, taking his time to clean and dress the wound, often shaking back his hair as he stole glances up at Jack, a secret smile playing about his lips. Jack felt at times aroused, at times suffocated and confused. Hasan was incurious and ponderous, rarely understanding any of Jack's jokes. He was clumsy and unable to perform any task alone unless carefully directed. But the cruel and sudden loss of Salim, of Sofya, had left an aching vacuum, a strong, dark undercurrent that easily undermined the conscious mind that told Jack, rightly, that he didn't even like Hasan, who began to take liberties, turning up late, disappearing for long cigarette breaks, perhaps to test his power over Jack. And yet Jack continued to schedule the two of them together. When he and Jack were alone, Hasan became increasingly feminized, his hands straying out to straighten Jack's hair, to pluck an eyelash from his cheek, scrape smut from his shirt. He'd even begun, sometimes, to pluck the cigarette from Jack's lips, drawing a deep drag before slipping it back. Jack was finding it hard to sleep. He still thought with such longing about the white room, the playful grapple of young animals, the nerve-fizzing release of desire. He loved Sofya. But that was a hidden world, forever closed off now.

One evening, he and Hasan worked late on a broken water pipe in someone's home. The tension between them built to an almost unbearable pitch, becoming absurd as Jack tried grimly to ignore Hasan's incessant glances and touches. It was dark as they left the house. A two-week curfew had ended the previous night. They both lit a cigarette. After a moment, Hasan said, "Let me show you something."

Mutely Jack trailed after Hasan until they arrived at a concrete factory hit by an Israeli shell during construction and never completed. Hasan pressed a finger to his lips as he led him cautiously through an opening in its surrounding fence. They entered the clinker storage building, a circular concrete silo covered in graffiti. Littered with bottles, it stank of urine and people had built fires that streaked the walls with ashen shadows. A stained straw mattress lay beneath the words "I fucked your mother's cunt here."

Hasan sat on the mattress, wrapping his arms around his knees, all coy glances, like a naïve and fearful schoolgirl. Jack realized that it wasn't in Hasan's nature to be the active pursuer, only to be seductive and to wait. His rational mind was in full alarm, begging him to leave, to run. But a deep current had caught Jack; to struggle against it would only drown him.

Kneeling in front of Hasan, who was affecting to tremble, Jack kissed him without tenderness, his whole being ambushed by an arousal that seemed the lurid flower more of anger than desire. Anger at coy, breathless, schoolgirl Hasan; at himself for being helpless. Though Salim had also wanted to be the woman, Salim himself was always there, a diamantine glint in Sofya's eyes, playful, ready to push back, to demand his own needs satisfied. But Hasan had lost himself entirely in this melodrama of the ingenue being cruelly deflowered. Jack roughly stripped off Hasan's clothes. As he shoved him naked onto the filthy mattress, Hasan briefly broke character to hiss into Jack's ear, "Slap me, call me a whore, force me to do whatever you want."

Calling him all the filthy names he could think of, Jack, not wanting to see his face, wrenched Hasan over onto his front, roiling with a disgusted desperation. It was not even an animal lust, for what animal is driven by hatred? A hatred fueled by circulated scraps of Western pornography, blond cheerleaders in locker rooms, those stories of sexual conquest from the men who traveled abroad, often related with a cynical curl of the lip, as if this were covert revenge on the West, on women themselves. Jack felt drunk, his very blood activated by the gathered yeasts of sweaty nights. To have someone, even in this sordid fantasy, utterly in your power, was sickening and delicious, accessing something deep within him that longed to degrade and destroy not just this other, but himself.

Suddenly they were raked with flashlight beams. "You dirty cunts, you filthy sharmootas, animal bastard sons of whores. May God curse you."

Kicks and punches rained down until they were finally dragged to their feet, Hasan naked, Jack with his pants around his ankles. No doubt someone had informed one of the Islamic groups of two possible spies or collaborators entering the factory. Since the start of the intifada, the bodies of collaborators were turning up all over the city.

A gnome of a man, who couldn't have been more than five-foot-five, looked half insane with fury, spit foaming on his heavy beard as he screamed at Hasan, "The penalty for this, by God, is death!" A few of the men looked wolfishly excited; others appeared embarrassed and confused.

"Let them get their clothes on," their leader said. He was older, perhaps sixty, with a black skullcap on a close-shaven head and a streak of white in his beard.

The gnomish man screamed, "They should be killed here in the evidence of their sin. God wills it!" as he suddenly swung the butt of his Kalashnikov into Hasan's face, sending him crashing back onto the mattress, blood spurting from his nose.

"That's enough, by God!" the leader shouted. "We need to question them."

After they'd pulled on their clothes, Jack and Hasan were shoved along toward an old Mercedes and a truck at the opening in the fence. While Jack was slapped a few times on the head as they walked, Hasan received the brunt of the punches and kicks. Jack sensed it was Hasan's effeminacy that set the gnome and some of the others off: his long, pale hair, that soft, pear-shaped body and pigeon-toed walk. The gnome jabbed the muzzle of his Kalashnikov hard between Hasan's buttocks, hitting his tailbone at one point with a loud crack. Hasan howled and collapsed to his knees.

The older man again shouted "Enough!" annoyed less at the abuse than at being slowed down.

Sacks were shoved over their heads as they were bundled into the old Mercedes and driven away, to be dragged out ten minutes later and guided down steps. Jack was pushed into a chair as a door slammed and the sack was yanked off. He sat in a windowless concrete room, four of the militants with him. The only other piece of furniture was a small desk holding two pieces of paper and a pen. A bucket sat in one corner. He could hear Hasan's voice from an adjacent room behind him. One of the men bound Jack's wrists with a rope threaded through a pulley in the ceiling and then tugged on this rope until Jack's arms bore his entire weight, his toes barely touching the floor. Jack could hardly breathe, and pain shot through his arms, shoulders, and back. Behind his insomniac-looking, overweight interrogator, two of the others slouched against the wall hugging their Kalashnikovs while the one who'd secured him to the rope—a skinny, sickly-looking fellow—took up a length of heavy-duty electrical cable. As this skinny man thrashed Jack all over his body with the cable, the interrogator barked questions, *Who are you having sex with? Do groups of men do this? Who are they?*

Which ones are the men and which act like women? Where do you meet these men? What's your relationship to God?

Over and over, Jack repeated that there was no one else, the pain from being suspended by his wrists becoming so unbearable that the whipping actually alleviated it. These blows were halfhearted, though at one point the skinny man, growing tired and not paying attention, struck Jack's testicles, exploding gut-wrenching pain, and was scolded by the interrogator.

Hasan's screams were also torture. He could hear the shouting of the gnome, clearly in charge of interrogating Hasan. The intensifying screams became so vividly evocative of increasingly monstrous acts that the men in Jack's cell began to stare at each other with confusion and concern. Then came a howl so agonized, the militants leaning against the wall flinched, wrapping their arms more tightly around their Kalashnikovs, and the man whipping Jack with the cable stopped and said, "By God, what is that son of a bitch doing to him?"

The insomniac man didn't respond, but Jack could see concern in his face also.

Finally lowering Jack back onto the chair, they untied his wrists and dragged the desk in front of him. His interrogator slapped the pen down onto a blank sheet of paper. The other sheet held a list with seven names. Jack recognized a couple of them as prominent Fatah men from his neighborhood, political rivals to the Islamist groups.

"Now, you write down here"—the interrogator tapped the blank sheet—"that you've had sex with these men"—he tapped on the list—"or, as God is my witness, we'll strip your skin off."

"But I haven't."

"God curse you and those who gave birth to you, you son of a whore. These filthy acts are punishable by ten years in jail. Section 152 of the penal code. Do you want to spend the next ten years in a room this size?" the man shouted as he slapped Jack's head.

Jack was crying. "I don't know these men."

"You'll write their names and say you behaved like an animal with them, you goddamned deviant. Do it!" he screamed, slapping Jack's head again, but they were no harder than the slaps his father often gave him. The Islamists wanted to jail these men or destroy their reputations. But he could sense that his captors didn't have the heart to torture him much more, and in truth he wished they would kill him. He couldn't bear the shame of his parents or Salim knowing about him and Hasan.

The door banged open and the vicious gnome strode in, his blue shirt stained with sweat at his chest in the disconcerting shape of a perfect heart, his jeans spattered with blood. He looked high, out of breath, frantically overexcited, murderous.

"That pervert sharmoota son of a whore signed," the little man said triumphantly. "What about this little fucker?"

"He will," Jack's interrogator said.

"He hasn't?" the little man declared with incredulous fury, not needing an answer, since he could see the blank sheet.

Pushing aside the desk, the gnome took hold of Jack's ankles, snatching him off the chair, Jack's head smashing onto the concrete.

"Hold his legs and keep him down," the gnome barked at the skinny man who'd been whipping Jack. Snatching the cable from this man's hand, the gnome whipped the soles of Jack's bare feet mercilessly, sweat pouring off him.

Jack howled, begging him to stop, burning pain flooding his body. Finally, his assailant told the skinny man to lift Jack onto the chair and dragged the desk in front of him. He tugged Jack's head back by his hair, clotted with blood from where he'd hit the floor. The gnome seemed intent on ripping his hair out, but suddenly thrust Jack's head forward, slamming his face into the desk. Pulling a Makarov pistol from the waist of his jeans, he screwed the barrel into Jack's temple.

"You write this confession or I'll send you to the seventh level of hell right now, you pervert son of a whore."

All Jack could think of was his father's disgusted face and willed the gnome to shoot him, refusing to take hold of the pen thrust into his hand. The little man then took off his leather sandal and slapped Jack repeatedly on the head, showering him with spit and sweat.

"This is not doing any good," Jack's original interrogator said.

The gnome, so out of breath he was hardly able to speak, managed to puff out, "Who is he?"

"His name's Jamal Shaban, son of Ali Shaban. They live in Beach Camp."

"Ali Shaban," the gnome declared delightedly. "I know that name. He's a Fatah man, uh? High up. High."

"Okay, I'm going to get that deviant next door to add Ali Shaban to his list." He bent down to Jack. "How do you like that, boy? The son of a goose is a swimmer, uh. Everyone's going to think your dad fucked his own son."

Jack called the man back before he left the cell. Dizzy, his eyes bleary, Jack copied out the confession they dictated to him, swearing by Allah that these men were perverts and had corrupted him as a boy into their deviant life.

Jack and Hasan were kept locked up overnight and into the next day. Finally, the door opened, and a man carried in a bucket of water.

"Get the blood off your head," he said. "Clean yourself up."

Jack did nothing, still wanting to die, so the man took tight hold of his hair and roughly scrubbed the wound at the back of his scalp. As this was being done, the older leader from the previous day appeared in the cell, seeming irritated.

When they closed the door, Jack heard him say outside, "Tell the boy's family he's still being questioned, and keep him here until some of the bruising in his face has gone down. Make sure he doesn't harm himself. Before he leaves, dress him in fresh clothes. The other one's family know he's a deviant. They want nothing to do with him, so just take him and throw him in the street somewhere."

Jack spent five days in the cell, four of them naked because one of the men found him unconscious after Jack tried to kill himself by knotting the leg of his pants around his neck and tugging as hard as he could before blacking out. He considered smashing his head against the wall, but feared he might just end up brain-damaged and his mother would have to look after him. On the fourth day he thought of drowning himself in the urine that had built up with his shit in the bucket, but the bucket was too narrow. He would have had to tip it, and when he passed out, it would just spill.

On the fifth day two men entered with soap, water, and a coarse-bristled broom. They told him that if he didn't wash himself, they'd do it for him with the broom. After he was dressed, they thrust a sack on his head and drove him home.

His mother was waiting anxiously outside their house, and the unfailing Arab telegraph filled the street with nosy neighbors. Jack broke down the moment his mother took him into her arms as the men shoved him out of the car.

Jack was pulled from his memories by the giggle of the butterfly girl beneath him. Wondering what her story was, he thought of Danh, a little boy with a GI father, incarcerated with his collaborator mother for years before suffering the horrors of that squalid refugee camp. He felt suddenly almost weepily happy that these two had found each other.

Jack didn't think he'd ever heard his father laugh. He tried to remember if he'd ever seen him smile. After the Islamists had returned him, his father refused to share the dining table with him, so his mother brought his meals to his room. She often touched the fading rope burns around his wrists, her face betraying her desperation to know what happened, but Jack couldn't bring himself to talk about any of it. She slept on the floor beside his bed until the end of the first week, when she told Jack that she and his father had found him a wife: Dimra Ageel, seventeen, educated through fifth grade. He was to meet her the next day.

Even through his continuing numbness, he'd been apprehensive. There had to be something seriously wrong with her. What kind of parents would sacrifice their daughter to someone like him?

His mother led him into the kitchen, where Dimra sat at the dining table with her back to him, her parents slumped in chairs behind her. His own father sat behind where Jack was to take his place at the table. It was the first time Jack had seen him since his release, a grim effigy, refusing even to look at Jack. Jack felt faintly nauseous as he made his way around the table to his chair, but the moment he took his seat and saw Dimra, it was as if the sun had instantly burned the morning's fog away. He almost laughed at the absurd phenomenon of such a youthful, lovely, and ardently receptive face within the grim arena of these miserable adults. Not that there wasn't a deep sadness in her, but beneath that reached something irrepressibly open to joy, love. She returned him to himself enough that in their conversational foray, he made some silly joke and was gifted with her delighted if slightly surprised laugh, as if she wasn't used to humor.

Her parents, though, remained stone-faced, and before he knew more about their situation, he assumed them to be ultra-orthodox. He'd noticed this about fundamentalist Muslims, such as the men who'd captured him. Humor was a satanic gift, haram, like all colors but black for a widow. Dimra's mother couldn't produce three words without a *bismillah* or *inshallah*. But a Palestinian without humor, as his mother said, is a hairless cat. Even though so much of the humor was cynical, Jack thought, the humor of the hopeless. Dimra's innocent laughter, though, felt like a resurrection, her gorgeous, obsidian eyes glittering with subversive joy. Unfilial joy. The joy of his wife.

He would later find out that their name wasn't Ageel. Her father's father, a Turkish deserter from the Ottoman army during the Great War, had married a woman from a clan called Masri, descended from Egyptian migrant workers living on the outskirts of Dimra's namesake village in what was called the Egyptian neighborhood. This clan could own no land, and had no voice, banned from the diwans held by the village mukhtar. After being expelled by the Zionists in '48, they found a place in Gaza where they were not known and assumed the name of Ageel, one of the larger clans. Their shame ran even deeper than his own.

After Dimra and her parents were gone, his father left the house and Jack and his mother returned to his room. She sat on the bed beside him, combing the hair back from his forehead with her fingers, searching his face for something she half dreaded, half hoped to find. She was always touching him tenderly now, as a sculptor might touch the contours of a just-finished work. As a mother, she'd taken eighteen years of her life to make one thing: him.

"What do you think?" she said, lifting his hands to kiss them.

"Well, her mother's a joyful soul, isn't she? I didn't know you could mention God's mercy and beneficence that many times in one sentence."

She winced, as if she'd dropped something precious and fragile inside herself and was waiting for it to smash. Somehow, miraculously, it didn't, and with an expression of exhausted relief, she said, "Well, habibi, when you have nothing, you have God."

Only much later would Jack discover that the naked, tortured, hogtied body of Dimra's older brother, Nafiz, had been dumped on a garbage heap the week before, his throat cut, a urine-soaked sack over his head, and "traitor" carved into his chest.

"What do you think?" she repeated.

He shied from the intensity of her searching look. Jack now wished he'd kept his eyes upon that handsome face he so loved, with its deep emotional intelligence; wished he'd taken every moment to remember his mother in every shade of feeling.

He pretended indifference: "She seems nice enough."

"She's *beautiful*, isn't she," his mother urged.

He shrugged, but couldn't help smiling, "Not bad."

"She's a good girl. She'll be a good wife." His tearful mother embraced him, kissing his forehead. She knew what it was to be a good wife.

For Jack, the wedding was a humiliating sham, only immediate family and a few old friends in attendance. Not so for Dimra. With her hands intricately hennaed, wearing a traditional thobe from her village and a headdress of gold Ottoman coins, her face conveyed as much pride and solemn joy as if Jack had been led in on a white horse and her parents' entire village were singing, trilling, and dancing the dabka.

Salim attended without his wife, claiming their baby daughter had a fever. Jack had thought about his cousin that morning as he shaved himself. In the old world, it was tradition for the groom's closest friend to shave him, making him new for his bride. At the wedding, Salim, glanced often at his watch. Remaining less than an hour, he begged leave to check on his child, and only just remembered a stiff "Mabrouk" before he vanished.

That was the last time Jack ever saw or spoke to his cousin.

It was strange to lead Dimra into his childhood bedroom, fitted now with a new queen-size bed. His parents were staying with Salim to give them privacy. After their first kiss, standing beside the bed, she stepped away from him, began to clap in a slow rhythm and sang,

> *Say to his mother rejoice and be glad,*
> *place myrtle on the pillows and henna on our hands.*
> *The wedding is here, the men are all dancing,*
> *this home is my home and the rooms are all mine,*
> *We are as one, let the enemy die!*

She sang it with a haunting mix of joy and sadness, as if in memory of all those who might have sung it, the scattered fellahin of her namesake and vanished village. She sang it alone, and this morning he'd shaved his own face, as if they were the first of a new tribe, beginning again. Their wedding had felt to him like a wound, but here was the wedding in all that mattered, sanctified by her lovely young voice, and it was in this moment that the love gestating within him stirred for the first time.

She removed her headdress to release her mass of black ringlets and he helped her slip off her thobe. She was trembling, so he took it slow. He loved the soft skin of her breasts, the swift tautening of her dark nipples. Her mother had instructed her enough that she could help him with his own ignorance, guiding him, but the moment he entered her she flinched and gasped with pain. Though he insisted they could take their time, she shook her head, lifting her legs around him. It was over quickly, and he felt a rush of love for her as he realized he would be a father. God willing, the best father, the best husband.

In the following weeks, he was ravenous for her, and so she seemed for him, urging him to bed, loving to kiss him, but as hard as she tried, she couldn't hide her pain. And not only when they made love. Nothing helped, and her suffering became constant during her period. Afterward, lying awake in bed with her asleep beside him following yet another difficult physical encounter, he often recalled the playful sexual joy of the white room.

On the day Jack determined to ask his mother to take Dimra to see a doctor, a gentle knock came at their front door late in the evening.

It was Abu Faris, their neighbor, who'd been a fedayeen with his father in the early years. He looked troubled, almost angry, refusing coffee and glancing at Dimra in a way that made Jack's mother ask her to go upstairs. Jack and his mother sat on the couch, his father in his armchair, kitty-corner to Jack, while Abu Faris took a chair opposite them. He told them that several key Fatah men had been accused of being perverts, and that a new Islamist group called Hamas claimed they possessed signed confessions from Jack and Hasan, and that Jack had confessed he was corrupted as a boy by these men and would stand witness to this.

"The families have vowed revenge on you and Hasan," Abu Faris said directly to Jack. "I told them who your father was. I said, as God is my witness, you wouldn't have signed anything."

Jack still hadn't told his parents about the confessions, sinking everything that happened in that concrete cell deep into his mind like the memory of a bad dream.

"Yes, this is not true," his mother declared, looking anxiously at Jack.

The split moment of Jack's silence threatened to plunge them all into an abyss before a blinding blow to his cheek threw his head hard against his mother's shoulder. His father then seized him by the collar, ripping his buttons as he dragged him awkwardly over the arm of the couch and punched him again in his face. His mother jumped up, screaming as she tried to shield Jack, but his father shoved her away and dragged Jack onto the floor. Seeming at a loss for what to do, his father snatched up and flung down at Jack an ashtray, a bowl of almonds, and a full cup of tea, stopping only when his mother had finally managed to cover Jack with her body.

Abu Faris was standing now, shocked, glancing from Jack and his mother on the floor, to Jack's breathless father. "I'm sorry, Ali," he murmured, and left.

Later, sitting in bed with Dimra, his nose throbbing, probably broken, the skin under his eyes already blackening, the two of them listening to his parents screaming at each other, Jack felt like a child. What was he doing with this girl, this stranger in his bed? He examined her lovely face, those large depthless eyes that seemed hardly to blink, always with a question in them—one that, as her husband, it was now his responsibility to answer. There was nothing accusatory or critical in this question. It was like the question of a child during that time when every answer you provide is met with another "why?"

He couldn't bring himself to explain to her what was going on, and she didn't ask, simply lay her head on his shoulder.

The screaming stopped and his mother knocked and entered, beginning to cry again at the sight of Jack's bruised and swollen face. Calming herself, she sat on the bed.

"Habibi," she said to him, "your baba wanted the two of you to leave right after the wedding. I made him delay, but it's too dangerous now. The two of you must leave Gaza right away."

He couldn't help but smile bitterly. "Yes, yes, we'll fly to the beach in Honolulu tomorrow."

"You'll go to Egypt," she said.

"They won't let us in there either."

"You were *born* in Egypt."

"What are you talking about?"

"Your father and I were there because my brother died."

"Your brother?" He hadn't even known she had a brother.

"Of course, I wouldn't have been welcome at the funeral, but I wanted to go to his grave. Your father tried to stop me because I was heavily pregnant, but I told him, as God is my witness, he could divorce me if he wanted.

"I went, and the stress of the journey and the grief caused you to come early. I convinced your dad to have you registered as Egyptian."

When Jack looked more directly at his mother, she couldn't meet his eyes. He guessed she must have known she'd give birth to him there.

"Baba let you?"

"On condition I never told you."

"So, I'm Egyptian."

"Don't ever say that to your father."

Two days later, the day before Jack and Dimra were to leave Gaza for Cairo through the Rafah crossing, Jack snuck out of the house and wandered through the streets of the city where he'd spent his whole life. Rude, vibrant life had recolonized the rubble left by Israel's response to the intifada, like the plants and grasses of Beirut's Green Line. He passed a troop of Israeli soldiers sitting on a halftrack, speaking too loudly, out of fear or bravado. It would be good to be free of the small throb of hatred he felt for them.

He found himself at a small mosque in the Zaytun Quarter of the Old City. From his earliest memories, he'd never felt anything spiritual in a mosque or church. For him, as soon as you submitted yourself to hierarchy, ritual, dogma, even just to the necessary social acknowledgment of another person, God vanished. It was a good thing to face others in love and community; but God you faced alone, wrestled with him like Jacob, spoke to him like Moses, and never on your knees. You made him, as he made you, in the image of your soul. But on that final day, Jack entered the mosque just at the time of the midday prayer, and joined a small crowd of local men, less to pray than to smell the mats, the rich loam of Gaza in those bodies, holding their secrets, and to feel for once aligned with the life of his home in the voice of the imam. Just after he slipped his shoes back on and was about to leave, he felt a gentle touch on his shoulder.

"Jamal. Do you remember me?"

It took him a moment to recognize the young imam who taught Islamic history in the UNRWA school when Jack was younger, and he nodded.

"I remember you because you were one of the few students who paid attention and asked questions. I was sure—I'm still sure—you're destined for college and great things, God willing."

"Yes, God willing," Jack said.

He could tell by the imam's searching look that he knew Jack's shame.

The imam rested a gentle hand on his shoulder, "How are you, my brother?"

The secret softness of his voice, its pained concern, made Jack tearful. He nodded, unable to speak, and then managed, "I'm fine, shaykh. Thank you."

Reaching behind his own neck, the imam removed a necklace that appeared to be a gold Quran.

"It's made of brass," he said. "Even so, I probably shouldn't wear it." He smiled ruefully. "Some years ago, the Israelis jailed my brother for six years, releasing him on a prisoner exchange. He was back for only three days before the IDF smashed in our door and arrested him again. I was fifteen. The next day I asked around for a pistol to kill any Israeli soldier I could find. When I returned home, a young theological scholar working with our local imam was waiting for me. He'd heard what I was doing and told me I could kill a man or I could devote my life to bringing people to God. This necklace was his."

Quickly, the imam slipped it over Jack's neck.

Jack protested, "No. Please. It's yours."

"I've found my way, Jamal. May Allah give you peace and protect you."

Jack spent much of the rest of the day in the British War Cemetery among those boys from British cities and villages now buried in the sand and blistering heat of Gaza, the dead of a war that led to Ottoman defeat, Sykes–Picot, the betrayal of the Arabs, Balfour, the Mandate, the partition, and now this juncture of a single life. Lying on a grass verge between rows of tombstones, feeling the stillness of those men beneath the boiling surface of humanity, it calmed him that the peace of death would be his one day.

Toward evening he wandered up the beach all the way to the broken house. He stood at the shoreline staring at the window, thinking of the room and all it once held. Recent shelling had destroyed part of the fence and widened the crack. It was pockmarked with bullet holes.

"Fall," he murmured quietly as the sea hissed and curled about his feet. "*Fall.*"

When he returned home, his mother was frantic. "Where have you been?"

"Just walking." The pain in her face made him realize how selfish he'd been: of course she'd wanted to be with her son on his last day.

His father joined them for the final dinner, remaining silent, and but for Dimra's bright and lovely face, the meal would have felt funereal. When they'd eaten, his mother asked him to come to her room. They sat on her bed. After she kissed his hands, she reached over and picked up the copper-wire scorpion on her bedside table. Intricately made, bigger than his palm, it had a complex green patina and the copper wire of its back, claws, and stinger caged fragments of dark-blue sea glass.

"I know you have a lot to carry, habibi, but please find a place for this."

"No, Mama, it's yours."

"You must take it. You'll never meet my mother or father, but they were not the most affectionate or attentive of parents. I remember once my little brother, the one who died, pointing at my father during some big function, a wedding I think—he was six—and asking me who that man was. I was much closer to Zuhur, the Nubian who drove me back and forth to my school. I was a very fearful little girl, afraid of the dark, of dying, of being alone, of the other girls in school. One day, he gave me this. He told me scorpions were guardian spirits, even protected the dead on their journey to the underworld, and he'd made this one specially to protect me, with blue sea glass to ward off the evil eye. No one had ever made me anything. I took it everywhere with me and kept it under my bed.

"It's the only thing I own that means anything to me. Your father lost his home, I lost my home, and now my son has—" She became emotional and took some deep breaths. She kissed his hands again. "Sleep, habibi," she said. "It's going to be a long day tomorrow."

His parents drove them to the Rafah border crossing in the hardware store's van, all of them squeezed into the front. Jack was sure Salim would come to say goodbye, but he didn't.

His father helped him unload their suitcases amid the chaos in the arena of human misery that was the border, hundreds wilting in the sun, sitting on their luggage, waiting for their passports to be returned and their taxi assignments. Jack felt a little sick, knowing the border would be a nightmare to get through, praying they didn't close it.

Setting down the last suitcase, Jack's father spoke for the first time since Jack had been returned by Hamas.

"Salim is my son now. The business will be his, as will our home and all we have after your mother and I have gone."

Jack nodded, but his father wasn't looking at him, only down at the battered suitcases on the sand, then at the crossing itself.

He assumed this would be the last thing his father said to him, but his father lifted his eyes to Jack as if his gaze were a heavy weight he was hefting up with every ounce of his strength.

"Do you know why you could become an Egyptian citizen?" he said.

Jack shook his head.

"You can become one if your father's Egyptian or if your mother's Egyptian and your father's unknown—or stateless, like me. It means a Palestinian father is the same as the bastard who's abandoned a woman he's made pregnant. A Palestinian is nobody. As far as Egyptian law is concerned, you're nobody's son. I didn't want that for you," he said, "but now I'm glad your mother persuaded me."

Jack thought that was it, but his father maintained that heavy gaze, beginning to tremble beneath its weight, and said, "Remember that you're not nobody."

14

Jack finally entered his home to the delicious smell of the food Dimra was preparing for the condo meeting that evening. In the kitchen, he almost fell over the carry cot, where Aiden sat playing with his toes.

"Where were you?"

"Oh," he said, "just chatting with Bernard."

Feeling guilty and overcome suddenly by a surge of love, he wrapped his arms around her.

"Oh, God preserve us, you're *freezing*," she said. "And you've been smoking."

"I'm sorry." After releasing her, he shied from her interrogatory look.

Returning to her cooking, she said quietly, "I Skyped with Mama today."

"How are they?"

"The situation's terrible, no fresh food, electricity constantly going off. Mama has an ulcer and can hardly look after Baba. He's yellow from his cirrhosis, and his legs are badly swollen and discolored. The doctor said he won't last more than a year. I think we might need to pay for someone to look after them."

"Okay," Jack said. Jack had no idea how they were going to afford that. As frugal as she was, they were hemorrhaging money: for her parents, for the fertility treatments, for all the building issues.

"Do you want me to join you next time on the Skype call?"

"No, no," she said, suddenly very present and vehement. "They understand you're working, busy."

Dimra talked to her parents now only when Jack was away. He guessed she wanted to spare him his mother's litany of misery and her sniping at him for neither making her pregnant nor providing the wealthy life her nephew had forged for himself in America. He'd suggested trying to get her parents U.S. citizenship, but they said that they were too old to leave their home, and didn't want to risk even a short trip, terrified the Israelis wouldn't let them back in. Jack and Dimra mentioned visiting Gaza, a place for them both of shame and pain, but the blockade made it impossible, and her father was adamant his daughter never return.

Glancing at Aiden, who'd managed to get most of his foot into his mouth, he said, "Would you consider adopting a child?" Lulu suggested this to him, since she wanted to bring up the idea of adoption to Valeria.

Aiden started to grizzle and Dimra, gently freeing herself from Jack's embrace, lifted him out of his cot, rocking and kissing him.

"I wish I could adopt this one," she said, adding after a moment, "I feel that Allah the all-knowing and merciful has not intended for me to have children."

She handed Aiden to Jack, turning away from him to begin shaping falafel into balls, and sighing, said, "When I was little, in the camp, there was a woman called Um Mazim. She was from our village. Mama told me her story. Her two teenage boys went to fight the Jews in the '48 war. Lots of fighters vanished in that war. She'd already lost her husband to it and had to join the household of her husband's brother. He was devout, slapped her when she begged Allah for her boys' safe return. It was haram, he said, to make agreements with the Lord of the Universe who ordered all things. All was as Allah willed it. She didn't listen. She went to the door of the mukhtar's madafa to ask questions about the war and where her sons might be. All the men, they shouted at her that this was no place for a woman. Her brother-in-law beat her harder. He locked her in her room. But she got out, wandered the village, searching for someone who could tell her where her boys were.

"Years later in the camp, when I knew her, she looked like a beggar. She exposed her body. Urinated in the street. I didn't know to look away when I was little. She shouted curses into the mosque. She demanded God return her sons, and she constantly called their names. She was always muttering, and as a child I thought her a witch, conjuring a new god. People cursed her, threw stones at her. They hated her because she"—Dimra hesitated, her hands shaking as she wiped them with a dish towel before pouring oil into a pan—"because she was the truth of what we'd lost; of who we were. She shook people's faith in our cause and in the Almighty. It meant nothing to her anymore to be a Palestinian or a Muslim. Even, I think, to be human. All she wanted was her boys."

Jack, who'd never heard Dimra speak like this, experienced the dizzying sense that he had no idea who his wife was.

"I've never forgotten her face, Jamal. I never forgot her eyes. What they demanded of me, of everyone; what they said about the love of a mother for her children. For weeks, I've been trying to remember the name of her second son. Last night, it came to me. Harb. How had I forgotten that? I feel her inside me, Jamal. It's like she's wandering around my barren body, this woman looking for her children. A woman willing even to make herself a new god to get them back."

She removed the spinach fatayer from the oven, but nearly dropped the tray on the stovetop, flinching and clutching her shoulder.

"Are you okay?"

"My shoulder. It hurts all the time," she said, trying to rotate it. "And I've been feeling bloated and nauseous."

The bloating and nausea, they knew from long experience, were symptoms of her worsening endometriosis.

"We'll get you an appointment with the doctor," he said, gently massaging her shoulder.

She nodded. "If it gets any worse."

= 15 =

Aiden began to grizzle again and Dimra wanted Jack out of the kitchen, so he took the baby to the back bedroom, walking him around the trundle bed, rocking him. For a while, Dimra filled his mind. He was worried about her pain, but also thinking about how little they'd shared that was truly intimate, haunted by her inner life. Aiden finally started to drop off, and feeling the boy's downy hair in the hollow of his neck, Jack thought of his father again. Had his father ever held him like this? Had he ever been able to love his son in any pure way, rather than as a new Nasser or a boy forced to learn that his home wasn't his home? He tried to remember the name of the child he'd invented to hurt his father in that angry letter. After a moment it came to him. Fayez. The phantom child. Again, he saw his father's face that final time before the hellish trip across the Rafah border. *You're not nobody.*

When had they crossed, in '88? No, early '89, and somewhere deep within him, Jack had been excited. A chance, at last, to shed that old skin. When they arrived in Cairo, they had just enough money to rent a place and he hoped he might be able to secure employment at a hotel, since he could speak French, English, German, and Hebrew, but these were plum jobs, obtained through family connections or bribes, and he had no qualifications or references, and little money. Jack finally found a position as a hospital orderly, the pay barely enough to cover their rent.

One day a German tourist who'd been hit by a car was trying to explain to a confused nurse where he was hurting, so Jack translated. As Jack was about to leave, a middle-aged Egyptian man recovering from kidney-stone surgery in the same ward called Jack over and introduced himself as Mahmoud El Tayeb. Mahmoud spoke with a coarse accent, his snarl-like smile revealing a gold front tooth. When he found out that Jack could speak other languages, he offered him a job as a tour guide. Though Jack thanked him and said he'd keep it in mind, there was something wolfishly intimidating about this man, and the job's only pay was tips.

A couple of evenings after this, on Jack's returned from a shift at the hospital, Dimra told him that a woman had come to their door that afternoon. The woman's cousin lived in Beach Camp. She said she'd tell Jack's boss, their landlord, and everyone in the neighborhood that Jack was a traitor and Dimra was the sister of an Israeli collaborator unless they gave her a quarter of Jack's pay at the hospital every month. Jack searched Dimra's eyes, wondering if the blackmailer also told her he was a sexual deviant. Dimra had never asked about Abu Faris's visit or why Jack's father had beaten him up, never questioned the necessity to leave Gaza, and he hoped her parents were too ashamed to admit they were marrying her off to a pervert.

Before the blackmailer could return, they moved, this time to live among the rural poor of Upper Egypt in the dense maze of unpaved alleyways and shacks that constituted the Imbaba neighborhood on the east bank of the Nile, a place that reminded Jack of the camp.

He met Mahmoud at his office, a glass-enclosed fishbowl in a rotting warehouse full of contraband near the river, with his brothers, Tarek and Omar, who looked even rougher than he did. Two half-starved Alsatians locked in a cage became frenzied when Jack entered, tearing at the bars.

Mahmoud told him that he and his brothers ran several businesses and were moving into the increasingly lucrative tourist trade, where they could charge in foreign currency. They'd invested in tour buses but struggled to find people with languages. Jack would soon discover from the other tour guides that the El Tayeb brothers' businesses included running prostitutes, brokering summer brides, and loansharking.

Jack, however, had little more choice than those exploited girls. Dimra's endometrial pain had progressed to the extent that she was bedridden during her period. The healthcare system was hopelessly overcrowded, and they sold the last of Dimra's small stock of bride gold to see a private gynecologist who told them the only solution was a $2,000 operation to remove the adhesions. Jack took every tour shift he could.

Though Jack was shy, almost throwing up with nerves before his first tour, the sight of Dimra trying to hide her pain forced him out of himself. He studied history at the library in his free time to provide as many interesting facts as he could, but also developed comic routines involving absurd, made-up history delivered in a charming, slightly goofy persona that earned him decent tips. Without wages, though, it was still hard to earn much more than he had as an orderly. To perform all day made him feel dissociated, and after work he needed time and silence to let his scattered soul return like bats to a cave. He had nothing left for Dimra, who said that women stopped her in the street, curious about who they were and why they were living in that neighborhood. Fearful of being found out, she slipped into total isolation. Both knew they'd soon have to move again.

Then one day a tour-guide colleague told him that his brother, now living in Colorado, had paid a man $15,000 for a green card. The colleague introduced him to the man, who explained that his cousin, an American immigration lawyer, worked with several officers inside the immigration system who could be bribed to approve a faked application.

That night, Jack couldn't sleep. America, the great Satan, was also the place of dreams, where he could at once disappear and become somebody. He'd also be able to find better medical treatment for Dimra. But it was an impossible sum, and they hadn't saved even half the amount for Dimra's operation.

It was here in Egypt that the pattern of their life became established, Dimra withdrawing from the world out of fear and shame, while he was thrust upon a little stage amid the swarm of humanity, emptying himself, returning home to a wife in pain, often curled up in bed, and ravenous for human contact. They lived on beans, saved every penny.

Sex became an insisted-upon ordeal, Dimra desperate for a child. At work, American and European women (and not a few men) flirted with Jack, and his moral constitution felt besieged. With that combination of performing every day and the hunger of desire, he couldn't center himself and felt as if a suffering and depraved creature lived within the cracked white room of his own soul.

Then one day he was told by the youngest El Tayeb brother, Tarek, to run a tour with a pickup at the Blue Nile Hotel. When Jack arrived, the bus wasn't there. He called the warehouse, but no one answered, so he trudged all the way back.

When he entered, the Alsatians tearing at their cage, all three brothers seemed to be waiting for him, sitting on the office desk. Hadn't they heard the phone? Mahmoud asked why he didn't turn up for his tour at the White Nile Hotel. Jack said he was told to go to the Blue Nile, but Tarek denied this.

"You lost us a thousand dollars," Mahmoud said. "You need to pay it back."

A few days before, one of Jack's colleagues told him that news had filtered down to the brothers that one of their tour guides had received $300 in tips from a bus full of Texans. Jack guessed the brothers had convinced themselves that the tour guides were earning a fortune, despite them being frequently tipped little to nothing. This, Jack realized, was their way to secure a cut of this illusory action.

Jack felt the heat of outrage in his face. He couldn't believe they were doing this to him, their most popular tour guide. But extortion was all the brothers knew, and the notion of anyone but them earning any real money from their enterprises was unacceptable.

"Unless you can pay it all at once," Mahmoud said, "we'll arrange a payment schedule at a fair rate."

Jack knew they charged 40 percent for loans.

The brothers seemed to be waiting for his response, feigning nonchalance, scratching their noses, scraping dirt from under their fingernails, at once slack and coiled, like a pride of lions. It occurred to Jack that even gangsters required justification, however skew, for their actions, and that if he reacted, as he was about to, furiously, at these morons who believed they could eat their golden goose and still have her eggs, the anger he provoked would provide it.

Despite his burning face and the shuddering piston of his heart, he forced himself to nod gently and say, "*Tamam*. I'm sorry, Tarek, I must have misheard you."

The three brothers didn't know what to do with this, casting questioning, almost guilty, glances between themselves. Jack recalled watching a wildlife show once where a lioness caught a newborn gazelle. In confused terror, the gazelle pushed its head under the lioness and began to suckle. The lioness, baffled, wandered off, leaving its little captive to return to its mother.

Mahmoud jumped off the desk, slipping his arm around Jack. "Look, we like you, Jamal, so I'll tell you what, habibi, we'll make it five hundred, no interest, spread out over ten months. You can manage that, can't you?"

When Jack said, "Yes, God bless you, brother," Mahmoud seemed to shiver, as if, for the first time, he felt a frigid breeze at his back rising from the abyss of his own iniquity.

Even with this small victory, he and Dimra wouldn't be able to save anything during those ten months of paying off the $500.

Now desperate, the only solution Jack could come up with was his mother's family. She once told him about her childhood home in the Zamalek district, a limestone mansion with Corinthian columns holding up turret-like structures at either end, one with a crenellated roof, the other with a dome. He found it with relative ease one evening after work. Standing at the mansion's wrought-iron gate with its Ottoman tulip pattern, he felt that the careful pressing of his old-fashioned suit, and the layered polish on shoes worn shapeless as potatoes, was more indicative of his poverty than rags and bare feet. The servant who answered regarded him with suspicious contempt. Jack asked him to inform Mr. Zohry that his daughter Yasmin's son would like to see him.

The servant made him wait in a liwan off the side of the entrance hall. The house astonished him, its vast lobby lined in blue tiles with flower motifs rising to a gorgeously painted dome with a Coptic cross at the center. He waited a long while and could hear voices echoing, even a shout. Finally, the servant returned, looking disturbed and confused, a frayed nerve of this home, to announce that the family was ready to receive him.

He entered another reception room, the family seated at the far end, like royalty, upon ornate, gilded chairs, his elegant grandparents at the center, flanked by his willowy aunt, whom he knew was named Mona, with her nervous-looking daughters, perhaps fifteen and ten, and her husband, stiff as a Nutcracker soldier. His grandmother was full-figured, like his mother, with a Queen Elizabeth hairstyle, his grandfather tall and thin, like Jack, with a neat, sharp goatee and immaculately coiffed hair, dyed a little too black. The moment Jack walked in, his aunt began crying, and a shock rippled even through the stone-faced hostility of his grandparents.

No seat was provided for Jack: this was to be a brief audience under sufferance. Jack's grandfather ordered his aunt Mona to control herself and asked Jack's uncle to take the girls away. When they were gone, he coldly addressed Jack. "What do you want?"

Feeling abject, Jack quickly explained that he found the house from a description his mother provided him as a child, and that she knew nothing about his visit. "I've left Gaza and now live in Cairo with my wife."

"What's that to us?" his grandfather demanded.

"Baba," his aunt softly appealed, but her father barked at her to be silent or leave.

"My wife is sick. I want to borrow money for an operation."

His grandfather's lips curled with a smile wrought from the satisfaction that all his expectations for a son of his traitorous daughter had been met.

"I'll sign a contract," Jack said.

"You have collateral for this loan?" His grandfather's mocking tone made it clear that Jack didn't need to answer.

But his aunt then interjected with sympathy, "What's wrong with your wife, Jamal?"

"Don't you dare call him Jamal," the grandmother hissed, staring at Jack with confused pain.

"*Nothing* is wrong with his wife!" his grandfather shouted.

"She has endometriosis. Sir, you can pay the surgeon directly if you wish," Jack said. "Send someone to witness the operation."

His grandfather stood. "You wanted to see us. We've seen you. Now, go tell your mother that if she was starving I wouldn't give her the soles from my shoes."

At the click of his fingers, the manservant who'd been standing behind them hurried over and firmly shepherded Jack out of the building.

After lingering at the wrought-iron gate, crushed, wondering how much longer Dimra could endure her pain, Jack headed away. Moments later, his name was called and he turned to see his aunt clutching a leather satchel.

She stopped, breathless, in front of him, staring at his face incredulously, tears slipping from her eyes as she pressed a hand to his cheek. "My mother and I thought my brother, Jamal, had returned from the dead."

"His name was Jamal?"

"You didn't know?"

Jack assumed he was named after one of his father's lost relatives. "Mama told me once she'd come back here to see her brother's grave, but that's all I know."

She retrieved a black-and-white photograph from the satchel, and it was as if Jack were looking at a photo of himself sitting as a smiling fedayeen in the shade of an olive tree, his Kalashnikov lying across his legs, an ardent innocence in his eyes.

"My parents blamed Yasmin for radicalizing him. Jamal worshipped her and your father. He ran off to Jordan when he was fifteen to join the fedayeen and was killed on a mission to attack Beisan."

A ticklish tightening in Jack's scalp as the foundation of his faith, the golden idol of his mother, tilted upon its axis. It appalled him to realize that guilt was as much her legacy as grief. He now understood not only the nature of her banishment but the elegiac quality of her love for him, as if she was always experiencing not the joy of his presence, but the pain of his loss.

His aunt handed him the satchel. "These are your mother's, habibi. I don't know why she didn't take them with her. Will you tell her I love her and I miss her."

Before he could figure out a response, she jumped in, "Well, of course you can't, darling. She wouldn't want you to have come here, would she." Kissing his cheeks, she hurried back home.

He found a small square and sat on the edge of a fountain to investigate the satchel. He was expecting more photographs, keepsakes, but it contained jewelry boxes. The first held a matching gold-and-emerald bracelet and necklace; the next, enormous pink diamond teardrop earrings; the last, a slender Cartier Tank watch with a diamond studded band. There was also a roll of bills that his aunt must have slipped in herself, just over $2,000.

A miracle.

He took these treasures to several jewelers in the souk, but they angrily turned him away or threatened to call the police. Only one led Jack into the back of his shop. Nothing could convince him these were legitimately obtained and he would offer no more than $3,000. Jack said he needed $15,000, but the man could see he was desperate and told Jack he'd hold the offer for one more day.

The next morning, when Jack picked up his tour assignment at the warehouse, he saw Mahmoud in the glass-sided office talking to a fellah in a gallabiyah and white turban, accompanied by a girl who looked no more than fourteen. As Jack approached the office, Mahmoud caught his eye and lifted a finger for him to wait. After a while, Mahmoud produced an impressive wad of dollars and peeled off a half dozen for the fellah, who hurried out, leaving the girl.

"That was her uncle," Mahmoud said as Jack entered the fishbowl, glancing at the poor girl who clutched her hijab tightly around her childish face. "Took less than a quarter of what I was prepared to offer. Not pretty enough for a summer bride," he said ruefully. "The uncle guarantees purity, filthy old dog, may God curse him and those whose seed made him."

"Mahmoud," Jack ventured, having to clear his throat from nerves, "I want to ask a favor."

Mahmoud raised his brows, a surprised smile creeping over his lips, as if this were a wonderfully novel request.

"Where might you suggest someone go if he had something to sell that people might think was stolen?"

Mahmoud's gaze immediately tautened like a muscle, and Jack witnessed a struggle in his face between his predatory nature and that troubled look that had afflicted him at Jack's passive acceptance of their extortion. Glancing over to his brothers, doling out tour assignments in the warehouse, he hastily scribbled a name and address onto a card and slipped it into Jack's pocket.

Mahmoud's fence, enormously fat, with a great mop of nappy hair and paranoid eyes, ran a newsstand. When Jack mentioned Mahmoud's name, he called a boy over to take charge and led Jack into the dusty back room of a cluttered house behind the stand. The fence unbuttoned his jacket to reveal a Webley revolver, and Jack feared Mahmoud had sent him into a trap until the man slipped on a pair of jeweler's magnifying glasses and examined every piece carefully. Without asking a single question, he offered twelve thousand. Jack said he needed eighteen. The man insisted thirteen would starve his children. They settled eventually on sixteen.

When Jack was far enough away from the fence to no longer fear he was being followed, his adrenaline and initial sense of triumph became slowly infiltrated by the bitter realization that his mother's jewelry was worth perhaps fifty times what he'd sold it for. He'd just thrown away his legacy, the legacy of his children, for pennies on the dollar. This is where poverty led you. He felt suddenly angry, desperate, and for a moment thought of returning to demand the jewelry back, before he remembered that the only thing his mother took from her home was a scorpion fashioned by her driver from copper wire and sea glass. He recalled the bitterness of her father, the fermenting atmosphere of anger and pain that made that beautiful house feel more like a mausoleum than a home. He thought of that poor child who was not pretty enough to be a summer bride and would spend her life in a sweaty tent servicing construction workers. Jack had the money he needed for his wife's operation and for a future in America. What price could be placed on the freedom to be whoever you wanted to be?

Aiden stirred in his arms and settled again. Jack noticed a rash on the back of one of the boy's hands because he sucked on it. He needed to buy some binkies. He lay down on the trundle bed, cradling Aiden against his chest, a cursed feast that only made him hungrier, hollowing him out, the soft, fleshy weight of this boy. And how much more intense, he thought, must this feeling be for Dimra.

Eighteen years before, when they'd passed through immigration at O'Hare on a bright late-September day, they had been particularly hopeful for a child. After the operation to remove her adhesions, Dimra was nearly pain-free, and the surgeon said it might be years before the adhesions returned.

They were met by Dimra's cousin, Wafiq, and his slender, strawberry-blond wife, Amy. Amy took point in dealing with them, quickly netting and clubbing the heads of any questions, even those aimed at Wafiq, who remained an éminence grise wearing a smile of formal, rebuffing stiffness. Swallowed into the leather bowels of a Chevy Suburban, they were driven by Amy, Wafiq beside her in the front, to a Greek revival mansion in Wilmette, a northern suburb of Chicago. There, Jack and Dimra were briefly introduced to the squirming five-year-old Fuad, called Freddie, and prim nine-year-old Emily, before the children were led away by Nina, their live-in Ukrainian nanny.

After an early dinner, just the four of them on the terrace of an immaculate garden, Amy maintaining her role as Wafiq's vizier, they were encouraged to take a walk to the lake. They assumed Amy and Wafiq would join them, but Amy needed to supervise the children's bedtimes, and her darling Wafiq, she said, required his "decompression" time.

After Gaza and the Imbaba neighborhood, it felt as if they'd been spewed from chaotic whitewater onto a sun-dappled bank, their ears ringing with the quiet of this place. They walked beneath bright autumn trees lining the sidewalks. The massive houses—Dutch colonial beside Tudor beside French country—were fortresses of privacy with a palace guard of women vigorously marching up and down the sidewalks, alone or in pairs, some of them, for some reason, running.

They discovered that Lake Michigan was as vast as a sea, the pristine, white-sand beach all but empty.

"There's no smell," Dimra said, meaning salt. "It doesn't seem real."

On the way back, Dimra stopped at a sprawling Spanish colonial, wrapping her hands around the bars of its ten-foot wrought-iron fence, like a prisoner at her cell window, and took in the achingly green lawns, immaculate flowerbeds, and a fountain with a man-sized brass Hermes at the center.

"I want to live here," she said. "It's like being dead."

Jack would have laughed, but she wasn't being humorous, the knuckles of her small hands white with the pressure of her grip.

Dimra had always been a woman of faith, but something about Wilmette and those wealthy northern suburbs intensified her religiosity. She began to pray constantly. He found the place to be a kind of winter, a dormancy that both starved and concentrated his senses. For him, the silence and almost militant privacy of this place, with its immaculate, ersatz beauty, felt devoid of God. He remembered sensing God in moments of silence snatched from a crowded, chaotic city, looking out of the blue-framed window of the cracked white room, but here, though the silence could be intense (in the intervals between the din of landscaping crews with blowers, committed to the fairytale task of removing every dropped leaf), it was a silence where he'd suddenly feel himself falling, as in a childhood dream, into a shock of emptiness from which he woke desperately clutching to life.

Hispanic men tended to the gardens, Hispanic or Filipina women cleaned the houses, reminding Jack of day-laboring Palestinians, like his uncle, in Israel.

Amy became irritated at Dimra for cleaning, particularly after she dulled the finish on a granite sink top in one of the bathrooms by using the wrong cleaning solution. Amy didn't want her to cook either. Amy cooked with the help of a Filipina woman and was fastidious about nutritional balance and fat content. She didn't eat carbs, particularly bread. Always forcing down pint glasses of lemon water, she hurried to the bathroom dozens of times a day.

Wafiq's mother and father had come to the U.S. a decade after the Nakba. Wafiq, born here, was now a partner in a large corporate accounting firm. Wafiq would return from work at six or seven, and after a quick hello to the children, a kiss from his wife, a princely inquiry to Jack and Dimra about their day, would retreat to a small media room, where he'd slip on a pair of headphones, listen to jazz, and eat sunflower seeds. The room itself was the only messy room in the house, containing scraps from the past. The table beside his Eames lounge chair was of the type you'd find in many Middle Eastern homes, made from a ceremonial brass tray upon a stand. On the sideboard lay a scattering of gold Ottoman coins, a wooden backgammon box with elaborate marquetry, needlepoint Quranic calligraphy, and a foxed black-and-white photograph of a couple Jack assumed to be Wafiq's parents on their wedding day, wearing traditional village dress. This fading aperture into the past was the only picture of Wafiq's parents or anyone else from his Palestinian family anywhere in the house. Apart from Fuad's dark eyes, you would never have guessed Wafiq's children had any Middle Eastern blood, both possessing the same straight hair and pale skin as their mother. It was as if the past had been almost entirely washed out of Wafiq's life.

Wafiq would appear at dinner, ever maintaining his defenses, never quite meeting Jack or Dimra's eyes.

At one of these meals, Dimra asked if it might be possible for Jack to become an accountant.

"There are night classes," Wafiq said simply. Wafiq never extended his responses, no doubt fearing the doors such incontinence might risk opening.

Dimra looked at Jack hopefully. "Jamal is clever with numbers, a hard worker. He can speak—how many languages?"

Jack rested a gently restraining hand on her arm. "Just a few and some very badly."

"Your English is certainly excellent," Amy graciously conceded. She always gave the impression they were sitting beside each other on a long flight and had made the mistake of beginning a conversation.

"So," Dimra continued, undaunted, "he could go to night classes to be an accountant?"

"I'm sure Jamal could do whatever he wished," Wafiq declared generously.

"Then maybe he could work for your company," she said.

At this, Wafiq huffed out a friendly but studiously neutral chuckle.

Later that night, exploring a library at the side of the house where the books were color-coordinated, Jack heard Amy and Wafiq in the garden from the open window, Amy hissing, "When are we going to get rid of these people? I have to spend all day with that woman. She's always trying to talk to me, fussing around my kitchen."

"That's all she knows," Wafiq said, frayed insulation about a live wire, using the same rebuffing and careful neutrality with her as he used with them.

Jack took the next job he could find, manning the Fly Fresh stand in O'Hare's international terminal. Not wishing to impose upon them any longer, he accepted Wafiq's offer to lend them the deposit for a place to rent. As soon as they moved in and bought sufficient furniture, Dimra invited Wafiq and Amy to dinner. Dimra spent much more than they could afford on food and gifts for the children, and cooked for two solid days, making every traditional dish she knew. But Amy and Wafiq didn't bring the children, ate little, drank the wine they'd brought themselves, declined the cardamom-flavored coffee and handmade sweets, refused to take anything with them for the children, and left early. This was a severe blow to Dimra. They were family: wasn't family everything?

It took them five months to save enough to mail Wafiq the check for the deposit, but it wasn't cashed. Jack telephoned, leaving a message, and received a call from Amy to tell them to consider it a gift for their new life in America. The cool lack of welcome when they were staying with Amy and Wafiq had aggravated Jack's endemic shame, depressing him, but this call ignited a small flame of anger at the core of his being that seemed to feed upon his shame. He'd developed no mechanism by which to make use of anger, to focus it. Consequently, he felt constantly agitated. Finally, Jack asked Dimra to bake a tray of sweets. He withdrew the money from their account and after work took the Metra to Wilmette and walked to Amy and Wafiq's house. Amy met him at the door, hardly hiding the disappointment in her surprise at his visit. He felt like something stuck to the bottom of her Manolo Blahnik shoe. He asked to see Wafiq. She invited him in, but he refused. Wafiq finally and cautiously appeared. Jack placed the cash for the deposit into his hand, together with an extra $100 for interest. He handed the tray of sweets to Amy and said that if they didn't want them, they could throw them away.

As he closed their gate behind him, his anger slowly burned itself out, leaving him at last only with the familiar and functional discomfort of his shame.

16

When Dimra entered, Jack was almost asleep on the trundle bed. Gently scooping Aiden from his arms, she told him the food was ready and asked him to send Aisha to her when Marcia arrived for the meeting in a few minutes. Standing, he slipped his arms around her, the child between them. For the first time, it seemed to him, her eyes met his without a solicitous, anxious, or yearning question in them. More than exhausted, she looked extinguished.

Once, Jack recalled, he and Birdy had held a baby just like this between them. A flight to Denver. They were helping a woman whose infant had thrown up all over her. Birdy was holding the perpetrator, a chubby girl. As Jack cleaned the child with wet wipes and tissues, Birdy said, smiling, "Wouldn't we have an awesome baby?"

That evening, they landed in Denver during a blizzard. Later, they ventured through three feet of snow to a nearly empty all-night diner close to the hotel, sliding themselves into a booth. The diner, a '50s-style double-wide fishtank, all red vinyl and sparkling chrome, was a distinctly American lifeboat drifting in time and space. Birdy, slumped over her plate, devoured a Reuben and fries, lips glistening with grease. He went around to her and knelt.

"Are you proposing?" she said, her cheeks bulging with food.

He gently cupped her chin with his hand.

Her eyes widened.

"Birdy," he said, "you're *beautiful* and you're beautifully tall, but you're always stooping or slumping. You're going to have a widow's hump before you're thirty. And you eat as if you're terrified someone's going to snatch your food away. Your brothers aren't here."

He knew this was condescending, but it seemed to him essential to eat as if the people you were with mattered, not the food. Bread was always about communion, even when you were alone, requiring you to recognize the presence of some other, of God if you wished, with gratitude for the one who made us, in so many ways, hungry.

"You should be proud of yourself, Birdy, proud of your height, proud of your body. Eating is intensely social; and just as we don't squat down on the floor to have a shit in front of someone, we don't eat in front of them as if we're dangerously late for hibernation."

She huffed a laugh through all the food in her mouth.

After giving her a few moments to swallow, he said, "Think about it like sex. There's nothing wrong with a bit of quick, sloppy, ravenous sex sometimes, but eat in other modes also, getting to know the food, taking a little time, tasting it, bringing yourself just to that point where hunger and satiation touch."

"You're making me so wet right now," she said.

"You're *impossible*."

She put a cherry tomato between her teeth and bit down, bursting it all over her chin.

"Oh, piss off," he said as she crossed her eyes and rubbed a stale dinner roll over her boobs until it broke into crumbs.

As he removed his hand, she quickly snatched it into her own and said, only half-joking, "Jack if I cut my hair short and dress like a man, could you fall in love with me?"

"I *am* in love with you, Birdy," he said.

Returning from that trip was the first time he'd mistakenly called Dimra Birdy.

He now kissed Aiden's forehead, then his wife's.

"What's wrong?" she said.

"Nothing. I've just been thinking about how we got here."

"Here?"

"I mean Chicago. Here."

Jack glanced down at Aiden, so deep in sleep he seemed to be sinking back into the world before birth, before life, and said, "We're lucky. Aren't we lucky?"

When he looked up, she was examining him curiously, as if he were behind glass in a museum, an artifact for an arcane rite or purpose she was trying to fathom.

A loud knock, and their front door opened. Aisha, shouting for Dimra, thundered down the hallway.

The condo meeting went smoothly, for once, because he had good news to deliver. Since the mortgage crisis had collapsed the construction industry, he'd found a company who'd not only rebuild a new back deck for half last year's estimate, but would accept monthly installments. He reminded everyone, studiously avoiding Marcia's eyes, that the $3,000 special assessment was due by midnight.

That night, Jack couldn't sleep. The lees of the past stirred up in him, and he was rife with anxiety about his wife's health, her parents' survival, their own dire finances, the growing realization that he'd never be a father. This life of being no one, nowhere, would go on and on.

The next morning, he made his own coffee. For the last few weeks, Dimra had stopped waking up before him to prepare it. Even in sleep her face looked wrought with pain. And while he was glad she allowed herself to be relieved of this task, it revealed just how ill she must be. For months he'd been trying to convince her to see the doctor, but she refused. He stepped onto the deck into a salmon-pink and gunmetal-blue sunrise and took deep, smoky breaths to calm himself.

Just as the cold was penetrating too deeply for him to stay much longer, his cell vibrated.

It was Marcia. As soon as he answered, she screamed, "That bitch emailed me a fine last night for not giving her the three thousand. I put the fucking check in that box outside her door four days ago. It's the only time I've ever paid anything early, and I worked my ass off to get that money together."

It took him a while to calm her down, the anxiety recolonizing his body. He texted May to see if she was awake and a little while later entered the lush foliage and vibrant colors of her apartment.

"I didn't get her check," May said. Above her on the vast television stood a reporter at the scene of a West Side murder.

"She told me she delivered it four days ago."

"She's a liar. We need to get *rid* of her, Jack."

As he remained silent for a moment, face-to-face with his obdurate neighbor, wondering if she'd deliberately destroyed the check to stir up more trouble, something occurred to him. "May, is your son around?"

"What's that to you?" she said fiercely.

"I saw him with his girlfriend before the meeting yesterday. Are they still here?"

She shook her head.

"Did they leave last night, during the condo meeting?"

"So what?"

"I was just curious," he said, and told her he was going to talk to Marcia again.

Instead, he knocked on Gunther's door, and when Gunther opened it asked if anything was missing from his place.

"Missing?" Gunther looked perplexed, and just as he said, "What do I have to take?" seemed to realize and hurried into his bedroom.

"Oh fuck," Jack heard him shout, "fuck fuck *fuck*!"

All his artifacts were gone, the mineral samples, the prehistoric insects in amber, the twelve-million-year-old crab.

"The stone baby?" Jack said.

Gunther nodded, "But that doesn't matter," he said. "No one knows it exists. The rest of it's going to put me in jail. Those insects in amber have to be back for an exhibit in three days."

Jack guessed that Danh thought he could pawn or sell them somewhere. The amber had to be worth a decent amount. He called Lulu. On the phone he could hear her moving around her apartment, opening drawers. Her turquoise bracelet and the diamond studs she received for her quinceañera were gone. She told him to wait a second. Jack heard her opening another drawer, and then had to tip the phone away from his ear as she screamed, "No mames! Chingado! Ese drogadicto hijo de puta!" Danh had found her stash of nearly $1,000 earned for cash-in-hand massage therapy for people in Pilsen's Latino community who didn't have health insurance.

Ken discovered his small collection of antique watches missing, none crazily valuable, but all together worth close to $1,500.

Hurrying down to Marcia, Jack asked her to call the bank. She discovered that her check, made out to a woman called Emma Durant, had been cashed at a PayNow on Howard the previous day. He'd heard Danh call his girlfriend Tash while he was coming out of the basement one time, so he guessed she was using a fake ID. Danh knew when the checks were due and how long it took his mother to deposit them. No doubt he took Marcia's early check from the box outside his mother's front door. May had the keys to all the apartments, and Danh must have then slipped down to Marcia's, found her checkbook, and made one out to Emma Durant for $3,000, forging her writing and signature, knowing she had sufficient funds and wouldn't question the money disappearing from her account. Danh risked staying for the condo meeting because he knew they'd all be at Jack's apartment, avoiding only Pauline's because of Bernard.

Jack returned to May. She seemed to have already realized that her son was responsible for the missing check, her body rigid, her fists clenched, as if frozen between fight and flight.

She begged him not to call the police. Before he could answer, there was a sharp knock at her front door and Marcia burst in.

"Your drug-addict son stole my fucking money."

"I'll pay." May looked frightened. "He's on probation. He'll go to jail."

"That's where he belongs," Marcia said.

"No. He can't go to jail. No." Her eyes spilled tears and she looked frantic. Jack thought of those years she and her young son had spent incarcerated, the abuse they'd endured.

Jack told May about all the other things he stole, not mentioning that Gunther would go to jail if they called the police.

"I'll pay, I'll pay," she said. "Whatever he stole, I'll pay."

Marcia drove her advantage home: "And you'll get rid of those fines and stop fucking persecuting me?"

May nodded. He sensed with relief that Marcia also didn't want the police involved and wondered if she or Ryker had a record. It was hard, despite everything, not to feel sorry for May.

After Marcia left, he asked May to tell him where she thought her son might be. All she could tell him was where he went to his NA meeting and that his sponsor was a man called Rod.

Jack hurried to a meeting scheduled for that morning, arriving just as it was breaking up. Someone pointed him to Rod, a squat, shinily bald white man, perhaps in his sixties, who looked like a piece of gristle life had chewed and spat out. His raw-red face was so mashed you could barely see his eyes, though they still burned bright and sincere.

When Jack told him what was going on, he heaved the sigh of Sisyphus back at the base of the mountain. "I knew those two would lose their way. Been in this game long enough, I can tell when people aren't ready."

"But they were bound to get caught." Jack was trying to understand.

Rod laughed. "Ain't thinking that far ahead, chief. You ain't talking about criminal masterminds, here"—he picked up his large backpack—"them there's addicts."

"I need to find them," Jack said.

"That's for sure." Rod rummaged around in his pack. "A pair of junkies with a ton of cash ain't going to end well." He handed two boxes of naloxone to Jack. "I'm guessing they're at Tash's."

"Danh's girlfriend?"

Rod nodded. "Just lost her sister, Emma."

"Emma Durant?"

"That's her. Overdosed on the El a month ago. Other passengers just watched her nodding out. Her dead body rode the Blue Line all day." He explained that NA didn't take people's contact info, but he called Tash's sponsor, entering into a long and in moments heated conversation before scribbling an address on a torn-off piece of his cigarette packet.

As he handed it to Jack, he said, "Tash came to meetings but never said a word. Emma let it all out, though, and the shit that happened to her and Tash as kids was the worst I ever heard until Danh told me what happened to him and his mom in that Malaysian camp."

The address was a run-down blond-brick apartment building a few blocks west of Loyola, surrounding a courtyard that was a sunless patch of cracked dirt, broken toys, vials, and trash. Ancient air conditioners immured in the brick bled rusty stains down the walls. Luckily the main doorway to the apartments was propped open with a shoe, since no one answered the intercom, and he found Tash's apartment at the top of the first flight of stairs. But Jack's knocking received no reply, so he went around to the rear of the building. There he could see her back door and window, accessible via a swing-down fire escape. Standing on a dumped shopping trolly, he climbed onto the stone windowsill of the ground-floor apartment and managed to lever the fire escape down just enough to pull himself up onto it.

The window in Tash's back door looked in on a galley kitchen scattered with Chinese takeout boxes. Through the bedroom window beside it, he saw Tash lying on the bed in a Metallica T-shirt and underwear, asleep. He knocked, trying not to be too loud, terrified someone might call the police. She didn't wake. He tried to pull the sash window up, but it was painted in. The upper frame, though, had slipped down enough for him to jam his fingers into a gap at the top and rock and wrench it until it stuttered down sufficiently for him to snake himself in, tumbling to the floor.

It felt so weird being in this bedroom with an unconscious, half-naked girl. He quickly checked the other rooms. Danh wasn't here.

Then he tried to wake Tash, shaking her and softly calling her name, but she didn't respond. She looked drained of blood, even her lips pale. He checked for a pulse, and for a while couldn't find one. Calming himself, he rested two fingers gently upon the artery at her neck and finally felt it, extremely faint and slow. His hands were shaking as he followed the instructions for the naloxone, injecting one milliliter into her skinny, scarred thigh. Within a few minutes she made a noise, as if she were having a bad dream. He tapped her cheeks, calling her name. Now her breath was coming jaggedly, and her eyes slid open.

"It's okay," Jack said as she pulled herself up against the headboard.

He knew he should call an ambulance but was desperate not to involve the police.

"Can I check your pulse again?" he asked.

She didn't respond, fearful and bewildered, but also aggrieved to be conscious, perhaps even to be alive. He remembered what Rod said and didn't want to think about what she'd been through in her short life.

She let him touch her neck. Her pulse was strengthening. He noticed then that she was wearing Lulu's diamond stud earrings.

"I'm not going to call the police," he said, "but we need all the stuff back. Where's Danh?"

She shrugged.

He told her he was going to check the apartment. The small bedside cabinet was full of fentanyl patches, Vicodin, and baggies of what he guessed might be heroin, bought, no doubt with Marcia's $3,000 and Lulu's stash. At the bottom of the hallway closet, Jack discovered a good deal of what they stole from Gunther, which he put into the bags the Chinese takeout had come in. The amber, Ken's antique watches, and Lulu's bracelet were nowhere to be found.

When he returned to the bedroom, she was as he'd left her, as if paralyzed. It was cold in the apartment, so he pulled the covers around her, feeling an intimation of how exhausting it was to love—to care about—people so victimized, wounded, and fragile that it was impossible to imagine anything could ever change. She would die here, *wanted* to die here, perhaps, like her sister, carried off by those butterflies to some painless oblivion. He suddenly recalled flushing that strange, jellied, tadpole life down the toilet, and was seized briefly by the weird impulse to pick Tash up and carry her back to Dimra, as if he'd retrieved her from the sewers: *Here she is, our child*.

"I need these." He touched his earlobes.

Removing the diamond studs, she handed them to him.

"I don't want you guys going to jail. Where's the stuff you took that's not here? Where would Danh take it?"

She shrugged helplessly.

"When's he going to be back?"

The same pathetic shrug.

Jack thought for a moment and then fetched another one of the takeout bags. Returning, he sat on the bed beside Tash, opened the nightstand and filled the bag with the drugs. Suddenly Tash found the strength to protest and even reached over to try to stop him. Jack held her back. He could feel his heart harden, and was aware, even, of the slenderest tendril of pleasure in his resolution and strength, and in her desperation.

"If I don't get the other stuff you stole back, you don't get your drugs. Where would he take it?"

Just as he said this, the front door opened, and Danh walked in.

"What the fuck," Danh said, trying to look as vicious as he could, though he resembled a wet cat, and was clearly high.

"He's taking our shit," Tash mewled.

Danh glanced down at the open and empty nightstand as Jack stood up from the bed and said, "Where did you sell the stuff you stole?"

Danh charged him, catching Jack by surprise, both of them landing on top of Tash. Danh, who weighed almost nothing, was instantly shaking from the exertion, and perhaps from fear also. Jack lifted him off as if he were a child, pushing him facedown athwart Tash, who was issuing a low, keening sound. Pinning Danh with one hand, Jack rifled through his pockets, retrieving more drugs and $200 in cash. He threw everything into the bag containing the other drugs. His physical power over Danh and Tash evoked an unsettling, nearly erotic feeling that seemed to crack a thin but deep fissure. Through this fissure, a long-pressured anger surged to his surface: anger at all he'd lost and where he was in his life, the children they'd flushed down the toilet, his innocent wife's endless pain, his days spent nursemaiding refractory passengers, sleeping alone in hotel rooms. These two useless people pathetically writhing around on the bed, what did they cause but pain? How much better the world would be if they both took an overdose right now. He lifted and turned Danh over, shoving him down onto his back against Tash with a roughness that shocked Jack himself and clearly frightened Danh, who was quietly crying.

Jack lifted up the takeout bag full of their drugs and the cash. "You bring me to where you sold the stuff you stole, you'll get this back, understand?"

Danh nodded, murmuring, "You need money."

"We're picking up your mother on the way."

This didn't affect Danh in the slightest. Only one thing concerned him: "And we'll get our stuff back?"

Jack nodded.

They stopped off so May could go to the bank. Danh told them he'd sold everything for $600. May withdrew $1,100, the last of her savings, and they drove to a pawn shop in West Garfield Park between an African food and liquor store and a storefront church called God's Battle Axe Prayer Ministries. The wide boulevard had a desolate quality, many of the stores boarded up, trash everywhere.

"I'll stay in the car," Danh said.

"You're coming in." Jack wondered if he'd have to manhandle him again. Without a pawn ticket, Danh was all they had to show.

A heavyset, bearded, vaguely Middle Eastern–looking man appeared at the desk as they entered, his face as pitted as the moon.

"I need to get all that stuff back, Vartan," Danh said meekly.

"What stuff?" Vartan fixed dead, reptilian eyes on Danh.

"Look," Jack said, taking over, "I don't want to involve the police. This is Danh's mother."

"My condolences," Vartan said, his eyes remaining murderously fixed on May's son.

"You paid six hundred," Jack went on. "We'll pay you a thousand. I told his mother we'd give this a try. If you're not interested, I'll call the cops right now."

Slowly the man turned, briefly settling his eyes on Jack before glancing at May, clutching her bag to her chest. After a speculative moment, he said, "Three thousand."

"We don't have three thousand."

May dug around in her bag and threw all the cash she had on the counter. "Eleven hundred sixty-five dollars," she said desperately.

"Twenty-five hundred." Vartan insisted. "Call the cops if you want."

"Wait," Jack said. Hurrying out to the car, he retrieved the bag containing all the drugs and the rest of the money from the trunk. He put it on the counter.

"You can't give him that," Danh screamed, lunging for it. Jack pushed him back.

"Another two hundred in cash in there and at least three thousand in drugs."

Vartan didn't touch the bag for a moment, and Jack saw him scanning the outside of the store. He then surveyed them all again with those lifeless, saurian eyes, reassuring himself that they were far too pathetic to be a risk. Taking the money and the bag, ignoring Danh's sobbing insistence that it was his, he slunk into the back.

Vartan returned with a Jewel Osco shopping bag containing all the prehistoric amber, four of the five antique watches, and the bracelet.

"I gave one of the watches to my nephew for his birthday," he said.

Just over an hour later, Jack returned the artifacts to an ecstatic Gunther.

"Everything but the stone baby," Jack explained. "The pawnbroker didn't want it, so Danh threw it away."

"I don't give a shit about that. No one's looking for it. You've saved my fricking *life*." Gunther snatched him in for a bearish hug. "It's all going back tomorrow," Gunther declared, as if he were making a covenant with God. "I am a reformed man. I will never, *never* take anything again."

Jack couldn't sleep that night, lying next to his wife, whose dreams were making her whimper. He felt wired, as if the way he'd behaved with Danh and Tash had altered his body chemistry. The memory of holding Danh violently down against a softly keening Tash kept vividly returning in throbbing surges either of shame or fury; or of a darker feeling he didn't want to acknowledge writhing up from even greater depths. Close to morning, his and Marcia's bodies became slickly intertwined, and Jack startled awake from the first wet dream he'd had since he was a young teen.

= 17 =

"I think Papa's going to our old home in Skokie."
Before Pauline's frantic call, Jack had planned to spend his day off on this gorgeous May afternoon reading in Dawes Park. Micah, who ran the shoe-repair shop on Howard, had called her at work. He'd spotted her father catching the 97 bus.

Bernard's dementia had rapidly worsened. Jack had shut off the gas to Pauline's cooker, removed the stoppers from the two baths because Bernard forgot he was filling them, and drew up a schedule so he, Dimra, Lulu, and Ken could check in on Bernard while Pauline was working to make sure he was eating and safe. Despite the new signs fixed to the inside of the back and front gates—Papa, tanpri pa kite. *Father, please don't leave*—he began to wander. Usually, neighbors recognized him and led him back, or they'd find him perusing the aisles of Jewel-Osco or in Amit's corner shop on Howard, sitting on a chair next to the counter, chatting to the schoolkids buying chips and candy. Bernard carried a special phone with everyone in the building on speed dial, and his pockets held laminated sheets with his address on them. Pauline, aware this wasn't sustainable, was looking into nursing homes.

Pauline was tied up at the hospital for at least another hour. Jack told her not to worry. He'd round up a posse. She gave him their old address in Skokie.

Soon Jack was in his car with Ken and Lulu. Dimra, who was babysitting Aiden, sat vigil on the deck in case Bernard returned.

Bernard's previous house had been replaced by a Lubavitch Hebrew Day School. Jewish refugees from the Second World War once made up 60 percent of Skokie's population, and it still retained a large Jewish community. A big project was under construction there for the Illinois Holocaust Museum, slated to open in a year.

They fanned out looking for him along the bus line until Jack received a call from Pauline to tell him that an Irwin Bynes had called her. Bernard had tried to enter Irwin's house with his old key. Irwin and his wife were returning with him in a taxi. After texting Dimra, he gathered the troops and sped back.

They found Dimra, holding Aiden, waiting at the front of the building just as the taxi pulled up. The couple, who looked to be in their eighties, stepped out with a confused and distressed Bernard.

"You're home now, Bernard," Mrs. Bynes said. "This is your home. We talked to your daughter."

"I don't know why I'm here," Bernard pleaded, at the verge of tears. "I just want to go home."

"Bernard, you are *home*," Mr. Bynes seconded his wife, patting Bernard's shoulder with an arthritic hand. "*This* is your home."

Pauline's father regarded them all with fearful confusion before Dimra handed Aiden, who was chewing on a set of plastic keys, to Jack, hurried over, and hooked her arm through Bernard's. "Come, let's all have some tea," she said, asking the couple to please join them. Jack insisted he'd drive them home and, brushing off Mr. Bynes's protests, paid for the taxi.

They all sat on Pauline's deck, Lulu helping Dimra to bring down tea, coffee, and plates of cookies and savory pastries. Aiden, who was in a happy mood, delighted the couple, and Mrs. Bynes asked to hold him.

As they all sat enjoying the pastries, Bernard calmed down, glancing around him with an expression of fragile speculation. His neighbors were blank to him now, souls who might yet become anyone.

"Delicious cookies," Mr. Bynes said.

"My daughter," Bernard gestured proudly toward Dimra. "And my grandchild." At last, he'd begun to assign them an identity, anchoring himself.

"You have a lovely family, Bernard," Mrs. Bynes said, dangling the plastic keys above the transfixed baby in her arms.

An hour later, Jack drove the Byneses home, Mrs. Bynes beside him, Mr. Bynes in the back seat.

"You have an adorable son," Mrs. Bynes said. "I wanted to steal him."

"He's our neighbor's son," Jack said. "My wife's babysitting."

"You have children?" she asked.

"Unfortunately, we . . ." he stammered, "haven't been blessed in that way."

She nodded. "Do you have family here?"

He shook his head.

"Your parents?"

"They've passed," he said, wondering if his baba was still alive.

"And where are you from?"

He was about to say Egypt, but felt suddenly tired of lying, "Gaza."

Mrs. Bynes filled the momentary vacuum of silence: "We pray every day for peace in the Holy Land."

Jack smiled at her. "I think I've given up praying."

She patted his knee. "Never give up, my boy."

Jack asked if they had children.

"We have a son, Ezra," she said.

"Here in Chicago?"

"No."

The silence extended again until Mr. Bynes spoke up from the back. "He's missing."

"Missing?"

"He went to Nepal to hike the Annapurna trail," Mrs. Bynes said. "This is more than thirty-five years ago now. He was a world traveler, couldn't get enough of different people and cultures; he went everywhere."

Jack nodded.

Mr. Bynes added, "No one knows what happened to him. People can get lost in those mountains."

"I'm so sorry."

"We used to go every year," she said.

"To Nepal?"

She nodded. "Still, Jack, you know, when anyone rings our doorbell or knocks, I often think it's Ezra. Today, when Bernard knocked, I don't know why, but I was just sure it was him. I got chills; I became scared and happy." She laughed.

"I'm sorry," he said again.

She tapped his leg with her old hand. "Don't be sorry. When I was there among all of you, your lovely wife, all those people from such different places, together, I felt Ezra had led us there. I felt his presence."

Jack saw Mr. Bynes's hand come to rest on his wife's shoulder, perhaps to calm her.

"And here you are, Jack," she said, "driving us home."

They'd arrived. He helped them out. Mr. Bynes was such a contrast to his wife. While she was aglow, her eyes glistening with intense emotion, he seemed weary of his wife's hope, the light of faith dim in his eyes.

"You're very welcome to visit us any time," Jack said.

"Thank you," Mr. Bynes said. "And thank your wife for her hospitality. You're very lucky in your choice of wife."

He agreed that he was.

After Mr. Bynes shook his hand, Mrs. Bynes embraced him emphatically and Jack found himself as emotional as she was, suddenly clutching to her as she did to him until each released the other to rejoin the life to which they'd been assigned.

18

As Chicago's festive, muscular summer began, Dimra's stomach and shoulder pain worsened. She suffered from abdominal pain, nausea, and either constipation or diarrhea. She was also losing weight because eating was making her uncomfortable. Jack finally managed to convince her to get checked out by a doctor.

He accompanied Dimra during her appointments because her English broke down when she was stressed. He sensed that her hijab caused doctors to assume she was unfulfilled, unhappy, and attention-seeking. Their GP, Dr. Papadakis, was a leonine Greek American man in his fifties who always looked hungover. When Dimra related her symptoms, his eyes became glazed, and following a quick examination he diagnosed her shoulder issue as bursitis. After Dimra stepped out to provide a urine sample, Papadakis, speaking to Jack in the manner of a mechanic explaining what Jack could do to eke a few more years from his junker of a car, told him that the best word for his wife was "neurasthenic." He prescribed Lexapro and suggested she volunteer somewhere so she could feel useful.

A few weeks later they secured an appointment with Dr. Pandit, Dimra's gynecologist. An Indian woman full of impatient, heroic bustle, she mustered even less respect for Dimra, speaking solely to Jack, as if he were the one in charge of his wife's body and treatment. Jack was called back to the examination room after barely ten minutes, Dr. Pandit hurriedly typing up her notes while confirming that Dimra's stomach pain derived from her endometriosis. When Dimra dared assert herself, inquiring about her exhaustion and nausea, Dr. Pandit became angry, snapping, "You have chronic endometriosis. Period. You've had it all your life. You want me to tell you you have something else?" Turning back to Jack, she suggested surgery to remove excess tissue, and then asked Jack, as if Dimra wasn't sitting right beside him, to convince his wife to undergo a hysterectomy for a more permanent solution.

Jack begged Dimra to have the surgery to alleviate her pain, but she refused. They would have had to pay a few thousand out of pocket, and she wanted to send everything she could to her parents.

Jack noticed areas of their apartment becoming dusty, even dirty. Dimra was forgetting key spices in her cooking, and ate little herself, since food made her uncomfortable. She suffered spasms of pain so intense she'd have to support herself against the wall or the kitchen counter with her eyes tight shut.

One lazy Sunday morning, lying in bed together, Dimra said she was sorry she couldn't be a good wife to him. She touched him tentatively on his thigh and suggested she help him. He told her he was fine. He kissed her lips, and then, gently, her neck and chest, careful not to go too far, since it would only frustrate them both. Without the energy to adhere to the Sunan Al-Fitrah, she'd let the hair under her arms and between her legs grow back, which he much preferred, and for the first time he could smell her body.

They spent a lot of time like this, lying quietly together in bed, smoothing each other's naked bodies with tender, sculptural hands.

"You know what I was thinking about today?" she said.

He was gently combing her hair out of her face with his fingers.

"This tissue." She touched her belly.

"The endometrial tissue?"

She nodded. "It's like every part of me wants to be a womb. And because of that somehow, because I want it so much, because my body wants it so much"—she paused, sinking away from him for a while before resurfacing to declare with desperate intensity—"it doesn't make sense, to be barren because you're too full of what gives life."

His phone began to ring on the dresser beside the bed. It was Gunther, who rarely called.

"Hey, Jack," Gunther said. "Look, I don't want to be in anyone's business, but you know what these apartments are like. Lulu's been crying for about six hours. I mean *really* crying, like a baby. She was throwing up as well. Throwing up *while* she was crying."

Valeria. It had to be. She'd completed her move into her duplex in Hyde Park yesterday. Jack felt a little filament of hatred ignite in him at just how coldly and efficiently that woman had made use of Lulu.

He and his wife dressed. Jack called Lulu and when she didn't answer, texted that Dimra was at her front door with Lulu's favorite ma'amoul cookies.

He waited inside his door until he heard Lulu's door open, a gush of sobs, and his wife's soft "Habibti, habibti."

A few days later, Jack helped Pauline move her father into a memory-care facility in Uptown. Bernard no longer knew her. When Jack visited with Dimra, Bernard's canny charm would reassert itself at first, but increasingly faded into a kind of catatonia, disturbed only periodically by small, troubling impulses, dust devils gathering out of his past, swirling in his mind, sometimes sending him marching through the facility's hallways toward people and destinations known not even to himself. A kindly nurse would quickly intercept, appeasing him until that willful dust settled and the nurse could lead him back to his small bedroom, where a television softly played old musicals on a loop. Just weeks after he entered the facility, he contracted pneumonia and died. None of the signs in the condominium were removed for a long time: *Papa, please don't leave!*

19

Emergency! Flood!

The text was from Marcia. Jack was driving home from the airport on a scorching July afternoon. Terrified by images of another ejector-pump disaster, he floored his poor old Honda.

Marcia's door opened the moment he knocked. Wearing a camo tank top and olive-green cargo pants, she resembled a guerilla leader. Glancing with confusion at his luggage, she snapped with a harshness that didn't bode well. "Are you moving in?"

"Your text sounded—"

Without waiting for him to finish, she hurried inside and he followed.

A pile of soaked towels lay on the floor in front of her flooded dishwasher. "Look at this shit. Is it ever going to fucking *end*?"

Glancing around, he saw she hadn't painted the drywall he took his entire day off to replace after the ejector-pump flood; carpet remnants still covered the damaged floor. He guessed Aisha and Aiden were with his wife.

"Can't you sort out the plumbing in this shithole? Isn't that what I fucking pay you for?" She was screaming into his face, her nose almost touching his. "I've got a full-time job and two fucking kids. I don't have time to deal with this shit. I put the dishwasher on before I left for work and look at my fucking floors."

The cheap, engineered-wood flooring had turned white, curling away from the raw-concrete subfloor upon which it had been laid with no moisture barrier.

She began to poke him in the chest repeatedly with a sharply manicured fingernail. "How come you guys up in your apartments don't have to deal with any of this? Shit flows downhill in this building and right into my *fucking* home. I'm going to get a lawyer and sue all of you for discrimination." The poking in his chest was painful. When he tried to gently push her hand away, she clutched angrily to his fingers. "I went to the alderman's office yesterday and—"

"*Stop* shouting at me," he cut her off with quiet fury. "I am *not* your landlord. I'm *not* your fucking maintenance man. I'm *sick* of having to deal with this. I have a job too. I have to pay my fucking underwater mortgage just like you. I get paid *nothing* for responding to these abusive, angry texts from you and everyone else in this shitty building. My wife looks after your children. Bizarre as it might seem to you, I have my own *life*. I do every fucking thing in this place and not once has anyone thanked me. All I get is . . . *people*" (he'd been about to say assholes) "like you screaming in my fucking face."

For a fraction of a second, it looked as if she were about to tear back into him, her eyes widening with fury, but all at once her rage drained and she became human again, looking at him as if she were actually seeing him for the first time. Still clutching the fingers of his right hand in the space between their chests, she now raised her other hand to take hold of his in both of hers, as if in supplication.

"Jack" she said. "I thank God every day that you're in this building. I thank God *every* day."

Her anger drained further, and she looked despairing, releasing his hands. They were almost chest to chest, both breathing hard, his heart pounding with the emotion of his own outburst.

He gently placed one hand upon the face of her Día de los Muertos beauty, the other over her rose-entwined dagger, and it seemed the most natural thing in the world, after the kind of fight he never had with his wife, for them to kiss; to do so gently at first, as if in a kind of mutual assuagement and sympathy, as if they were kissing a place on a child's body that was hurt.

Afterward they sat naked together on her bare mattress sharing a cigarette, the sheets tugged free and on the floor following their frenzied coupling. Jack was appalled, his thoughts unable to cohere. And yet the sex had brought him back, if briefly, to the joyous releases of the white room.

She had returned to equilibrium, her anger no longer cornered and desperate, but redistributed evenly through her long, pale, muscular limbs, gathering its strength.

She seemed absorbed in thoughts of her own, but then asked him, "What was your first sexual experience?"

"You tell me yours first," he said, still trying to think about what he'd done, or perhaps just stop thinking.

Handing him the cigarette, she leaned over her knees to rub her shins, and said, "Well this isn't sexual, exactly. Erotic, I suppose. When I was thirteen, my mom had this handsome Hispanic boyfriend who smelled of Old Spice and wore these really fancy leather cowboy boots. And one time while he and my mom were asleep, I took one of his boots, rubbed Old Spice all over it, brought it to bed, and had a fine old time."

"With a boot soaked in aftershave?"

"It was lot sexier than most of the men I've known. What about you?"

He went blank for a moment, taking a drag and handing the

cigarette back, thinking about everything he couldn't tell her, but then remembered.

"One time, my cousin, Salim, and I were walking down one of the narrow alleys of the camp, Beach Camp, where I grew up."

"Why do you call it a camp?"

"It was a refugee camp."

"Refugees? From where?"

"From, well, *there*." He laughed at the absurdity of it. "It's a long story, habibti."

"What does that mean, 'habibti'?"

He shrugged. "My dear, my darling."

"I can call you habibti?"

"Yes. Well, no, you call me habibi, but . . ." though he wanted to ask her not to, it seemed rude. "Are you interested in my story?"

"Of course," she said, "*habibi*."

He was glad, at least, for her mocking tone.

"So, this young woman, she suddenly runs out of one of the houses. When I say houses, they're more like breezeblock shacks with tin roofs. Anyway, she came screaming out into this narrow alley on fire—"

"On fire?"

"Gaza's a poor place, so a lot of things for sale in the markets is stuff no one else wants or that's illegal to sell anywhere else. There were these acrylic-cotton mix dresses imported from India that were banned there because they were notorious for going up in flames.

"I'm guessing her dress had caught on her kerosine burner, so she ran out, screaming, right in front of me and Salim. Then her husband runs out after her, tackles her to the ground, rolling over her and tearing the dress away because it's sticking to her skin. You could smell her burnt skin and charred acrylic. And a woman who'd seen it from another house rushes out with a basin of soapy water she'd been washing clothes in and flung it, covering them in this kind of slick, soapy afterbirth. I'll never forget it. It was . . . I mean it was *awful*, but it was also"—he could feel the heat in his face—"erotic: they were both out of breath, moaning, and her naked body was covered in these blackened shreds, like a half-shed skin. So, there it is, my first erotic experience: a woman on fire."

"Well, that beats my Old Spice–soaked cowboy boot." She was staring at him curiously with a smile that was, if reluctantly, impressed. "God, I thought the place I grew up in was rough."

She gave Jack the last drag of the cigarette, and as he leaned over her knees to put it out in the cup, he said, "There was plenty of joy in Gaza too. But even as a little boy I always felt that human life was . . . tragic, I suppose. But I was never cynical. I hate cynicism. I feel the miracle of life often, feel awe, which I suppose is a kind of faith. But some people are made, as my mother once said, to sing at the wedding, others at the funeral."

Shaking her head with a skeptical look, she said, "You're so fucking weird."

They were quiet again for a moment. She sat with her wrists draped over her knees like a war chief at a tribal meeting. He recalled the edge of violence in their sex as she resisted his search for tenderness.

"When Dimra brought Aisha back down to me yesterday," she said, "Aisha wouldn't let go of her, and kept saying, 'Mommy, Mommy, Mommy.' To Dimra. She won't eat the food I make her. And do you know what that fucking asshole, Ryker, did yesterday—"

Turning toward her, Jack pressed his hand gently on her chest, just above her breasts, saying, "I wish you could stop being so angry."

Knocking his hand aside, she stood and shouted, "Don't fucking tell me what I should feel."

Jack touched his finger to his lips, pointing into the ceiling.

"You don't think I know when Ken's upstairs. I can hear him fart."

Slipping her clothes back on, she left the bedroom. Quickly dressing, he followed her.

She'd turned on the kettle to make coffee.

He looked inside the dishwasher. Wincing at the rancid smell, he reached into the flooded base and removed the filter.

"This is your problem." He hurried the dripping filter to the sink. "Your filter."

"My what?"

"You need to clean it every couple weeks."

"Fuck. Why didn't I know that?"

After running hot water over the food-and-grease-choked filter, he scrubbed it with her dish sponge.

She put a restraining hand on his arm, her red face expressing something between irritation and embarrassment. "You don't have to clean it. Just show me what to do."

"I'm *showing* you." He continued to clean the filter before demonstrating how to reinstall and remove it.

"I'm sorry about your floor," he said.

She responded with quiet anger at herself. "You mean you're sorry I'm too fucking dumb to know a dishwasher has a filter."

They were standing close again, face-to-face, and he could feel desire intensifying; he needed to go.

Sighing, she said, "I've never had a dishwasher."

He nodded, picking up his suitcase. As he walked toward the door, she called, "Jack." He turned back. "You know I didn't fuck you so you'd fix my dishwasher."

As he walked upstairs, he realized that he'd have to bring Aisha and Aiden back down. His wife was finding it hard to carry the children because of her bad shoulder.

The shift was jarring between Marcia's dark, faintly mephitic basement and his own warm, sun-lanced great room smelling of fresh-baked cookies. Equally jarring was the glance Dimra gave him the moment he entered. Aisha was reading *Six-Dinner Sid* to his wife, the two of them cuddled up on the couch, Aiden asleep in his carrycot on the carpet. Dimra always looked a little troubled now, a permanent pinch between her eyebrows from her constant pain, but this glance seemed anguished, and for a scalp-tingling moment he felt sure she knew what had just happened between him and Marcia.

She said, "I thought your flight arrived two hours ago."

"Yes, Marcia had an issue with her dishwasher. It flooded. I'm sorry, I should have texted you. I'll take the children down."

Still that look, searching and tortured.

Normally, he would have cast back a questioning glance, but he just busied himself with the children.

"I'll help you," she said, lifting Aisha off her onto the floor with obvious difficulty as she stood.

"No, no, it's easy to carry them both."

Now her glance took on another dimension, as if she were aware suddenly that something was wrong with him. She was so intuitive about him it was terrifying, reading every nuance of his voice and manner with native fluency. He felt entangled in the delicate tentacles of her sensibility. He hoped she merely assumed he was upset by Marcia's usual abrasiveness.

"Aisha and I have made dinner, haven't we, habibti."

Aisha nodded and then raised her arms, calling "Up, up." Dimra lifted her onto her hip with a stifled flinch of pain. Aisha's jealousy about the baby had made her regress. She spoke in baby language and insisted on being carried everywhere.

"You've been smoking," Dimra said.

"Yes, I'm sorry."

Aisha, squeezing and poking at his wife's cheeks with her plump little hands, said, "I don't want to go."

"Your mommy's waiting for you," Dimra said.

Suddenly Aisha clamped her arms violently around Dimra's neck.

"Habibti, that's hurting me," Dimra cried, flinching even more intensely with the pain.

It took Jack and Dimra a long while to unhook Aisha. Finally, Jack settled the now-grumpy little girl on his hip and lifted the baby's chair.

He knocked on Marcia's back door and when Marcia opened it, her expression hard and distant as ever, he managed a meek "Special delivery."

He lowered Aisha to the floor and as she entered, the little girl said huffily, "It *stinks* in here," causing a tiny surge of pained humiliation to redden Marcia's cheeks before she was rescued, as ever, by her anger, snatching the baby chair from Jack and slamming the door.

= 20 =

Jack ascended the back stairs with a heavy gait. His whole life was a lie. As he arrived at his door, he hesitated, turning around to face his small slice of the city, the Metra rattling downtown, the airplanes circulating to and from O'Hare and Midway like illuminated prayer beads. Feeling like a condemned man, he was desperate for a last cigarette, but didn't want Dimra to wonder where he'd been again.

The viscous dread pooling in his chest vitrified to shards about his heart and lungs when he found Dimra weeping on the couch. He was sure now she knew. He sat next to his wife, not venturing to touch her. Then she slumped her body against his, and sobbed, "Baba is dead."

Her mother had called to tell her just after Dimra received the text from Jack that his plane had landed, but Dimra didn't want to upset Aisha. Wrapping his arms around her, Jack thought about that heavy, sad man, who existed in Jack's consciousness as little more than an ironic counterpoint to his wife's lamentations.

"I need to be with my mother," she said.

Though a bolt of cold fear sliced through him at the thought of returning to Gaza, he responded evenly, "I'll arrange our flights," and kissed Dimra's forehead. With what had just happened with Marcia, everything—his calm voice, this Judas kiss—felt like a performance, at once meaningless and melodramatic.

Jack found a flight leaving late the next day and arranged for time off.

That night, as Jack lay in bed performing the act of reading in a bedroom that felt as alien to him as the world must have seemed to Bernard with his dementia, his wife called Jack into the bathroom.

He found her sitting naked at the edge of the bath in the dark, having failed to pull her nightdress over her head. Jack kept forgetting to install lower-wattage bulbs into the four lamps above the double sink, and they rarely turned on those blazing, unflattering lights.

"Will you help me?" she asked. "I can't move my shoulder very well."

"I think it's inside out." He slid it off her arms. "We need to get you back into physical therapy."

Dimra had stopped going because even with insurance it was too expensive, and her bursitis hadn't improved.

Trying to find the label on the nightdress, he flicked on the bathroom light and was shocked by the sight of his wife in that unforgiving glare, her face distorted by pain, her eyes bruised with sleeplessness, ridges of bone surfacing between her shrinking breasts, a belly so swollen with endometrial tissue she looked five months pregnant, this bulge rapidly tapering to matchstick legs. Food triggered her pain, and he guessed she was eating too little, particularly when he wasn't around.

"Let's go into the bedroom," he suggested. The softer light allowed her to appear just a little thin and bloated, though the suffering brutally evident in her face filled him with a vertiginous feeling, all the time she'd spent alone in this apartment yawning wide as a canyon in his imagination. Overwhelmed with love, regret, and sorrow, he lowered himself to his knees, kissing her legs as she regarded him with anxious curiosity, and stated simply, "You're in pain."

"Once they cut out this tissue, I'll be fine," she said.

"So you'll have the surgery?"

She nodded. "And then we can try again, Jamal. We *need* to try again."

No doubt it was her father's death that made her want this.

She cried out as he lifted her arm to slip her nightgown over it.

"W'allaw," he said, "what could you have done to it?"

She shook her head. "Maybe I lifted Aisha up too quickly."

"You need to sleep. We have sixteen hours on a plane tomorrow."

Jack wondered if his baba were still alive. In the fishbowl of Gaza, Salim and his father would soon know he was there. And what about the people who believed Jack responsible for the shaming and arrest of their family members? He also remembered how adamant Dimra's father was that she never return.

He helped his wife into bed, and while he brushed his teeth he could hear her crying softly and murmuring, "Baba, Baba."

As he returned to bed, he heard the buzz of a text. May.

> Has she lost ANOTHER baby!?

It sickened him to imagine May sitting directly beneath them on her own bed, listening. Switching his phone off, he slipped in beside Dimra, holding her as she convulsed with tears. Finally she calmed. Her eyes were still open, and after a long while, she said, "My baba forgave me. He shouldn't have, but he did. I don't think my mother can. It's why she has to show me how much she's suffering, so I can never forget."

Jack was confused. "You mean he forgave you for leaving them?"

She remained quiet for so long, it surprised him when she spoke again. "Shabak knew my brother was involved in armed resistance, but never had any real evidence. When they threw Nafiz in jail for whatever trumped-up charge, it only made him more popular. He never worked. Expected Baba to support him. Nafiz even picked out a husband for me, a man high up in the resistance; a father figure for him. Nafiz thought Baba was weak and a coward; said so to his face. Said he wanted my children to be the children of a true Palestinian hero. I didn't like this man. I was to be his second wife. He was old and ugly, and seemed very cold. Because of my brother, it became a regular thing for Shabak officers to break into our house with soldiers, tell us they were looking for weapons as an excuse to smash up everything; to terrorize my mother. And she was frightened of her own son. Then the Israelis destroyed Baba's business. He ran a cooperative sewing shop making clothes for export to Israel. They held up his goods at the border, intimidated his workers, fined him for violations in his workplace, and convinced his Jewish customers to drop him. They were destroying our lives because of Nafiz.

"When I was out shopping one day, a patrol appeared and arrested me. They said I'd slapped a soldier. At the jail, female officers strip-searched me. They laughed at me. Said I stank like an animal. They kept me awake. They put me in a cell without water and I became so thirsty I was going to drink the water in the toilet. A Shabak officer later interrogated me, a big man with a mustache who called himself the Jackal. They were looking for my brother, but I didn't know where he was. They wanted me to give them information about him and his comrades. At one point a man entered wearing a hood with holes for eyes, a collaborator, they said. They told me they wouldn't touch a filthy, ugly girl like me themselves, but this man was going to rape me and they were going to film it so everyone in Gaza would know. What could I tell them? I didn't know anything. But there was one young Shabak officer, Danny. He stopped the collaborator from raping me, shouting at the Jackal. He brought me water. He gave me ointment for my wrists, from where they tied me too tight. He sat in my cell and talked to me about how he longed for peace between the Israelis and Palestinians, or just about ordinary things, how his parents were always badgering him to get married, or about his trips to Europe. He told me he'd love to take me one day. But always the Jackal would take over again, and my life would be hell for a while. Danny told me that a grenade thrown into a settler's house had murdered a mother and two children, and a recent ambush of an IDF patrol killed two soldiers. They knew my brother and his group were responsible, and his superior officers would go to any length to bring these killers to justice.

"Danny began to talk about his life, his feelings. I'd never heard anyone speak like this. He encouraged me to talk. I told him about the arranged marriage. He told me I was the kind of beautiful girl most men could only dream of marrying. He told me that people like my brother and the Jackal were the ones who prevented peace. I remember him taking my hands and saying, 'Look at us. There can be peace, love even, but then someone like your brother gets some poor kid to throw a grenade into a house, and it all goes to hell.'" She hesitated again. "I can still see his eyes. The same brown as an almond, with flecks of gold in them. He was the first man whose eyes I ever dared look into; and when I did, I couldn't stop looking. He had beautiful hair, too, thick and dark blond." She was silent for a moment. "I think I fell in love with him. Or something. I don't know. It was so strange to be in that awful place, to not know if Danny or the Jackal would come through the door. And when it was him, I felt more joy than I'd ever felt in my life.

"Finally, they let me go. All I could think about was Danny. He came to my cell the night before I left, gave me his number—his private number, he said—and begged me to let him know if my brother or his comrades were going to cause any more trouble. He embraced me and told me we needed to find our way to peace so that people like us could be free from all those who wanted to destroy love. He kissed my forehead.

"My brother would enter our house through a fake water tank on the roof with a door in the bottom. I'd come in, and there he'd be, my poor mother scraping together what she could to feed him; Baba giving him whatever money he could spare. Nafiz was going ahead with my marriage. I protested. When Baba also protested, my brother punched him, knocking him down. Baba is a very gentle man. I *hated* Nafiz. One day he came in with a new recruit, just a boy who seemed to idolize my brother. I heard him showing off to this boy, talking about an arms shipment his group were bringing through one of the new tunnels the next evening. So I called Danny from a payphone. I told him all I'd heard, the time and place, and who was involved.

"The IDF ambushed them; killed or arrested everyone. My brother was still at home. Though I'd told Danny this, they didn't break in and arrest him. Instead, a few days later, Palestinian resistance fighters arrived in the night through the secret door wearing balaclavas. They said they were rescuing him. My brother and the young boy went with them. A week later, Nafiz's naked body was found on a garbage heap. They'd broken out all his teeth, castrated him; carved 'traitor' into his flesh. The Israelis had used collaborators to spread rumors that my brother betrayed the resistance. The body of that poor young boy was with him. I'd killed him too." She hesitated. "I'd done it just to hear Danny's voice again.

"Baba knew something was wrong with me, and one day got me alone and asked. I told him everything. He told Mama because he had to convince her to marry me to you; someone who was leaving Gaza. 'If you can't have a marriage made in heaven,' he told me, 'then what choice do you have but one made in hell?' He knew Shabak might try to blackmail us into more collaboration, despite us being shunned. He knew the resistance might find out what I'd done. He knew no one now would marry me."

"Sounds like I was quite a prize." Jack was trying to be funny but felt almost dizzy with shock at these revelations, kept from him for all these years.

She put her hand gently on his cheek, staring into his eyes, as he could imagine her once, thrilled at her own lack of shame, staring into Danny's.

"How could I ever have been luckier?" she said. "Is there a better man in the world?"

= 21 =

Dimra had finally closed her eyes. Jack couldn't sleep, his mind chaotically kaleidoscopic: images of Marcia's strong, slender body wrapped around his; of Dimra's father's besieged life in Gaza; of Dimra in that filthy cell waiting for Danny to fill her teenage heart with love. He examined Dimra's face, anxious even in sleep. What a fool he was to believe anyone could have emerged innocent from that world. It appalled Jack how important his wife's innocence had been to him. He'd always craved innocence. Was that why he'd been so drawn to Birdy? He thought of Georges. When did he first meet him? Six, seven years ago? It was nearly a year after Birdy's abortion and breakup with Nick. They were returning to Chicago from Dallas and Birdy told Jack she wanted him to meet her new boyfriend, who was picking her up at O'Hare to whisk her off to Door County for the weekend.

"He's Lebanese," she said, "a Maronite, which I guess is a kind of Christian, and I'm *crazy* about him."

Jack followed her to the Starbucks at arrivals, where Georges El Khouri waited. He kissed her cheeks. When he shook Jack's hand, Jack could see Georges quickly repressing how unsettled he was, as was Jack, by something Birdy seemed oblivious to: they were doppelgängers. The same height and slenderness, the same thick, wavy hair, the same large, slender nose, the same somewhat delicate wrists and strong, oversized hands. The difference was that one of Georges's delicate wrists displayed a Patek Philippe watch. Behind his gracious, transactional smile, Georges seemed, to Jack, to be assessing him for weakness and advantage, and upon him Jack projected, unfairly perhaps, a particularly Lebanese type: a mercantile core within European elegance supercharged with Arabic hospitality. Manicured and coiffed, he oozed a cosmopolitan slickness. Jack could see it all: the Ottoman-era mansion in Achrafieh; the stone family home in an idyllic town in the Chouf surrounded by snowcapped peaks; a beautiful, pale-skinned and Europeanized family speaking French as they dined in the mottled sunlight beneath grape arbors. The world of the Lebanese wealthy before the war. The Maronites might say, before the Palestinian influxes of '48, '67, and '70. Georges held Jack's hand for too long, telling him that Krysta never stopped singing his praises and what a pleasure it was finally to meet him. Jack felt light-headed with jealousy.

Georges bought them coffees, and despite them insisting they didn't want anything to eat, a plate of every pastry Starbucks had to offer. He owned three Lebanese restaurants in Chicago and its suburbs and was about to open a fourth in the Loop. He kept touching Birdy's arm possessively, and Birdy, this towering Junoesque blonde, had never looked more captivating. Jack was no Professor Higgins, but for better or worse, just as Jack's mother once smoothed the rough Gazan streets out of her son, he'd helped Birdy suppress her clumsy, cubbish essence to deport herself more elegantly. She was also educating herself, devouring the novels he suggested (most recently *The House of Mirth*) and talking about them with increasing sophistication.

When Birdy went to the bathroom, Georges spoke to Jack in his singsong upper-class Beiruti Arabic.

"I have a cousin in Cairo. Where did you live?"

"In Dokki, near Abd al-Salam Arif Street," he lied. This was near one of the hotels where he'd often started tours. He could hardly tell him he lived in the Imbaba neighborhood with his wife.

"Almost in Giza," Georges said to show how well he knew the city.

"Almost." Jack let the silence swell.

"She told me you liked to swim in the sea with your friend."

Jack felt exposed, a slender filament of annoyance beginning to burn in his head as he realized how much Birdy had told Georges, and that he was being tested. "The Nile. She misunderstood."

Georges sat back, widening his legs and narrowing his eyes with a forensic glance: the body language of a man assuming control.

"I adore Krysta," Georges ventured, "but don't you find it shocking sometimes how ignorant Americans can be?"

Not wanting to concede anything to this man, Jack said, "There are ignorant people everywhere, but Americans have power, so their ignorance can be especially destructive."

Georges nodded vaguely, as if he weren't really listening to Jack's responses, at least not to their specifics. "You have an interesting accent."

Though Jack was trying to keep his accent middle-class Egyptian, he wondered if he'd slipped into the Gazan Arabic he used with his wife, or the "bumpkin" accent, often mocked on Egyptian television, of the Sa'idi people of his old neighborhood. "I don't speak Arabic too much anymore."

Georges nodded in that same abstracted way. "In Egypt, I understand, there's no law against..." He gestured toward Jack, as if that were sufficient.

"No written law," Jack said, and before Georges could continue his investigation, asked, "How did you end up in Chicago?"

"My brother attended the GSB at the University of Chicago and married an American. We had a hotel and restaurants in Beirut, but the civil war left them in pieces. And then I lost my wife and three-year-old son to a"—he hesitated—"leftist shell. Leveled my home while I was picking up our visas for America."

"I'm sorry," Jack said, though he couldn't feel it, recalling images of the carnage in Karantina and Tel al-Zaatar early in the civil war, and the bloated, fly-wreathed bodies of Sabra and Shatila during the Maronite collaboration with Israel in '82. How sad and bizarre, he realized suddenly, that his irrational hatred of this urbane Maronite should make him feel truly Palestinian for the first time in his life.

"You'd never think of returning now the war's over?"

"Over?" Georges laughed. "With cancer you can have a remission, a few good days, even years, here and there, but it's always going to return. Always. My beautiful country has suffered from a cancer for forty-four years and now . . . now it's everywhere."

They stared at each other for a tense moment before Birdy appeared, fresh and flushed, smiling and smelling of municipal soap. Instead of sitting back beside Georges, she sat next to Jack, clutching his arm and pressing her head affectionately against his. "Now," she declared, "the two of you must be the *best* of friends."

Jack and Georges found respite from each other by turning their eyes to her lovely face.

"What?" she inquired innocently, smiling. Neither spoke, and glancing back and forth between them, she repeated with more intensity, "What?" And the three of them, for some reason, began to laugh.

A few months later, working a flight to Vancouver, Jack and Birdy sneaking a snack in the galley of a 757, she asked with a frown, "What's a Palestinian?" And then, "Why are you laughing?"

He shrugged. "I'll try to find a good book to explain it to you. Why do you want to know?"

"Georges and his mother *hate* them."

He nodded, said nothing.

"No more English," she insisted, switching to Arabic to tell him that the setting red sun outside the window was the same color as his tired eyes. He thanked her, laughing, and said that the fluffy clouds beneath it were of the same consistency as her brain.

When she'd asked him the day after that first tense meeting with Georges to teach her Arabic, intending to surprise Georges and his mother when she was proficient enough to converse fluently, he replied, with a sarcasm she didn't understand, that she'd be better off learning French. He then, with equal peevishness, toyed with the idea of teaching her to speak Arabic with a thick Palestinian accent. He wouldn't do that, of course, but didn't think he'd have to do much of anything. Yet, like everyone in Birdy's life, he'd underestimated her, and was astonished by how diligently she studied and how quickly she picked up the language. This revelation of how much her relationship with Georges meant to her saddened him. It also made Jack feel exposed, as if she were levering open that tightly sealed entrance to his own past. Having Birdy speaking to him in Arabic, just as his wife did, playfully calling him habibi, often shifted him into that dissociated dream state that seemed his true world, Birdy an ectopic love curled ever more tightly about his heart, twin to his embryonic wife, who was always waiting, within those strangled chambers, for her life to begin.

Birdy often stayed with Georges now at his brownstone in Lincoln Park. His mother, Roselle, occupied a self-contained apartment at the back, and Birdy began to piece together Roselle's conversations with visiting Lebanese women, often relating remembered fragments or words for Jack to translate. If Birdy was present without Georges, Roselle, ever basting Birdy with her sickly smile, would tell these women in Arabic that this was the American girl her son was wasting his time with, a donkey with no degree, whose job was to serve and clean up after people on airplanes. She'd say that when she first met Birdy, she thought this giant was a man dressed as a woman.

Just recently Georges was teaching Birdy to make baba ghanoush in his kitchen, roasting the eggplant on the gas stove's burner, his mother looking on with twitchy annoyance as Georges ignored her Arabic comments that American girls could never learn how to cook. He spooned the baba ghanoush into a beautiful hand-painted bowl, releasing it a fraction too soon as he handed it to Birdy so it slipped out of her grasp and smashed on the floor. Though his mother pretended to be as sweet as ever, telling her not to worry, Roselle said to her son in Arabic that if he wanted to play around with this stupid, fat American whore, he should have the decency not to bring her home. Birdy was at the verge of blowing her cover to use some of the choice Arabic insults Jack had taught her when Georges, helping Birdy clean up the mess, told his mother in Arabic that the only whore in this room was the one who'd given birth to him, and that if she ever insulted Krysta again, she could pack her bags and, as far as he was concerned, go to hell.

Underestimating Birdy again, Jack had never believed Georges could be serious about her until Birdy ran up to him in O'Hare's Terminal 2 flight-assistant lounge to show him her engagement ring set with an enormous diamond. She flung her arms around him, sobbing, his own face, which Birdy couldn't see, so stricken that a couple of the girls rushed over with concern, assuming Birdy had received bad news.

Georges flew Birdy and her family to Lebanon for a formal engagement party, and Jack couldn't imagine it would seem any stranger to Birdy's family if she were marrying a djinn who lived in a cloud castle. Birdy begged Jack to come, but he managed to convince her that it was important for her to meet Georges's extended family on her own. The only thing Jack wished he'd been there to witness was Birdy standing up unexpectedly after the engagement dinner to deliver, in fluent Arabic, the speech he'd helped her compose. How exquisitely painful it was for Jack to teach her, in his own language, to declare her love for someone else, and to have to stand in for Georges countless times as Birdy delivered this declaration with trembling emotion. Jack would, however, have relished the appalled realization surfacing even through the Botox and bovine collagen in Roselle's face that her daughter-in-law-to-be had understood every word she'd said.

Jack couldn't, however, excuse himself from an informal engagement party at a rented beach house in Michigan. This party was just for Birdy's closest friends, mostly flight attendants, all women but for Jack and Georges.

Again, Jack had to lie to his wife about where he was. A safe pair of hands, since he didn't drink, he drove four of the girls to the beach house near Saugatuck in his old Honda, Georges bringing Birdy and the rest in his Range Rover. The house was midcentury modern, all glass on the lake side, with a private beach at the bottom of a steep dune between pine trees. Jack just wanted it over. The moment he met Georges again, he felt a repulsion between them akin to that between like poles of a magnet. He loathed the polite, formal stiffness he provoked in Georges, and worried that Georges suspected or had found out something about him. He realized, though, this awkwardness might also derive from Georges's discomfort with homosexuality and with his wife's intimate friendship with a man Georges wouldn't want many of his friends or relatives to meet.

In Georges's world, everything was perfect. When they arrived in the late afternoon, the sun obliged with an operatic death over the lake until the stage was mobbed by a horde of stars led by a full moon, the night bringing just enough of a chill to enjoy the fire pit by the water. They emptied bottles of Delamotte, dancing in the sand to music from a boombox, plucked exotic amuse-bouches from picnic hampers as Georges grilled lobster tails and steak.

The tension between him and Georges intensified, perhaps because Georges was drinking as much as the girls. When they were near each other, Georges avoided his eyes, but periodically Jack would glance up to find Georges staring intensely at him. And yet he also saw a different side to Georges, working so hard here to make everyone happy.

When Trudy, a squat bottle blond with a thick Alabama accent, helped Georges plate up the food from the grill, he heard Georges tell her he loved feeding people, but that running restaurants was the closest his family would let him get to his true desire to become a chef.

Jack had thought Georges stuffy, but when he was pointed at, he jumped happily into the middle of the dancing circle and flung himself about like a marionette whose strings were being worked by a three-year-old. When the girls, dipping their toes into Lake Michigan, declared it too cold for a swim, he flung a beach ball into the lake, stripped naked, and dived in after it. Standing in the shallow water, the ball held jealously in his arms, he announced that anyone who could pry this ball from him and bring it all the way back up the dune to the porch of the house, without someone else taking it from them, would be rewarded with a full weekend spa experience at the Chicago Hilton. Clothes frantically flung aside, an hour later all of them lay scattered up the steep dune, panting and coated in sand, except for Jenka, a husky Ukrainian from Bucktown, who took the honors.

The party continued around the fire, the girls staggeringly drunk and unabashedly naked, Georges with his pants back on (Jack, numbingly sober, hadn't stripped his off). At three in the morning, Georges asked if Jack wouldn't mind helping him return the grill to the porch. As the two of them struggled up the dark, tree-shadowed dune, Jack felt the tense silence grow increasingly pregnant. They arrived out of breath, and Georges asked him to come see the cake he'd made and help him prepare Arabic coffee for the final ritual of the evening.

Jack attended to the coffee using a large traditional brass dallah. The cake was a beautifully decorated three-tier creation.

"You made this?"

Georges nodded.

"I heard you tell Trudy you wanted to be a chef. Why didn't you do it?"

"I'm the head of my family, responsible for everyone. Like me, many in my family lost loved ones. Compared to a life, a vocation is a small thing to lose."

Then Georges asked, "What about you? What do your family expect of you?"

Having prepared himself, as if for a blindside blow, for a final resolution of the tension building between them, Jack interpreted this question as scornfully rhetorical. Georges clearly knew exactly who "Jack" was: a filthy Palestinian rejected by his own family and community, a carnal brute forced into a shameful marriage, a man who lied to everyone, including his beloved Birdy.

Jack's answer, accompanied by a sharp glance at Georges, was a curt "Luckily nothing."

But Georges didn't seem to be listening, sadly absorbed in the silhouettes of the naked women dancing around the fire at the base of the dune.

Georges sighed. "I wasn't fetching my family's visas for America, I was in a hotel in the mountains with my girlfriend, mistress, whatever you want to call her, Farida, a married woman. She's from one of the leading Palestinian Sunni families, her father high up in the PLO. I don't need to tell you what it would have meant if we were caught, a Maronite and a Palestinian during the civil war. I didn't even like her. Spoiled and self-involved, she'd published a couple of awful roman à clefs, like every educated Beiruti. But she was sexy, and I was compelled, even though it always left me with a kind of hangover." He began to cover the cake in sparklers. "I remember the artillery starting up, pounding from somewhere in the mountains, and Farida and I wandering out onto the balcony of our room with glasses of Dom Pérignon, and all the people out on the hotel terrace below holding cocktails and looking down at Beirut lit up with tracer bullets and rockets. We could see towers of fiery smoke when the shells struck, the sound of those explosions not reaching us for what seemed like minutes; and even from all the way up there we could smell the acrid scent of the shells." His gaze returned to the dancing women, the full moon opening a glittering road into the heart of the dark lake. "Farida poured me more Champagne as I stared down at the burning city. I remember her watching it with the face of an excited child, saying it was beautiful, which is exactly what I was thinking, Jack, until I realized how many of the shells were landing in Achrafieh; and just as Farida gently bit my ear and whispered that it made her want to fuck me again, a terrible premonition turned me to ice."

Georges audibly drew and released a breath. "It didn't stop me fucking her." After another struggling breath, as if a great weight sat upon his chest, he murmured to himself, "We all stand on mountains looking down at burning cities."

He then turned to Jack. "The only recognizable part of my wife was a piece of her hand with her wedding ring still on it. My son, Émile, was intact, covered in concrete dust, like the kind of little statues people put on a child's grave."

Now they both returned to staring down at the women's infernal silhouettes. Behind them lay the moon's dreamlike path across the dark lake. To take it demanded a faith beyond either one of them.

"I love Krysta," Georges said. "No one in my family wants me to marry her, but she's the only person who's taken my pain away. Whenever I'm with her I feel hope. I feel clean again. I was moved that she learned Arabic, but I wish she hadn't. I don't want her to be a part of that world."

He went quiet again for a moment as the house filled with the rich smell of Arabic coffee, and though Georges turned his head toward Jack, he couldn't look at him, and instead glanced back at the cake, wincing.

"She talks about you all the time," he said. "Do you know how we met? I was sitting in a café downtown. She was at the table opposite with a couple of her friends, and when I looked up, she smiled at me.

Then she joined me and said, 'I'm sorry if I'm staring. You remind me of a friend of mine.'

"I can't tell you how often she mistakenly calls me by your name. She wants children, a family. I want that. With her. She's agreed to give up her job as soon as we're married, so she's not away all the time, but it was hard to convince her because of you. The truth is I'm always having to step out of your shadow, Jack. I think Krysta and I could be happy, but..."

Georges looked directly at him for the first time that night, his expression helpless, cowed, pained. Jack understood what he was asking and realized that the only thing Georges knew about Jack was that Birdy loved him.

Jack looked past the dancing women at that shimmering path across dark waters into a light that seemed to him now like the light of a heart gone cold.

"I'll bring the cake," Georges said. "Can you manage the coffee and those cups?"

"Of course," Jack said. "No problem."

After that, Jack found excuses not to work with or meet up with Birdy, and then stopped responding to her texts.

22

He and Dimra left for Jordan late in the afternoon of the next day, Jack sweaty with dread. Their Gaza IDs had expired, and Gaza was almost sealed off by the Israelis. He thought of the two hellish border crossings. If they made it through Al-Jisr, they'd then have to endure the Eretz crossing. He'd convinced Dimra to dress like a Western woman, and it was strange to see her in jeans and a blouse, her lovely dark curls loose around her shoulders. It surprised him that she agreed so readily, but she was desperate.

The flying time was sixteen hours, with a five-hour stopover in Washington, D.C. Dimra seemed not only emotionally and physically wrecked, unable to hold any food down, but became increasingly agitated as they approached Amman.

Just after the pilot announced their descent, Dimra laid her hand upon his, and turning to him, though unable to meet his eyes, whispered, "Jamal, I told my parents you're a pilot. I couldn't tell them you served people."

He understood now why Dimra was so adamant he not join her on Skype calls with her parents. The hurt impulse to snap back that he was sorry she was so ashamed of him soured to a bitter "Well, I hope no one asks me how to fly a plane."

A few minutes later, as Amman's ugly sprawl of concrete beehive buildings came into view, she again took hold of his hand, gripping his fingers hard and trembling as she said, "I told them Aiden was our baby."

"What?" Again, he experienced that dizzying sensation. With this added to her revelations about betraying her brother, he realized that the wife he'd always viewed (*dismissed* perhaps) as a paragon of truth and innocence had been deceiving him and her parents for years.

"They have no one," she explained, "no family left but me. My baba wrote to me once to say that he longed for an American child who'd never have to know what it was like to live in their world. It sometimes felt as if it wasn't a child he wanted me to give birth to, but a passport."

It struck Jack that Dimra must have conceived of this lie after that last miscarriage, unable to tell her parents and hoping that Marcia, who could hardly manage Aisha, would need her to look after her baby. A little shiver of fear snaked through him as he realized there was a touch of madness in this, though his wife was sane enough to have pulled off this deception; and to feel shame.

"I read your letter," she said, "years ago."

"My letter?"

"To your father."

He was still perplexed.

"I found it in the back of the filing cabinet when I was looking for Scotch tape. I shouldn't have opened it."

"A letter to my father?"

"Fayez," she said. "That's what you called him, our son."

Now it came back to him, that letter he'd written after his mother's death, the baby conceived out of his grief, bitterness, and fury as a weapon to hurt his father.

"That's why I kept trying," she said.

"Trying?"

"To have a child. I kept dreaming of having a boy and calling him Fayez. So that it could be true."

"Did you call Aiden Fayez?"

She shook her head. "I wanted to make my baba happy, so I named him Umut, after my baba's father."

A Turkish name. Jack remembered that her grandfather deserted from the Ottoman Army during the First World War, resulting in the marginal, low-caste life her family led in that Palestinian village. He knew what the name meant: hope.

"So, what have we done with him?"

"I told my mother he had an ear infection and with the long flight and everything going on in Gaza right now, I didn't want to risk bringing him. I said Lulu was looking after him."

He nodded slowly, sad and bewildered, just as the plane came to a bumpy landing.

At Al-Jisr, they waited nervously in the passport line manned by a slender blond woman whose acne made her look a lot younger than she probably was. She took their passports and asked their purpose for entering Israel. Jack said they were here for his wife's father's funeral in Gaza and handed her their ID cards.

"These are expired," she said.

"We were hoping we could renew them or just secure a travel pass. We're only staying a few days."

She gave him an ironic smile, "You were *hoping*?"

The acne looked painful, a vivid bloom on each cheek and across her forehead; a strange contrast with her somewhat colorless features: limp, ash-blond hair, watery blue eyes, severe, slender lips.

"When was the last time you entered Israel?"

"We haven't entered since we left in 1989."

"You haven't been back in twenty years?"

"No."

"Why?"

It was as if this young woman were asking them to expose all the secrets of their lives. "Just . . . we now live in America."

"What about your family?" she asked him. "Are they still in Gaza?"

"My mother's dead. I'm not sure about my father."

"Not sure?" Clamping the dry rinds of her lips together, she squeezed from them what meagre bitter amusement remained.

"We're not in touch."

"You must have siblings, cousins, uncles?"

"I'm not in touch with my family."

"Why?"

"Just . . . we lost touch, I suppose."

"You *suppose*?" Now her tone was both mocking and suspicious.

"We're here because my wife's father died two days ago. Her mother is unwell and needs help with the funeral." Though he'd never expected to be treated with dignity, he hoped that reminding her they were in mourning might recall her at least to a professional tone.

It didn't work. The girl's mouth was still distorted with ever-souring amusement as she beckoned Dimra with a crooked finger. "So you're here for your father's funeral?"

"Yes," Dimra murmured.

"Speak up," the girl snapped, irritated.

"Yes. For my father."

"You haven't seen him in twenty years, but now you're here to see him buried. Did you not like him?"

Jack could see that Dimra didn't know how to respond to this.

"Hello?" the woman called, her tone sharpening, "Twenty years in America and you don't speak English?"

"No. I mean yes. I speak English. I am here for my father. My father died."

The woman took a bunch of details, and then beckoned another officer over.

"You need to wait now," the woman said. "We'll call you."

When Jack asked for their passports, the woman told him they'd get them later. It panicked Jack to be without his passport, as if to return to Gaza one had to become stateless again, nobody again.

The other guard then led them to join the rest of the damned, all Arab, in a dismal concrete room that reeked of despair, containing, as it did, the potential abortions or miscarriages of this bloated creature of the border.

As hours passed, Jack tried a few times to talk to the soldiers guarding the room but was angrily ordered back. All the others knew, as he should have, that if you struggled in the web, it only bound you more tightly. America had robbed him and Dimra of some of their immunity to being trapped in this hellish no-time, no-place. Six hours later, a sad-eyed, middle-aged man who'd retained all the gangly awkwardness of an adolescent, with a mop of rusty brown hair and a large Adam's apple, appeared and called their names. Sighing often, he embodied the congealed time of this place and asked them exactly the same questions the previous woman had asked, pecking the answers into an old computer terminal with agonizing slowness and lengthy moments of myopic confusion about what was on his screen—family names, names of fathers and fathers' fathers, where these family members were born, where they lived, where they died—but instead of sharpness and sarcasm, the questions were asked in a hopeless tone. He didn't want to give the impression that this was anything but a waste of time.

They were then asked to identify their bags from a huge pile and directed to take them into another bleak concrete room, where they had to place them, open, on a large steel table. The floor was scattered with the detritus of countless searched bags, a mound of spilled talcum powder, hair clips, a child's shoe capsized in one corner.

There they waited another hour, sitting on the steel table, since there were no chairs. Finally, two young IDF recruits entered. These two boys, like vultures, pecked at and disemboweled Jack and Dimra's suitcases, spilling their innards onto the table. Jack and Dimra watched as every item of their toiletries was opened and examined, lids left off as they were flung onto the pile of clothes. At last, one of the boys told them to repack.

As Jack and Dimra disentangled their clothes, picked a few things up from the floor and tried to reconstitute and seal their lives once more, the recruits talked in Hebrew, which Jack could still understand, about someone called Uriel whose father had died and left him a big apartment in Tel Aviv right on the beach. Amazed by how many tourist girls this Uriel had sex with in it, they fantasized about what it would be like to own their own apartments.

Jack and Dimra were then led back to the waiting room they'd started off in, joining the same people who seemed to have been there for an eternity, most not bothering to look up, but a few glancing at them enviously, since at least *something* was happening to them. He wondered if some of these people had nowhere to be deported to, the world's unviable humans.

Some hours later they were fetched again and taken to a cubicle manned by a heavy, stern-looking woman with a formidable bun of dark hair almost as large as her head. Let down, it seemed that her hair would be as long as Rapunzel's, and he felt he was in a place full of characters not from Disney fairy tales, but from the older ones, written as terrifying warnings to children.

After ordering them to sit down on the two steel chairs in front of her cubicle, she said to Jack, "Your father, he was arrested many times."

"Mostly when he was young," Jack said.

"And it says here you don't know if he's alive or dead."

"I'm not in touch."

"He's dead," she said in a dismissive tone, though she glanced at Jack with an expression that seemed almost to suggest she'd killed him herself.

Jack nodded, trying to remain stoic, not wanting to give her the satisfaction of knowing she'd detonated a depth charge of sadness in him, seething out to his extremities, numbing his head.

"You don't know where your grandfather is buried?" she asked.

Jack shook his head.

"So what, he just vanished? Was he a magician?"

"He tried to return to his village inside."

"Inside?"

"I mean in Israel. We don't know what happened to him."

Now she leveled her gaze at Dimra. "And you, you're here for your father's funeral."

Dimra nodded.

"What do you think of Israel?"

Dimra clearly didn't know what to say and glanced at Jack.

"Don't look at him. You look at me. Answer my question: Do you hate Israel? Do you want to destroy it?"

"No," Dimra murmured.

"Speak up," she shouted.

"No."

"But you belong to BDS, isn't that right?"

Dimra, confused, shook her head. "I don't know what that is. I don't belong to anything."

"You don't belong to anything? BDS is a group that calls for people to boycott and disinvest from Israel. It wants to destroy Israel."

"I don't belong to any groups."

"Then why do we have your membership details?"

Jack remembered the protest. "She just thought she was signing a petition—" he began.

She cut him off furiously. "In Israel, men don't speak for women. In Israel women matter. You understand? So, you keep your mouth shut."

She turned back to Dimra, and from a manila file on her desk slapped down a printed piece of paper. "What's this, then, on the front of their newsletter? That's you, isn't it?"

There it was, a printout of Dimra's image, with the headline, *Fahrenheit 451 Palestinian style: woman named after her destroyed and ethnically cleansed village.*

Now the officer produced printed-out newspaper clippings.

"You said we're like Nazis uh? Do you deny that?"

"I didn't mean it like that," she said.

"So, when you said, quote, 'Jews are like the Nazis,' you meant what? That Jews are like angels? Do you understand how obscene this is to us?" The woman, now red in the face, began to shout. "Do you understand? Or does your husband do all your thinking for you as well as your speaking?"

"I didn't mean—"

"You want to come back for your father's funeral, I *shit* on your father's funeral. Do you understand that? If you don't understand the shit coming out of your own mouth, do you at least understand what I'm saying?"

Dimra's face was flushed and desperate. "I don't want to go to Israel," she said, tears streaming down her cheeks as she tried to ignite her grief and fear into anger, her voice growing louder. "I don't want to go to Israel, I want to go to Gaza. I want to bury my father. I want to see my mother. I want to go home. To Gaza." She clasped her hand to her chest. "To *my* home. I haven't seen my mother in twenty years. I want to go home. My father's dead. You can't stop me going home." Dimra had stood up now, and Jack touched his hand to hers, but she snatched it away. Dimra glanced around at the door behind them, looking for a moment as if she might make a run for it, try to find her way, as in a nightmare, through this concrete labyrinth back to her mother and her home.

The woman, contemptuous of Dimra's trembling, tearful attempt at self-assertion, said, "I can do whatever the hell I want." And with pettish forcefulness, stamped their passports with DENIED ENTRY.

It had taken nearly ten hours for them to be disgorged back out into Jordan, where, after a long, tearful phone call with Dimra's mother, they caught the next flight back to Chicago.

23

Though Lulu had been waiting with lasagna and a tray of brownies when they arrived, Dimra was too ill and exhausted to eat or stay up and collapsed into bed. Jack recited the whole horror story as he and Lulu ate. Though Lulu tried her best to express outrage and sympathy, she seemed slightly distracted, even impatient, and Jack realized why when they sat on the couch with a cup of mint tea and she slapped onto the coffee table a $10,000 check Valeria had mailed her. The note with it tersely explained that the money was to cover Valeria's share of the mortgage and other expenses during her stay with Lulu, ending with, *Warm Regards, Val.*

"As if I were a *fucking* hotel with benefits." Lulu half stifled the "fucking." Her parents had always been strict about not swearing and she was never comfortable doing it. "She broke up with me on the *day* the last piece of furniture was moved into her place in Hyde Park."

Jack suddenly recalled that beautiful snakeskin Gunther had shown him, preserved as if, perfected, it had shed the corrupt and mortal life within. It was a soft July day, blue sky through the swell of bright, fresh leaves outside the window. He was trying to listen to Lulu and respond but his whole being felt like a city after relentless bombing, the buildings mostly flattened, dogs pawing at the rubble. Here and there remained preserved chambers opened to the world, his memories like those half-shattered diorama rooms in ripped-open buildings: there Salim on the white bed slipping a scarf over his head, there his uncle with a glass of rakija like Van Dalen's *Bacchus*, there his mother cradling little Jack as she reads him *The Fantastic Mr. Fox*, and there his father at the kitchen table, a bitter, brooding wreck, *You are not nobody.* Jack's gallery of ruin.

Luckily Lulu didn't need too much response from him, and it struck him through the fog of his own being that she was moving in the right direction, pinballing now between sadness and anger.

"She never told me she loved me," Lulu said, her eyes not on him but searching frantically inward. "After sex, she'd always say, *¡Eso fue divertido!* like we'd been on a carnival ride."

She flinched as if suddenly seized again by a sickness of longing, a chronic fever.

Jack knew it had always been hopeless. For Valeria, Lulu was in her rearview mirror, like some poor critter she'd run over on the highway. Valeria would hardly have noticed the bump or have any awareness of the half-crushed creature struggling for its life.

Lulu was asking him a question.

"I'm sorry," he said.

"You and Dimmy," she repeated, "you were very young when you married, right?"

He nodded.

"Was there anyone before her?"

At his hesitation, she said quietly, "She told me about her difficulties. I mean, sex."

What she was angling to know, he realized, was how he managed to live without passion. He guessed she'd always wanted to understand this about him and now felt that her heartbreak gave her the right to ask.

"I'm sorry," she said at his continued silence. "I shouldn't have asked you that. But you're so *good*," she asserted with almost perplexed emphasis. "I don't know how you can be so good."

"There *was* someone before Dimra," he murmured, afraid his wife might hear. "Please don't say anything to her."

"Sofya?"

"What?"

"Dimmy said you sometimes called her Sofya, early on."

It unsettled him how much his wife had revealed.

He nodded and told her he knew what it was like to have a broken heart. He also knew what it was like to confuse performance with reality but didn't say this.

She wasn't listening anyway, having lost herself in a surge of pain and longing that again distorted her face. "She's all I can think about." She struggled to catch her breath. "Every time my telephone or the door buzzer rings, I think it's her. She won't return my calls." Suddenly, she cried out, "She's such a *coward*."

He put a gentle hand on her arm.

Trying without much success to laugh, she said, "I deserve it. I've broken a few hearts. But it always felt like it didn't have anything to do with me, like it was a nasty accident or something. I'll never feel like this for someone again."

"You will." Jack's head echoed with the dull thud of that blandishment.

"When I told her I was going to put my apartment on the market, she told me not to. I didn't have the courage to ask her why not."

"You think she would have told you?"

She nodded. "She never lied to me."

"A lie isn't just about what you say." He immediately regretted this. He didn't want to encourage Lulu to be angry. There were some people whose central energy was anger, whose landscape had been fashioned by it, for whom anger was vitality, inspiration, even beauty; but Lulu wasn't constituted for anger any more than he or Dimra were. It would only corrupt and enervate. It could not save her.

"You *knew*, didn't you?" she said. Almost an accusation.

He wanted to say, *You knew too*. It seemed to him that people always knew. He wondered if there was a true life that lay beneath the lives we live. If some manage always to remain connected to it, while others drift inexorably away. If what some called a soul was a sixth sense attuned to this true life, a way to navigate back to it.

He shook his head. "You never know," he said. "What do any of us really know?"

24

Just a few days after his return from Jordan, Jack was working a flight to San Diego with Melissa, one of the girls who'd been at the engagement party and who was still close to Birdy. He always felt guilty with Birdy's friends. They all knew how confused and devastated she was when he cut her off. Melissa was easygoing, though, and they worked with a warm cordiality. As she was breaking up a bag of congealed ice in the galley, she glanced at him in a way that suggested she was weighing whether or not to say something. His softly questioning frown encouraged her enough that she asked, "Did you hear about Krysta?"

Stricken just by the sound of Birdy's name, he worried that something terrible had happened. He shook his head.

"That bastard she married ran off with another woman."

"What?"

"Yeah, some mistress he'd had for years in Lebanon. I guess that's not unusual for these guys. She's Palestinian and Muslim, though, which Krysta says is a huge deal with his family. It's sort of *Romeo and Juliet*; or would be if they hadn't shat all over Krysta. They ran off to Paris; he opened a restaurant there. The woman was pregnant; they have a little boy."

"He *left* Birdy?"

She nodded. "I guess their families cut them off. They fucked up their whole lives. Krysta made out like a bandit, though. Got the house, control of the restaurants, a shitload of cash."

"Is she okay?"

Melissa sighed. "She was in a really bad way for a while, but she has to get on with it; she has two little kids. She still asks about you, you know."

Jack recalled Georges telling him about Farida, that spoiled Palestinian princess, and him, the Maronite prince, in that hotel in the mountains looking down upon the City of Destruction, the burning city, unaware that they were burning too. It made sense they were together. How could they ever become disentangled? There is no way out of hell. Quite a punishment, to have to make love, for as long as you live, to a person you hate.

And yet, Jack knew this wasn't Georges's fate, and felt that he knew even when Georges was telling him the story of the burning city that he loved Farida, loved her, as she did him, enough to risk their lives for each other. It was himself Georges hated, for being unable to stop loving her.

25

In August, three weeks after their abortive attempt to return to Gaza, Jack and Dimra sat in the waiting room of an imaging center on Cicero just east of the Edens Expressway, a dismal-looking place like a concrete bunker, painfully evocative of the Al-Jisr border crossing. A slightly deflated metallic red helium balloon ominously declaring "We see what others can't!" banged its exhausted head against the receptionist station.

Dimra's stomach pain was so intense, she'd fainted a few times, but they hoped the surgery to remove the excess endometrial tissue, scheduled in three weeks, would solve this. Dimra refused the hysterectomy despite Dr. Pandit's melodramatic exasperation.

They were here to figure out what was going on with Dimra's shoulder. Lulu was worried because Dimra's pain was worsening and spreading down her back despite Lulu's massage therapy. There was tenderness in places all along Dimra's spine, as well as a slight bump Lulu suspected might indicate a disk issue. Aware of Dimra's determination to save as much money as possible for her mother, and given their GP's refusal to believe it was anything other than bursitis, Lulu suggested he take Dimra to an imaging center and pay out of pocket for an X-ray of her spine. Jack lied to Dimra that their insurance would cover it.

Dimra had almost abandoned cleaning the house, saving her energy for looking after Aiden and Aisha, though this would often leave her trembling and weak with pain. Jack knew he should have put his foot down, demanding she stop babysitting at least until after her surgery, but he hadn't the strength to do so.

Jack had turned up at Marcia's door again a week after his return from Jordan. When she opened it, he wasn't able to say anything. She stared at him for a moment with a complicated expression (tinctured with her signature anger), as of someone surprised by an inevitability; disappointed perhaps.

Being with Marcia had the quality of lucid dreaming. A life beneath his life. It had always been there. It was as if he'd returned to the condemned house, the room with the cracked wall. Their sex was almost violent at times, as if skin were a kind of surface tension that could, that *must* be broken, plunging them to cool depths, a place this fire could not touch. Then came that exquisite pain. A chemistry: he'd felt it with Birdy when she kissed him on the first day they met, all the misaligned vectors of his being polarized into goose-stepping ranks of desire.

And not only desire.

A nurse called their names and led them to another sad room under fluorescent lighting. There, Dr. Park, an older Korean American woman, waited. After shaking their hands, she asked a few questions about Dimra's symptoms and then illuminated the X-ray.

"You'll need an MRI for full confirmation, which I'd recommend. We have a special on at the moment. If you combine it with our online coupon for ten percent off, the price of an MRI is reduced by nearly six hundred dollars."

They were both staring at her bewildered, so she turned her attention to the X-ray, touching her finger to it. "There," she said, "between C4 and C5, you have a tumor."

26

Dr. Papadakis was neither apologetic nor particularly sympathetic, filling Jack with rage.

"My wife might have received the right treatment years ago if you hadn't been incompetent," Jack shouted.

"Abuse of staff is not tolerated in this hospital. I'd suggest you calm yourself down, Mr. Shaban. The simple fact is that your wife's endometriosis made accurate diagnosis impossible, and no doctor in the world would diagnose a tumor from a sore shoulder."

"A sore shoulder without any cause that became more painful over time. Didn't that ring any bells?"

"I'm sorry, are you a doctor, Mr. Shaban? There's my degree." He pointed to his University of Washington diploma.

Jack succumbed to a moment of towering hatred for this man-child, with his floppy hair and fashionable glasses, who drove a vintage Shelby Cobra and probably hadn't read a medical journal since receiving that diploma a quarter century before. Jack could hear his uncle's cynical voice: *Behold one of the monkeys in charge, the true inheritors of the Earth.*

No doubt Jack's tense silence and murderous stare conveyed all this, as Dr. Papadakis glanced toward the door as if assessing his escape. Jack felt his wife's hand on his arm.

"Jack," she murmured soothingly, her enervated look saying, *What good is this anger?*

Sighing, she turned back to Dr. Papadakis and said, "So, what's next?"

Dr. Wasim Bhutta was next. A second-generation Pakistani immigrant, he had the conflicted manner of someone who longed to be a stand-up comedian but was, in fact, an oncologist—an excellent one, by all accounts. He showed them the MRIs, used with a contrast agent, and PET scans. These provided a better image of Dimra's spinal tumor. They also revealed tumors in her liver and colon. The latter was the primary cancer, the tumors in her colon large and inoperable.

As they all stood looking at her body constellated with those illuminated tumors, Jack thought of the California firestorm two years before, nine thousand separate wildfires visible from space. She was on fire everywhere and he couldn't throw himself upon her. Dimra, though, saw it differently. Huffing out a little grunt that wasn't quite a laugh, she murmured, "I've become the Occupied Territories."

Dr. Bhutta refused to assign her cancer a stage. *Cancer's a ham: give it a stage and it'll play Hamlet.* His little conflagration of chuckles was doused by Jack and Dimra's perplexed faces and he quickly and more seriously assured them that everyone was unique and responded differently to treatment. This treatment began with radiation to shrink the spinal tumor; then chemo at the end of July, "turned up to number 11," Dr. Bhutta declared, looking for their laughter before remembering again that he was an oncologist.

Then they were helplessly sucked into Cancer World, the most dismal theme park ever conceived. It was as if they'd been invited to a dinner party with enthusiastic hosts so afraid that conversation might flag, the party fail, that they'd arranged an elaborate game of charades, each couple given a pile of cards telling them what they had to act out. His and Dimra's cards, of course, all said the same thing: Cancer. Not wanting to let down their anxious hosts, they did their best to perform it in every way they could. While Dimra lay locked in and mummified, he acted out MRIs, PET scans, targeted radiation with fingers wiggling through the air; but mostly it was left to Dimra to look washed out and hopeless, hooked up to FOLFOX in dismal rooms with other members of her new tribe.

= 27 =

Marcia's text woke him at close to midnight.

Ryker is in the parking lot.

She must have just returned from a late shift. He was glad Dimra was in the back bedroom with Aiden.

Jack was worn out. After completing a long six-leg trip, returning from Las Vegas that morning, he'd immediately driven Dimra to her chemo at the Kellogg Cancer Center. Strange to be at work for these last two months of his wife's treatment, feeling devastated and guilty, but unable to say anything to his colleagues. He wished he could be with Dimra full-time, but they needed his health insurance. Lulu and Pauline arranged their schedules so they could take Dimra to her other appointments. Today, driving back from Kellogg, he had to pull over and shove the car door open so his wife could vomit in the street. The vomiting had wrecked her, each retch like a punch in her stomach, so when they returned to the condo, he lifted her into his arms, ignoring her weak protestations, and carried her up the deck stairs, appalled by how little she weighed. May stepped out of her door to water her deck plants just as they arrived at her landing and was so horrified and embarrassed, she nearly fell back into her apartment. May seemed to understand that something was expected of her, a kind word or expression of concern, but this only made her sharper and more officious with Jack whenever they met, as if to ward off any mention of Dimra.

Jack quickly dressed and picked his way across the treacherous floorboards down the hall. Aisha was asleep in the second bedroom under her My Little Pony bedspread crowded with stuffed toys. She was surrounded by decals of fairies and rainbows on pink walls. He glanced into the back bedroom, where Dimra lay asleep with Aiden cradled in her arms, his bottle of milk tumbled to the floor. She'd painted this room yellow and had hung butterfly mobiles she made with Aisha from the ceiling.

He and Dimra had argued again today about the children, Jack insisting she was too sick to be looking after a six-year-old and an infant, and to be responsible for a baby overnight. Dimra was frantic, begging Jack not to tell Marcia about her cancer, fearing Marcia might feel she needed to find someone else to look after the children, though Jack knew Marcia couldn't afford anyone who wasn't free. Dr. Bhutta had told Jack that it was important for cancer patients to have something to live for, and Jack suspected, sadly, that Aiden and Aisha were Dimra's primary purpose and joy.

Just before he slipped out of the back door, he recalled his dream—half dream—of the previous night in the Las Vegas Marriott. He was kissing the constellation of beauty marks on Dimra's back, kissing her soft, round behind, her legs, her belly, her breasts. She was young and laughing, no endometriosis, no cancer, no pain. As he was kissing her lips (no one had softer lips than his wife), the two of them intertwined, her body lithe, delicious, responsive, a scream had woken him, his heart pounding: he was back in Gaza, still a child, his entire adult life only a dream. Screeching laughter followed and he drew the hotel curtain to see a crowd of drunken women staggering back to the hotel in pink T-shirts that said LIBBY'S HEN PARTY, EIGHT CHICKS, NO COCKS, the bride holding a helium balloon in the shape of a penis declaring, ONE DICK FOREVER!

Another buzz of his phone.

Are you coming?

He found Marcia sitting in the parking lot with Ryker's head in her lap. It was late October, winter's chill in the air. Ryker wore his usual outfit, the sleeveless leather biker vest open to his bare torso, jeans, and biker boots. His "days sober" button, capable of going up to 9999 was back at 0001. She was in her work uniform, a blue suit with a pencil skirt. Above them the full moon shone bright as a searchlight.

"He's pissed himself," she said. "I was going to call the police. I don't want to keep picking him up."

Jack hunkered down, shaking his head with sympathetic exasperation. "Let's get him on the cot bed in the basement and then you need to tell him when he wakes that no matter how many days, months, or years sober he gets, you're done."

She thought for a moment, "No bed, no blanket," she said. "We'll put him in the basement so he doesn't get eaten by the rats, but that's it."

Jack nodded, hooking Ryker under his arms as she took his legs. Hefting him into the basement, they lay him on the cold and musty concrete floor.

"I feel like you've helped me bury a body," she said, glancing up at him, the two of them breathing hard.

In the dim basement, her angular face took on a baleful beauty, like an avenging goddess, her eyes glimmering with the moonlight shining through the basement's back door.

"*Would* you help me bury a body?" she asked.

He made a performance of thinking for a moment. "Is it May's body?"

She ceded a smile.

Leave, he thought. *Walk away.*

A half hour later, he found himself crying. He tried to hide it from Marcia, but she pulled his face around and said, "You can be such a girl sometimes, Jack."

They could see that astonishing moon out of her narrow bedroom window as they lay on their backs, shoulder to shoulder, naked, sharing a cigarette. The other views available to them were singularly depressing. Nasty-looking stains had bled through the ceiling and unpainted drywall. Almost all of the wood veneer on the floors had curled away from the damp concrete, the ones that had come loose entirely kicked or brushed into small drifts in the corners of the rooms. The house smelled rank, the sink piled with unwashed pots and pans, here and there a forgotten coffee mug growing mold, a half-empty wineglass with a cigarette in it, an insidious base note of sewer gases. For bare feet, the floor was a minefield of toys from Happy Meals and cereal boxes. The bathroom was shocking; he'd once cleaned the toilet himself. She'd called him a girl then too. The carpet of her tiny bedroom was strewn with clothes and shoes. This home she'd been so proud of had become little more than a musty bed in a basement.

As he glanced out again, for respite, at that moon like God's X-rayed skull, it was erased by the blaze of the motion-sensor floodlights. *Shit.* Someone was walking along the side of the building. They'd be seen. It had to be May, Lulu, or Pauline. He couldn't imagine which of them would be worse. Jack looked around frantically, trying to find the sheet they'd flung off, but then just jammed his head under the pillow.

"It's too late," Marcia said. She hadn't moved and when he finally lifted the pillow to glance up, she was taking a careless drag.

Panther stood staring at them through the window with magisterial contempt before leaping effortlessly over the fence. The lights switched off.

Jack jumped up to lower the blinds.

"Don't," she said. She was staring at the moon, its light illuminating her pale body. "I feel like I'm buried in here if the blinds are down. No one's going to come. It's against the fucking rules, remember."

It was the compromise he'd forged: the motion-sensor lights could remain, but no one could walk along the side of the building after eleven.

In that moment of fear, he'd felt his nakedness intensely; still standing by the window, he looked at hers as if for the first time. She was sitting cross-legged, her cruel, lovely right hand hung slack over her knee, the cigarette unspooling itself between her fingers. He loved her body, loved its lean muscularity, loved those strong shoulders, loved the hummingbird tattooed beneath her right breast with the words *Time for Everything* encircling it, loved the slightly crude monochrome tattoo of the phases of the moon that ran along her spine, loved her bony, wide-set hips, which set her legs at the striking separation responsible for her sturdy, mannish stance, loved the strange little hieroglyph on her right knee from when she'd fallen from her bike into gravel as a child. Love surged in him because he needed it to, in the same way that he sometimes needed anger, even aggression, when those feelings had lain dormant too long. Love surged and found expression in this moonlit body upon a mattress in the dead womb of this half-abandoned, wrecked, and impossible home.

Absorbed in her, he'd forgotten himself, forgotten he was standing naked there at the window. He never felt naked in front of her; rather, always felt naked, but never ashamed.

She glanced from the moon to Jack, taking a moment to coolly examine him also.

"Is Dimra okay?" she asked. "She looks like shit. She said it was eno . . . endo . . ."

"Endometriosis."

"What is that?"

"It means there's a lot of fertile soil in places nothing can grow."

She frowned: it was beneath her dignity to ask him to explain. "She said she'd be okay after an operation."

He nodded.

"Looks like it's really painful."

He suddenly wanted to tell her his wife was dying. He wanted to tell her that Dimra didn't have the strength to peel an orange, that her eyes had swollen shut after one chemo treatment; that after another, she'd shitted out the lining of her colon. He wanted to tell her about what had happened when Dimra threw up after chemo today. When he flung the passenger door open, he glanced up to see a pregnant woman passing on the sidewalk. Responding to Dimra's swollen stomach, the pedestrian called in a comradely way, "How far along is she?" Not wanting to embarrass the woman, and perhaps to dignify their own situation, he called back, "Four months."

"It'll be over soon, then," she said.

"Yes, it'll be over soon," he responded.

He wanted to tell Marcia that while he was here with her, his wife was upstairs with Marcia's baby lying in her arms. He wanted to tell Marcia that *this*, the two of them, was unforgivable.

She was looking into his face now, examining it with unwonted uncertainty. "Would you ever leave Dimra?"

"No."

"Why not?"

"Because she's my wife. I love her."

For a moment, she stared through Jack, as if she could sense rather than see him, before her eyes met his directly again with that baleful intensity he'd experienced earlier, the silence between them becoming precipitous. Nauseous, furious at himself, he wished he could tear his skin off.

"I have to go," he said.

"You could stay longer," she said.

Lies, lies. Marcia's gaze softened. She stood, rising to the height of her long limbs, approached, wrapped her arms around him, her hard, angular face struggling with her weakness, a little angry at him for it.

"Just a little longer." She kissed his neck.

He slid his arms around her. Their bodies fit perfectly together. They kissed, tender and slow, a kiss more expressive of love than desire. Tears again.

"For fuck's sake stop being such a girl?" she said.

"I've got to go."

"Goddamn you!" She flung herself, frustrated, back on the bed.

He dressed quickly and as he made his way to the door, she called his name.

When he turned back, she said, intending humor, perhaps, but looking serious, "I don't care if you're a girl."

As he made to leave again, she called his name with even more feeling and urgency. This time she just stared at him, unable to formulate or articulate whatever it was she wanted to say. Finally, she murmured, without heat, "Fuck off," and turned back to the moon.

He exited through the basement, Ryker still passed out on the concrete floor. Among Ryker's possessions, piled up near the water heaters, he saw a blanket. Retrieving it, he brought it over to this man sleeping in a way Jack envied. Death could hardly be deeper. He looked at those blacked-out tattoos and, lifting the back of Ryker's vest, uncovered more of the past Ryker still needed to erase: a swastika, an image of a naked woman on her knees with her mouth open. Ryker's whole being embodied failed resolutions, that button he wore ever climbing, ever tumbling down. At sixteen days sober a month ago, Marcia had been at the point of allowing him to return. But sixteen days to zero, to eleven days to zero, to one day to passed out in the parking lot. Jack turned the button's dial back to 0000. He held the blanket over Ryker but found himself hesitating. After a moment, Jack returned the blanket to its original place in the detritus of Ryker's life and left the basement.

28

Jack scoured his body in the shower with no more luck than Lady Macbeth, Marcia's scent haunting him. Then he couldn't sleep, unable to rid himself of the image of Marcia in the moonlight.

The next morning, bone-tired, he packed a lunch for Aisha, who sat singing some six-year-old version of "Hakuna Matata" to herself at their kitchen island, eating Cheerios while Dimra fed Aiden, who was starting to look like the Michelin Man's baby. Marcia worked a double shift today and would be sleeping at the hotel tonight. It angered him, as it always did, that Marcia just assumed his wife would look after her children for days at a time. But Dimra seemed to be experiencing one of her brief reprieves from pain. It was as if a slender beam of sunlight had found its way through a chink in the wall of an oubliette and she was lifting her face to it. He could almost see the sting of light in her half-blinded eyes, the awful hope.

Though he protested, Dimra insisted she take Aisha to kindergarten. They had a routine, and since Aiden's birth, Aisha needed more than ever to feel secure. Dimra did call him, however, when she returned, to help her back up the stairs with Aiden. He could see that the fragile beam of sunlight on her face was fading, though not entirely gone.

She headed to their bedroom, he assumed to lie down, so Jack took charge of Aiden, who was an easy baby. After slipping him into his walker, Jack even managed to read a little, despite the flashing lights and interminable "Twinkle, Twinkle, Little Star" as Aiden careened around the room.

An hour later, lifting Aiden from the walker to look in on Dimra, he found her in the bathroom vigorously scrubbing out the tub.

"Marcia—Dimra," he corrected himself, "why are you doing this?"

"The bath was dirty," she said, struggling for breath.

He quickly lowered Aiden to the bedroom carpet, detonating an outraged wail. Kneeling beside Dimra, he removed the sponge from her trembling hand and pulled off her rubber gloves.

"The house is so *dirty*," she sobbed, still unable to catch her breath.

She struggled to stand even with his help, so he carried her to the bed, her body shaking with exhaustion. That she would choose to use this fragile reprieve to clean their bathtub broke his heart. She reached toward Aiden, who was still crying, and Jack carried him over. Though he calmed down immediately as she kissed his downy hair, Jack could see that even this was too tiring, and sitting beside her against the headboard, he lifted Aiden into his own arms. He stared into her face, the face he loved, now gaunt and hollow, Death's face, and for the first time it seemed to hold a desperate appeal, as if asking him to help her. He touched his forehead to hers.

"Marcia," he said. "*Dimra*," he corrected again. "I'm sorry," he scrambled for an explanation. "It's because Aiden's here. Marcia *should* be here. I had to help her with Ryker last night. He'd passed out in the parking lot. I'm so sick of it, *sick* of her."

Dimra was looking at him without reproach, though somewhere beneath this neutral surface lurked the flickering shadow of a question.

She glanced away from him into the bathroom. He followed her gaze. Framed in the doorway, her flaccid gloves over the rim of the bath beside a cannister of Vim, the bleach-spattered cushion she knelt on, the sponge tumbled onto the floor, a still life: *The Rapture Comes While Cleaning the Tub.*

"You know, you haven't called me Birdy in a long time," she said quietly, turning back toward him. With her face grown thinner, her skin increasingly translucent, her large, dark eyes had become otherworldly.

"Oh, Birdy's long gone."

She nodded, a slow nod through the thick mud of her fatigue and pain. "Between Sofya, Birdy, and Marcia, I'd choose Birdy. I like it, the name, and whenever you called me Birdy, you seemed happy, or something, as if it were the name of someone you"—she had to wet her dry mouth—"really liked."

He could see it wasn't much use saying sorry again.

"My name," she said, "is a place I've never been. A place that doesn't exist anymore." She took a moment to breathe. "It was the place before . . . before everything. Where everyone was happy."

"Where the figs," Jack ventriloquized Dimra's mother, "were the size of a man's fist, as God is my witness, oranges the size of a man's head, cucumbers the size of a man's—" He widened his eyes with a lewd look. She smiled and, if she'd had the strength, might have laughed.

After another pause for breath, the smile evaporated, and she said, "Now I'm not going to exist anymore."

He didn't know how to respond. Not only was the chemo brutal, it was useless. While the radiation diminished the spinal tumor a little, the tumors everywhere else were ripening apace, colonizing all the soft tissue, crushing what little hope was left for Dr. Bhutta to display his comedy chops.

He took her hand and kissed it. "Where's your ring?"

"I take it off when I clean. It's in the soap dish. I don't think I'll be able to get it back on. It's hurting me."

The edema caused by the cancer in her liver and the chemo had made her hands swell.

They sat quietly, Aiden now lying back against Jack asleep, Jack rubbing the deep compression where her wedding ring had been.

After a while, she said, "If you're going to call me anything, call me Birdy."

29

It was just a few weeks to Christmas. For Jack and Dimra, the game of charades at the dismal dinner party continued. Dimra was sometimes used as a prop in someone else's performance, becoming a grim puppet manipulated by a dinner guest whose card read "Oncology nurse with patient not even God can save" (most guessed, kindergarten teacher with naughty five-year-old). And soon it was hardly worth bothering. When their turn came, all his wife had to do, with her bald head, her hollowed features, the rashes all over her skin, the canker sores that made it hard for her to speak, was to stand up and everyone at the party would point and scream, "I've got it. Cancer. It's cancer!" Then he and Dimra had to wait their turn again, glancing at the clock, wondering when they could politely make their excuses and leave, feeling bad for hosts who had gone to so much trouble and expense.

The only thing that lifted Dimra's spirits was a drive into the north suburbs. They explored all the side streets, often stopping to look at a particularly lovely home, or to sit in a quiet, manicured park, or in the gardens of the Bahá'í temple. They found one street where every house was a Frank Lloyd Wright imitation. If she had strength enough, they might walk to the lake: vast and moody, merciless, becoming ice-fanged, winter's maw. No garbage on the streets, no madmen screaming of God's hellfire, demanding repentance, no tumbledown houses guarded by vicious dogs. Many of the houses seemed uninhabited, the families diffused into their vastness.

Dimra said it felt peaceful, safe, a high-class anteroom between this world and the next. He felt guilty having ever delayed their plans for him to attend night school, to become an accountant and earn enough to live there. Not in one of the lakeside mansions, of course, but a nice little house in a leafy Wilmette side street. It's all she dreamed of. That and a child. Here, she was the odd one out, a Muslim woman looking ancient and hollow in her drab abaya and hijab, sullying that immortal place with her dying. He'd see young children, safely buckled into the back of Escalades or Land Rovers, and thought of his own childhood, one of the million children buzzing like flies about Gaza, and wondered what it was like for a child to grow up in Shangri La, to be chauffeured back and forth to practices and play dates. That had been his mother's life, from which all that remained was a copper-and-sea-glass scorpion.

One day, he returned from a two-leg trip to find Dimra asleep with Aiden in the back room and Aisha on her own with the oven on, the kitchen looking as if it had been hit by a tornado. She'd made a pretend cake from everything she could reach in the cupboards, packages and jars open everywhere, and was preparing to bake it.

Jack dealt with the tears resulting from his insistence that she pretend-bake it; and the subsequent tears because Dimmy was asleep and couldn't perform their usual bedtime ritual. As soon as she was down, he texted Marcia, asking when she'd be home.

He waited up, receiving the text that she was home at nearly one in the morning. After checking once more on his wife and the children, he hurried down. Marcia opened her door topless but for her bra and still wearing the pencil skirt and tights of her work uniform, a cigarette dangling from her lips. She'd not turned on the overhead lights, only a dim floor lamp in a far corner, and hurried back to the sink to continue scrubbing at a stain in her work shirt.

"Mustard," she explained, as he walked up behind her. They hadn't been alone together since the night of the big moon. She smoked indoors now, in part, he guessed, to disguise the headachy, damp smell. The dim light, hardly better than a candle, cast into shadow the apartment's irredeemable mess. The sink, cataracted with grime, held little turds of ash. Her Calavera Catrina tattoo stared at Jack with seductively malevolent eyes. He wanted to kiss Marcia's shoulder, her neck; the lit tip of desire peeled and eddied inside him like the smoke of her Red Label.

"Aisha got chocolate all over my other good shirt." She bustled past him to throw the shirt into the washing machine and turn it on.

She hadn't looked at him yet, even when she'd opened the door.

Returning, she slipped her cigarette between his lips, providing the excuse she seemed to need to meet his eyes at last. As he took a drag, she slid her arms around his waist and laid her head against his chest. In this moment, with the feel of her quick breath at his neck, he understood how hell could seem worth it even just for skin, bone, and sinew: her stark clavicles, the hollow of her throat, the snaky sink and surface of her spine. He sensed a shift in what was happening between them. Her nervousness even to meet his eyes and that elaborate performance with the mustard stain to distract him from her vulnerability had provoked the sensation of something deep within him, uncoiling from long slumber.

From which he saved her, saved himself, by wrenching from his throat, "Dimra can't look after the children anymore."

Pulling back, she examined him with an anxious, searching, angry look, perhaps wondering if Dimra suspected something or if he was trying to sever ties.

"She's just too sick right now."

"What the fuck, Jack," she said. "What am I meant to do?"

"Dimra passed out with exhaustion today. I found Aisha on her own with the oven on."

"What about her operation?"

"What operation?"

"For that endo-thing."

Just tell her, he thought, but he couldn't bear her to realize they'd been down here making love while he knew his wife was dying.

"It's too far gone," he said, a confession of sorts.

But Marcia was hardly listening, lost in her own trouble. "I have a shift tomorrow morning."

"Look, I'm taking the next few days off," he said. "I'll see to the kids, but I'm sorry, by Monday you need to find someone else."

He moved toward the door but couldn't stop himself looking back. She was leaning against the sink, the dim, fragile light of that lamp losing its struggle to keep her above the darkness.

Dimra couldn't muster the strength even to protest the loss of the children. When the doctors began talking vaguely about quality of life and palliative care, leaving weighty silences, Dimra, sick of this dinner party, sick of this game, sick of being polite, stood up and said to the hosts (themselves secretly relieved, though they feigned disappointed surprise), "It's time for us to go." To Jack: "I want to die in my home."

After the hospital made them sign countless indemnity forms, Jack transported all the equipment they needed to their condo. It was left to Jack, then, with visits from a palliative nurse, to see her through what Dr. Bhutta said could not be more than two weeks.

30

The day Dimra arrived home from the hospital, she and Jack Skyped with her mother. The Gaza War, which had started just after Christmas, was ongoing, and Dimra's mother lived in an area near the fighting, the connection hazy and unstable. Enrobed in black, she appeared out of a lost, ruined world upon that brown-and-orange flowery '70s couch beside the empty space where Dimra's father used to ameliorate her operatic laments with his covert, kindly irony.

The camera shook, her mother lifting her hands to cover her head. It took a moment with the delayed feed for them to hear the explosion and her mother scream, "They're killing us! As God is my witness, they're killing us all!"

When relative calm returned, she launched into her litany of the usual miseries exacerbated by this war: no cooking oil, little water, she would die but for the kindness of her neighbors, that she *should* die, with no place for her in this world. With the delay in the transmission, it was hard for them to get a word in edgewise.

After a while, she interrupted herself to say, "Where's Umut?"

It was astonishing that she couldn't see how sick Dimra looked.

"Mama," Dimra all but shouted, "I have cancer."

Her mother said nothing, looking confused. When Dimra explained that she'd stopped treatment and was not expected to live for long, her mother began to rock and let out a low wail, tugging at her clothing.

This went on for a little while, through another shuddering of the camera and delayed explosion, but it wasn't really her daughter she was worried about, and with a frightened look she said, "If Jamal doesn't take care of me, I'll last even less time than you. I'll be dead too."

"Jamal will look after you." Dimra was becoming too out of breath to shout. "Don't worry."

"Jamal will marry again, have a family. What will I be to him?"

"Of course I'll look after you," Jack shouted. "The money will keep coming. Please don't worry."

"Who will look after Umut?"

"There is no baby," Dimra admitted softly as the camera again vibrated with an explosion.

Her mother cried out, "The sky is falling on our heads!" She had not heard what Dimra said and the connection was lost.

Dimra could hardly stand, so Jack carried her to their bed.

"I'll tell her," Jack said. He didn't need to add, *When you're gone.*

Lulu and Pauline came every day. Dimra generally lay on the couch covered in a duvet, since she was always cold, a spectral figure, her hair just beginning to regrow. Every time she opened her eyes from sleep, it felt to Jack like a minor resurrection. The cancer had spread to her lungs. A cannula now connected her to an oxygen tank. Every inhale was a struggle.

"I think I'm in love," Lulu admitted to them one day with a fragile, slightly guilty joy. She was sitting behind Dimra on the couch, gently massaging his wife's shoulders. Jack made tea, brought cookies, then sat in the PELLO armchair. He wasn't surprised. Gunther had told him with a wink that things were getting rambunctious in the bedroom above him.

They congratulated her. Strange how life went on. Jack glanced out at the grayscale world: leafless branches above a street of dirty snowdrifts and bundled-up people.

"Her name's Andy. When I asked her about children, she said I could have a dozen if I wanted."

Lulu spoke as if children were everywhere, ready to be snatched up by the armful. Jack glanced at Dimra, who was looking tired.

Lulu's eyes were wide, her breath as short and snatched as Dimra's.

Suddenly tearful, she said, "I want one day to have what you two have."

A few days ago, Jack had been helping Lulu rearrange her living room furniture with NPR on as background noise. Suddenly they were listening to Valeria's slightly nasal voice. She'd become WBEZ's go-to expert on all things queer and Latino. In her clumsy rush to turn it off, Lulu knocked her radio halfway across the room. Jack returned what was left of it to her trembling hands.

The crack through Lulu's heart would never fully heal, and yet now he often heard her laughing in the front stairwell or out on the deck, sometimes even through the walls, like the song of a bird species thought long vanished. He recalled those European flowers still waiting after three million years for a hummingbird to appear. Samood, steadfastness. But faith also. And love.

= 31 =

A week into Dimra's home hospice, Jack, as the condo's registered agent, was served with notice of the bank's foreclosure on the basement apartment. When Marcia answered his phone call, he could hear music and lots of voices.

"Marcia, where are you?"

"Disney World," she shouted, moving herself to a quieter place.

"Disney World? Do you know the bank's foreclosing on your apartment?"

"I haven't paid for six months," she said. "My place isn't worth shit."

"Did you find someone for the kids?"

"No one I could afford."

"So you took a vacation?"

"The hotel fired me."

"What? Why?"

"I was taking stuff. I mean stuff everyone takes, soaps, shampoos, shit like that. Some bitch there I didn't get on with ratted me out."

"Marcia, if you've been fired for stealing, how are you going to get another job?"

Her anger flared, "You know what, Jack, I really don't give a shit anymore."

He couldn't believe she was jobless, about to be homeless, and spending what little she had on a trip to Disneyland. It struck him then that she was doing this for Aisha. To win her back.

After a moment, he said, "Thanks for paying your monthly assessments."

Now he could hear Aisha whining and Marcia calling, "Sweetie, we're going in a minute." To him, then, with a sigh, "I haven't been paying them, May has."

"May?"

"I told her if she didn't, I'd tell her son's probation officer what he'd done."

"Why? Why would you do that?"

The husk of a laugh. "Well for one thing, she's a total bitch." After a hesitation: "And I knew if I didn't pay, you'd have to deal with that shit. I guess . . . I guess I didn't want you to not like me." To Aisha: "Sweetie, you got to stay here with Mommy. One more minute."

He could hear Aiden getting fussy.

"Marcia, what are you going to do?"

"Right now, Jack, I'm going to enjoy three or four or five mojitos at the T-Rex Cafe."

= 32 =

Jack had wandered out to the local Dominick's. Joan, his favorite of the palliative nurses, a no-nonsense, but genuinely empathetic sixty-year-old, had relieved him that morning. He didn't need groceries, with Lulu and Pauline stuffing their fridge with food. But he did need to escape his stiflingly warm apartment into the bracing cold of a Chicago winter. The short walk there and back was punctuated with adjurations to repent, written by Preacher Morris in colored chalk on the pavement. Dimra had been home now for nine days. The airline allowed him ten working days with pay, but he was too numb and tired to be anxious. At this point, filled with painkillers, Dimra was barely coherent, but her body had, so far, refused to let go of life.

As he entered the bedroom, Joan said, "She's asleep now. She's been a little delirious. She keeps asking for Danny. Who's Danny?"

The name shocked him, and he found himself quickly saying, "Our child. We lost our child."

"Oh, I'm so sorry."

The concerned hand Joan laid on his arm caused Jack to flinch. "Don't say anything to her about it."

"Jack, I don't think I'll have the opportunity anyway." She met his eyes with a look of deep sympathy. "She's just about there."

He nodded.

"Do you want me to stay?"

He shook his head. "Thank you." It was strange to feel both dread and a kind of excitement, as at the culmination of some long and arduous event.

After Joan left, he sat with his sleeping wife and thought about Danny, the Shabak officer who seduced a Palestinian girl in the hope she'd give up her brother and his organization. He wondered if Danny, or whatever his real name was, had a family he returned to after his days with that girl in the cells. He wondered briefly how that man could do it, before realizing he knew exactly how. Exactly.

A half hour after Joan left, Dimra's eyes opened.

"Danny," she called frantically. "Danny."

"It's me," he said.

She looked at him, running her tongue around her dry mouth.

"Jack," he said. This didn't seem to clarify anything. "Jamal, your husband."

"He promised he'd be here." She looked grief-stricken.

She continued running her tongue around her mouth, so he fetched her an orange popsicle. She'd asked him to keep the blinds in the bedroom always open. She couldn't bear feeling enclosed, she said, as if she were already in her coffin. He'd set the television up beside the bed, on the opposite side from the window, and she spent most of these final days, as she had so much of her life, wired into this new war in Gaza. The Arab press called it the Gaza Massacre. The Israelis named it Operation Cast Lead, after a line from a Hanukkah poem by Bialik: "My teacher bought a big dreidel for me, Cast of solid lead, the finest known. In whose honor, for whose glory? For Hanukkah alone." As if this new convulsion in a sordid, senseless conflict, with over a thousand Palestinians already dead in the first two weeks of 2009, were somehow equivalent to the defeat of the Seleucid Empire and the inevitable rededication of the Second Temple.

Before she became too sick to leave the apartment, she split her time, his dying wife, between trips into the ersatz heaven of Chicago's north suburbs and staring with a horror and despair that had never diminished throughout her life at that hell of camera-shaking explosions, stone-throwing children, corpses, and weeping mothers.

But in this moment, she didn't ask him to turn it on. She stared out at the eternally tarped roof of the neighbor's tumbledown house, lazy flurries of snow, the branches of bare trees veining up through the sky's livid flesh like the dead nerves of a cataracted eye. From one of the streets nearby they could hear Preacher Morris, his voice ringing so clear in the cold, unmuffled air, testifying to terrified passersby, begging for forgiveness by accusing the world of sin.

"Why won't he ever shut up," she said. "I've spent my whole life listening to him." And for a moment, she seemed to be back to herself. She suckled on the orange popsicle he held for her, her eyes glazing a little.

"Danny," she said, "do you know what I've always wanted?"

After a moment, Jack said, "What?"

She opened her mouth as if to speak, but nothing came.

"I'm here, Dimra."

She frowned, shaking her head at some internal grievance. "They'd always say it."

"Say what?"

"A woman's reputation is like gold. If you did anything wrong, if you even glanced at a man, 'Where is your shame? Where is your shame?'"

"Don't upset yourself."

"Danny?"

"I'm here," he said, not knowing what else to say. He brought the popsicle to her lips again and she seemed to calm a little.

Then she lay back and looked suddenly in pain and scared.

"Do you need more Dilaudid?"

She nodded, and after a while calmed again. "In the village the word for spring was 'grass,'" she said, as if happily surprised she'd remembered this. "Its green was spring. My favorite month was February, high waves and still cold sometimes, but I could smell summer in it. In March I'd make myself a wedding dress out of almond blossoms stuck to paper. My father loved green almonds."

"So did mine. And sour grapes with salt."

She looked at him with a weak smile.

And then she seemed more troubled again. "Will God know I loved him?"

"Of course."

She faded out for a moment, and then, turning to him, her eyes widened, and she said, "Danny, Danny, I have to go."

Jack assumed she wanted the bathroom, though she was too weak for him to take her.

"Danny, I have to go," she insisted, tears now. "You never came."

"I'm *here*," Jack said, taking her hand. She squeezed his hand for a few moments before her grip slackened and her eyes seized. Dropping the popsicle, he put his hand to her chest. She was no longer breathing, her heart no longer beating. He kissed her and closed her eyes.

With her lips bright orange from the popsicle, she looked like a little girl.

33

Jack returned to work less than a week later. Manny was on crew for his first leg to Seattle. Birdy's friend, Melissa, was assigned to business class. There was also a new girl, Chantelle, from a town called Mountain Home in Arkansas. Short and sturdy, she'd pulled her mousy hair back so tight it resembled a seed coat from which the plump, pale legume of her head was about to pop. Her face had been impastoed with base, eyebrows plucked almost to nonexistence, her false eyelashes dramatic, her lips garishly red. Chantelle's eagerness and small-town innocence reminded him of young Birdy.

Manny quickly intuited that something was wrong with Jack and asked him if he was okay. Insisting he was, Jack felt sickened by all his lies, thinking of everything Manny had revealed in the confessional of the plane's galley. Now Jack had nothing to hide: the wife he'd never mentioned no longer existed.

A few hours into the flight, after sending Chantelle, who was desperate to do something, up the aisle with a tray of water and orange juice, Jack said, "Manny."

Clearly sensing something in Jack's tone, Manny met his eyes with concern.

"I've been lying to you."

"Lying to me?"

"To everyone. You asked me what was wrong. My wife died four days ago."

"Your wife?"

For a moment, fighting tears, Jack couldn't speak, and then it seemed that what he had to say was absurd. "I'm not gay. I never had a partner called Mario." He shook his head and rubbed his eyes, perplexed at himself. "Hard to explain, but all of that was made up."

Manny looked as if he wanted to laugh but was too confused. "You mean you're coming out as straight?"

It was just then that Jack noticed Melissa at the entrance to the galley.

"I'm out of Bloody Mary mix. Everyone's having Virgin Marys," she said. "I hope it's not a bad omen."

As Jack put a half dozen cans on a tray for her, he wondered how much she'd heard.

"And guys," she said as she headed back, "can you calm the new girl down. She's giving some woman a neck rub. You know how important it is for us to keep expectations low."

They both gave her a thumbs-up.

Chantelle appeared moments later. "Gosh, they were thirsty," she declared, replenishing her tray and heading back out.

"Tell me the rest in Seattle," Manny said. "We'll have dinner. And, well, I'm sorry about your wife, Jack."

"Dimra," he said. "That was her name." As he struggled with tears again, Manny rested a gentle hand on his arm.

An hour later, during a quiet period, Jack sat reading *Suite Française*. Manny was also reading, and Chantelle, who leapt up every time a passenger pressed the call button, was knitting restlessly. She clearly wasn't someone who coped well with silence. Since Dimra's death, Jack felt as if his voice had slipped down a deep crevice.

"So, what are you reading?" she asked Jack. "Is that even English?"

"Oh," Jack said, "it's an incomplete novel, originally written in French. It's by a Ukrainian Jew who was murdered in Auschwitz. The manuscript was found some time after her death."

"That's lucky," Chantelle said. "I mean that they found it. Did they ever catch who murdered her?"

Jack laughed nervously, glancing at Manny, who'd peered over his reading glasses at Chantelle. It was clear she wasn't joking.

"My dear," Manny said, "Auschwitz was a concentration camp where just over a million people were murdered, most of them Jews."

"Oh," she said, shocked. And after a tentative silence, "Was that a long time ago, then?"

Manny was quiet for a moment, and then said with a slightly glazed look, "Yes, my dear, a *very* long time ago."

Relieved, she returned to Jack. "Is it good?"

"So far," Jack said.

"I don't have the patience to read," she said.

"*Good* for you," Manny said. "It's a filthy habit."

Jack lowered his book. She was sitting right next to him, her hands moving furiously. She was just eighteen, as Birdy was when he first met her. He could see clotted mascara on her eyelash extensions. Like Birdy in those days, she still had the look of a girl, rather than a woman.

"I have to be busy," she said, glancing at Jack. She showed him the knitting pattern.

"I'm making a sweater for my sister; she has Downs. It's going to have a rabbit on it. Emma loves rabbits."

Now she looked straight at him, producing a wide smile expressive of an innocence so appallingly absolute it seemed sinister, before returning to the relentless machine of her hands.

34

So strange for Jack to enter his apartment after that three-leg trip, having finally spoken Dimra's name into the outside world. He was as sure as he'd ever been that she'd be waiting for him but entered a place where every familiar and intimate object was now an artifact. Within moments he felt shipwrecked upon this island of her absence. Unraveling her prayer mat, which at the end she hadn't been strong enough to use, its pile worn at her knees and head, he set it toward Mecca, as if to release the built-up pressure of her devotion. He then took one of her scarves out of the drawer and lay on their bed holding it to his face. He could hear the loudspeaker at Jordan Elementary, followed by the uproar of the children streaming out to their homes. Nothing had changed in the world. He thought of what was going on in Gaza, that eternal flame of embittered remembrance, a flame that might, at any time, set the world on fire. He fell asleep, waking in darkness.

He suddenly recalled that Marcia had returned from Florida today. He checked the time. Nearly ten. Wrenching himself off the bed, he went to what had been Aisha's bedroom, retrieved the stuffed Simba she left behind, and headed down. Outside Marcia's back door, he texted her and waited. As he was about to give up, setting down the big-eared lion cub, the door opened and there she stood, in black silk boxers and a red tank top.

"I just got Aisha to sleep," she whispered as he followed her in. "She wanted to sleep up in your place."

Again, that dim corner lamp provided the only light, the two of them within a Caravaggio-esque darkness.

"What are you going to do?" he said, standing opposite her as she sat on one of the stools at the kitchen island.

Staring off into the darkness with an expression that suggested she'd long lost hope of finding whatever she was looking for, she said, "We're moving in with my mom." She glanced back in his direction but couldn't meet his eyes, remembering, perhaps, that she'd told him she'd rather die. "At least until I get straight."

"What about your sister?"

She didn't respond to this. Jack knew it would be agony for Marcia to confirm the opinion she believed her sister already had of her.

"She's going to know you're there."

"No, she won't. She and Mom don't talk. She told me Mom's a black hole and there's no fixing a black hole."

He thought of reminding her that her mom lived in a miserable one-bedroom yellowed with tar. "When are you going?"

"Tomorrow."

"Tomorrow? How are you going to get there?"

"We'll catch the bus."

"What about all your stuff?"

"The bank's welcome to my fucking couch."

"I'll take you."

Before she could protest, he said, "Marcia, you've got a baby and a six-year-old. I'll hitch a small U-Haul trailer to the back for anything you want to bring. Okay?"

She sighed but didn't say no. Her hand rested on the dark countertop, a lovely hand, suited to a more privileged and elegant life. He wanted to take it in his, this living hand. The sensation of Dimra's slackening grip had never left him. He worried, though, she'd interpret it as desire; worse still, as pity.

"This is the only place I ever owned," she said. "Never really had a home. After Dad fucked off, Mom moved a lot. We lived with her boyfriends, mostly, and when that didn't work out, friends' floors. We even lived on a campsite in a van someone loaned her for a while. I guess I never really owned this." She laughed. "Didn't pay off a cent of the principal. That mortgage guy fucked me over." She sighed again. "You and Dimra have a great place."

He nodded. "We're still underwater, like everyone else. And Chicago was never home for Dimra."

"Does she miss—what was it called again?"

"Gaza. I guess. Nothing good there for her, but she never let it go."

"Do you miss it?"

He saw the white room, that crack splitting the wall above and below a blue-framed window filled with the azure sky, open to the scent of the sea, mixing with that of Salim's sun-warmed skin. "Some things I miss."

"Home is home," she said.

"That's the odd thing. We were in a refugee camp. None of us were home. The people there wanted to return to the places they'd been from."

"Why couldn't they?"

"Oh, that's a long story," he said.

"I have time," she said.

They were quiet for a moment, and then Jack said, "I was once snowed in, in St. Louis Airport, and I needed to come home because Dimra was unwell." (It had been one of her miscarriages.) "So I got a ticket on an Amtrak, a reserved seat. And this Amtrak was just crammed: two canceled trains earlier in the day; lots of people who couldn't get their flights. I got to my seat and there was this young man sitting in it. I told him it was my seat, showed him the reservation. He said someone was in his seat. I said that wasn't my fault. He told me that circumstances had meant Amtrak's rules had changed and all reservations were void. I was already upset, because of Dimra, and tired, and people were jammed all around me. I became so furious. I had the ticket, the reservation; the two of us argued, everyone looking away, clutching to their own seats. And I was filled with this terrible sense of injustice, of everything in the past, of all the trouble of my life. And all of it became this little guy in my seat. He was choking my life. I *hated* everything about him: his little bum-fluff mustache, his greasy forehead, his ugly green Crocs. And I suddenly just wrenched him out of the seat—which I *know* I wouldn't have done if he was some big, scary guy. And we had this humiliating scuffle, with him trying to push himself back into the seat and me forcing myself under him, and him landing in my lap for a few seconds." Jack laughed sadly. "Finally, he got up. He was shaking and shuffled off into another carriage. I remember one woman shouting, 'Was that *really* necessary?' I *hate* violence. I saw so much of it when I was young. And I just sat there for ten hours feeling raw and ashamed, as if I'd violated myself."

Marcia was frowning at him, no doubt wondering why he'd told her this. Finally, she just shrugged and said, "Why would *you* feel bad? I would have pulled him out of that seat by his fucking balls."

He laughed and she smiled.

After another silence, she said, "My sister once punched one of my mother's boyfriends in the balls. He was calling our mom nasty names."

"She sounds tough, your sister."

"She was."

"Sounds like you both had to be."

Marcia looked off into the darkness, renewing that hopeless search for whatever she'd lost, and after a few seconds said, "Kelsey always told me I was all hiss and no bite. She said I was like our mom, always the fucking victim. No matter how shitty your life was, Mom's had been shittier, and that excused all the shit she pulled. Why did she even have kids? Sometimes I feel like I caught that bitch like a fucking disease."

"You tried to make a home for your kids."

"Don't make excuses for me," she hissed, turning back to him, her anger flaring. "Dimra's the one who made a home for them. Aisha's been crying for her every fucking night. Now I'm bringing my kids back to my mom and all the shit I had to deal with. At least she's too fucking old and ugly for boyfriends." He could see she was close to tears, but he was too emotionally drained to comfort her. Glancing at her lovely hand on the black countertop, starkly pale in the dim room, he let the ghost of his hand take the ghost of hers.

"I'll come at ten tomorrow."

As he headed to the door, she said vaguely, "How's Dimra?"

He hesitated. "She's away."

If she'd asked him where, he would have told her the truth. But she didn't. Too lost in her own anger and sadness, she'd become hardly more than the shape of a woman at the precarious edge of a dim well of light.

35

As Jack climbed the back steps, still thinking about Marcia's pale hand, he felt his phone buzz with a text. May, he assumed, some fresh outrage. He sat on his deck in the piercing cold, not wanting to bring her voice into his home, lit a cigarette, took a few moments to watch the lights of planes coming across the lake like a stream of ants carrying fireflies, and finally checked his phone.

> I hope you don't mind me texting you Jacky. Mel said she saw you on the Seattle run. You know my life crashed and burned. Georges is with a woman called Farida. Palestinian Muslim no less in Paris. He's written me lots of pathetic letters. In one he said he asked you to step away from me. I knew you wouldn't have just dropped me. Mel also told me she heard something about your wife (?!) being dead. I'm so sorry, of course. And confused. Can we meet? Just for a chat. I've missed you every day.

A surge of joy, to hear her voice again; and hard upon that, shame. How could he respond after all this time? After all those lies? Wasn't it better just to leave it, to expunge the past, to vanish? He'd never be able to sell his apartment in the current market, but he could rent it. United had hubs in Denver, San Francisco, even Guam.

He thought of Georges escaping to Paris with Farida, the woman with whom he'd watched Beirut burning as they'd sipped Champagne while delighting in the beauty of the tracer shots, missile trails, and pluming shells. Making love as the odor of the artillery and rockets vined through their own heated scent, the percussion of the very shell that killed Georges's wife and son infiltrating the rhythm of their cleft bodies. *We all stand on mountains looking down at burning cities.* Isn't that what Georges had said?

Jack stared out at Chicago. How peaceful it seemed, that patchwork of lights, each person reduced to no more than a flicker of the conflagration that lay beneath. Lining the streets, surrounding them all, winter trees lifted empty arms to a moonless sky. The last Metra rolled by, holding a few passengers in amber light, like those insects. He became aware suddenly of all the sirens swelling out of the city, endless tragedies falling upon leaden ears. From the apartment building adjacent leaked the anesthetizing sounds of television, its occupants drifting through fitful blue light. All those planes in the darkness, as if the stars were being mined out of the heavens on ponderous conveyers. He thought of the Chicago riots, a year after Al-Naksa. Martin Luther King said he'd never in any city, even in the South, encountered the intensity of racial hatred he'd encountered in Chicago, still the most segregated city in America. All these years later, the West Side remained scarred, patchworked with vacant lots from that burning city.

He reentered his apartment, expecting still the smell of whatever Dimra had cooked counteracting the bleachy, lemony scent of all her cleaning. She had been his home, he hers. She waited ever for his return: an ancient story.

Jack hadn't eaten and fetched a plate. The plates were once patterned, he remembered, with cherries. Only a few pink smudges remained. The nonstick had worn off the pans, every surface dulled by her cleaning, her prayer mat scarred by her shins, hands, and forehead, the old IKEA couch they'd owned for fifteen years worn almost through to the stuffing where she'd sat every day to watch the news of her childhood home itself being expunged. They had been living in the slow erasure of their home. The child was meant to change everything, to bring spring to their winter garden, to take Dimra out of this apartment and into life, and to return Jack home for good. Everything would follow from the child, night school, a job where he earned enough for them to live in an adorable house in a leafy, quiet, safe northern suburb. Waiting, waiting, waiting ever for the child who would not come.

Returning the plate, too tired to eat, he pulled out his phone and texted Birdy, saying he'd missed her, too, and suggesting they meet on Saturday evening anytime after five, wherever suited her.

He went to bed, dropping his clothes on the floor, and lay staring up at the ceiling dizzied by the swirl of memories and thoughts: Dimra's open and innocent smile when he first met her, filling him with hope; Birdy in those early years when they'd wrestled like children. And then, just before he drifted into sleep, he imagined a young Kelsey (what was the posh name she called herself now—Katy, Colleen?) punching one of her mother's boyfriends in the balls; or rather, he imagined her younger sister, crouched behind Kelsey, frightened and learning the power of anger.

= 36 =

The next morning, he helped Marcia fill his trunk and the U-Haul trailer, trudging through the four inches of snow that had fallen in the night. May sat on her deck looking on with an expression of vicious triumph. When Jack went up to fetch some old blankets and towels for cushioning, she hissed, "Bye-bye white trash!" He didn't respond. She'd not yet said a word about Dimra's death, and during Dimra's last weeks had texted endless complaints about the noise the wheelchair and the nurses made.

When he returned, Aisha asked him where Dimmy was, and he said she was away, but had told him to give Aisha a hug. It made him tearful again to see the little girl staring up at their apartment as if expecting Dimra to emerge with a Tupperware full of cookies.

His ancient car struggled to pull the trailer on the slippery streets, the whitewater of Chicago traffic roaring around them. Marcia sat beside him, Aiden asleep in her arms, Aisha in the back sucking her thumb. Forty minutes later, when Jack pulled into a space near her mother's apartment building, it struck him that anyone who saw them would assume they were a family arriving at a new home.

"Oh God, there she is." Marcia pressed her head back against the seat rest, closing her eyes tight, as if hoping she might wake into a different reality.

Her mother, perched on the swept-clean stoop of her apartment building's main door, wore a pair of men's duck boots and a huge moth-eaten fur coat over her nightdress, her face wizened and cured, her hair yellowed by two packs a day for over fifty years. She was smoking now, despite the cannula attaching her to a wheeled oxygen tank.

Marcia noticed Jack checking his watch and glancing up and down the street. "Do you have to get back?"

"No," he assured her, "I don't start work until late tonight."

"Are you just desperate to get rid of us?" She was giving him a half-smile, and for once there was no gathering storm around those sea-glass eyes.

"No," he said. "I'm going to miss you—all of you." He glanced back at Aisha, who was in a world of her own, staring out of the window.

Reaching into his pocket, he produced his mother's copper scorpion and handed it to Aisha. It broke her from her dream. Smiling, delighted, she took it.

"Dimra told me you always asked to play with it, so she wanted you to have it. Her name is Serket. She'll watch over you."

"What do you say?" Marcia warned.

Aisha whispered her thanks.

Turning back to Marcia, he found himself impulsively removing his Quran necklace.

"No, Jack." She put her hand out to push it away.

"Please," he said. "Someone gave me this when I was in a tough place in my life; someone had given it to him."

Her hand wilted, and she let him slip it around her neck. They sat quietly for a moment looking at each other, not knowing what to say.

"Well," he declared finally, with one more disappointed glance up and down the street. "Shall we?"

Marcia fetched Aisha from the back and began walking over to her mother with the two children. But just as Jack unlocked the trailer, a pearl-white Escalade pulled up. Out of it stepped a tall, full-figured woman in a brown lambskin trench coat. Her platinum-blond hair was cut in the kind of bob that beautiful alien women wore in '70s science-fiction movies. She was followed by her college-age daughter—the one with MS, Jack recalled—wearing an oversized hoodie and yoga pants, her hair ponytailed.

The idea woke him in the middle of the night, and this morning Jack had searched the internet for Marcia's sister. He didn't know her married name, but knew she ran a Century 21 real estate franchise in Highland Park and remembered that she'd changed her name from Kelsey to something posh. He found a Colette Stern, who somewhat resembled Marcia. After emailing her work account he left her a phone message, apologizing if she was the wrong person, explaining Marcia's situation, and providing details about when they were likely to arrive at her mother's place.

Marcia shot him a furious, betrayed look. "Did you do this?"

"Are you Jack?" Kelsey/Colette said, approaching them, her daughter trailing sheepishly behind her.

He nodded and then said to Marcia, "I'm sorry. I just thought she might be able to help you."

Their mother watched them all disinterestedly, as if they were strangers arguing in the street.

"Hello," Kelsey's daughter said, hunkering down to Aisha. "Last time I saw you, you were a little baby. I'm Felicity. I like your scorpion."

Aisha smiled shyly at her.

"This is your cousin," Jack said.

Kelsey and Marcia stared at each other for a tense moment. Kelsey, regal in her stance, was taller and more filled out than Marcia. He could see her as the tough, protective, and bossy older sister, partly because her presence provoked a childish look of recalcitrance in Marcia.

"Who's this?" Stepping close to her sister, Kelsey rubbed the baby's cheek.

"Aiden."

"Can I hold him?"

Marcia, struggling not to yield her refractory stance, handed him over.

Kissing his forehead, Kelsey cooed at Aiden, "Aren't you a big, handsome boy."

At this, Aiden stopped chewing on his colorful plastic keys to give her a dreamy smile.

Looking up at Marcia, Kelsey said, "We have a nice big granny flat in the back of our house. It's got its own kitchen, separate entrance. It would be perfect for you guys, just until you're on your feet."

So strange for Jack to see Marcia as baby sister, powerless before Kelsey, her face brightly flushed, a spill of treacherous tears. Kelsey quickly embraced her with her free arm, the baby between them. Felicity had picked up Aisha, who was letting her admire the scorpion.

"Give me your address," Jack said to Kelsey after she'd released Marcia. "I'll try to follow you, but I'm very slow."

They all headed to the Escalade, but partway there, Marcia broke off and hurried back to their mother, squatting in front of her, showing her Aiden and talking quietly for a moment. Kelsey, who hadn't even acknowledged their mother's presence, called impatiently to her sister. Kelsey—no, it was Colette now. Colette had severed her childhood like a gangrenous limb, making good use of her own white-hot anger. Hers was anger as a superpower. It gleamed in the immaculate futuristic metallic bell of her hair, her glossy lambskin coat, the pearl white of her tanklike SUV. He'd been wrong about Marcia: anger was not native but invasive, dangerously unbalancing her indigenous landscape. Never in control, it had only ever attracted disaster.

The Escalade quickly lost him. When he arrived, Colette and Marcia were waiting. Aisha had already found some girls her age from the neighboring houses, and they were playing statues with Felicity. Aisha looked so happy, which filled him with sadness as he realized how quickly she'd forget Dimra. He vaguely remembered this street from his many meandering explorations with his wife before she became too sick to leave the house. Jack had tried to resent these suburbs as sterile and even grotesque, places where the kind of men who'd just undermined the entire economy could store their svelte wives and children in houses sometimes large enough for a half dozen families, kept immaculate by immigrant gardeners and cleaners. But it was beautiful. And peaceful. Colette's house, at the end of a cul-de-sac, just three blocks from the lake, wasn't ostentatious. It had an elegant, slightly Italianate design, and was part of a real neighborhood, with lots of people out on their porches watching their children building snowmen and having snowball fights.

It took less than a half hour for him, Colette, and Marcia to move the few things Marcia had rescued from her apartment into the granny flat at the back, with a large picture window looking out onto the snow-covered garden, ending in a wooded ravine. Though the trees were bare now, he could imagine summers of watery spangled sunlight, the children exploring the ravine or spending days on the beach.

Marcia followed him out to the car. As he came to a stop at the driver's-side door and faced her, she said, "I'll send you the money for the trailer."

"Don't send me anything," Jack said, resting his hand on her upper arm just beneath her Calavera Catrina. "Just . . . be happy."

She lifted the arm he was holding and took gentle hold of him in the same place, locking their arms together, and for a while they stood there coupled like that in silence.

Finally, he called goodbye to Aisha, but she was being chased by Felicity, too caught up in running and screaming with delight to hear him. The copper scorpion lay abandoned on the sidewalk.

Marcia quickly retrieved it. Seeing that she was about to scold Aisha, Jack said, "Don't. I hope she forgets everything. You too. Forget that place," he said. "Just look forward."

Her face instantly took on an expression of hurt surprise. "I don't *want* to forget."

Their hands released, their arms falling limply. He slipped into the driver's seat, turned the car very slowly around, and negotiated his way carefully out of that street of happy children.

37

When he returned, he sent an SMS to Dimra's mother. She responded that the fighting seemed to be mostly over and her internet was working, so he Skyped her. They were the only family each other had left. For an hour he gently nodded, not managing to interject a word as this old woman swathed in black, heavy in her body and sorrow, either sang the litany of her suffering in a high, atonal, cracked voice or wept silently, as if her tears were an intense intermittent pain she was endeavoring to endure and subdue. Her agonized face conveyed the dreadful and unanswerable *Why?* She'd lost her home, her family, her husband, both her children, and even a grandchild who'd never existed, though Aiden's picture still hung on the wall beside the yellowing Polaroid of Jack and Dimra at their sparsely attended wedding. As she spoke, her hands, otherwise pressed to her sides, flared periodically, as if she were trying to grasp something, or perhaps let something go. Dimra had been worried that her mother would die soon after her father, but Jack knew she'd endure if only to honor her suffering. For Jack's wife, Gaza had become bodies removed from shattered homes, wreathed in blood and concrete dust, an infernal cityscape scattered with pyres of black smoke like active volcanoes: the City of Destruction, the burning city. For Jack, twice a week, for years to come, he knew, his computer screen would open its eye to a great black bird singing her soft, atonal arias, or crying without a sound, or flaring her stunted unfledged wings as if recalling, though she'd been falling for most of her life, the old imperative to fly.

For the rest of the day, he lay on the couch staring out of the window. He hadn't told Marcia that Lulu had been vigilantly following the foreclosure process. The market was flooded with foreclosures and short sales, so the company the bank had put in charge accepted the condominium association's offer of $26,000 for the basement. Everyone willingly paid their portion of this so they could expunge the existence of that unviable and accursed place.

His phone dinged at close to ten at night.

You up there?

It was May. He thought of not answering, but his car was out back, so she knew he was home.

Yes

After a moment, she responded.

Can you pls move around.

He imagined her sitting down there alone in her beautiful apartment. His wife had always been home and never as careful as he was traversing the floors. He thought of how loud Dimra's silence must have seemed to May.

Rolling off the couch, he headed to bed, making sure to step on every forbidden floorboard.

38

Birdy had asked him to her house, reasoning that any restaurant on a Saturday evening would be too crowded and loud. He drove straight from the airport, and it took him an age to find a parking spot. As he climbed the capacious steps to the grand front entrance of her three-story brownstone in Lakeview, he felt a near panic attack at the prospect of seeing her. His grief for Dimra was a ragged pulse, by turns numbing and aggravating, the routine of his life constantly ruptured by a deep sense of chaos. It felt as if he hadn't slept in days.

The instant he rang her doorbell, he could see her blurred figure swimming up the hallway behind the door's Art Deco stained glass. Abruptly, there she was, taller than he remembered, a little slimmer, a great deal more fashionable, but with all her old clumsy intensity as she almost headbutted him with the enthusiasm of her embrace. She led him by the hand through the hallway and into a large open-plan kitchen, dining, and sitting area. Birdy was so nervous she was speaking compulsively, causing his raw loneliness to tighten its grip. She told him the lamb tagine would be ready in a half hour or so, inquired where he'd flown in from (Washington), asked about a few of their old crew, told him her son and daughter were upstairs teaching their taita to play Mario Kart and that she couldn't wait for him to meet them all later. She fetched him a glass of mineral water, herself a glass of red, and led him into a sitting area with an impressive gothic fireplace.

They sat kitty-corner to one another, their knees almost touching, Jack on the couch, Birdy in an armchair, leaning toward him, her elbows on her thighs, her hands cupping her cheeks. She couldn't seem to stop talking. Farida, she said, had attended their wedding. A tiny, dark-skinned woman Birdy had thought was Indian. "I could be his first wife's twin. I wonder now if that's why he married me." She told him how hard it had been on their son, Kyle, who was four, and especially their daughter, Brigitte, who was nearly six. Georges's mother still lived with them. "She loves me now!" She'd helped Birdy when Georges's brother wanted to take her kids to Lebanon. He also wanted to take the restaurants. "If I'd never met you, I might have let him. You gave me confidence, Jacky." Birdy began to speak to Jack in fluent Arabic. She was one quarter away from completing a master's in Arabic Language and Literature from Northwestern's SCS. "Can you believe that? Me!" Breathing hard, she was clearly becoming distressed at his bewildered reticence, unaware that he felt as if his own voice were choking him.

Suddenly, a high-pitched cry: "Daddy!"

Jack turned around into the delighted and then confused face of Birdy's daughter.

"Darling," Birdy called, "this is Jack, a very good friend of mine."

Brigitte had Birdy's blue eyes and pale skin, but a great deluge of black curls, like Dimra's.

At his "Hello, habibti," Brigitte smiled, twining coyly as she pushed herself back against the wall before vanishing at a call from her grandmother.

Bravely now, Birdy let the silence between them deepen and extend for long enough that the constrictor of his grief and loneliness slackened its hold. When he felt he could breathe again, Jack gently peeled her hands from her cheeks so he could hold them and have an unobstructed view of the face he loved.

"Oh Birdy," he said, "I have so much to tell you."

39

It was nearly three a.m. by the time he returned home from Birdy's. As soon as he shut the door, silence rushed in and he felt for a moment as if he could reach through the rupture Dimra's death had left in this world to touch God, or whatever lay above or beneath the surface of this life. He could sense it right here in the dark apartment, its silence becoming a singularity, a fissure into the stars if he could just have faith enough to close his eyes and find his way to it.

"Where are you?" he said quietly. Dimra could answer only as stars answer when you lie on the Earth, staring at them for long enough that they begin to pulse with the beat of your own heart. He went to the bedroom and retrieved the box from the bottom of his bedside table. Sitting cross-legged on their bed, he lifted out the lithopedion.

He'd found her—it had always been a girl—in Tash's apartment. Tash and Danh probably weren't sure what to do with it, looking as it did like a clumsy clay model, half-crushed. Jack examined, as he had a dozen times before, her slightly flattened, pugilistic face and fisted hands. He had no idea why he hadn't returned her to Gunther. No idea why he wanted to hold on to her, this besieged, walled-up infant who'd refused to be discarded, this helpless, indomitable being who looked as if she were bravely confronting a nightmare from which she could never wake. This child who'd cause her mother so much pain. All Jack knew for sure was that every now and then he liked to take her from her box and hold her, as he did now, upon his joined palms. To hold her as if opened hands were all that had ever been required to give her birth.

ACKNOWLEDGMENTS

Many thanks to fellow writers, friends, and family who have been loving and supportive throughout: Pippi, Sammi, Rory, Alan, Eliza, Fiona, Sheila, Shauna, Elizabeth, Bette, Lloyd, Penelope, Tony, Nancy, Craig, Cliff, Deena, Judy, Charlie, Dick, Lynn, Kimball, Audrey, Paul, Katrina, Mai, Maya, Rachel, and John.

While I've read too many books to mention on the history of Palestine and Israel, and on the Israeli/Arab conflict, the following books were particularly helpful for this novel: *Drinking the Sea at Gaza*, Amira Hass; *My Father Was a Freedom Fighter*, Ramzy Baroud; *Beyond Intifada*, Haim Gordon, Rivca Gordon, and Taher Shriteh; *Surviving the Siege of Beirut*, Lina Mikdadi. Also: "Freedom. Money. Fun. Love.": *The Warlore of Vietnamese Bargirls*, by Mai Lan Gustafsson.

My profound gratitude to the following: my wonderful family, particularly my mother and brother for their faith and loving support through everything; Uncle Badie and Uncle Bishara for sharing their stories; Myla Goldberg and Fred Leebron for their generous advice and support; Chris Wiman and Danielle Chapman, beloved friends, brilliant readers; Ellen Levine, my indomitable agent; YJ Wang for her kind enthusiasm; Alane Mason—I couldn't imagine a better editor; and, of course, my wife, Averill, for her unstinting love and faith.